The Time of Her Life

About the Author

Kate Fenton was born in Oldham, brought up in Cheshire and read PPE at St Hilda's College, Oxford. A former features and documentary producer for BBC Radio 4, she lives in the North York Moors near Whitby with her husband, a GP. She has written radio drama and journalism as well as seven novels, one of which, *Lions and Liquorice*, was serialised on *Woman's Hour*.

Also by Kate Fenton

The Colours of Snow
Dancing to the Pipers
Lions and Liquorice
Balancing on Air
Too Many Godmothers
Picking Up

KATE FENTON

The Time of Her Life

HODDER &
STOUGHTON

First published in Great Britain in 2020 by Hodder & Stoughton
An Hachette UK company

1

Copyright © Kate Fenton 2020

The right of Kate Fenton to be identified as the Author of the Work has been
asserted by her in accordance with the Copyright, Designs and Patents Act 1988.

A CIP catalogue record for this title is available from the British Library

Hardback ISBN 9781529358582
eBook ISBN 9781529358599

Typeset in Plantin Light by Hewer Text UK Ltd, Edinburgh
Printed and bound in Great Britain by Clays Ltd, Elocraf S.p.A.

Hodder & Stoughton policy is to use papers that are natural, renewable
and recyclable products and made from wood grown in sustainable
forests. The logging and manufacturing processes are expected to
conform to the environmental regulations of the country of origin.

Hodder & Stoughton Ltd
Carmelite House
50 Victoria Embankment
London EC4Y 0DZ

www.hodder.co.uk

For clever, funny and altogether wonderful Ed – who might think fulsome tributes are neither obligatory nor desirable, but stuff that. With my love and amazed thanks to him for making these Senior Railcard years absolutely the time of my life.

(. . . and equally amazed gratitude to Carolyn Mays, not just for remembering who I was – after such a prolonged arid spell – but improving this book immeasurably).

I

'Today is the end of an era,' declared Annie Stoneycroft. 'And I'm here to tell you it's a black day for me. A very black day. Not because, at the last minute, I'm having to stand up here in place of the best man. By the way, I'm really sorry about that, folks. Here you are, expecting a celebrity turn, and all you get is little old me. What a let-down, eh? At least you can have a laugh if I topple head first into the cake.'

Anyone who happened to have observed Annie's activities before she embarked on her speech might have wondered if she spoke in all seriousness. After rising from her seat at the top table in the silk-swagged marquee, her trim figure could have been seen craning from side to side like a sea captain on the bridge and stretching unsteadily up on tiptoe before she subsided with a frown to summon a waiter. Within minutes, a beer crate had been borne across to be upturned in place of her chair, and what appeared to be one of the groom's mighty wooden chopping blocks hauled out of the kitchens and squared-up on top of that. With a thumbs up to her sweating assistants, Annie had scrambled aboard this improvised platform. Whereupon, wobbling a little but confident now of commanding every last silver-cloth'd, flower-frothing, sequin-spangled table in the tent, she had grasped the microphone, ready to address the assembled crowd.

Her fellow guests, meanwhile, were topping up their glasses and angling their chairs towards the top table with the stoicism of a theatre audience who have found the slip of paper in their programmes regretting that the leading role today will, perforce, be taken by an understudy. The absence of the groom's father from his side in the front pew had already led to a most unchurchly buzz of speculation, indignation and dismay. Word had rustled round the congregation that a medical emergency – supposedly – accounted for the no-show. No, not himself. His missus. Yes, *her*. Bloody shame. There were sighs now mingled with the laughter when Annie recommended them to look on the bright side. At least, she said, with no time to prepare a speech, she couldn't bore them for long.

'Get on with it then,' shouted a stout gent at the back. However, they were all mellowed by several gallons of Dave Eastman's excellent champagne, and if one or two amongst them reckoned Annie Stoneycroft was inclined to be a bit full of herself and her grand ideas, she was – bottom line – one of their own. A Bucksford lass, born, bred, and long since returned to her native roots.

As someone had been recalling only a minute or two earlier, it had to be the best part of thirty years, think on, since the lass had come skittling back home. With no husband, two squalling littl'uns and, it was widely reckoned, barely two halfpennies to rub together – although she'd never let on about that. Say what you like about Annie, she'd grit, had that girl; proper Yorkshire grit. Never a one for mithering and faffing around. No, she'd just pulled up her socks and got on with it. Before you could say Farrow and flipping Ball, she'd expanded her dad's little decorating business into *Annie's Interiors*, charging an arm and ten legs for telling folk what colour to paint their walls. Next thing you know, she'd set up shop in a damn great old warehouse, all trendy brick and wormy beams, selling everything from four-poster beds to stinky candles. And rumour had it she'd come away with a very tidy sum indeed, now she'd flogged the place to a flashy property developer – who must have more brass than sense, by the sound of it. *Harrogate* firm, mark you. Enough said.

Still, good for Annie – that was the consensus. Because while running her business and bringing up her kids, she had also looked after her mum and dad through to the end like a Trojan. Done the same for her scallywag of a husband, too, only for him to go and die on her as well. Aye, she'd done right by one and all, had Annie.

And no one thought the worse of her now for claiming that she couldn't have managed any of this without Bernadette Saville. Or rather, as they would all have to get used to calling her, Mrs David Eastman.

'Give over blathering, you great eejit,' spluttered Bernie, who had just taken a mouthful of wine.

'I meant every word,' declared Annie into the microphone, while smiling down at her friend. 'How am I ever going to survive without you?' She was hitting her stride now. After doing her oratorical duty at three funerals within the past five years, she had become all too accustomed to public speaking. A wedding made a blessedly welcome change. 'I still remember the day you and I met as though it were yesterday.'

'You'll be after making me weep if you carry on like this,' Bernie wailed. 'Spoil all the fancy make-up you've plastered on me.'

'Twenty-seven years ago,' she continued imperturbably, turning back to the guests. 'I was nine and a half months pregnant, or that's what it felt like. With Dominic, who you can see over there, trying to sink under the table because he's scared stiff of what his crazy mother might say to embarrass him.' She grinned that way, raising her voice theatrically.

'Don't worry, my precious, you're not born during this anecdote. You don't have a speaking part.' She returned to her audience. 'Now he's an *actor*, of course, he thinks I should leave the performing to him.' She paused, enjoying the ripple of amusement.

'So there I am, in the maternity outpatient clinic of a London hospital. The place is packed tighter than Oxford Circus in the rush hour and, this being mid-August, hotter than a sauna. What's more, I was desperate for a pee, crossing my legs and hopping around like a demented elephant. But I couldn't go in search of the ladies' because my handbag strap had just snapped, spewing all my worldly goods over the lino, and my infant daughter was lying in the midst of the rubble, drumming her heels and having screaming hysterics.'

Bernie, magnificent in crimson satin with her wild red hair whipped up into a chignon ('like a feckin' ice-cream cornet,' she had moaned, when Annie was supervising the hairdresser earlier) grimaced up at her and hooted. 'Glory, yes, I'll not be forgetting that day in a hurry, will I now?'

'And you,' said Annie, smiling back, 'in spite of being even more pregnant than me, and all of seventeen years old to my thirty-whatever, asked if I could use a bit of help at all, at all? Then, before I can so much as blink, Martha stops screaming. Total hush. Just like that. And I think she might actually have choked and died and at that moment I don't care. Because a calm Irish voice is telling me the loo's down on the left, my bag's here with everything inside, and I'm not to fret about my little cherub, she'll be fine, so she will.' Annie is now on a roll. 'By the time I get back, my hell-babe is cuddled on Bernie's knee, chewing Bernie's thumb, clearly wondering how she can trade in her useless mother for this miraculous creature who has not just spotted instantly that she's cutting a tooth but knows exactly what to do about it. And since it

4

would obviously require a crowbar to separate my daughter from her new guardian angel, I collapse into the chair beside them and ask her if she wants a job. I'm joking, of course I am. But blow me down if this slip of a girl with a bulging belly doesn't look me straight in the eye and say—'

'When can I start?' cried Bernie, swabbing her tears with a bunched-up starched napkin. 'At which exact moment, God's honest truth, my waters broke.'

'And since there was no way I was going to let this Wonder Woman escape, I followed her trolley into the cubicle – we never had time to get to the proper ward – and I ended up holding her son even before she did,' said Annie. 'Yes, Liam himself. Who I can assure you was almost as gorgeous then as he is now.' She craned round to shoot a mischievous glance at the undoubtedly handsome, six foot three Dr Liam Saville, who cast up his eyes, blushing adorably.

'You sure as hell sorted out that stroppy cow of a midwife,' muttered Bernie. 'Who still reckoned girls like me belonged in the workhouse.'

'And we've been a team ever since, Bernie and me. Let's face it, we've lasted longer than most marriages. It's more than a quarter of a century, dammit, that she and I have lived together, during which she's cuddled, cajoled, cooked for and cared for Martha and Dominic alongside her own lovely Liam, never mind my mum and dad—'

'Don't forget Jakey,' chipped in Bernie, 'bless his wicked old soul.'

'But most of all, always, through all these years, she's looked after me. OK, so I haven't needed my nappy changing. And I don't throw screaming tantrums. Well, not often. She has just been my friend, my best mate. The very bestest of best mates. We've laughed, we've cried, we've shared our kitchen, kids, hearts, souls . . .'

'And a – a bottle or two,' gasped Bernie through thick tears.

'And a ton load of bottles, you betcha, because we've stuck together through thick and thin, through all her grown-up life and most of mine and I'm sorry if I sound like the soppiest, tackiest greetings card, and so help me I'm making myself sob too, but I can't be flip about Bernie. She is fantastic. Dave is the luckiest man on earth. *However* . . .' Here Annie halted, confidently stretching the expectant hush. 'I could not have invented in my wildest dreams a better, bigger-hearted, more worthy husband for my comrade-in-arms than Dave. Yup. It's a tragic loss for me, as I said, a black day indeed. But I have to admit this truly is a marriage made in heaven. And it is absolutely not going to be spoiled . . .' she caught Bernie's eye and winked, 'because the best man's lovely wife ate a lousy peanut.'

A roaring tide of laughter exploded from all sides, a storm of cheers and clapping. Annie beamed through her tears as she raised her glass high. 'So, join me, please, in drinking a toast to – this *very* happy couple.'

Several hours and a good deal more champagne later, she threaded a purposeful path through the smokers huddled in the gap between the marquee and the rear door of the Hopkirk Arms. She was wondering what had become of her son – but, no, he did not appear to be out here with the fag brigade. Probably snoring in a corner somewhere. A punk-haired waitress stopped her to ask if she knew where a new bottle of Baileys might be found. Tempted to suggest that whoever wanted it should just cultivate better taste, Annie said she'd see if she could locate Bernie. She was dog-weary, but happy still to accept kisses and plaudits on her efforts as she squeezed her way through, because she did feel this day had been one hell of a triumph of planning and persuasion – as well as flat panic and last-minute improvisation.

Weather fab, church overflowing, bride sumptuous, bridesmaids adorable, groom jubilant, feet killing me and Dominic pissed. How about U?

So ran the text she had just sent to her lifelong friend, Rob Daley. Three years her junior in age but – dearly as she loved him – occasionally inclined to fancy himself her senior in wisdom. It was time he acknowledged that, far from taking to gin or daytime telly since flogging her business, Annie had invested her newfound freedom in masterminding Bucksford's wedding of the year. Down to the last sodding buttonhole.

The sunshine was the only element for which she could not claim credit. The sun had blazed as beautifully as the bride – and Annie was undoubtedly responsible for the latter. No way had she been prepared to accept her friend's protests that, at forty-four, she was too old for fuss and fancy feckin' frockery. Fortunately, Dave Eastman, noted chef and proprietor of the Hopkirk Arms, had notions of hospitality that accorded with Annie's. The size of marquee he had deemed necessary to accommodate just his immediate family, closest friends and favourite customers barely fitted on the grass behind the pub. And while he might not have roasted the giant hog himself, he had presided over the carving of it, with ruddily beaming face and a vast striped apron knotted over his wedding finery.

That marquee now glowed like an alien spacecraft in the darkness and throbbed to the beat of the DJ within. Annie's head was also throbbing, just a little, as were her feet, her left big toe in particular. But she would no more admit that she was too old for loud dance music than she would have swapped her Jimmy Choos for driving loafers. The day a woman even thinks of resorting to flats at a wedding is the day that woman has given up – and given in. Annie had done neither. Six weeks it had taken her to starve into this dress, which was sharp-cut to bare one shoulder and both knees at a height

7

precisely calibrated between matron and mutton. Her legs were buffed and bronzed, her blondeish hair carefully glued into careless disarray, and fingernails, which were not her own, had been lacquered a fashionable but dignified mauve. Small wonder, as she halted in the canopied entrance to the tent, that a strawberry-nosed cigar chomper, one of Dave's late-night regulars in the side bar, told her thickly that she was looking a proper picture, not a day over twenty-nine.

'Time for a new pair of specs, Len,' she returned, blowing him a kiss. Before she could move onwards, however, he grasped her arm.

'What's the real story with Dave's dad then?' he said. 'You reckon we're ever going to clap eyes on t'bugger?'

Her smile stiffened. As far as she was concerned, this no-show by the best man was the only worm in the otherwise perfect apple of the day. Of course, she felt the disappointment as keenly as she did purely for the sake of Dave and Bernie. It had nothing to do with herself. She had not lavished so much care (and cash) on her appearance today just because she had – she would admit this much – anticipated sharing a dance or two with Dave's glamorous parent. Although it was also true that she had never expected any other male present to be worth a leg wax. Well, she'd been right about that. Having done her duty with the familiar round of sweaty hands and wobbly beer bellies on the dance floor, she had found herself this past couple of hours sorely missing Rob, stuck as he was at some bloody conference abroad. Crap dancer, but at least they could have shared a laugh. And she was sick to death of deflecting questions about the absence of the best man. She was about to say, with what was by now well-practised indifference, that she was sure they would all get to meet him sooner or later, when she was diverted by a commotion from within the marquee.

There was a splintering crash; some woman shrieked; the music stopped and, amongst a babble of voices and raucous laughter, Annie thought she detected her son's voice. Groaning? With a hasty apology, she spun away and plunged into the tent. Fairy lights twinkled, hot bodies pressed forward to see what was amiss and the DJ's voice crackled over the speakers that there was nothing to worry about, guys, a minor mishap, that was all.

A table was overturned on the far side of the dance floor amid a tangle of chairs, glasses and flowers. A shaven-headed gorilla in a tuxedo was stamping on a flicker of flame from a spilled candle, while his chum, in an ill-advised tartan cummerbund, was clumsily trying to shake wine and glass shards from a feather boa.

'Fuck knows what got into him,' snapped its owner, a female with improbably black hair and a sun-leathered bosom, rather too much of which was exposed by a spangled, tight-laced corset which struck even Annie as a bold choice for a female of mature years. 'Dickbrained kid.' She was glaring down at the floor at – yes – at Dominic, whom Annie now spotted, prostrate behind the toppled table.

Even flat on his back, with a leg caged in medical Meccano, his waistcoat rucked round his neck, and his shirtfront splattered purple with wine, he looked beautiful. That was not the view of a besotted mother – rarely had this mother felt less besotted – Dominic Stoneycroft really was something to behold. Long-limbed, lean-bodied and peachy-skinned, with a thicket of dark curls, he was blessed with the profile of a Greek statue and the lashes of a baby Alpaca. That noble head, however, was skewed at an unnatural angle against a chair leg and the lushly fringed eyes were shut.

'Oh Lord, did he trip over his crutches again?' Annie dropped to her knees to retrieve one of these and tuck it under her son's limp arm.

The two men eyed one another.

'He stood up – a bit sudden like,' offered the cummerbunded one. 'No harm done, eh?'

The black-haired woman snorted and folded her arms over her bulging cleavage.

'Come on you, up we get,' said Annie. Then more loudly, 'Dominic, love?' There was no response. She leaned over him but could hear nothing.

'He hasn't knocked himself out, has he?' enquired the gorilla.

'He's been drinking,' she said distractedly. 'Like a fish. He's – not used to it.'

'What's wrong with . . . ?' He was indicating Dominic's splinted leg.

'Knocked off his bike, last week. Damn nearly got himself killed.'

'Christ. Like, uh, should we get a doctor?'

Annie shook her head, staring down, chewing her lip. This really was not like Dominic. The antics of his late father, however, had trained her in the management of comatose males at social events. She clambered to her feet, straightened her frock, smiled brightly round the assembled company – and kicked her beloved child in the ribs. Sure enough, his eyes flipped open. He had his dad's eyes, too, as fabulously blue as the sky on a seaside postcard. Little sod. He squinted up at her, then at the other faces around her, as though struggling to remember where he was. Even as his exasperated mother reached down to heave him to his feet, however, his bleary gaze fastened on the ageing belle in the spangly corset and all at once his face contorted. 'Shit, iss her,' he wailed, twisting to grab Annie's ankle. 'Keep'r away. Chrissake.'

The woman gasped, the men guffawed, Dominic gulped – and threw up copiously over his mother's feet.

She closed her eyes. 'Ah,' she sighed. 'I think this might be home time for us Stoneycrofts.'

'Shorry, Ma. I'm really, really—'

'So you keep telling me.' Annie peeled off one stinking, vomit-spattered stiletto, then the other, and flung them into the rear well of her car before shrugging her feet into her saggy old driving shoes with a whimper of gratitude. One steadying hand on the doorframe, she lowered herself into the leather-scented cockpit of the vehicle. Her son was already slumped in the passenger seat. 'You're a monster, of course. And you will deservedly feel like death tomorrow morning.' She sighed. 'Mark you, I don't suppose I'll be dancing round like a spring lamb.'

She was blinking at the array of dials on the dashboard and wondering where the ignition key plugged in. No, she was *not* drunk. This was just a strange car, her new toy, barely two days out of the showroom, less than fifty miles on the clock – her little treat to herself on selling the business – and, oh God, yes of course, you didn't actually insert a key at all, you just pressed a button. Which was where exactly?

'You're missing the party,' Dominic moaned, well into the maudlin phase of inebriation by now. 'All cos of me.'

'Things were winding up. More or less.'

Annie leaned back in her seat and closed her eyes while he fumbled for the seatbelt. 'So. You going to tell me now what actually happened in there?'

'Nothing.'

'Nothing? With that woman clearly ready to murder you? And it wasn't even her feet you were sick over.'

'Yeah, well . . .'

'Come on, *give*. What'd you done to her?'

'Me? More like wha' she did.' This burst out so vehemently Annie opened her eyes again and turned towards him.

'Yeah?'

'She – oh.' He wouldn't look at her. 'Shit. 'Fyou must know, she, uh, put her hand on me.'

'I'm sorry?'

'You know.'

Annie stared at him in the semi-dark. His head was resolutely turned away. 'You're telling me she *groped* you? That – that cougar-in-a-corset made a pass at my little boy?'

''Snot funny. So, m'be I over-reacted, bit, but, like—'

'A bit?' She was still laughing as she pressed the starter button and the engine roared like a tiger loosed from a cage. 'Oh my precious snowflake. Lucky Mummy was there to protect you.'

'Piss off.'

'And although I don't suppose it's so much as crossed your tiny mind,' she continued chattily as she craned round and began very cautiously to reverse, 'no, I should *not* be driving. Not legally, anyhow, so let's just hope I can manage to get us home safely. You'd be amazed how mopping up vomit and broken glass clears the head.' She braked too hard, flinched, pushed the gear lever into first, took a deep breath and barely touched the accelerator. The car surged forward.

The schoolboy in a cheap suit who'd sold her this baby had intimated that the spec of the sports model generally made it more of a, you know, young person's car? He had been struck gratifyingly dumb when she had tartly asked how soon he could deliver.

'Just keep your fingers crossed this isn't the one day a year the North Yorkshire Constabulary ventures into the wilds. An hour and a half for a bloody taxi, can you believe it? In Bucksford?'

'So? Could've had 'nother drink.'

'Exactly. And since when did you acquire such a taste for booze? Please God it isn't hereditary. *Hey!*' Preoccupied with trying to flip the headlights up to full beam, she had only just noticed that the breathing beside her was thickening. 'Don't you dare go to sleep, Dominic Stoneycroft. We'll be home in ten minutes, and you're going to get yourself and your crutches out of this car and up the stairs because I certainly can't do it for you.' She stabbed what she thought was the radio, heard a dialling tone and cursed as she stabbed it off again. 'Remind me to read the handbook in the morning. So come on, my lovely, if I can't get loud music out of this machine, we'll just have to talk. I need you wide awake. One pretty amazing humdinger of a wedding, huh?'

'Sorry? Oh. I guess.'

'Don't over-enthuse.'

'Yeah, well. Dunno what Bernie sees in . . . Not really.'

'Are you kidding?'

'Dave. You know?'

'I bloody well do not know. Dave Eastman is single, solvent, straight – and sane. Which makes him rarer than rubies amongst blokes his age. Plus he's a darling, and crazy about our Bernie. And vice versa. Shagging away like teenage rabbits, from what I gather.'

'Whoa!'

'I thought that'd wake you up,' she said, steering smoothly onto the Bucksford Road. 'Hard for you to believe, I realise, that the old Adam can still stir in the over-forties, but—'

'Huh. 'F you knew.'

'Knew what?'

'Nothing. Just – 'nuff about, y'know, sex.'

'What'd you think I was going to say? Ask when you last had any? Worse, tell you when I did?'

'Ma. *Puh-lease.*'

'Yes, well, maybe this isn't the time for ancient history. Ever noticed the way magazines go on about how liberating it is when your children finally metamorphose into adults? When at last you can talk freely and frankly about absolutely anything?'

'Look, if you really wanna know—'

'Makes you wonder what planet they live on. Because in my experience your generation curl up into a ball if anyone so much as—' She broke off. 'Shit.'

'When I – when I—'

'*Quiet!*'

'Thing is, 'slike—'

'No. No, please God no. *Please.*'

'Mum?'

Annie had dropped the car's speed to a crawl and her voice to a whisper. 'Tell me I'm not seeing this. Behind, in the mirror. There's a blue light. Flashing. D'you think . . .?'

2

'OK, let me get this straight,' said Rob Daley. 'You were drunk as a skunk, doing forty-plus in a built-up area? With your hazard lights going.'

'I didn't know *that*. I'd pressed the wrong button. Apparently.'

'So you were flashing away like Blackpool Illuminations. With sonny boy here's coat-tails flapping out the side of the passenger door.'

'I didn't know that either. And God knows what that'll cost me, because it's hired morning dress, of course.'

'And that's all? Well, I can't imagine what made the boys in blue think they should pull you over.'

'Oh ha ha. You know sarcasm's going out of fashion?'

'That right? The classic line used to be that it was the lowest form of wit. There was always some smart Alec at the front of the class trotting that out with a huge smirk, like I'd never heard it before.' He grinned. 'Well, I always said you'd be desperate for stimulation without your business. Never thought you'd resort to getting yourself arrested, though.'

Dominic lifted his head. 'It was all my fault, Uncle Rob. I made an arse of myself. Mum had to get me away before I – well, whatev. I don't remember much. To be honest.'

'He was sexually assaulted,' offered Annie. 'By an ageing harpy in a very tight dress.'

'Not funny,' he said, flushing.

'And before your Uncle Rob chips in with a politically correct chorus about abuse always being abuse and not to be joked about, blah-diddly-blah, can I just say, sweet of you to fall on your sword, kid, but it wasn't your fault.' She sighed. 'Not really. I was the one climbed into that driving seat. Unlike you, I knew what I was doing, and it wasn't just that I wanted to get you home. Fact is, I was dog-tired, hoarse from shouting over the disco and I couldn't face hanging around until after midnight, waiting for a cab. So here I am.' She shut her eyes. 'With a splitting head and forty-odd grand's worth of new car sitting in the drive. And very soon no licence to bloody drive it. The only question is for how long. And my tea's gone cold.'

'Poor old Nan,' said Rob. 'What an idiot. D'you want me to cook you up some breakfast then?'

It was past noon. They were in the kitchen of The Red House, Deerbourne Lane, the sprawling Edwardian villa that had been Annie's cherished home for so many years. The terrifying sum she had scraped together to buy such a property would now, of course, scarcely purchase a garden shed up this desirable end of town, and her many improvements and enlargements had only inflated the value further. This kitchen alone was bigger than the entire flat that Dominic had recently been sharing with two other struggling actors in Camden Town, and its splendours had regularly featured in the advertising for Annie's design services. The vaulted ceiling rose to an intricately wrought atrium; the floor was flagged in stone venerably pocked from service in a Lancashire cotton mill; and two whole walls of glass doors folded open into the garden. There were solid banks of cupboards and shelves, artfully washed in assorted greys and topped with marble gleaming smugly in the midday sun, while a battle-scarred refectory table, big enough to seat twelve, presided in the centre of the room.

Annie and Dominic had been slumped round one corner of this table when Rob arrived. They were still swaddled in their dressing gowns, with half-drunk mugs of tea, tumblers of water and various analgesics scattered between them.

As ever, he had barely bothered to knock on the back door, just clattered in across the flags on bowed legs, thanks to the plugs protruding from the soles of his cycling shoes, with his stocky frame shrink-wrapped in the inevitable Lycra. Annie had more than once observed in his hearing (with only the kindest of intentions) that she had yet to meet the man who looked anything other than a plonker in cycling gear. And even though, as she had remarked just now while squinting up at him through red-rimmed eyes, Rob was blessed with a shapelier bum than most middle-aged male cyclists – in fact, quite a fine bum – it bloody well wasn't enhanced by the bulge of padding all these bikers wore stitched into their ballet tights. What was more, his chin was bristling as blue and square as a Brillo pad, his thicket of grey hair stuck up like a lavatory brush and, as she had squawked when he leaned down to kiss her, he was dripping with sweat.

'But you love me really,' he had said.

'Can't think what gives you that idea.'

Once she learned, however, that the carrier bag he had dropped by the door contained the necessary components for a full English along with the Sunday papers, all of which he'd had the forethought to purchase before pedalling up Deerbourne Hill, she was moved to declare that there were times when, yes, she could feel quite fond of him.

'Well, I knew I'd likely find nowt worth eating in your fridge,' he commented, briskly tumbling the contents of his bag across a marble worktop. 'Not these days. The place's gone to the dogs since Bernie moved out.'

'I shan't rise to the bait,' she said, rocking back in her chair and propping one leg languidly over the end of the table. 'Just pour us a large orange juice and hand over the *Sunday Times*. What about you, Dom?'

'I'm going out for, um, some air.' He was already reaching for a crutch with one hand while patting his pockets for his cigarette packet with the other. Before he limped out, Annie saw him shoot a wary glance at Rob, whose back was towards them as he opened one cupboard door after another, whistling under his breath. Dominic had only the other day remarked to his mother that you could never quite forget Rob used to be a headmaster. Not that he *said* anything, exactly. It was just his look.

'Tell me about it,' Annie had responded. She said she got that look every time she refilled her wineglass or said 'fuck'. However, it was water off a duck's back if, like her, you could remember Dr Robert Daley, MA (Cantab), as a scabby-kneed, snotty-nosed kid, three years and twenty paces behind you, badgering to be let in to your gang.

Annie and Rob went back a long way. Indeed they had known one another for many years before her younger sister married his elder brother, Annie having started at Sandy Hill Primary on the same day and in the same class as Philip Daley. However, while Annie's family had lived in a trimly hedged semi up towards the park, the Daleys were squashed into a council terrace situated, quite literally, on the wrong wide of the track. As well as the long defunct railway, the canal and river ran nearby in what was then very much the rougher end of Bucksford. Nowadays, of course, with every last city and town rediscovering its waterways, this quarter of town was smart, almost hip – well, by Yorkshire standards. Suffice to say

Annie's former warehouse was down that way, overlooking a canal long since cleared of supermarket trollies.

The old Daley home had vanished under a sports complex, however, and Rob's parents dead these many years. All Annie could remember of his dad was a gurgling cough, the oxygen cylinder beside his chair and a smell of stale beer. His mum was a very different character. A cleaner by day, a dressmaker by night and a tiger mother round the clock, she had determinedly propelled her two boys onwards and upwards. Gratified as she had been by Philip's degree from Manchester, her crowning triumph had come with little Bobby's cap and gown at Cambridge. By the time she died, he was head of a thousand-pupil comprehensive with a growing reputation for taming the wilder outposts of the education system. While Annie's mockery was a flimsy disguise for (slightly amazed) pride in her old playmate's distinguished career – 'is it bleeding social conscience or d'you just like marching into playgrounds with your sheriff's badge and guns blazing?' – she had quite seriously asked if he wasn't tempted by a quieter life in the kind of joint where they wore blazers and played violins. He was not. He had, however, retired from his last headship three years ago. Annie said he must be finding it too easy by now to batter schools into submission and up the league tables. At fifty-five he was a respected consultant and pundit on education policy, advising governments and public bodies both at home and internationally. It was a long-booked conference in Chicago where he was the keynote speaker that had kept him away from Bernie's wedding.

'I told her how gutted I was to miss all t'fun,' he remarked now, slapping a frying pan onto the hob with a clang that made Annie flinch and grope for the paracetamol. 'Seems you gave a cracking turn, standing in for Dave's dad. Shame about him not showing up, though. For the Eastmans, anyhow.' He began breaking eggs into a bowl. 'Scrambled suit you? They weren't saying much last night, but I could see they felt it.'

She looked up from her newspaper, surprised. 'You actually got to the Hopkirk Arms last night?'

'Sure. Managed the earlier flight by the skin of my teeth and drove like the clappers. They reckoned you'd only been gone ten minutes.'

She groaned. 'God. If you'd been just a whisker earlier I wouldn't be in this mess. Because as sure as eggs is eggs – and yes, scrambled's great, thanks – you'd have had those car keys out of my fist before I could say welcome home.'

'Happen I might at that. Two rashers?'

In spite of a double first from Cambridge and the Order of the British Empire from Her Majesty for services to education, Rob Daley had never felt any need to smarten up his accent. Quite the contrary. According to Annie, he damn well revelled in his rough, gruff man-of-the-people image. She herself had sensibly chucked her flat vowels along with her fag ends out of the train window on the journey down to her own university in Bristol. She regularly pointed out that Rob's eeh-bah-gummery was a bit rich coming from a bloke who, even as a spotty teenager, had been sounder on sonnets than whippets.

More privately, she had sometimes pondered the mysterious way Robbo had metamorphosed from irritating kid brother into (occasional) Dutch uncle. There had been the occasional twitch of disapproval from him when they were in their twenties and sharing a flat in London. He had been manning the chalkface in some forlorn outer postcode while Annie was employed in the epicentre on various glossy interiors magazines, hurtling from party to party, job to job and, at even giddier speed, man to man. Rob would sigh and roll his eyes but he remained her sturdy comrade, always ready with a laugh or a comforting shoulder when, as must happen to a young female careering through the 1980s, she occasionally crashed.

Yes, Rob was reliably good fun to be around in those days. She reckoned the rot had set in with Frances, the woman who became his wife and was the only person on earth other than his mother ever to call him Robert. She could always remember when that pair first hooked up because it wasn't long after she herself had lost her heart (also her head, her job and a stone and a half) to the mad and fabulously bad Jake Stoneycroft.

However, six months ago, after nigh on thirty years of a marriage everyone had believed to be as stoutly dull as the Bank of England, this same Frances had walked out on her husband. Just like that. With no advance warning nor, so far as could be ascertained, any whiff of a secret lover in the Georgian terraced house she had quietly purchased and furnished for herself in York before detonating the marital bomb. Shock? Annie was still reeling. She had been fond of Fran. Well, fondish. She would have been the first to tell you how attractive Fran was (if you like the skeletal look), how stylish (in a beige carpet throughout sort of way) and clever – oh, seriously, *seriously* clever. Barrister, QC, all that. Also a model mother to three delightful kids, intimidatingly competent at everything from jam-making to sudoku-cracking and never less than impeccably civil and helpful to Annie herself.

In fact the only charge Annie could make stick against Frances Daley was her dustily lawyerish sense of humour. For which read, lack thereof. But perhaps that was saying no more than that she didn't laugh much at Annie's jokes. Probably not clever enough for her. Also, it had seemed to Annie that Rob, too, laughed less when the wife was around. He was more the starchy headmaster than the brat who had kidnapped her

Sindy doll. And buried her in Dad's rhubarb patch, what was more. Not that Annie bore grudges.

'Dearest and best beloved old friend?' she said.

He glanced over his shoulder. 'What you after?'

'Pot of coffee?'

'Some vegetarian you are,' said Annie, half an hour or so later. 'How many pieces of bacon is that?'

'I never said I was vegetarian,' returned her son. 'I just try to avoid meat. Mostly. It's all about a healthier, more sustainable lifestyle, yeah?'

'Like riding a bike round central London?' she said, through a mouthful of toast. 'And look where that's got you.'

'Proper little bundle of sunshine you are this morning, Nan,' said Rob, reaching for the butter. 'How'd you actually come off, Dom – pothole? Your mum never got round to the backstory. Too busy thanking God you were alive and cursing me for being abroad when she rang us from the hospital. Oh, and ranting about the machine coffee. That's when I thought maybe I didn't need to hop on the next plane.'

'I was in shock. What'd you expect, after I'd gone pelting down to London in the middle of the night, not knowing whether my son was alive or dead?' Annie swept on before her son could answer. 'He had an argument with a Bulgarian container lorry, that's what, so he's bloody lucky to be here eating bacon. Hyde Park Corner at night, I ask you, with dodgy lights and pissed out of his skull. And don't you dare turn that back on me, Rob Daley, because I might have been driving illegally last night but I could still string a sentence together, whereas when I found this maniac trussed up and bloodied to the eyeballs in a hospital bed, legless with drink and inches away from ending up legless full stop, I mean—'

'It wasn't drink.' Dominic pushed back his chair and stumbled to his feet. 'Well, not just drink.'

Annie's eyes opened very wide. 'Now he tells me. Stoned, too?'

'*Stoned?*' Dominic grimaced as he wedged a crutch under his armpit. 'You're showing your age, Ma. Um, thanks, Rob, that was a lifesaver. The scrambled eggs were awesome.'

'My pleasure,' said Rob. 'Just a whisper of cayenne, that's the secret. And not overcooking, of course.'

Annie finished the last fragment of toast as Dominic limped off into the garden. 'Since when did you turn into Heston Blumenthal?'

'I'm having to learn fast, aren't I?' Rob shrugged. 'Now that I'm shifting for myself.'

'What? Oh.' She bit her lip. 'Sorry.'

'Don't beat yourself up. Statement of fact. Fran's gone, old house's gone, I'm still unpacking boxes in the flat, with sole care and control of a shiny new kitchen. And I'm here to tell you the cookers these developers put in nowadays are so bloody complicated you need a degree course just to turn the grill on.' He took a swig of tea. 'Matter of fact, I've always quite liked cooking. It was Fran used to hustle me out of the kitchen. She said I made more mess with one supper than she did in a week.'

Annie's eyes flickered towards the pans, tools, pots and crumpled packaging strewn across her own worktops. 'No, really?' She did not pursue this line of attack, though, because she sensed an opportunity. They – which is to say Annie, her sister Jennifer, Bernie and even daughter Martha on the phone from New Zealand – had been speculating amongst themselves at length but largely fruitlessly as to what lay behind the collapse of the Daley marriage. The older women had talked to Rob, of course, variously offering sympathy, surprise, solidarity or shepherd's pie. He had responded with polite impenetrability all round. The most revealing admission any of them had prised out of him was that no, he couldn't honestly say he'd seen this coming. Gobsmacked would about sum him up. But there you go, eh? Naturally, Annie was not prepared to accept such blokey stoicism at face value.

'So how's Fran getting along?' she enquired now. Very casually. 'In her new house?'

Rob had just taken a bite of toast. 'Fine,' he said thickly. 'So far as I know.' He swallowed and met her gaze squarely. 'And before you ask, yes of course we're in touch. All the time. We've three kids and the thick end of thirty years joint finances to sort out for the divorce agreement. And no, we're not at war. It's fine, she's fine, I'm fine, any other questions?'

Now or never. 'Why'd she leave you, Robbo?'

At least this silenced him, if only for a moment. He glanced at her rather oddly. 'You got any suggestions?'

'Apart from you being impossible for any sane woman to live with? Oh, don't give me the kicked-spaniel look, you know I'm joking. No, I haven't the foggiest, how should I? We all thought you two were rock solid.'

He looked down at his hands, at the left hand where, for the first time, she noticed a pale indentation where his wedding ring had lived. 'Yup,' he said quietly. 'Reckon I did and all.'

This was so different from his usual brusque tone that Annie was moved to put her hand over his and was as much surprised as touched when his fingers twisted to return her clasp. 'Poor old Bobsy,' she said. 'We'll have to find a nice little friend to cheer you up, won't we?'

Considering she had spoken from the heart, in a one hundred per cent genuine surge of affectionate sympathy, she was not expecting him to snort and snatch away his hand. 'I was being nice to you,' she protested.

'Yeah, well. It's unnatural. Frightened the life out of me.'

'Idiot. I'm concerned for you, that's all.'

'Finished with that plate?'

'For Pete's sake, can't we have an adult conversation for once? I've been feeling guilty for weeks, actually, but what with winding up Jake's estate, selling the business, the wedding – and now Dom crashing home – it's been one blessed thing after another. I've had no chance to talk properly, see how you're getting on, be a friend in need, all that.'

'In need of what?'

She grinned. 'How about a woman?'

He rose to his feet and eyed her satirically. 'You offering?'

'Be serious, you pillock. Female company, if you'd sooner call it that. I refuse to talk about girlfriends and boyfriends—'

'Thank God for that.'

'—because with the best will in the world, we're not young-sters any more, are we?' She rose too. Scooping up mugs and side plates she followed him across to the sink. 'But I'm sure it must be tough, finding yourself rattling round in a strange flat . . .'

'The flat's great.'

'If you like operating theatres. No, no, don't jump down my throat, your, um, apartment's fine, lovely. What I'm talking about is being on your own. For the first time in decades.'

He glanced up from the dishwasher into which he had begun to thread cutlery. In the wrong rack, but she let it pass. Some things in life are even more important than the correct stacking of dishwashers. 'So are you, with Bernie gone,' he said. 'Living on your tod. For the first time.'

'Actually I'm not, not now Dom's back. And with all the ironmongery in his leg and zilch in the bank it looks like he'll be around for a bit. Plus he's bust up with his girlfriend, did I tell you? Not that she's any great loss . . . Anyway, that's beside the point. I'm a woman.'

'You don't say.'

'Whereas it's well recognised that men aren't good on their own. Scientific fact. They die younger.'

'Been reading the *Daily Mail*?'

'I'm offering to help, OK? Come on, I did a pretty amazing job pairing up Bernie and Dave.'

Rob straightened and turned to stare at her. 'You're never claiming credit for that marriage? Anyone with half a brain could see those two were made for one another.'

'Ha!' Annie leaned back against the sink, folding her arms. 'It's all very well saying that now, but who spotted the potential in the first place? Who was sending Bernie up to the Hoppy night after night to help with the little girls? And you know it isn't easy forging relationships after a certain age. The game's different. No one knows the rules. People are terrified of making a fool of themselves.'

Rob returned to the dishwasher. 'Tell me about it.'

'See? You do know what I'm talking about. And getting Bernie and Dave together I felt like—' She broke off. 'What's that barmy Scottish sport where they chuck boulders along the ice?'

'Curling?'

'Exactly. With those two, I've been like one of the broom-swishing minions, whizzing out in front, sweeping all the crap out of the way. Don't pull faces, Rob Daley, it's true. I was forever throwing them together, including babysitting his kids so they could go out on their first proper dates. In fact, if you'd been at the wedding yesterday, you'd have heard Dave saying all this and more in his speech. I was very touched.'

Rob was studying a dismayingly egg-encrusted pan. 'I heard Dave spent most of his speech quoting the email his dad'd sent, instead of turning up.'

'His bloody wife was taken ill. Allergic shock or something.'

'Yeah? Well, much as I hate to say I told you so . . .'

'Only your favourite phrase,' said Annie, seizing the pan from him and filling it with water.

'How much did I bet you the guy wouldn't show?'

'I can't remember,' she said, untruthfully. 'But very likely about what it'll cost me to replace this saucepan. So shall we call it quits?'

3

Annie used to say that Dave Eastman's life story was more the kind of tear-jerker you boggled at on the telly than anything you expected to encounter in the real world.

Where to start? Perhaps with his first wife expiring in downright Victorian fashion during the birth of the second of their two daughters, conceived only after an agonising and expensive decade of fertility treatment. And that wasn't all. Thanks to years of slaving and saving through assorted tenancies, she and Dave had just managed to buy the country pub of their dreams in a pretty village outside prosperous Bucksford. Of course they were swimming in debt with the business barely established. To cap it all, his widowed mum, who'd done her best to help out for a couple of years, began sinking into a final recurrence of cancer.

Having long since determined with gloomy Northern relish that there was no way poor old Dave could carry on alone at the Hopkirk Arms – with two kiddies, one of 'em barely started at nursery? – the locals were now comfortably certain of his imminent bankruptcy and departure. Nor were they prepared to abandon their dire prognostications when Bernadette Saville took to lending a hand with the motherless bairns. And the bar. Then the staffing rotas, the VAT, the refurbishment of the letting bedrooms and – finally – the lonely landlord himself. Whereupon they were not in the least surprised. Hadn't they been telling Dave all along things would come right in t'end?

Many a pint of his expertly cellared ale was raised in celebration of his newfound happiness, because there could be no doubt Dave Eastman was once again a happy man. Most wholeheartedly had he loved his first wife and his mother, most sincerely did he mourn them, but his was not a nature to dwell in the vale of tears. Life goes on, and there's forty-odd booked in for dinner.

This summary, however, omits the most intriguing – and most talk-show worthy – strand of Dave's history. It begins on a quiet autumnal evening not long before his mum's demise. She is by now drifting high in the morphine clouds, and while her other children and grandchildren have been attending in shifts what is tearfully recognised to be her deathbed, only her eldest son Dave is by her side at this crucial moment. He is flicking through a copy of the *Radio Times*. This may sound prosaic, but deathbeds, as Annie herself has learned, can last for days, weeks and even years. You can't just sit around weeping as you await the end.

His mum gasps, 'There's your dad.'

And Dave says, gently, 'No, Mum. Dad passed on a long time ago, remember?'

'No,' she says, more loudly, sounding agitated. And he realises she's pointing one wavering finger at the cover of the *Radio Times*. Having opened it to see when the football might be coming on, Dave has already twigged, with some disgust, that it's a very old copy, years out of date, which for some reason was stuffed into his mum's bedside cabinet. The cover features a full-colour photo, in tweeds and trilby, of handsome Doctor Cockerdale. Remember *Country Doctor*? Every middle-aged, middle-England woman's essential Sunday evening viewing around the turn of the millennium? Not that Annie would have admitted to being middle-aged back in 2000. She will scarcely admit to it now, when she's about to qualify for a senior railcard. Even so, she regularly used to find herself curled in a corner of the sofa alongside Bernie, with a mug of coffee and a fond smile, watching the charmingly bashful doc tootle around the calendar-pretty villages of what purported to be 1950s Yorkshire in his well-polished Morris Minor, saving lives, delivering babies, fluttering hearts.

'Simon, whatshisname, uh, Spencer?' says our Dave to his ailing mum without interest. He knows the face well, without ever having been what you'd call a fan. At eight o'clock of a Sunday evening he'd be at work in some steaming kitchen or other. Besides, his notion of good television generally involves guns, gags or balls. Very much a boys' boy is Dave. He is not suspecting, not for an instant, the bombshell his dying ma is about to drop. 'What about him?'

Of course this tale was well polished by now. Dave had been recounting it in strict confidence to a new best friend in the bar at least twice a week. His teenage mum apparently met the equally juvenile Simon Spencer at a Butlin's camp. His mum was on a family holiday. The young Spencer, already an aspiring performer, had wangled some kind of job backstage at the camp summer show. They were both kids, however, too young and too madly in lurve to give a thought to contraception. The inevitable happened. This was the 1970s, so Simon wasn't marched to church at the end of a shotgun, but he was certainly expected to stick by young Lorraine.

And he would have stuck by her, he *would*, Dave now insisted. He only went off to work on that cruise ship to earn some money to support their child. It was his mum broke off the relationship because, with Simon away on the high seas, she took up with the man he had always known as his dad. A nice man, a good man, bit strait-laced maybe, and older than Mum, but offering to bring the unborn babe up as his own, with no bugger the wiser. Just so long as she gave the order of the boot to slippery Simon. Which, after a lot of heart-searching (said Dave) she did. In fact, she did more than break off with Simon. She wrote to him, care of P&O, and told him she'd had a late miscarriage. So that was that.

When Dave reached this suspenseful juncture in the tale, it always triggered a blizzard of questions. Had he never suspected his dad wasn't actually his real father? How did he feel? Had he rushed straight off to contact this Simon Spencer? If not, why not?

Dave would respond that he had never suspected a thing, was knocked sideways, backwards – every which way – by the news. He confessed that the possibility of this famous actor being his biological father quite, you know, tickled him. Nothing against his other dad, you understand, but the old man had been dead and gone a long time. However, no, he had not immediately tried to get in touch with Simon Spencer because ... Well, was it all true, for starters? His mum had been away with the drug fairies by the time she came out with this extraordinary tale. Plus there were his brothers and sisters to think of, because they were never going to be half-brothers and half-sisters to Dave, no matter what his parentage turned out to be. Naturally he was chary of springing the news on them, particularly when they were all still grieving for their mother. What he did not admit, perhaps even to himself, was that the composition of a letter or email to this Simon Spencer broaching such a sensitive issue was a challenge for someone whose literary endeavours did not generally stretch beyond a scrawl on cheques and Christmas cards.

Then Bernie swept into his life. She heard the story. She marvelled, she shed tears, she laughed, she hugged the great steaming eejit – and she went straight back to the Red House to consult Annie. Naturally. Annie had pondered for a full five seconds before decreeing that Dave most certainly must act upon his mother's startling revelation. The sooner the better.

Her advice, of course, was quite unrelated to a charmingly absurd vision that may have flickered across her mind of handsome Dr Cockerdale driving his shiny Morris Minor up Deerbourne Lane. Nor was she in the least influenced by the regular tittle-tattle in the gossip mags about rifts in his real-life marriage. She never read such rags. Well, perhaps she glanced at the odd article when in the hairdresser. That must be how she came to know that this Simon Spencer was – what a coincidence! – almost exactly her own age.

What is certain is that she was prodding busily at her phone even as she instructed Bernie that an email needed to be despatched, forthwith and immediately, care of Mr Simon Spencer's agent – look, she had already Googled the contact details, piece of cake. The text must be brief, and she was inclined to think it should come from Bernie herself on behalf of her shy husband-to-be—

'Shy?' her friend had squawked. 'Are we talking about my Davey here?'

—because delicacy of phrasing was essential, nothing must be stated as fact, they must just open a door to the possibility ... Look, would Bernie like her to draft something? After an hour of condensing long and hard thought into short and soft words, Annie took a deep breath and watched Bernie press *send*.

She had not been unhopeful of some sort of response, given she could swear she'd seen a piece during her last cut and blow-dry about Mr and Mrs Simon Spencer's sadness that their marriage had never been blessed with offspring. Inevitably, the feature had concentrated more on *her*, since there could be no competition as to which of that couple rated top billing, but amid the usual guff and fluff about their gracious Hollywood mansion, there was a coy hint that their menagerie of dogs, cats and parrots – was there even a miniature pig? – might be a substitute for the nursery full of children she and her husband had hoped for. Which sounded promising, did it not?

Even in her wackiest fantasies, though, Annie had never anticipated that the actor himself would telephone the Hopkirk Arms the very next evening. Yes, within twenty-four hours and all the way from California, Simon Spencer had called. And he had talked to his newly discovered son for an hour and three quarters. And what a conversation that had been. When the man learned he had two little granddaughters as well as a son, he had actually wept down the phone. Well, actors are emotional creatures, aren't they? Even if they were born in Yorkshire. Simon Spencer wanted to know every last thing about his new family and could hardly wait to embrace them all. A gloriously happy ending appeared to be imminent. Except . . .

This life-changing conversation had taken place months ago, back in the spring. And while barely a week had passed since then during which Dave had not been in touch with his newly discovered dad via phone, email or Skype, all the many plans for Simon to come and acquaint himself with his family ahead of the wedding had, one way or another, failed to translate into a visit.

It was not hard to identify the spanner in the works. Anyone who has ever opened a newspaper, let alone *Hello!* magazine, will guess. Simon Spencer, after all, was married to an ageing Hollywood goddess more newsworthy by now for her tantrums than her talents. Countless stories were written about her maladies, if not her movies, about her collapses, mental and physical, along with her 'addictions', recoveries, relapses – survival of all of which she was famously ready to ascribe to anything from avocados to Aztec astrology. With a sackful of crystals thrown in. She had become the patron saint of health cranks and tabloid hacks alike. Yes, this was the Deptford Diva herself, born in London, immortalised in Beverly Hills – none other than Dame Viola Hood.

There should surely be a drum roll, a dimming of the lights and a storm of applause as the divine Vi makes her entrance onto the page. Her lustre may have faded in recent years, but whose does not, sooner or later? And once a star, always a star. Except Viola is not about to appear, not in the flesh. Even Dave Eastman, an optimist to his bones, never seriously hoped Viola would accompany her husband to little old Bucksford. He had, though, truly believed his dad would be there to support him at the altar. But what had happened, barely hours before the wedding?

'Nut allergy my arse,' said Bernie, some ten days later, after she and Dave tottered home from what passed as a honeymoon – with kids, at Disneyland Paris. 'You ever heard of anyone over the age of eleven allergic to peanuts? Jaysus, allergies hadn't even been invented when I was a kid. Get yourself inside, woman, we need to talk. I am so big with news I could *burst*.'

She had already seized Annie's arms and was tugging her into the bar. This being a balmy late July morning, the doors were thrown wide even though the Hopkirk Arms was still closed to custom. A basket stuffed with newly purpled heather had replaced the fire in the grate, sunlight glinted from the racks of bottles and glasses, and there was a sweet tang of beeswax and orange peel in the air, usurping the more usual public house miasma of beer and chip fat. This was down to Bernie's artistry, as Annie knew well. Premises under her care were more than spanking clean, they glowed, they smiled, they blossomed. Bernadette Eastman was also one of the few women she had ever known who not only quite naturally took your hand or threw an arm around your shoulders but was able to sustain the intimacy without awkwardness.

'Not a word until you've a coffee in front of you,' she said, pressing Annie into a chair. 'Two minutes. Don't move a muscle.'

Bernie was as tiny and fine-boned as a sparrow, with wild gingery hair, currant eyes and a sharp nose, childishly freck-led. From afar, her slight figure could be mistaken for that of a schoolgirl, rather than the mother of a hulking, rugby-play-ing registrar in a London teaching hospital.

'I,' she said, returning with two brimming mugs, a dish of flapjacks and a couple of sheets of A4, close-printed, 'have received an email. Addressed to me, myself, personally, not to Davey Boy. No, don't say a word, Annie Stoneycroft. You can guess who it's from, and I can see from that lemon-sucking look on your face you're going to tell me it's only more blather. Which it is not. At least, yes, he does apologise all over again, to be sure he does, but ... Well, you must read it for yourself.'

Annie rummaged in her bag for reading specs. Since they were sparkly pink and jokily oversized – more a toy, obviously, than a necessary prop for ageing eyes? – they were not hard to locate. She was just playing for time. Whatever they said, she had known how deeply Simon Spencer's absence from their wedding had wounded Bernie and Dave. Looking at the glow of hope in her friend's face now, she felt she could not bear to witness another let-down. Annie was still seriously cross with this man.

Dear Bernie – My Very Dear MRS EASTMAN!!!

'Exclamation marks are a tool of the illiterate,' she muttered, taking a sip of coffee. 'Ditto capital letters.'

'Hark at Miss Smarty-Pants. Have a flapjack and stop scowling.'

Just writing your new name brings a smile to my face, reminding me afresh that I now have not just a son and two grandchildren, but also a lovely daughter-in-law! I'm sorry that all you get in exchange is one sad old thesp!

'Laying it on with a trowel, isn't he? Exclamation mark, exclamation mark.'

'Will you shut up and read?'

Seriously, Bernie, for all I've told Dave again and again how sorry I am, I feel I still owe you such a massive apology I hardly know where to begin. It was YOUR wedding day, above all, and ...

'... desperately upset, blah-blah, terribly mortified, yeah-yeah-yeah ... we've got the message, you smarmy sod. You're sorry you didn't turn up.'

'For Pete's sake—'

'Well, he doesn't use one word where twenty will do, does he? Oh, here we go.'

I can honestly say it was one of the most miraculous moments of my life when my agent forwarded that first email from you, Bernie. Thank God you sent it. And I'm eternally grateful to the wonderful friend who Dave tells me gave you the courage to write.

'See? You're in there too.'

'Huh,' said Annie. But she did settle her specs more firmly up the bridge of her nose.

Even now, I can hardly express what it means to me, learning I have a son. That I've been a father all these years. I can't wait to put my arm round Dave, around all of you.

'So what's stopping you, sunshine? Oh, keep your hair on, Bernie, I'm reading.'

You, I'm quite sure, will be asking why I haven't arrived on your doorstep long since.

About to comment, Annie glanced at her friend and thought better of it.

That's why I wanted to write to you particularly, Bernie.

*I know you'll understand that what I'm about to tell you must
be in confidence. I don't want to give more fodder to the ravening
jackals of the tabloids over in the UK. Of course, you must share
everything with Dave. I'm only emailing you instead of him, for
once, because I'm hoping that you, as a woman, might understand
more easily the situation I'm in, and maybe help him to understand, too. Talking to Dave on the phone, man to man, I've never
quite found the right way in to this conversation. You know what
we chaps are like, especially Yorkshiremen. We josh, we banter, we
take the mick. We don't – bluddy hell, eh? – bare our hearts. It isn't
easy for me even now. I'm down in my den with the door locked
because I've a bottle of Jack Daniel's, which I confess is sinking
rather fast. Officially we don't have alcohol in the house, and I
have to keep bottles well hidden.*

She raised her eyebrows. 'So the wife really is an alkie, like
they say?'

'Just keep reading, cherub.'

The fact is, my poor darling wife and I . . . No! Let's cut the crap.

Annie blinked and put down her mug.

*I'm so used to talking about my 'Darling Vi', I do it on autopilot
and it's meaningless. Worse, it's a lie. It might have been true once,
but that was long ago. Do you understand, Bernie? Everything
you must have read in the bloody papers about our miserable shell
of a marriage is true. And, God knows, a lot more besides.*

'Blimey,' breathed Annie.

'What'd I tell you? Food for thought, hey?'

Food for thought indeed. So absorbed was Annie in pondering the content of Simon Spencer's rambling missive that she
drove the length of the Bucksford Road before realising she
had, for once, passed the spot where the police had pulled her
over without so much as a shudder. She was due in the

magistrates' court on Monday, too, to answer for her misdemeanours. Today was doubtless the last chance she'd have to drive herself out to the Hopkirk Arms for a long time.

She banished this lowering reflection by returning her thoughts to the email.

It was true, as Bernie had pushed her into admitting, that what he had written went some way to excusing his wayward behaviour. Annie must always feel for the spouse of a drinker, and it seemed Viola Hood was not just the modern Californian notion of an alcoholic (OMG, you drink a whole glass of wine every day?) but the real old vodka-by-the-litre McCoy. If given the chance. Prescription drugs, too, from what Simon wrote. He claimed things only got seriously out of hand, however, after their failure to have children. But as he said, they'd married too late, were too busy, too often apart.

...Vi's eight years older than me, of course ...

'Is she now?' Annie had said, with just the flicker of a smile.

...for all she's never looked it – still less admitted it! – but once she was heading for fifty, I knew it was hopeless. She was obsessed, though, and the bloodsucking clinics over here will let you try anything if you have the money. She put herself through hell – both of us, to be honest. Ours isn't the only marriage to crumble under the strain. But then we had the cancer scare ...

'Just because you're a raving hypochondriac doesn't mean you can't be sick,' had commented Bernie, and Viola Hood certainly had been sick, surviving heart trouble, hip surgery and some gut problem as well as breast cancer – along with more than one overdose of painkillers.

...although her doctors and I believe she only wanted to frighten us. I'm telling you all this, Bernie, because the most recent time she resorted to a fistful of pills was the day after I received your wonderful email. My fault. In my excitement I blurted out the whole story. Desperate as she'd been to have a family, it's hardly surprising she

was less than thrilled to hear I'd just acquired one, ready made. And I'm trying not to think how she'll react if and when the press get wind of my long-lost love child.

In the light of the above, however, you may not be entirely surprised to hear that, far from accidentally swallowing a nut hidden in a sandwich, Viola appears to have consumed an entire tub of peanut butter ice cream. She denies it, of course, furiously, but I can't imagine how else an empty carton came to be stuffed, rather pathetically, at the bottom of the cupboard where she used to stash her bottles. I found it three days after your wedding, checking the old hidey-holes for hooch, before they let her out of hospital. She hadn't touched peanuts in decades, ever since a reaction covered her in the most hideous red lumps, which held up filming for a week and nearly bankrupted the producer. That's all it was, though, a swollen mouth and hives, nothing life-endangering and – whatever she claims about the cleaner's son and the ice cream – I believe that's what she was intending now. To make herself just convincingly ill enough to keep me at home.

I'm sorry if you're shocked that I could even suggest my wife would play such a mean-spirited trick – worshipped, as she is, by all those fans – but I have to tell you her health crises have often had an uncanny knack of striking just in time to scupper some plan of mine she didn't like. She misjudged badly on this occasion, though. She went into full anaphylactic shock, and it really was touch and go for twenty-four hours. Having scared herself nearly to death – literally – she'll never touch another nut, that's for sure. She's even had people round inspecting the labels of every jar and packet in the kitchens. I'm tempted to say that the only nut left in this house now is Viola herself!

But that's a cheap joke. And I can't prove any of this – I just thought you deserved the full story.

'So why doesn't he leave her?' Annie had exclaimed.

'Maybe he's scared she'll hit the pills again? That's a terrible thing to have hanging over your head, isn't it now? Anyway, get on to the last bit, about the play she's planning to do over here next year, where he hints this might be his chance to quit.'

Annie bent her head to the last page again. 'Sounds dodgy to me. If a marriage is dead it's dead. You don't put "leave the wife" in your diary for next May, do you? Besides, he says he's coming to the UK to look after her.'

Bernie beamed. 'And won't that be just great? He'll be over here for months.'

'Except he then says not to hold your breath, because she's notorious for pulling out of jobs at the eleventh hour. Even so . . .' Annie put her head on one side. 'He writes persuasively, I'll give you that. And yes – yes, I think I do believe he really is keen to come and see Dave, meet you all. I can see why you're excited.'

Bernie winked at her. 'And aren't you?'

'Sorry?'

'Excited? Oh, come on, Annie Stoneycroft, this is me you're talking to. So don't even think of pretending you haven't always fancied the feckin' pants off my father-in-law.'

4

Bucksford was not a large town. Once upon a recent time, Annie would have described it as conveniently compact. At its heart, Victoria Square housed the town hall and a blackened but still visibly unamused statue of the eponymous queen. A quaintly cobbled high street was broad enough to host a market and sufficiently populous to rate a branch of Boots, if not of Marks & Spencer. Any shopping other than the most mundane thus entailed a journey, but the railway line which had once connected Bucksford to York was now a cindered footpath, and Annie exasperatedly declared that the bus timetable required the decoding talents of Alan Turing. The two large supermarkets serving the town, moreover, were exiled to retail sites on the bypass, the nearer of which, by the shortest route she could devise, lay 2.6 miles from her front door.

She was viewing her home town through new eyes. Deerbourne Lane wound a leafy way up the south-facing side of the valley and the Red House perched close to the summit, with just enough hill behind to shelter it from the worst of winter's blast. Annie had always delighted in the prospect this situation commanded: a pleasing tumble of roofs, chimneys and trees below, threaded with an occasional twinkle of river and canal. Beyond, a patchwork of fields stretched up to High Buck Moor, which, at this time of year, lined the horizon with purple. She was taking less delight in the elevated location of her home now, when she found herself slogging up Deerbourne Hill on foot, particularly with a bag of shopping.

The inevitable had happened. She had lost her driving licence. As an upstanding citizen whose last formal punishment had been to write out ten times Portia's quality of mercy spiel (for the record, it was not actually the young Annie Royd who had dropped that fag packet out of the art-room window) she was ashamed to find herself in both the dock and, no question, the wrong. Immediately after her court appearance, the relief of getting the legal procedure over with had buoyed her spirits for a time. She was also grateful to have received only the minimum ban of one year. As a lifelong looker on the bright side, she even began lecturing herself – and everyone else – on the health benefits of walking. That was before she tried climbing Deerbourne Hill with a watermelon in her bag.

A standing contract with a taxi firm was easily arranged, although she was soon swearing she would scream if another well-meaning friend told her how much cheaper using cabs was, long term, than running a car. Setting aside the tedium of waiting for taxis and the small talk of drivers who made Donald Trump sound like a liberal intellectual, the maths of these wiseacres failed to factor in ownership of a brand-new, top-of-the-range car. This extravagant toy was sitting in her drive, losing money faster than if she were standing out there herself, ripping up tenners in the breeze. And she simply could not understand – as she said more than once – why her son, after a single half-hearted attempt in his teens, had never bothered to retake his driving test. OK, with his injuries, driving might be forbidden by the orthopaedic surgeon at present. But, as she tersely pointed out, if only Dominic had applied himself to the business, like any normal young man, she could at least be looking forward to climbing into the passenger seat of her car. To which he had retorted—

But enough of that, perhaps. There's no need to rehash every little tiff between mother and son. Suffice to say, their enforced confinement was beginning to chafe on them both. However if Dominic seemed resigned to wallowing in apathy, she was not.

'I know,' she said one drizzly morning, while supervising his exercises. 'We'll have a dinner party.'

He scowled. 'Why?'

She balanced a weighted bean-bag across his ankle as prescribed by the physiotherapist. 'Lift and straighten, far as you can. See some friends, cheer ourselves up? Keep lifting, kid, you have to do a dozen of these.'

'I don't need cheering up.'

'Yes, you do,' stated his mother in tones that admitted no dissent. 'We both do.'

It was no surprise the Eastmans couldn't escape for a night, with a pub, young children, and – so Annie learned – a sous-chef off with tendinitis. It was nevertheless a disappointment. She was feeling Bernie's loss with renewed sharpness, and not just as a chauffeur. That was the least of it, although her frustration at being unable to jump in a car and see her friend at will was doubtless why the house was only feeling so disconcertingly silent and empty now, months after Bernie had finally moved out. With Dom morose when he wasn't asleep, Annie was rattling around, feeling like the last biscuit left in the tin, even before Rob told her he was about to embark on a lecture tour of Bolivia or Buffalo or somewhere equally outlandish. So he wasn't available for dinner dates either.

'But you've only just got home.' She was rocking back on her chair, feet on the kitchen table, phone clamped between shoulder and ear. 'I haven't seen you *properly* for ages. I'm missing you.'

43

'Bloody Nora, you must be bored. Well, I always said you'd regret packing in the day job.'

She crashed the chair legs back to the floor. 'Oh for God's sake, how many times? I sold up because I want to *do* things, different things.'

'Like?'

'Have fun. Get out. Give – dinner parties.'

'Very stimulating.'

'Piss off. I could travel. Learn Italian, tap-dancing, water-colours, you name it. Go to the theatre, galleries, meet people – new people.'

'What's wrong with the old ones?'

'They're always bloody going off abroad when I want them.'

'Yeah, because I need to make myself useful. Look, give over snarling. All I'm saying is, sure, have your fun, but I still reckon you'd be happier with some kind of worthwhile occu-pation alongside all that.'

'Don't you get it?' she cried. 'I have been solidly, worth-while-ly occupied for so long I can't even remember what it's like *not* having to be somewhere, do something, see to some-one, morning, noon and middle of the bloody night. Now, I've no clients or staff, kids are grown up, no dad, mum – or Jake. I'm free as a bird. At last. But my problem – my only problem, old friend – is not having wheels.'

'But—'

'I'm going crackers, Rob. All these things I want to do, and it's impossible without a car. No, seriously, d'you know how long it would've taken me to get to that exhibition at the Hepworth by public transport? Five hours, and what is it – forty miles? God, I've been so desperate I nearly joined the book club Trisha bangs on about, only I missed the meeting because the taxi firm screwed up. Again. And don't you dare mention walking. Of course I can walk; I am walking; I have walked so many sodding miles I've nearly worn out a pair of trainers already, but even if it's not raining – which it has been doing solidly for the whole of this past week in case you haven't noticed – it takes hours. *Hours*. Half your day's gone and all you've done is buy a few loo rolls and had a coffee. And if that's you sniggering I can hear, you can stop right now.'

'Poor old Nan. You thought about a bike?'

'Ha!' she cried. 'Bet your life I've thought about a bike. For at least ten minutes. Until I also thought about pushing it up Deerbourne Hill, because I've had to climb that bastard a few times recently on foot and I'm here to tell you pedalling up it would make the Tour de France look like a stroll in the park.'

'I cycle up there all the time.'

'Exactly.'

He laughed. 'Look, I gotta run, I'm late for a meeting. You'll be seeing the Houghs at your thrash, won't you? Tell Trish I'm really sorry I didn't have time to drop round at the weekend.'

'Actually, no, I wasn't thinking of inviting—'

Rob had already rung off.

'This is a fab party,' bellowed Trisha Hough. 'Isn't this fab-ewe-luss, Joey?'

Her son, lolling in his wheelchair, twisted his head round to squint up at her with a gargling noise, which she did not hesitate to translate as enthusiastic agreement.

'Bit of a madhouse but I'm glad you're enjoying yourselves,' shrieked Annie, with gritted-teeth gaiety. 'Excuse me, Trisha, the hordes are roaring for bread.'

They were in the garden where a warm harvest moon was obliterated by strings of flashing lights. Skinny young bodies in everything from wrecked denim and shrunken T-shirts to gold bras and tartan hot pants were entwined on the crowded terrace. Forty had been invited, but Annie reckoned this mob must number half as many again. Bottles were being passed over heads, viscous grey smoke wafted from a hired barbecue and reggae throbbed from black and battered speakers, also rented for the night. This was not the civilised dinner party she had once envisaged.

With a resolute smile she elbowed her way across to a paper-cloth'd trestle littered with empty cans and improvised ashtrays, banishing wistful imaginings of the table over which she might have been presiding this evening, a-flutter with candles, a-glitter with glasses and sweet with the scent of exquisitely arranged flowers. Was it so middle-aged to prefer conversation you could hear? Mozart to Bob Marley? Witty repartee and roses to burnt sausages and gnats?

'Hello, hi, I wonder if you could just . . .? Look, *PLEASE WOULD YOU MOVE YOUR BAG SO I CAN PUT THIS BREAD DOWN?* Great, thanks, terrific.'

According to Dominic, no one in their right mind actually enjoyed formal dinner parties – no one under forty, anyhow. Giving them was just a competitive sport for pretentious old farts with too much time and money, wasn't it? Having prided herself on throwing some of the smartest dinners in town, Annie had smiled sweetly, loaded an extra weight onto his ankle and told him to do another twenty lifts.

'The music is rather loud, isn't it?' said a well-brought-up female voice close behind her ear. 'If you're clearing plates, shall I follow with another pile? I'd be much happier making myself useful.'

'Please do,' shouted Annie, without looking round or drawing breath.

Naturally she had disregarded her son's infantile opinions. However, while being by no means as incompetent in a kitchen as Rob Daley liked to joke – and an expert navigator of the high-end ready-prepped market – Annie had found herself reflecting that a sit-down job for twelve might be a stretch without Bernie alongside. Besides, with neither of her most cherished kindred spirits able to attend, her enthusiasm for inviting lesser souls had ebbed. Ever one to turn obstacles into opportunities, however, she decided Dominic needed booting out of the doldrums even more than she. So she had announced that this was now to become his party. His friends, his food, his music, OK?

It could not be said he had jumped at the offer, but his phone must have been busy. All the old crowd seemed to be here. She had blinked on seeing his schoolfriend Kit Grayson's pierced nose and studded brow, never mind the marijuana leaves which were not just tattooed up his scrawny arm but, by all accounts, flourishing in his attic. Such a nice little boy he used to be. He'd been chatting to a couple of people she half recognised from the Woolshed, Bucksford's new arts centre. The Roxy, the Picture Palace and the velvet-swagged Little Theatre were long gone. Bucksford now had this *space*, as Dominic approvingly termed it, all exposed scaffolding and black shuttered lights in a converted mill, hosting every-thing from Bertolt Brecht to Walt Disney, with Pilates classes thrown in. Rob, too, spoke highly of the Woolshed, but that was hardly surprising, since he was on the board of trustees. Ah well, Annie had told Dominic to invite whom the hell he wanted, had loaded a taxi with booze, burgers, bangers and (inevitably these days) their veggie equivalents and promised to keep a low profile.

'One good thing about a barbecue,' she remarked over her shoulder, as she led the way into the relative quiet of the kitchen, 'in fact the only good thing if you ask me, is that people cook their dinners for themselves. Or cremate them, to judge by the stink. Thank you, that's really helpful—' She broke off, surprised, because she had assumed that the willowy figure carrying a stack of plates behind her was just another of Dominic's twenty-something cronies. Under the brighter light indoors, though, she saw that what she had taken for blonde hair swept into a bird's nest of a bun, was in fact silver, and that the woman already opening the dishwasher was of her own generation, although her complexion was as pink and enviably smooth as a child's.

'Liz Jones,' said this newcomer, competently relieving Annie of her jumble of cutlery. 'I know who you are, of course. Oh glory, isn't this kitchen to die for?' She circled slowly, gazing up and down. 'I used to think your store was bliss, you know. I'd just go in and wander about if I happened to be in town and wanted to cheer myself up. I say, I do hope you don't mind my tagging along tonight? Hank assured me it would be fine. But the crowd out there does make one feel frightfully old.'

'Tell me about it,' said Annie. 'I wouldn't care but they're not even kids. Heading for thirty, most of 'em, and still charging around like sugar-hyped thirteen-year-olds. I'm sure we were more grown up at that age.' As certain of the wilder antics of her own youth occurred to her, she felt obliged to add: 'In some ways.'

'I certainly was.' Liz pulled a rueful face. 'I was married before I was twenty.'

'No, really? That's pretty extraordinary. Now look ...' However, just as she was about to offer this unusual guest a glass of decent wine, such as was most certainly not available to the hooligans outside, Trisha Hough's mountainous backside pushed through the doorway with her son's wheelchair following.

'I thought I saw you heading in here, Annie,' she panted, swivelling the chair round. 'I told Dominic ten to one this is

48

where you'd be hiding, and he said . . . Oh, would you credit it? Here's Liz, too. I'd no idea you were here, Lizzy, such a mad pack as there is out there, real needle in a haystack time. Look, Joey, here's our friend Liz – you remember Liz, don't you? Are we going to say hello?'

Annie was unsurprised and rather touched that Dominic had invited Joey Hough, one of his earliest playmates. They had attended the same nursery, along with Bernie's Liam. But while Liam and Dominic had scrambled around, screaming with laughter and hauling themselves up climbing frames and down slides, little Joey could only roll on the floor. Twenty-seven now, stout and spiky-chinned, he was twisted in his chair, one eye pointing skywards, the other wandering, able to frame no more than guttural sounds which only his mother could identify as words.

'That's right, love,' she cooed, 'Liz was the kind person who helped us work the lift when we went to see that funny old play last week. I can't just remember what it was called, I'll be forgetting my own name next, but about a couple of soldiers it was, Annie – at least we thought they were soldiers, didn't we, Joey, from the clothes? Although you can't tell these days with everyone fancying themselves in camouflage gear, and what they wanted with the blow-up lady doll was a mystery – large as life, she was, and quite pretty except with a peculiar round-shaped mouth and you couldn't help worrying what'd happen if someone left a drawing pin lying around, or even a candle flame, you know? She really would have been a blow-up doll then, wouldn't she, as I just whispered in Joey's ear, very quietly you know, except, well, he laughed that much I nearly had to wheel him out, but I don't think anyone minded, not the people sitting near, any rate, because I reckon they were as puzzled as us, and a bit shocked, I shouldn't wonder, at the language which wasn't what you hear in church, if you get my drift, but never mind, we had ourselves a nice night out, didn't we, lovey?'

Bernie had once said that if God took an interest in the affairs of Bucksford (which she doubted) he had planted Trisha Hough in the town to make sure the rest of them counted their feckin' blessings.

'We think the Woolshed's great, don't we, Joey? The best thing that's happened round here for yonks, and they're really good to us, you know, special deals for the disabled, well, they will insist on calling it "wheelchair users", isn't that right, Liz? Because we're not supposed to say "disabled" now, are we? Which is a daft old carry-on if you ask me, because Joey knows there's things he can't manage, so what's wrong with disabled? He doesn't give a sausage, do you, pet?'

Even Bernie conceded, however, that their friend, while being a saint of course, could talk five legs off a donkey.

'. . . fab new studio space our Hank's planning, fingers and toes crossed we can raise the money,' Trisha was continuing, without drawing breath, 'at the Woolshed, I mean. Mind, Liz knows all about our fundraising, don't you, Lizzy? Though Annie might be wondering what someone like me's doing on the committee, but it's not just a theatre thing, oh no, we're promised a proper community facility, what d'they call it, outreach? Any road, space for clubs like our Joey's High Rollers, and the mums and tots, and old folk and . . .'

That Trisha Hough was a saint everyone agreed. It was a bloody marvel the way she had soldiered on single-handed, after her husband buggered off, with no forwarding address, when the demands of his infant son's disabilities became apparent. Even her beloved sister was settled away on the far side of the world in America, these days. But look at her. A cheery smile for everyone, had Trisha Hough, with never a squeak of complaint.

'. . . and did a little bird say you wanted to come to our book club t'other week, Annie? Now if you'd only asked, I'd have run up Deerbourne Hill to fetch you in two shakes of a lamb's whatsit . . . Sorry, what was that, lovey?'

Joey had grasped her arm. 'Oh, has your mum fallen down the old rabbit hole again? That's what we call it when I go rabbiting on, which I do sometimes, I know, I'm a terror for rabbiting. And we only came inside because, if you don't mind, Annie, please may Joey have another can of that nice sweet cider? He likes his tipple once in a while does my young man, and I always say a little of what you fancy never killed anybody. Your Dom said would I ask you for some more beer out by the barbecue, too. And, um, toffee kebabs?'

'Sorry?' Trisha's stream of chat tended to shut down Annie's higher brain functions. 'Oh, *tofu*. Well, if that pack of locusts haven't emptied the fridge already. Anyway why doesn't the lazy sod come and look for himself instead of sending messages with you?'

'Ah, we mustn't forget his poorly leg, must we?' Trisha sank into a chair at the table and began rummaging in the capacious patchwork bag she kept suspended from the handles of her son's wheelchair.

'Are these the kebabs?' said Liz Jones with a shy smile, lifting a tray out of the fridge. 'I'll take them outside, shall I?'

'Here we are now.' Trisha had propped an iPad on the table and was stabbing busily. 'You can see what you missed at our meeting, if you like, because I always make notes for anyone who's missed a session, but you'd probably sooner I email that along. No, I really got the old paddywhack out – that's what we call it, you know, and Joey laughs his head off, because we sing *iPad, paddywhack, give the dog a phone* . . .' She chuckled. 'Where were we? Oh yes, I thought you'd want to have a look through the photos of our trip to that literary festival back in

May, see what we get up to, and there's too many to email, even if quite a few seem to be pictures of the back of my hand or foot or summat, honestly, what am I like? We generally hire ourselves a minibus for our excursions, you know, and—'

'Can't wait.' Annie seized two six-packs of lager. 'But maybe I'd better deliver these first?'

5

Regularly, nowadays, women of a certain age complain that they have become invisible in the world. Annie Stoneycroft was not one of them. That might be because bossy cows, as she has been known to describe herself, are not easily overlooked. Tonight, however, she could have joined the chorus.

As she squeezed and shoved and excused herself round her son's guests, scooping up plates, extinguishing fag stubs and surreptitiously filling a bin bag with crumpled cans, she might have been a ghost. These youngsters were just not seeing her at all. Not that they were rude or difficult, far from it. Mostly the well-reared offspring of Bucksford's worthiest, several of whom she'd known since they were splashing in paddling pools on this very lawn, they would perhaps blink in mild bewilderment as she bustled past or beam bleary forgiveness when she stumbled over their outstretched feet, but that was all. One or two even passed her an empty bottle or can, but their gaze passed through her as through glass and their conversations never faltered.

It made her feel very old but at least banished any qualms about spoiling the fun by clearing up while the party swung on. As she remarked to Liz Jones, she could have stripped off and danced naked along the trestle table without this bunch so much as glancing round.

53

'You are funny,' said her charming new acquaintance, elbow-deep in the sink, washing glasses as fast as Annie could deliver them.

She had been a welcome support, even making the post-poned but inevitable trudge through Trisha's thousand and one snaps of her book club outing bearable – well, almost bearable – with a ready flow of comments and chuckles. Annie could only think such Olympian tolerance had been honed over years of attending to garrulous elderly parishioners, because she had now learned that Liz was the widow of a vicar. Since her own experience of the Church was confined to births, marriages, deaths and the sole occasion on which *Songs of Praise* had been televised from Bucksford Abbey, she found the notion of a clergyman's wife intriguingly exotic.

'Leave the rest of the washing-up,' she commanded as midnight approached. 'Let's take a drink outside. We've earned a break.'

The crowd was thinning, a creamy moon now floated overhead and even if the music was unrecognisably obscure it was at least quieter. Dominic was propped on the low wall of the fish pond in a group including a wiry young man sporting eyeliner, assorted ironmongery in ears and brow and a black trilby on the back of his semi-shaven head. Liz, with shy pride, introduced him as her employer, Hank Damon, apparently the artistic director of the Woolshed. Well, he certainly looked the part. Dominic was leaning perilously across him to light a cigarette from the glowing tip of Trisha Hough's while Joey flapped a protesting hand with a lopsided grin.

'Piss off, mate,' said Dominic to him as Annie approached, and she was glad to see her handsome boy throw back his head and shout with laughter at whatever Joey had grunted in return, sounding quite his old self. Well done, Annie, she said to herself. Had she not told her son that a party would do him good?

'Anyone for fizz?' she cried, holding up her bottle.

She was less gratified by the alacrity with which Dom thrust out his glass. This sudden thirst for alcohol was getting beyond a joke. For years he'd rarely drunk anything stronger than water, albeit of the most expensively mineralised brands, or snot-coloured cocktails of pulverised veg, while lecturing his mother on galloping cirrhosis in the silver-haired Sauvignon-swigging classes. Now he seemed to be making up for all that lost drinking time with grim resolution – and she was unmoved by any nonsense about post-traumatic stress. Pretending not to have seen his glass, she proffered the bottle towards Hank Damon and Trisha. While she told herself she was only imagining a certain self-righteousness in the swift refusal from both on the grounds of driving, she still felt the sting of a flush in her cheeks as she turned to Liz. 'Or are you in charge of a motor vehicle, too?'

Liz grimaced. 'I wish.'

Annie's eyebrows flew up. 'Hey, not another sinner like me?'

As she filled their glasses, however, she learned that Liz was merely without a car, her treasured old Fiat having been pronounced beyond repair that very morning.

'So what will you go for next?' she enquired with interest.

Liz sucked her lower lip for a moment. 'I may not, um, be replacing it. Not at once, anyhow. After all, in a small town like this, how often does one really need a car?'

'All the bloody time,' retorted Annie. 'Take it from me. I've eleven and a bit months off road still to go and I'm counting the days. If I were you, I'd be touring the dealers down the bypass tomorrow.'

'I can't,' the other woman burst out. Glancing round, she lowered her voice. 'To be honest, I – I can't really afford another car. Not just yet. I shall probably have to find a second job first. I adore working for Hank, but they can only afford to pay me for three mornings a week, and ecclesiastical pensions are . . . Well, you know what they say about church mice.' She smiled, but the effort was painfully clear. 'I can manage, naturally I can. It's just a shame my poor little car has given up the ghost because I do really enjoy driving. It's one of the few things in life I've ever been any good at.'

One of Annie's favoured faux-modest ripostes when congratulated on her clever ideas was to protest she was blessed with no more than a knack for spotting an opportunity. Therefore, before their glasses were even half emptied, Liz Jones had accepted the offer of Annie's motor to use as she pleased in exchange for regular, if ad hoc, chauffeuring services.

It would be hard to say which of them was the more delighted with the arrangement.

Hurray, hurray, ran her email to Rob Daley, *I'm back in the land of the living. Not only do I have my own personal chauffeur – should that be chauffeuse? – I have made a new friend. No substitute for Bernie, obvs., and couldn't be more different. Frightfully posh, shy as a bird, but very sweet and you would not believe the crap deal she's had in life, poor soul. Honestly, I sit in the passenger seat with my jaw on the floor as I listen to her tales from the vicarage.*

But thanks to her you can stop chuntering about me getting bored without the day job. Liz and I have put our names down for so many things, I don't know how we're going to fit them in. By the time you get home I could be painting abstract acrylics while scoffing home-smoked salmon and singing cantatas – in the original Italian! So Ciao for now, carissimo . . .

*   *   *

A fortnight later, Annie remained delighted, and this cannot have been just because her new friend so fulsomely admired her taste, her cleverness and all-round worldly wisdom. And giggled at her jokes. On the face of it, though, she and Liz would seem to have little in common beyond their sex and age. Even here, Annie was surprised to learn that peach-cheeked Liz was two years her senior. The benefits of pure living, obviously.

True, both had entered into less than idyllic marriages, but the idea of drawing a comparison between the Reverend Dafydd Jones and the irreverent – indeed downright irre-deemable – Jake Stoneycroft made Annie snort with laughter she wasn't going to explain to Liz. For while both women had recently tended these men through illness to death, she had already shocked her new friend by stating brusquely that she was no one's idea of Florence fucking Nightingale. She'd had to make clear that Jake had not been her husband by then. Just the ex she'd had the good sense to divorce a very long time before. She changed the subject before Liz could enquire further. She had not yet suggested that Liz might have had a happier life if she had likewise ditched her spouse. She was, however, working round to it.

They compared biographies during shopping trips (such a relief to escape the box-ticking tedium of websites); while throwing clay pots (messy fun, but who wanted to give house-room to the resulting lumps of solidified porridge?); when walking the Wrag Valley (too many cows) or the Moors Way (pretty scenery, ghastly hiking group); and even while attempt-ing to learn the tango. This so boggled brains and feet alike that they abandoned the class halfway through to head for a new wine bar in the high street. They agreed (which is to say, Annie declared, and Liz agreed) that ballroom dancing was hopeless without men. It was bad enough to clash toes, never mind bosoms. Sadly, they were too late to register for conversational Italian and, as time went by, their excursions did seem to drift more often towards cafes, pubs or tearooms, depending on the time of day.

As the daughter of a tradesman, with a cheerfully ordinary upbringing, Annie thrilled to descriptions of her friend's Dickensian boarding school and still more wretched home life after Papa decamped to South Africa with the nanny and the family money (yes, just like an airport novel). Her embittered mother apparently took refuge in God, Valium and an unheated hovel on the bleak Borders estate of her second cousin, a clinically bonkers (Annie's diagnosis) and legendarily miserly baronet. An entire floor in the aforesaid aristo's stately gaff had eventually crumbled under the weight of his stockpiled tins of food. What totally beggared her comprehension, though, was why, after a childhood of mouldy walls, daily Mass and all-round madness – never mind Christian summer camps and being so poor she had to cut up old sheets for sanitary towels – Liz had no sooner reached university than she hitched herself to another religious nutter. Dafydd Jones was then a curate with a gluey passion for model aircraft, chronic eczema and Asperger's. OK, this last was Annie's diagnosis again, but no two ways about it: that guy had issues.

This was where they got to the seriously interesting stuff, though. *Sex.* Annie did feel the odd twinge of unease when probing but, dammit, wouldn't you be curious? Here was a notably good-looking female of her own pill-gulping, *Cosmo*-reading, orgasm-counting generation who, like some Victorian maiden, had stumbled into marriage at nineteen with a beardy Bible-basher. To be strictly accurate, the Rev Jones' beard was thus far unconfirmed, although Annie would have bet a bottle of Moët the bugger had had one.

Even if Liz was too shy to be entirely explicit, Annie soon established that her experience of sex had been confined to the Rev's undoubtedly primitive fumblings under the marital eiderdown. A tempting hypothesis that no baby had resulted because neither of them knew quite what should go where had to be discarded when she learned that they had finally resorted to medical help. Her opinion of the Rev hit a new low, however, when she learned he had refused *in vitro* assistance, on the grounds that it was contrary to Divine Will.

'And I did so long for a baby,' admitted Liz, blinking rapidly and pretending to search for something in her handbag under the table so she could blot her eyes with a paper napkin. They were, at the time, draining their post-lunch coffees in the conservatory of the Moorside Garden Centre.

Annie's indignation was further stoked by Liz adding that at least her husband had not insisted on . . . *you know*, after it became clear there was no hope of children. Annie bloody well hoped he had not insisted, thereby adding marital rape to his charge sheet. Given that he was seven years Liz's senior, she already had him down as the next thing to a child abuser.

'So that was a relief,' whispered Liz, blushing vividly.

'Relief?' Annie was unable to contain herself. '*Relief?!* For pity's sake, Liz, sex isn't a duty. Sex is glorious – well, good sex is, anyhow. Fantastic. Mind-blowing, soul-shattering. It's – it's the magic glue that can bind you to the biggest bastard on two legs even if you know it's crazy, but you don't give a flying fuck. Ha ha, no pun intended. I mean, my ex, Jake, was a lying, cheating, drunken nightmare, no two ways about it, but sex with him was . . . *Ow!* Why are you kicking me?'

Liz was leaning so far forward over the table her necklace was dangling in the sugar bowl. 'People are staring at us?'

The cafe of the Moorside Garden Centre was a favourite haunt of the senior lunching fraternity and the tables were packed close. Glancing round, Annie noticed several grey heads either turned interestedly towards her or angled pointedly away.

She could hardly request the bill she was laughing so much.

'I'll never dare show my face in there again,' muttered Liz.

She backed out of the parking space at such swingeing speed Annie's head banged against the side window. It didn't stop her laughing.

That was one of the many differences between them. Liz worried *what people might think*. But Liz was a worrier, full stop. Her glass was always half empty while Annie's was not so much half full as in permanent danger of overflowing. And although her friend was generally quick to laugh with her, Annie was beginning to think, half the time, she didn't really get the joke.

'Lighten up,' she said. 'I'll bet we gave those poor old pensioners more entertainment than they've had in months.'

In spite of being retired from business herself, with pension securely in place, Annie would never have dreamed of describing herself as a pensioner. What an absurd notion. Similarly, she found no contradiction between her desire to become a grandmother (she tried not to nag, but it was time daughter Martha gave at least a thought to her biological clock) and her regular pejorative employment of the adjective 'granny-ish'.

Sad to say, 'granny-ish' was a term which occurred to her with regard to dear Liz's taste in clothes. She had a distressing penchant for wispy scarves and droopy brooches. As for her favourite pair of shoes – chunky, clunky, ankle-strapped flats in an unfortunate blue, all too reminiscent of the crepe-soled sandals in which Annie had started school – well, the less said about those the better. But what could you expect when the poor creature had never had the money to shop intelligently?

Annie was incapable of identifying a problem, however, without trying to mend matters. While she would readily admit to a catalogue of her own failings (or a little list, at any rate) her worst enemy could not accuse her of meanness. She liked nothing better than to give. It was just a nuisance she and Liz were such different shapes, she being a tubby dwarf compared to willowy Liz. Even so, a riffle through her over-stuffed wardrobe had identified several items she believed would work on her friend. Tact was essential, however. Certain of her nearest and dearest might claim she trundled through life with the sensitivity of a tank (and Rob Daley was a fine one to talk) but she proceeded here as delicately as a butterfly in a minefield.

She felt obliged to bide her time. She even humoured her friend's scruples by letting her fund the occasional coffee or entry to the kind of event that appealed more to Liz than to herself. An exhibition of patchwork quilts or a death-might-be-preferable dreary concert by a ladies' choir. The latter had at least served to dissuade her from any idea of taking up singing. However, she was slower than she should have been to query a proposal by Liz not merely that they should visit a flower and produce show over Richmond way, but that the outing was to be her treat. Annie must not argue, *she* was going to buy their tickets.

On the basis that entry to a village flower show was unlikely to strain even the slimmest purse, Annie did not protest. She did enquire, though, with more politeness than interest, what was so great about this event that they should drive forty-odd miles to Longbolton? They were, at the time, having an *après*-shop cuppa at her kitchen table.

'Don't you remember? Caradoc's dahlias?'

'Sorry?' Annie was guiltily aware that Liz's conversation, when not concerned with the juicy stuff, like her bonkers family or non-existent sex life, could flow past her ears like birdsong or the soothing churn of the washing machine. 'Was he the one you were going to ask about a rose variety to grow up the front porch? No, hang about, I know,' she declared. 'He's the cathedral guy. What is he, exactly, head gardener?'

Liz let out a peal of laughter so shrill Annie stared at her. 'Caradoc isn't the gardener,' she spluttered, and actually had to reach for a piece of kitchen roll to mop her eyes before she could continue. 'He's the bishop. Or he used to be. He's retired now.'

'Heavens,' said Annie, not inappropriately under the circumstances. 'I don't believe I've ever met a real live bishop. Does he wear purple underpants?'

It was a lame quip, absently uttered, because her gaze had already returned to the catalogue spread on the table in front of her, which featured chairs created from driftwood – intriguingly novel, or merely a novelty? She was struggling to visualise one of these artefacts in, say, the bigger guest bathroom when she realised Liz had fallen silent. Glancing up again, she saw her friend was flushed, and smiling to herself most peculiarly.

'Liz?'

'Gardener, oh my giddy aunt, that's such a hoot. I must remember to tell Caradoc. He'd laugh his socks off, really he would, he has a marvellous sense of humour. Although it's quite true, of course, people did sometimes mistake him for one of the gardeners, because he always used to wear the filthiest old overalls when he worked in the close, along with a hat you wouldn't give to a scarecrow. But he once told me it was a wonderful way to get to know his flock, because people would happily stop and chat to him about greenfly or geranium cuttings, with not a clue they were talking to the bish.

He was so funny about the things they came out with, too, he used to have us all in stitches.'

Not merely did this pour out in one breathless jumble, it was possibly the longest speech Liz had ever made, unprompted. And her face was alight, her eyes glowing, her cheeks prettily tinged with pink.

Annie shoved her catalogue aside. 'Did he indeed?' she said. 'Maybe you should tell me more about this Caradoc.'

6

Well, she had asked for it, hadn't she? By the time they were driving through the shaded lanes and golden-shorn fields towards Longbolton, however, Annie felt as though Liz had talked of nothing but the Very Reverend Caradoc Swallow for two solid days. The symptoms were unmistakable. Liz was like a teenager with a crush. Question was, did this Caradoc reciprocate? Annie sincerely hoped not.

Look, she had nothing against clerics, *per se*, but after a lifetime of penury and parish magazines, of coffee mornings and charity shops, of Siberian bedrooms and wonky cars – after an entire adult life, in other words, of slaving as an unpaid skivvy in the service of the Church of England – surely the last thing Liz needed was more of the same? Wasn't it high time she had some un-Godly fun instead?

What Annie wished for her friend – if only she could wave a fairy wand – was not just the odd classy frock and a decent car, but smart dinners and West End shows, champagne and silly shoes, sunset over the Nile, road trips across the States – a taste of life as it should be lived. So if Liz had to get starry-eyed, it would be much better to do so over a man with a bit of style and a lot of dosh. Admittedly a tall order. But the least Liz deserved (even if she didn't realise it) was a bloke who could show her that sex wasn't a marital chore on a par with putting the bins out.

If it wasn't too late? After all, Annie sometimes wondered whether her own working parts might be a tad rusty after more years of neglect than she cared to compute. And her situation didn't begin to compare with Liz's. Could someone who had never experienced a decent romp under the duvet really be expected to get the hang of the business in her sixties? She didn't know. She was very sure, however, that it would be tragic if Liz never had a chance to find out. Poor Liz. If only she'd been blessed decades ago with a sensible friend like herself, she might never have blundered into that frigid marriage. And since *The Joy of Sex* was unlikely to feature on a bishop's bookshelf, Annie would not just stand by if she seemed about to make another mistake with this Caradoc Swallow. Not that she was prejudging the bishop, you understand.

She had Googled him, it goes without saying, and found photos of a balding, beaming cove, with steel-rimmed specs, a gap between his front teeth through which you could drive a lorry, and a beard worthy of an ayatollah, never mind a prelate of the Church of England.

'Need to take the hedge clippers to that, bish,' she muttered. 'If the birds aren't nesting at this time of year.'

In short, the guy was seventy (too old), recently widowed (dangerously available), and the progenitor of no fewer than seven children (anti-contraception or just irresponsible?) along with a busload of grandchildren. Meaning there was a babysitting treadmill just waiting for an incoming Mrs Bishop. It needed only to be added that he played guitar and his hobbies included wine-making and steam railways. Annie would have laughed if the situation she saw unfolding weren't potentially so perilous for her friend.

According to Liz, this cheery, Kumbaya-strumming train buff was no more to her than the chum and mentor of her late husband. He had been a great support and comfort to her in her widowhood, she said, but if Annie was suggesting that there was, you know, anything else between the two of them, then she could assure Annie that she was barking up the wrong tree. Completely. Definitely. Utterly.

'Longbolton three quarters of a mile,' she carolled now, swinging the wheel left with joyous panache. 'Just beyond the church, apparently, so we're almost there.'

'Terrific,' said Annie. 'I can hardly wait.'

'Caradoc, this is my friend Annie. Annie, this is Cardy.'

They had run him to earth in a stiflingly hot marquee where the dahlia stand featured a forest of blooms the size of cabbages, mostly in the brown, orange and mustard shades that reminded Annie most unpleasantly of curtain fabric, circa 1975. In person, in the flesh, she had to admit this Caradoc wasn't quite as bad as she had anticipated. He looked reasonably limber. For a seventy-year-old. And he had to be a good six foot still. To be sure, the shapeless beige trousers, too high at the waist and too low at the crotch, were as grandfatherly as you'd expect, but his open-necked check shirt could be worse. Seemingly dog collars need not be sported when exhibiting at flower shows. However, while his pate wasn't as bald as had appeared in his photograph, the beard remained a disaster zone. Hairy chins were repellent enough when glossy and brown on handsome young hipsters, but they were as nothing compared to the wiry thatches of the grandparent generation, looking as if they might be harbouring the drips from last night's supper.

'I understand you're the owner of a vewwy snazzy little jalopy indeed,' he was saying, 'in which Elizabeth is cuwwently tewwowizing the woads awound Bucksford?'

Now in what universe today, exactly, would anyone utter the phrase 'snazzy little jalopy'? With a straight face and in an accent that made Pwince Charles sound common? Note also, the proprietorial claim implicit in his calling Liz by her full name. Liz to the world, Elizabeth just to him? Before Annie could take offence at his downright sexist quip about her terrorising the roads, however, it became clear Bishop Caradoc intended the joke against himself, since Liz had apparently taught him to drive and was, according to him, a quite bwilliant instwuctor.

'With the patience of Job,' he added, twinkling down at Liz. 'I was utterly hopeless I wegwet to say. Pushing forty, you know, and I'd failed my test thwee times before this marvellous gel took me firmly in hand.'

Even as Annie swallowed a snigger at this unfortunate turn of phwase, a plump, youngish woman with no make-up, a droopy brown frock and open-toed sandals of mountain-climbing robustness stomped through the crowd towards them with a wailing baby over one shoulder and a mucus-smeared toddler clinging to her skirt.

'Hey-ho stranger,' she hooted to Liz. 'Long time no see!'

Annie did not need her friend or the bishop to identify this as one of his many daughters. The woman had hearty young Christian written all over her and – no surprise – bundled her grizzling babe into Liz's outstretched arms before you could say all things bright and beautiful. The infant instantly sicked up on her shoulder, and Liz just laughed.

'Yes, it's been far too long,' said Bishop Caradoc, patting the toddler's head. 'We've all missed Aunty Liz, haven't we, Gideon?'

I'll bet, thought Annie, clenching a smile as she sidestepped a threatened embrace from the child, who was wielding an ice-cream cornet with lethal intent. Not that she didn't like

67

children, of course she did, she'd had two in quick succession, hadn't she? But having served her time in the vomit, poo and chocolate-everywhere wars, she now preferred a clean T-shirt. With a squeak of simulated enthusiasm for gladioli, she murmured something about leaving these old friends to catch up and dodged away into the neighbouring aisle. She studied the gladdies, then the chrysanths and then a display of mixed floral arrangements purporting to represent the atomic age – although what eggs and peacock feathers had to do with nuclear physics was anyone's guess – until she could bear the sweetly foetid air of the tent no longer. After a glance at her watch, which insisted that only half an hour had passed, she sighed, emerged into the autumnal sunshine for a dawdling circuit of the crafty stands, bought an artisanally sticky pot of honey, and stoically joined a queue which stretched from the tea tent to next Tuesday, texting Liz with her whereabouts.

She had drunk her stewed and over-milked tea while the cup she had bought for Liz grew cold on the other side of the rickety trestle table and, the scones being quite decent – better than the tea, anyhow – felt justified in polishing off the second of these before her friend finally appeared. Only for Liz then to insist on joining the queue herself to load a tray with sustenance for the bish and family. By the time this was delivered and shared over stilted smalltalk in the obliterating heat and noise of the Dahlia tent, a full three hours had passed and Annie felt she had seen – and suffered – enough.

The bishop quite understood her suggestion they escape the car park ahead of the main rush for the gates. He took Liz's hand between his own. 'Anyway, now you have a weliable set of wheels, my dear, instead of your beloved old boneshaker, we can hope we might see you again vewy soon.' He turned to Annie. 'With Mrs Stoneycwoft too, of course, if she cares to venture out this way.'

Mrs Stoneycroft? Was this just old-world formality or did he sense they were unlikely to become chums?

'Well, thank you,' she responded with a glittering smile. 'Although we all know how everything piles into the diary between now and Christmas . . .'

'He's a lovely man, isn't he?' said Liz, still smirking irritatingly to herself as she steered them out of the lumpy field which had been commandeered as a car park for the event. Annie winced in sympathy for her car's suspension at every rut and rabbit hole.

'I'm sure he is. Once you get to know him. What a shame for you, though, that he lives so far away.'

'Oh it's only forty miles, and now I've got the car . . .' She must have sensed something because she broke off. 'That is, obviously, when you don't need it . . .' Her words faltered, and she shot a glance at Annie before returning her gaze to the road. 'Of course, I'm terribly conscious that you wouldn't want me to put too many miles on the clock of your lovely motor, so you must always say if you think I'm, you know, taking advantage. Or – or anything?'

'How sweet of you,' said Annie smoothly, 'but truly you mustn't worry. When you need to be somewhere in a hurry, as I hope you know, family emergencies and so forth, you must hop in and drive yourself to Land's End, John o' Groats, wherever, don't give it a thought.' Did she hesitate here, just for an instant? Just to reassure herself that, however mean-spirited she must sound to Liz, she was, really and truly, acting only in her friend's best interests? 'But you've got a point, bless your heart. The way these cars lose value, it would be much appreciated if you could avoid clocking up the mileage for no particular reason.'

There. She had said it. And she could tell by the faint intake of breath from the driver's seat that she had mortified

Liz. Hurt her, dammit, but it was only for her own good. She had to be saved from herself. All the girly giggles and blushes had clearly shown how ripe she was for tumbling into Caradoc Swallow's elderly embrace, even if she didn't know it herself.

And, thought Annie, surreptitiously studying her friend's profile as they sped along, there was no use just *telling* her what she would be missing thereby. Liz had to see for herself. She had to be shown there were plenty more fish in the sea. Well, a few more fish, anyway. Oh, for goodness' sake, Annie could surely rustle up at least one or two blokes with enough spark to take her mind off a beardy old codger like Caradoc.

What was more, she would be happy to do so. This was a challenge right up her street.

'So what's with this new friend of Nan's?' said Rob Daley. 'Funny old carry-on, isn't it?'

He was sprawled on a bench in front of the Hopkirk Arms, with his eyes half closed, basking in the improbably warm sunshine of mid-October. His bike was lying on the grass, and there was a pint mug of tea on the picnic table in front of him, along with the crumbs from a slab of Dave Eastman's famously excellent game pie. He had been indulging his masochistic tendencies (as Annie was wont to describe his enthusiasm for strenuous exercise) by cycling fifty miles up, down and around the moor and had dropped in to see Bernie before pedalling home.

Bernie, perched busily upright on a corner of the table with one knee crossed over the other, had a pen in her hand. Reading glasses held together with Sellotape wobbled on the end of her nose as she checked through a wad of invoices between conversing with Rob and sipping her own tea. This, however, prompted her to lower her papers. 'Liz is a great girl,' she said. 'Don't be put off by the plum in her mouth, she's all right. Not a mean bone in her body.'

'I dare say, but—'

'I'll not be hearing any buts.' Tossing aside invoices and specs, she sprang off the table to replant herself beside him on the bench and tucked her arm through his. 'Listen to your wise old Aunty Bernadette, you misery-guts.'

'I'm ten years older than you, do you mind?'

'Twelve and what of it? Look, this Liz Jones is better than all right, she's a godsend, so she is. Weren't you worried that Annie was headed clean round the bend without a car, because I tell you I was. All that energy fizzing away with nowhere to go. Holy Mother, she'd be in meltdown by now without Liz. You know what she's like. She always has to be *doing*.'

'Too right. Which is exactly why she should never have sold up – as, you may recall, I said all along.'

Bernie tutted. 'We're never going to agree on that, are we? As *I've* always said, I trust Annie to know what's best for her, and she was ready for a change. Actually, d'you know what I think? Not that I'd tell her this, mind, so no carrying tales . . .'

Rob squinted sideways at her. 'Go on.'

'I'm thinking what she's really ready for is a fella. Hey!' He had straightened up so abruptly he almost knocked her off the bench. She mock-punched him as she hauled herself upright again. 'I know, I know, you'll say this is just newlywed talk, that folks like me with the old bluebirds still tweeting round their heads are always after marrying off the rest of the world. But don't you think I might be on to something? Seriously now? It's too long she's been on her own.'

'Come on, it's only back end of last year Jake Stoneycroft died.'

'Oh for God's sake.'

'What's that supposed to mean?'

'I'm talking about men, you great fat fool. Relationships, love, sex.'

'Hell, I wouldn't know about that side of things between her and . . .' To Bernie's amusement Rob coloured up and looked away. 'I mean, none of my business, their marriage and what have you.'

'What feckin' marriage? They'd been divorced for centuries.'

'So? Annie took him back.'

'Annie took him *in*,' she said. 'Which is not the same thing at all. And why are you gawking at me like I've just told you cows live in trees? Honestly, Rob Daley, I can't believe you ever thought anything different.'

'I assumed . . .' He shook his head wonderingly. 'Oh, God knows what I assumed. What do any of us understand about the workings of other folks' marriages?'

'Mine's blissful, thanks for not asking. At least it's bliss except when I want to throttle my lovely man, which is only about ten times a day.'

Rob gave a perfunctory grin, but his thoughts were patently elsewhere. 'You know, I used to reckon the trouble with Nan was that, whatever happened, she always came up smelling of roses. She's never learned what it's like to be on the losing side in a relationship.'

'What, falling pregnant by a scamp like Jake Stoneycroft?'

'Yeah, well, I never did get what she saw in him.'

'Handsome as a god, sexy as Mick Jagger and he wrote feckin' good books too. No, I can't imagine,' said Bernie tartly. 'And at least he did the decent thing, for once, and married her. Even if she couldn't hardly fit down the aisle, by all accounts.'

'But she was the one walked out, wasn't she? No hanging around hoping he'd mend his ways. Once she'd had enough, that was it. Next thing you know, she's back up here, giving us comedy routines about her poor bloody dates from the lonely-hearts columns.'

'Don't I just remember? Although that's all ancient history now.' Bernie chuckled. 'Cross your fingers we might not have to go through all that merry malarkey again.'

There was a silence. Rob twisted round towards her. 'What's with the cryptic smile, Bernie? Am I missing summat?'

'Take no notice.' She sprang up and gathered her mug onto his empty plate. 'I'm talking rubbish as per usual. Just a mad little notion of my Dave's. And will you quit glowering at me? Annie's fine. It's all fine.'

'Yeah?'

'I tell you, she's bouncy as a feckin' budgie. Go and talk to her, see for yourself.'

'Maybe I will at that.' Rising too, he reached for his helmet. 'Mark you, every time I've rung or texted these past few weeks, suggesting a drink or a bite of supper, she's turned me down flat. Seems she's booked solid.'

Bernie guffawed. 'Aha, the real truth's coming out, so it is. You're just sore as a bear because she's too busy with Liz to come out and play with you.'

'Give over.' He frowned as he buckled the strap under his chin. 'Whatever floats her boat, I guess. But I still say I'm surprised she's found a soulmate in this Liz. Don't bite my head off, Bernie, I'm serious. I was down the Woolshed t'other day and she was working in Hank's office, so I made a point of stopping for a word. As you say, perfectly nice woman, but come on. Hardly Brain of Britain, is she? Strikes me her biggest charm might be just that she obviously thinks the sun shines out of Annie's you-know-where.'

'Are you surprised? Thanks to our kind-hearted girl she's having the time of her bloody life.'

'Quite. And what happens when Annie gets her licence back and doesn't need Mrs Nice-But-Dim to chauffeur her around?'

'Sure, they'll still be friends. Why not?'

He cocked an eyebrow. 'You reckon?'

7

Considering Annie had been bewailing the lack of interesting men in Bucksford over the age of thirty-three ever since she returned to Bucksford (aged thirty-two), the confidence with which she began her quest to identify a suitable partner for her friend might seem surprising. She would never have admitted as much, but it's possible she felt that Liz would be less pernickety than herself. Look, anyone prepared to spend forty years in bed with the Rev Jones was hardly expecting to hook George Clooney next time round, was she?

Even so, trawls through brain, phone, address book and even old Christmas-card lists proved fruitless. Also rather depressing, because they made her realise how many people had died – and how many of the deceased were not nearly as much older than herself as she would have preferred. As October chilled into November, a bright notion of booking herself and Liz on a Bridge for Beginners morning at a local hotel (men like card games, no?) turned out to be a waste of time. Such masculine specimens as presented themselves at the tables were not just antique and acrylic-sweatered, they were closely (if unnecessarily) policed by their female companions. Nor was her mood improved by Liz showing more talent for cards than her. Must be all those years of parish whist drives.

On the way home, she was reduced to studying a flyer she had picked up at the reception desk. This advertised a monthly speed-dating event for 'senior singles', at the same venue. Fizz and Fun on Fridays for the Forty-plus. Apparently. Somehow Annie couldn't feel that a hotel with plastic ceiling tiles and ketchup on the tables was likely to attract the flower of North Yorkshire's mature manhood. There were surely more civi-lised alternatives.

'You ever thought about internet dating?' she enquired, without considering what she was saying, which was unwise in the car. Liz nearly drove into a hedge.

'Crikey pips, I'm so sorry.' She took her foot off the brake again, dropped a gear and curved safely back into line with the road. 'You're not serious. Obviously.'

Annie had not planned to promote this option now but, having begun, she felt she could only plough on. 'Why not? Everyone else does these days.'

Liz snatched a sideways glance. 'Have you?'

'You bet. I was in right at the start,' she said, with some pride. 'It was quite entertaining for a while, even if the ratio of frogs to princes was ten to nil. Or worse. But that was ages ago, before the big explosion online. The whole world's swip-ing whichever way it is now.'

'Are you looking for another husband?'

'Fuck no.' Annie laughed. 'After I got my decree absolute I swore I was never going down that particular road to hell again. Nothing against men, obviously, but why would I want to shackle myself to another? I'm in charge of my own life, and that's the way I like it. Time and money all mine, top on the toothpaste, channel on the telly – you name it, I call the shots. Yes, I'm a control freak. Yes, I dare say I'm a nightmare to live with, but who cares? Because I'm not inviting anyone to snore their way into eternity on the other side of my nice civilised bed. You surely don't think I was talking about marriage?'

'Aren't you? I thought—'

'I'm talking about . . .' *Sex*. Wisely, she caught herself up in case Liz drove them into a tree. 'Oh, the buzz of meeting someone new, someone worth dressing up for, the flirting, the fun, the fizz . . .' Lord, she was sounding like the ad for the senior singles night. 'The whole merry snap, crackle and pop of the relationships game, know what I mean?'

'Well, no. Not really.'

'There you are then. High time you found out.'

'At my age?' Liz squeaked.

She could not have uttered three more incendiary words. Annie was a passionate subscriber to the baby boomers' credo that ageing, far from being a biological inevitability, is a mere lifestyle choice – if not downright carelessness.

'Age is all up here,' she cried, clapping a hand to her forehead. 'Think old and you *are* old. Look at our parents – our grandparents. God, I've Box Brownie snaps of my gran in her hat and lace-up shoes on the beach at Scarborough, and she looks about ninety-three. She's on her bloody honeymoon. No, listen. The idea of my mum lathering on the warpaint and buying a plunge bra to go on a date when she was thirty, never mind sixty, is utterly ridiculous. As for Dad, bless his chequered cap, I think he hit middle age running at twenty-one.'

'But—'

'But nothing. We inhabit a different universe altogether. Sixty isn't just the new forty, it's the new twenty-five, compared to our grans. We should be out there gathering our rosehips as fast as we bloody well may.'

'You think so?'

Annie was not listening. 'Or is it rosebuds? And I mean both of us, you and me, because my own love life's due a reboot. Long overdue.' She flipped down the sun visor and scowled into the mirror. 'Calling Doctor Cockerdale,' she murmured. 'Serious case of neglected libido.'

'Sorry?'

'Nothing.' She tutted as she poked a hair daring to sprout north-west of her mouth. Then fluffed up her fringe and composed a determined grin. 'So what do you say, Mrs Jones? Shall we give the internet a whirl? Or if you'd sooner stick closer to home, I've a leaflet here advertising speed dating for senior singles. Which is it to be?'

There was no reply.

'Liz?'

'Oh, my dear Annie, you're so wonderfully sweet and kind, and please don't think for a moment I'm ungrateful, but . . .' She took a shuddering breath. 'I would as soon run naked down the high street.'

'Ah,' said Annie. 'Is that a no, then?'

The astonishing thing – the quite incredible thing – was that within the week Liz had stumbled upon a likely man all by herself.

Being Liz, of course, she did not realise she had managed anything of the sort, so it was as well she had Annie to super-intend developments. 'Stumbled' is the apt word. Seemingly she tripped on a kerb in the car park behind the market hall, saved herself but split her carrier bag, spilling fruit and veg everywhere. Which was how she had come to enter into conversation with the gallant chap who insisted on gathering up her carrots.

'. . . and he admired my car, although I told him right away it wasn't mine, of course, and that rather got us talking . . .'

She had arrived at Annie's front door, pinkly flustered with an armful of dry-cleaning. Such was her excitement she had yet to advance further than the hallway.

'. . . and obviously he knows you, because he looked at me, well, *significantly*, when I mentioned your name. Then quite out of nowhere he asked if I thought you might be interested in selling. The car, that is. So he must have heard you aren't, um, driving yourself at the moment. And without thinking, I blurted out that I jolly well hoped not. Was that awful of me?'

'You should have told him to sod off.' Annie took the poly-thene-swathed hangers and led the way into the kitchen. 'Sounds like a shark trying to snap up a bargain from a fluffy female who wouldn't know a carburettor from a coffee grinder.' She paused. 'Not that I'm entirely clear about carbu-rettors myself, but I'm well across car prices so he can't know me well. What's he look like?'

To her surprise, Liz let out a spurt of laughter. 'I have to admit he really is quite a dish. Hank says we only have to put his photo up in the foyer and the course sells out. The pension-ers' pin-up, he calls him. He is funny, Hank.'

Annie stopped stripping the cleaner's wrap off her winter coat and turned. 'Hang about. You know this guy?'

'No, no, I've never actually spoken to him, not before today. But he looks just like his pictures. He runs sessions in the theatre on meditating and – oh – mindfulness, that sort of thing. They're frightfully popular.' She giggled. 'Especially with the, you know, more mature women on our mailing list.'

'Married. Obviously.'

'Actually, I believe he was widowed, some time ago, back in Canada. He's Canadian, I know that much, but settled over here now.' Liz blushed vividly. 'The lady volunteers who sell the programmes talk about him rather a lot.'

'I don't believe it. And you say this ageing Adonis knows me? Don't keep me in suspense. Who is he?'

'Kelvin Parsons? He's a psychotherapist.'

'Oh, shit,' said Annie. 'Him.'

★　★　★

When Annie then went on to confess to having a bit of history with this Kelvin Parsons, she was quick to add she didn't mean *that* sort of history. Heavens no. The very opposite.

Such vehemence was perhaps surprising, given that she would concede Liz had a point: the man was easy enough on the eye. Tall and lean, with a long face and earnest eyes, he had a flop of white hair that contrasted not displeasingly with thick black brows. His clothes showed savvy, too, if a bit hipster-crumpled. Physically, aside from his fishy-fat lips, she had nothing against Mr Kelvin Parsons. Or rather, *Doctor* Kelvin Parsons. He was keen on the 'Doctor' tag, although it was not a medical qualification. And there lay the rub.

Kelvin was, as Liz said, a psychotherapist.

Now, Annie Stoneycroft was a modern woman. She prided herself on being tuned in to the zeitgeist, abreast of trends, *woke* even. (Whatever woke meant.) But this did not preclude occasional scepticism about, for example, the wackier effusions of contemporary (so-called) art. Or, indeed, about alternative (so-called) therapies. No Yorkshirewoman worthy of her birthplace would dream of shelling out good brass for an unmade bed or a spoonful of water in a homeopathic bottle.

As it happened, back in the spring at a crowded private view of some (allegedly) significant constructions of crumpled soup cans – about which comment had to be restrained since the whey-faced and disconcertingly androgynous artist was lurking about the place – conversation had turned instead to the holistic (so-called) healing centre across the road from the gallery. Afloat on Prosecco and surrounded by old friends – more accurately, by four old friends and one long-faced stranger – Annie had held forth exuberantly on the modern addiction to these so-called talking therapies. She hoped she was not just being an old fogey – 'As if!' chortled her chums

– but who did these self-styled therapists think they were? These hairy-sweatered snake-oil salesmen, peddling their soft-voiced, pseudo-scientific bullshit as they chomped their lentil burgers – 22-carat fruitcakes, most of 'em, far more screwed up than the deluded mugs they were purporting to counsel.

Oh, how they had all laughed.

All except one person.

'May I introduce myself?' had drawled soft-voiced Kelvin Parsons.

'And so we all managed to laugh it off,' Annie said to Liz, relating this excruciating encounter. 'Sort of. I've bumped into him since, of course. Place like Bucksford, you're bound to. He's all right with me – fine, in fact. Well, apart from once asking if I'd considered exploring my anger issues, which are apparently a classic symptom of, let me get this right, the unprocessed grief narrative. I mean, anger issues, *me*, how bloody ridiculous is that? I nearly punched him when I realised he had to be talking about Jake.' She saw Liz's face. 'God's sake, I didn't. I just politely set him straight that Jake Stoneycroft was my long-divorced ex by the time he kicked – by the time he died. We parted on cordial terms.' She hesitated. '*ish*.'

She had hesitated only because, for all the man claimed to be so cool about her gaffe in the art gallery, he was always ready to throw her embarrassing words back at her. As it proved, a few days later, when the doorbell sounded.

'Well, hi there, Annie Stoneycroft,' he said, as she opened the front door. 'It's your favourite 22-carat fruitcake.'

He handed her a single orchid in a slim cellophane cornet. Annie would have been more impressed if she hadn't seen a bucket of them at half-price in Sainsbury's that morning. 'And maybe you'd like to check out the non-hairy sweater, huh?'

'I'm never going to be allowed to live that down, am I?' she returned brightly, as he bent to kiss her, smelling expensively pungent. 'All I can do is grovel yet again for my appalling rudeness.'

Back in the spring, he had accepted Annie's scarlet-faced apologies with a smooth assurance that it was OK, he was cool, he guessed he knew when someone was just kidding around, yeah? But look at him now – was that friendly banter, to show all was forgiven, or a barbed reminder that it wasn't forgotten? However, she reflected, as she relieved him of a canvas shoulder bag printed with the words EMOTIONAL BAGGAGE – quite witty, actually – what he thought about her was neither here nor there. Liz was the only one who mattered this evening. Fingers crossed.

Her friend had been dumbfounded by Annie's brazen proposal that they invite the man round for a drink. What, just contact him out of the blue? When they barely knew him? Or rather, when she barely knew him. And, by the sound of it, he probably wished he didn't know Annie.

'So? This is me burying the peace pipe or passing the hatchet or whatever. Just make sure he doesn't think it's because I want to flog him my car.'

Liz's eyes opened wider still. 'You cannot be suggesting I do the inviting?'

'I'm not suggesting, I'm insisting. Come on, Liz, you must see it's tricky for me. But I promise to behave if you get him round here. Cross my heart.'

She'd had to spend the best part of half an hour soothing, cajoling and finally almost bullying her friend into making the call. So it was a relief to hear Kelvin had accepted with alacrity.

'Said yes almost before I suggested a date,' Liz reported as she replaced the receiver with a giggle.

'Did he indeed?'

There was a silence. 'Annie? Have I spilled coffee down my chin or something?'

'No, why?'

'You're looking at me – strangely?'

Head on one side, eyes half closed, Annie was indeed surveying her keenly. 'Don't take this the wrong way, my lovely, but . . . have you ever thought about getting your hair cut?'

8

As she ushered Kelvin into her sitting room, Annie surveyed her friend with authorial pride.

A daringly asymmetric bob showed off Liz's jawline to perfection, and a silk shirt from Annie's wardrobe – which she had sworn, poker-faced, was destined for the charity shop – clung charmingly to her slender frame. Even the cherished blue clodhoppers had been swapped for some plain but almost tolerable heels which Liz had been persuaded to unearth from her own wardrobe. A lot of tact, a little steel and a fib or two had been required to effect this transformation but to excellent effect. Annie reckoned her friend could easily pass for one of those silver-haired ex-models fashion editors occasionally yank out of retirement to prove they've nothing against the older woman.

To make up numbers, she had also invited two neighbouring couples long owed reciprocal hospitality but so dull she could not blame Dom for claiming an urgent date with the telly upstairs. There was guile in her guest list, however. The doggy-doting Brownes and the golfing Jacksons were unlikely to distract Kelvin Parsons, once she had delivered him to the sofa by the French windows, with a glass of Chablis, a bowl of olives – and the glamorised Mrs Jones.

Before ushering him into the sitting room, she slipped in a summary of those present, including the information that her delightful new friend Liz was recently widowed. 'Well, not *that* recently,' she hurried on, in case this sounded as though she might still be in purdah. 'A year now. High time to be looking outwards again and making, um, new connections, don't you think, after twelve months?'

He agreed. With slightly startling fervency.

She waited for him to settle beside Liz before moving away but kept them under covert surveillance while the Brownes showed phone movies of their latest puppy and the Jacksons ('Wacko Jacko, that's what my pals call me, eh, Sukey?') talked golf. And more golf. Umpteen holes and chewed slippers later, she was still heroically simulating interest, while speculating what might be engaging her friend and Kelvin Parsons in such satisfactorily close converse, when she saw the black eyebrows lift in her direction. Excusing herself, she picked up the wine bottle and sashayed across to the sofa.

'I've something of an issue to unpack with you, Annie Stoneycroft,' he said. 'Professionally.'

Uh-oh. But she smiled. Best behaviour. 'You do?'

'No, really, Kelvin.' Liz was as pink-cheeked and sparkly-eyed as a kid at her own birthday party, bless her sweet heart.

He patted her hand. Good. Excellent. Except he was looking up at Annie still. 'You know, when you and I first met, I believe I recall you describing me and my colleagues as, uh, a bunch of lentil-chewing snake-oil sellers, would it be?'

See? Banter – or deliberate bloody provocation?

'I'm sure she didn't really say that,' Liz was protesting.

She had promised to be good. 'Guilty as charged,' she returned gaily. 'Drunk and disorderly at the time, so go right ahead and put the boot in, Kelvin. Again.'

He chuckled. 'Whoa there, lady, no worries, I'm good, OK? Just kinda surprised to hear you're now setting up in therapy yourself.'

Annie had the Chablis bottle tilted over his glass but raised it again. 'I'm doing what?'

'Oh Kelvin, *really*. I never said—'

He silenced her with another squeeze of the hand. 'Yeah, our friend Lizzy here tells me you've had her sharing stuff she's never accessed in her life. Way back into childhood, family, marriage, the real deep routine. She said you'd been giving her' – he affected an upper-class English accent – 'a jolly good old spiritual spring-clean.'

'Oh, *honestly*, Kelvin, you are wicked.'

'Did you really say that?' Annie was rather tickled. 'And I thought I was just being nosy.'

'Now me, I'd say you seem to have enabled quite some journey of self-discovery.' Kelvin smirked like the swotty schoolboy who has spotted a mistake in teacher's sums on the blackboard. 'Assisted the verbalisation of authentic experience and—'

Pillock. Just look at that cheesy grin. 'You say therapy, I say friendship?' Her smile as she moved away again was saintly. 'Tomato, potato, let's call the whole thing off?'

He was never going to leave her with the last word, however. The guy clearly had an ego the size of Ontario. But why cavil? He was a big improvement on an antique bishop, and soon it wasn't only Liz listening, rapt. Doctor Parsons was only too ready to hold forth to everyone on the application of practical psychology to the perfect putt, even to the house-training of the imperfect mutt. And how they all chortled when he leaned across Annie and advised them in a stage whisper to disregard everything he said. It was, after all, only pseudo-scientific bullshit. According to their hostess.

Such a comedian. But she was not going to be provoked. He could say what he liked, just so long as he continued taking pains to include her friend in the conversation. Although she noticed he had a knack of recycling Liz's shy comments into sly snipes at herself.

'I mean, what's this garbage I hear about décor as a cure for depression? New one on me.'

'Don't listen to him, Annie,' chirruped Liz. 'You are naughty, Kelvin, I didn't say that at all. I was just trying to explain to him, you know, what you're always telling me about good design, and how it improves – well, improves everything in life.'

'You betcha,' said Annie, recklessly refilling her own glass. Best behaviour was thirsty work. 'One hundred and ten per cent.'

'Would that be a pseudo-scientific statistic? Or just plain old bullshit?'

'Who's been sleeping in the knife box then?' She was not going to be rude. Not. *Not*. 'Tidy house, tidy mind? Sunny room, sunny mood? It isn't what you'd call rocket science, but as my old dad used to say, a pot of paint beats a packet of pills.'

He looked at her squarely. 'I'd say talk beats both.'

Annie glared back. 'I had a client swear I saved her from the divorce court just by making her house work better.'

'Gosh, you sound like one of those makeover wizards on the TV,' said Liz hastily, looking from her to Kelvin. 'I love those programmes, don't you? I just wish they'd come and tell me how to brighten up my gloomy little house.'

He wrapped an arm round her shoulders. 'I don't believe it.' And now it was his turn for the glint of victory. 'Here's Bucksford's answer to Martha Stewart telling us décor's the solution to everything, and she hasn't even thrown you a few tips?'

For a moment, Annie could only blink. She was silenced not by his inane jibe, but by the sudden – and really rather shameful – realisation that she had not once set foot inside Liz's house. Oh, she'd seen it from outside, obviously, when her friend had called in for something. Bog-standard brick terrace, inoffensive enough, aside from the inevitable plasticky front door. But she had never even bothered to get out of the car. What kind of a friend was she?

'Maybe I should come take a look around,' Kelvin Parsons was saying. 'After all, if Annie's going in for psychotherapy, why can't I advise on wallpaper? Don't worry, only kidding,' he added hurriedly when Liz, torn between delight and dismay, squeaked that she, um, wasn't in a position to think about decorating, not at present.

'Nonsense,' interrupted Annie. Distractedly, because an idea was unfolding in her head, a rather clever idea – a scheme, in fact, of staggering genius. 'Emulsion and a bit of imagination goes a long way. Trust me. Decorating doesn't have to cost much.'

'Oh-ho, I'd take that with a large pinch of the old sodium chloride,' chipped in the idiotic Jacko, winking at Liz. 'These fancy-pants designers don't know the meaning of money. What did that fella want us to pay for a lampshade, Sukey old girl? Thick end of a hundred quid, wasn't it?'

'Is that all?' said Annie and everyone hooted. The fools thought she was joking. She, meanwhile, was fingering the waistband of her jeans. Too many garden centre flapjacks and National Trust cream teas. Painting would be bloody good exercise. Besides which . . .

'You're on,' she declared. 'I'll be down first thing in the morning, Liz. Don't look so alarmed, love, this is strictly do-it-ourselves. For peanuts. As for you, Kelvin,' she beamed at him, 'since this was all your idea, maybe you'd like to call round, once in a while, and give us girlies a hand?'

'Between ourselves, Bernie, it's a two-birds-with-one-stone job. Or rather, one decorating job to unite two lovebirds. All being well. Just call me Cupid.'

'Up to mischief – *moi*? Honestly, Robbo, you do talk tosh. I'm trying to help Liz, that's all. You wouldn't believe what a depressing little dump she rents. Off some churchy charity, too, which is disgraceful when you think about it, but that's why I'm ringing. I'm on the scrounge. Didn't you say you were still trying to find a home for some of the stuff from your old house?'

'Yup, Liz, our big project has to be the bedroom, deffo. A woman needs a stylish boudoir with seriously sweet lighting if . . . Well, she just does. And this room puts me in mind of a seaside boarding house in a 1950s British B-movie. Brown lino, for pity's sake. Pukesville. It will be a pleasure to roll up my sleeves.'

Embarking on the job truly was a pleasure. For the first time in many years, Annie pulled on her old paint-splattered dungarees – strange how storage had shrunk them – and spent a day gleefully filling a skip with swathes of ripped-up flooring and age-stiffened wallpaper, marvelling at the fun and splendid exercise she had missed for so long by outsourcing the hands-on side of her business to others. The next morning she could hardly get out of bed.

It was, of course, purely in an advisory capacity that a couple of the trusty tradesmen to whom she had used to delegate all this fun now arrived on the doorstep of 2 Station Terrace. The crumbling plasterwork required professional assessment, did it not? Still, it would have been downright unnatural of Nige and Trevor not to lend a hand with one or two other jobs since they happened to be here, as she airily explained to Liz. For some reason their visits thereafter coincided with Liz's working hours at the Woolshed. Exchanges of rolled-up tenners certainly did.

This is not to say that Annie herself did not labour long and hard. She damn well had to, because her amateur assistants were hopeless. Liz was willing, naturally, but it transpired that the late Rev Jones, when not glueing together his model Spitfires, had been quite the little handyman. As a result, his widow didn't know a screwdriver from a stick of rock and painted with such white-knuckled caution the job wouldn't have been finished by Easter, never mind Christmas, if Annie hadn't relieved her of the brush and redeployed her on curtains. She could, at least, operate a sewing machine.

As for Kelvin Parsons, a fastidious horror of dirty finger-nails and all-round cack-handedness made him about as useful as a crocheted condom. So Annie sourly reported to Dominic, while cadging a couple of his industrial-strength ibuprofen and tottering off to her bath. The best she could say was that he showed up regularly. Which, as she had to remind herself, was the important thing. And if his puerile notion of posting a photographic diary of their progress on Facebook kept returning him to Station Terrace with his phone on camera setting, he was welcome to candid snaps of her upthrust bum as she sanded a skirting board. He was at least handy for collecting takeaways and opening bottles.

That the job took a wearying three weeks rather than the one Annie had estimated will not surprise any DIY veteran. What will come as a surprise is that it cost even less than the minuscule budget she had agreed with Liz. Annie attributed this feat to the ruthless ransacking of the garages, tool sheds and attics of her own and her friends' houses for unwanted materials and furnishings. She did not mention the ruthless shredding of invoices and packaging from her late-night inter-net shopping sprees.

'Still, it's finished,' she announced in a weary phone call to Bernie. 'At long last. And with luck I'll be able to straighten up without yelping in a month or so. But if you ever catch me with a paintbrush in my hand again, just shoot me, will you?

However, I'm only ringing to say the great unveiling is at five tomorrow, which gives you plenty of time to get back to work for the dinner rush. Rob's home, too, so no excuses.'

'Well, you've done a grand job here, girl. This is one feckin' ritzy love-nest.'

'Watch it,' hissed Annie, glancing towards the open doorway through which a buzz of chatter rose from below, where Liz, Kelvin and Dominic were gathered in the kitchen.

Bernie was surveying the airy bower of creams, greys and dull pinks. Slubbed linen framed the window, rosy lamps glowed instead of a grim hanging bulb, and the lino had given way to artfully distressed paintwork, with a rug from Rob Daley's former marital home adding a patch of luxury. 'And who'd have thought that tatty old mirror from Martha's den would come up so fine with a dab of paint?'

'Six coats,' said Annie, 'plus waxing.'

'Ah, so you're a clever bugger, as if we didn't know it already.' Bernie lowered her voice. 'But tell me quickly, before they all pile back with the drinks. What's the score with the lovebirds themselves?'

Annie held up crossed fingers. 'But slow,' she whispered. 'Achingly slow.'

'Give 'em a chance, they're not sex-crazy teenagers, are they now?' Bernie chuckled. 'Tried oysters? Crumbling Viagra in his coffee?'

'Very funny. But it's getting beyond a joke. He's away to Canada in a couple of days, out there until Christmas almost, and who knows—' She broke off. 'Hey, look who's climbing the stairs.' She flung out her arms as Rob Daley put his head round the door. 'Bobsy-boy, you made it. Come in, come in.'

He returned her embrace with gusto. 'You know you've a gob of paint in your hair?'

'Oh, you sweet-talker, you. So.' Annie freed herself and gestured around. 'Mrs Jones' refurbished boudoir. Whaddya reckon?'

'Let me say hello to Bernie first, will you? And think on, Nan – I'm the guy you said had the aesthetic sensibilities of a warthog.'

'No, did I really? I must have been sober to come up with that. C'mon, put Bernie down and gimme some serious shock and awe.'

Grinning, he rotated on the spot. 'Ha, I recognise that rug. Recognise one or two things, come to that. Yeah, yeah, yeah, it's a triumph, Nan. As always. Hello, they're all coming up now.' He clapped Dominic on the shoulder and kissed Liz. 'Are you pleased, then? Where are you supposed to hang your clothes, by the way?'

'In the alcove, behind those curtains, of course,' said Annie.

'My old wardrobe was rather ugly,' offered Liz hastily.

'She made you junk it, did she?' Rob laughed. 'By, you're a hard woman, Annie Stoneycroft.'

'Ugly great looming box,' she said. 'I'm only sorry I couldn't chuck this monstrosity out at the same time.' Even with the treacle-varnished headboard stripped and streaked to a tasteful cream, the bed offended her deeply. She gave it a petulant shove and the iron frame squealed a rusty retort. Everyone laughed.

'Helluva passion-killer,' murmured Kelvin Parsons unexpectedly, just behind her ear.

'You're not kidding,' she said and shot him a conspiratorial grin before turning to the others. 'The maddening thing is Jen's got a spare queen-size she wants rid of, practically new. And bound to be top of the range, knowing her. Jennifer is my shopaholic sister,' she explained for Kelvin's benefit, 'forever throwing stuff out, so it's as well her husband earns my annual income every time he draws breath. But they're down in north London, so shifting the brute's the challenge.' She eyed Rob. 'I was thinking, actually, next time you go down that way . . .'

'A double bed? Oh sure, I'll just pop it in my boot, shall I?'

'Aha, that's the lucky thing. They've still got my old trailer down there, from when Ben borrowed it in the summer.'

'Smart idea. If I had a tow bar.'

'This bed's fine,' protested Liz.

Annie ignored her. 'That's just what your bloody brother said when I asked if they could tow it up at Christmas. And my idiot nephew has gone and flogged the car that did have one to fund his travels.'

'You know, it could be we've one of the old pine-framed doubles out back . . .' began Bernie.

'But Jen's would be so perfect,' said Annie disconsolately.

'Could I maybe help?' said Kelvin Parsons. They all turned to look at him. 'I'm flying from Heathrow when I go back home, so I'll be driving south. And I've a tow bar.'

'Oh Kelvin, you mustn't think of it,' cried Liz.

Oh Kelvin, you must, you absolutely must, thought Annie jubilantly. Course you must. After all, the last thing you want is to find yourself romping on this shrieking pile of scrap iron.

'Well, isn't that just marvellous?' said Bernie, straight-faced but avoiding Annie's eye. 'What a hero.'

'Indeed he is,' said Annie, planting a kiss on his cheek. 'Our knight in shining armour, eh, Liz?'

9

She did not see the bombshell coming, absolutely not.

Kelvin had flown off to Canada, promising to return with trailer and bed in good time for Christmas. This, however, was not the only circumstance prompting Annie to look forward to the festive season with even more pleasure than usual.

When all their children were young, it had been the happy custom of the Stoneycroft and Daley families for her sister and brother-in-law to transport their large brood back to Yorkshire for combined celebrations with her household and Rob's. As all their kids had grown into teenage and beyond, however, the annual pilgrimage became harder to marshal and eventually, with the arrival of grandchildren for Phil and Jennifer, impossible. And since the completion date kept slipping back of the shopping mall on which Martha was contracted in New Zealand (building it single-handed, according to her structural engineer daughter) there was no chance of seeing her before spring at the earliest. Annie was therefore particularly delighted that the London Daleys were planning to travel north again, for the first time in several years.

She gathered from Jennifer that this was an act of brotherly solidarity on Phil's part. It would, after all, be Rob's first Christmas since Frances left, and their children were spending the twenty-fifth with their mother.

'Not that my beloved husband would dream of admitting we're coming up for Rob's sake, obviously,' she added as they discussed arrangements over the telephone. 'You know Phil. He'd rather crawl over broken glass blindfold than admit to a normal human emotion. He claimed it was because he couldn't bear the idea of baby bro watching telly in solitary peace while he had to suffer the crackers, soggy sprouts and indigestion routine down south. Share the misery around, he said. Oh, ha ha ha, I said. I wouldn't mind but I have never served a soggy sprout in my life.'

'You'll be staying here, though?'

'We certainly will. We've only got the two nights and I've told Phil he's going nowhere near Rob's new flat. We'd never see either of them again. They'd spend the entire Christmas drinking beer in Yorkshire male silence, watching shoot-'em-up boys' movies on some giant screen. Because I bet Rob's got himself a whopping TV now, with no Frances to restrain him?'

'Probably visible from space,' confirmed Annie. 'What is it with men and size?'

Her sister's sigh rolled down the telephone line. 'So sad, though, him ending up in a miserable little bachelor pad, at his age.'

'Rob's place isn't bad, actually,' said Annie, with the damningly faint enthusiasm of one designer for the work of a successful competitor. You could be forgiven for not gathering from this that Rob Daley had snapped up the penthouse in an award-winning converted mill – a three-bed, three-bath palace of granite, steel and glass. Very stylish, as Annie said to her sister. If you liked that kind of thing.

'It still shocks me the way their marriage failed, just like that, out of a clear blue sky,' mused Jennifer. 'Frightening, actually. If a relationship like theirs can blow apart, it makes you think it could happen to any of us.'

'Not to you,' said Annie stoutly, tempted as she occasionally might feel to plant a stick of dynamite under her strong-minded brother-in-law. 'I agree though, mega-shock. So what time are you planning to arrive?'

Her happy anticipation of their visit was undiluted by the usual turkey-roasting anxieties. Dave Eastman had insisted the entire party come up to the Hopkirk Arms for dinner late in the afternoon of Christmas Day. Once he'd cleared the paying lunch customers out of the restaurant, he declared, nothing would give him more pleasure than to cook all over again for his family and friends.

'Don't argue,' Bernie had said. 'The boy loves it – the more the merrier.'

'And not only have they invited you,' said Annie jubilantly to Liz, as she clambered into the car beside her, with a bundle of empty shopping bags rolled under her arm, ready for a major pre-festive assault on the supermarket, 'but Bernie got a text back from Kelvin in Canada last night, saying he'd love to come, too. I suggested she invite him,' she added airily. 'After all, he's no family round here, and Christmas is a lousy time to be on your own, isn't it?'

Liz depressed the clutch and started the engine but did not release the brake. 'What a kind thought,' she murmured. 'He'll be grateful, I'm sure. Dave's cooking is out of this world. So sweet of the Eastmans to invite us all . . .' Her voice petered away. She was staring out of the side window of the car, but evidently seeing nothing because she didn't so much as blink when a motorbike screamed past the end of the drive.

'Liz?'

'I did say I'd come. I mean, I was thrilled you asked me, of course I was. And normally I wouldn't dream of being so churlish. But, oh, Annie, this is so . . .' She took a shuddering breath. 'I don't know how to tell you. I'm all at sixes and sevens.' She yanked the gear into reverse and was about to release the brake when Annie put a hand on her arm. She jumped like a startled fawn.

'Liz, love, what's up? Pete's sake, turn the engine off and talk to me.'

Her friend laughed, not her usual shy giggle but a jagged burst which sounded alarmingly hysterical. 'I can't believe it. At first, when Caradoc said it, I thought he was just inviting me to spend Christmas with them all. Which was typically thoughtful of him. And of course normally I would—'

'Hang on,' said Annie. 'The bishop? When did he say this?'

'Just now. This morning. He rang. On my mobile of all things. Because he'd already dropped into the Woolshed, hoping to, you know, surprise me. So he said. But of course I don't work on Tuesdays, and I wasn't even at home, because I popped out to get some stamps for my Christmas cards from the little post office on the corner and—'

'Yes, yes,' said Annie, with a touch of impatience because a mighty dread was beginning to seize her hitherto untroubled mind. 'And?'

'So he tried my mobile. Luckily I had it switched on. And I went to meet him for a cup of coffee in Rowbotham's.' Then she fell silent.

'So you had a coffee. And he invited you for Christmas, that's nice. But you told him you were coming to the Hoppy with all us lot?'

'He *proposed*,' Liz burst out. 'Marriage. He actually asked me to marry him. He said we'd always been such good friends. And he said he knew my marriage hadn't been easy. Actually he said more than that. I didn't know where to look. He said that although Dafydd had, um, many excellent qualities, he could be – difficult. And that he had always admired, very much admired, how I'd coped and how well I'd looked after him, and so forth. All nonsense, of course, but it was rather wonderfully comforting, someone actually—' She broke off and sniffed loudly. 'Anyway, he said he didn't want to upset me, but he felt I'd, you know, trodden quite a stony path, and he hoped I could be happier with him. Actually, he promised he would do his level best to make sure I was happy. Oh, and that his family were absolutely behind him, and couldn't wait to welcome me into the, um, tribe.'

'Really?' said Annie.

'That's rather lovely of them, isn't it? I mean, I was struck dumb. Simply didn't know what to say.'

Annie looked at her closely. She was quivering, poor thing, strung tighter than a violin, half smiling, half weeping. How on earth had she failed to notice any of this when she got into the car? 'Cheer up, m'dear,' she said. 'What's with the tears? It's very flattering. You don't pick up a marriage proposal every day of the week.' She realised Liz was staring at her in seeming bewilderment. 'Well, a bit tricky too, maybe. Yes, I can see you have to tread carefully. You wouldn't want to hurt the old boy's feelings.'

Liz did not respond. Annie swivelled to look at her, and she averted her head. The silence suddenly felt charged.

'Ah,' she said. 'Have I got the wrong end of the stick? Surely you weren't – I mean, were you actually thinking of saying yes?'

'He's a very good man.'

'I'm sure he is. Probably in his job description. Sorry, sorry, not the right time for jokes.' It certainly wasn't. This was tiptoeing on eggshells territory. 'Remind me – how old is, um, Caradoc?'

'Seventy-one next birthday.'

'Ten years older than you then.'

98

'Nine and a bit.'

'And he seems in pretty good nick. Odds are you'll get a few decent years together before you end up as a carer again.'

Liz's eyes widened. 'Oh, Annie, that sounds a bit bleak.'

'I'm only being realistic. But, if that's what you want . . .'

'I don't know what I want,' she wailed. 'I wasn't expecting this. It's – it's totally flummoxed me.'

'Well it's bound to, isn't it?' said Annie. 'Look, do you want my honest opinion?'

'Of course.' She gulped. 'I think.'

'It seems to me, from everything you say, you've really enjoyed spreading your wings recently. Getting about a bit, mixing socially with a livelier crowd than you're used to. Nothing against the Church as such, obviously, but I can't help noticing most of the people who turn out on a Sunday morning make you and me look like schoolgirls. Talk about God's waiting room.'

There was a watery giggle. 'You do have a comical turn of phrase.'

'Not that I want to influence your decision for one tiny minute,' she went on, with such conviction she could almost believe her own words, 'but I have to say that, if I were you, I wouldn't be in any hurry to slide back into that dreary old world. I'd be desperate for more new experiences, faraway places, interesting people – the kind of people who wouldn't be seen dead in church. At least, not unless they actually were dead.' Heartened by another soggy chuckle, she ploughed on. 'What I'd really want is to catch up on everything I'd missed in that forty-year stretch shut away in a bloody vicarage. Bet your sweet life I would.' Had she said too much? She bit her lip. 'But of course I'm me. And you're – you.'

Liz did not speak for some moments. But this silence felt promisingly pensive rather than dangerously electric.

'One of the things they advise, when you're widowed,' she offered at length, 'is not to jump into life-changing decisions. Not for the first eighteen months. And, I suppose, it is only a year – well, just over a year – since Dafydd died. So do you think . . .?'

'Absolutely,' said Annie. 'Far too soon. You, my dear friend, have a whole lot of living to catch up on. Forget shopping, let's go out to lunch. My treat.'

'You look fit enough to me,' said Rob Daley. 'Not a day over sixty.'

'I'm only—' began Annie. 'Oh, highly amusing. Look, you can't seriously be expecting me to get on this bizarre contraption?'

'Just try it, that's all I'm saying. Give it a whirl.'

It was a December morning, diamond bright, and they were in the flagged courtyard of Abbey Mill, the complex where Rob now lived, some five miles outside Bucksford. This mighty stone temple to the industrial revolution had been converted into offices and studios as well as apartments, and even boasted a pool and gym in one of the outlying buildings. Annie would have been quite happy to find herself in there, chugging up and down a few lengths before repairing for lunch. It was what she had anticipated, in fact, when Rob picked her up this morning with a promise of rejuvenating exercise, and she was surprised when he told her to forget the swimming cossie – comfortable jeans and trainers were all she needed. He had refused to tell her what he was planning. This was, he had said, a surprise.

Annie certainly was surprised. She was gripping the handle-bars of a shiny purple bicycle, of the latest battery-assisted design, peering warily at something resembling a sat-nav fixed to the handlebars. 'You do realise I haven't ridden a bike since you and I used to race down Lowgrave Hill? Way back in the last century?'

'And you always beat me,' he agreed, swinging one muscular leg over his own bike, which, in contrast to the relatively solid frame she was holding, was as thin as a blade and black as a stealth bomber. Just looking at the sliver of leather purporting to be a saddle on that beast made her eyes water. She was not, however, viewing the more generously upholstered seat of her own machine with much greater enthusiasm.

'Get on then.'

'Why am I doing this?' She heaved her leg over the crossbar. 'Don't answer. It's a rhetorical question.'

Once she had cautiously hoisted herself aloft, however, and was wobbling along behind Rob down Wearspring Road, she felt herself beginning to smile. From nostalgia, that was all. That well-remembered childish thrill of the wind rippling through your hair. As they rounded the bend and dipped towards the bridge across Abbey Brook, she couldn't resist standing high on her pedals to peer over the parapet at the water churning and frothing perilously far below. By the time she had pedalled halfway up the hill on the far side of the valley, overtaking a sweating Rob with battery-enhanced nonchalance, she was laughing aloud. 'Fantastic,' she yelled, as he caught up with her on the summit. 'Bloody brilliant. This is the best fun I've had in years.'

'Tell you what,' he panted, 'take a right at the end and keep going. We'll go the long way, round Lowgrave Hill. For old times' sake, hey? Last one to the bottom buys the ice creams.'

'Deal.' She was already out of the saddle, thrusting forward. 'And I'm telling you now, old friend, you're dead in the water.'

'You let me win, coming down the hill,' said Annie, as they flopped side by side on a low stone wall outside the Spar convenience store. Once upon a distant time, as they recalled in concert, this used to be Mrs Duckworth's newsagent, tobacconist and wool shop, where knitting needles mixed, seemingly at random, with the Woodbines and evening papers. In spite of a chilly December breeze, they were eating nut-crusted Magnums, and – to hell with nostalgia – agreed that these were an improvement on the pallid choc ices of their childhood.

'I didn't, not really,' said Rob. 'I just reckoned the speed you were tanking along at, I'd best stick behind, ready to scrape you off the road.'

'Ha! I never used to fall off. You did. All the time.'

'That's because I had a cruddy old bike with no brake pads and a broken saddle. You, as I well remember, got a brand-new Raleigh for your eleventh birthday, with a three-speed Sturmey. It went a lot faster than mine.'

'Not that you're bitter.'

He patted the vicious saddle of the bike propped beside him. 'Why d'you think I spent six grand on this baby?' He grinned at her gasp of incredulity. 'Serious wheels don't come cheap.'

'Boys and their toys,' sighed Annie. 'Still, this has been amazingly good fun. Let's do it again, when Christmas is out of the way. And once I've got my legs working properly, you won't see me for dust.'

He laughed and threw an arm round her shoulders to give her a swift hug. 'I'll hold you to that. We'll go round the old quarries up the dale. Remember how we used to take picnics up there?'

'Orange squash and sandwich spread? No thank you. But can you borrow this bike for me again?'

'It's yours,' said Rob.

She jerked round to look at him. 'It's what?'

'Your Christmas present. Early, I know. But the sun was shining this morning, and I thought you'd be too busy with a houseful of Daleys on Christmas Day, so – hey, hey, steady on, love.' She had clamped her arm round his neck and was embracing him.

'This is the best present – ever. Totally inspired. Bloody generous of you too, Robbo. I mean, what did I give you last year? Aftershave?'

'Don't get too excited. It didn't cost half as much as my bike.' He grinned. 'Still, I'm glad it's gone down well, because I knew I was sticking my neck out. But on this machine you really can pedal yourself up Deerbourne Hill so, if nothing else, I thought it'd come in handy when you lose your driver.'

'What?' said Annie. She looked at him in surprise. 'You talking about Liz?'

'Sure. Mrs Jones, soon to be Mrs Swallow. Very soon, from what Caradoc was saying.' He laughed. 'At his age, he reckons he should have "Carpe Diem" iced on the wedding cake.' He pulled a comical face. 'Uh-oh, have I let the cat out of the bag?'

10

'Watch it, Nan. You'll be catching flies in that mouth.'

'Hang on, let me get this straight. You *know* Liz's bishop?'

'Retired bishop.'

'Don't quibble.'

'Sure, I've known Cardy for years. Chair of governors at St Oswald's. One of the best chairs I ever had, in fact. Great guy.'

'Well, that's a surprise, coming from a card-carrying atheist like you.' Annie did not wait for a response. 'And the man actually told you he was marrying Liz? When, exactly?'

'He didn't give me a date.' Rob leaned behind her to aim the stick of his Magnum into a nearby bin. 'But I got the impression he was hoping to tie the knot soon as poss.'

'I meant, when did he tell you?'

'What's with the third degree? Last week sometime. We got talking after a Culture and Sport working group. Last Tuesday afternoon?'

She let out a long breath. 'Ah, that accounts for it.'

'I hadn't run into him for a good while. Probably since his wife's funeral, now I come to think about it. She was quite a character too, by the way. You'd have liked her.'

'Really?' Annie's tone was arctic, but he didn't seem to notice.

'So we'd some catching up to do, over a cuppa afterwards. He didn't know Fran and I had bust up, obviously. It was funny, actually, because we must've sounded a pair of pretty sad old codgers, sitting there, swapping notes on being home alone. How we neither of us knew what half the settings on the washing machine were for.' He shook his head. 'But he was saying how much he hated it.'

'Doing his own washing?'

'Hey, don't trivialise. He and Elinor were wed the thick end of half a century, poor sod. So I was really pleased for him when he let slip he'd found someone else. Even more so, when I twigged it was your mate he was talking about.' He pulled a face. 'I'm sorry if I've sprung all this on you, though. He did ask me to keep it under wraps, but I just assumed she'd have told you all about the guy long since.'

'Oh she has,' agreed Annie cordially.

He cocked an eyebrow. 'So why the big surprise?'

'The bishop may have popped the question, but did it ever cross his mind, or yours, that she might not accept?'

'Why wouldn't she?'

'Why wouldn't she?' echoed Annie. 'Why *wouldn't* she? My God, hark at the arrogance of blokes. You only have to offer, and we're expected to bite your hand off?'

'Spare me the feminist rant. We're talking about two old friends, fond of each other for decades. If I weren't, as you rightly say, a card-carrying God-basher, I'd be calling this a marriage made in heaven.' As an attempt to lighten the tone it failed. Annie remained stone-faced. 'Come on, Nan, what's not to like?'

'He's ten years older than her for a start. The poor woman's already nursed one husband through prolonged senility.'

'Rubbish. Cardy's fit as a flea. He still turns out for the village cricket team. Look, set me straight here. Are you telling me Caradoc has proposed, and she's turned him down?'

'Yup.'

'And you think that's a good thing?'

Annie lifted her chin. 'I do.'

Now he was staring at her keenly. 'You're not – leastways I hope you're not – telling me you'd owt to do with this? Encouraging her to turn down the best chance she's ever going to get, at her age, of—'

'My God, do you realise how patronising that sounds? The best chance she's got? At *her* age?'

'Best chance for the pair of 'em, I should've said. We're none of us spring chickens, are we? Is this just because you don't want to lose your driver?'

'What?' shouted Annie who, truth be told, was a little unsettled by her old friend's staunch support for the bishop. 'Let's get one thing clear. This has absolutely nothing to do with me and my car. How could you even suggest it?'

'But you egged Liz on to refuse? Don't deny it, I can see it in your face. Oh Annie, whatever were you thinking of?'

'Look, it's all right for your friend,' she said rapidly. 'He's had a happy marriage, by the sound of it. Lucky chap, good for him, maybe he's ready to sit back now and pull on his slippers and – and sink into the geriatric sunset.'

'The *what*?'

'Whereas Liz, she was shackled for forty years to someone she never even fancied in the first place, not really. She was too young, didn't know any better. They had sod all in common, not even kids, crap sex life, they just co-existed, functioned alongside one another for decades, can you begin to imagine that?'

'As a matter of fact, I think I can. Up to a point.'

He spoke grimly, but Annie wasn't listening. 'So now, OK, she and this Caradoc might be old friends, but does she love him? Is she *in* love with him?'

'I can't believe I'm hearing this – this Mills and Boon drivel. You honestly don't think that at our age—'

'Not that again, *at our age . . .*'

'Yes,' he shouted, 'particularly at *our* age, don't you think a partnership between two people who know and like each other, with all those years of friends and life experience in common, that this might not be a pretty bloody perfect basis for – for sailing into the sunset, or however you want to put it?'

'And how defeatist is that? Fuck me, on that basis you and I should be getting hitched. No I think Liz deserves more, as we all do, a lot more . . .' She faltered only because he had flinched, physically recoiled as though she had spat at him. Too late she recollected this was a man whose wife had left him recently. Even old Robbo, with the hide of a rhino, might be touchy on issues of love and marriage. She stared up at the sky for a moment and took a steadying breath. 'Um, have I put my foot in it?' she said. 'Look, I don't know quite what I've said wrong, but—'

'You never do. That's the trouble.' Rob stood up. He wasn't shouting any more. Shouting would have worried her less. Instead, he just observed quietly and even politely, as though talking to a stranger, that some marriages seemed to thrive quite satisfactorily on just such a foundation of mutual liking and respect.

'You've screwed up here, Annie,' he went on. 'Big time.' He swung himself back onto his bike and powered off up the hill.

He was out of sight before she had clambered onto her own bike. This time she did not catch up with him.

Their quarrel troubled Annie. It had been a real quarrel, not just one of their usual silly spats, resolved and laughed away in minutes. Rob had ridden off without a backward glance. She assumed he had headed home. She didn't know, because she had pedalled furiously back to her own house, not to

Abbey Mill. Once there, she had run a bath, poured a glass of wine and proceeded to soak, swig and sulk. She wallowed in the sulk for much longer than she did in the bathwater.

She was hurt, frankly. And still feeling sorry for herself several days later, however sternly and often she resolved to get over it. She had done nothing wrong. She had stuck up for her friend, that was all, and her friend's right to live her life the way she chose. Liz was not obliged to hop aboard just because the bishop had cruised along like a number 82 bus, was she? This was only one of several smart retorts she wished she'd thought of at the time.

She consoled herself with the reflection that if and when – fingers crossed – Liz and Kelvin got together, Rob would have to admit she genuinely had acted in the best interests of all concerned. Well, perhaps not those of the bishop, but you can't please everybody.

In the meantime, during Kelvin's frustrating absence, she was comforted as well as amused by Liz's delight in her home improvements. Annie did not attempt any more actual deco-rating – enough was enough – but she was ever ready to dispense advice, ideas and improving tweaks of a less person-ally exhausting nature throughout the rest of the premises. (Did Rob even begin to appreciate the many ways in which she was helping her friend to blossom?) Purposeless side tables and flimsy shelves were thrown out, dingy armchairs disguised under rugs and cushions, bleak overhead bulbs rendered redundant by lamps and candles.

'I don't recognise my funny old house any more,' Liz said wonderingly. 'Or myself, come to that.'

And when Kelvin at last returned from North America via north London, Annie's battered trailer, still emblazoned with her company logo, was packed tight to the roof not just with her sister's discarded divan – as luxurious as expected – but also with a charming chest of drawers, two pairs of lavishly interlined curtains, a rocking chair and assorted smaller items. Annie assured Liz with truth that she was doing Jen a favour by accepting all this largesse because it gave her retail-addicted sister space and licence to buy afresh.

'Some of her stuff's a bit frou-frou for my taste,' she added, peering at herself in a curly gilt mirror she had cleverly positioned to brighten a dismal corner of the landing with table and lamp below, 'but she's got a good eye.'

'It's all simply beautiful,' said Liz, gazing round like a child in a sweetshop. 'I've never had such pretty things. I don't know how to thank her or you enough.'

'You've never stopped thanking me. But listen ...' Annie peered down the stairs to reassure herself that Kelvin had not returned from the convenience store round the corner, whither she had despatched him to buy wine precisely because she wanted to have a word with Liz alone. A stern word.

Look, she had here a pair of prospective lovers, reunited after more than a fortnight apart. Both were in a high state of sexual excitement. Really, they were. Annie knew about these things, even if Liz hadn't a clue why she was so shiny of eye and short of breath. But Kelvin, too, was visibly hyper. His grin was goofy. Those thick black eyebrows had been all a-twitch as he gasped sadly juvenile double-entendres while they sweated and shoved together to manoeuvre the bed up the narrow stairs – *can't get it up! Too big to go in! Hard enough for you? Ha ha ha.* If Annie wasn't amused, she was prepared to make allowances for a man in lust. Particularly when, after they'd finally got the bed in place, he wrapped one of those long arms around a shrieking Liz and pulled her onto the mattress beside him. So enthusiastically did he pounce he could have toppled Annie, too, if she hadn't just happened to have ducked away in pursuit of a stray castor. He was, in other words, up for it.

But in this most feverishly fertile of situations, had either of the protagonists addressed a single sensible remark directly to the other? In three sweated hours of furniture humping, bed-dressing, picture hanging and what have you, this over-excited pair seemed capable of communicating only via herself. Liz asked her if Kelvin would like a glass of wine. Kelvin told her how cool Liz's house was looking. In fact, they both blathered on endlessly about her brilliant work. And while Annie was generally capable of soaking up compliments by the bucket-ful, she did wish they'd forget about her and concentrate on each other. Honestly, some would-be Cupids might be tempted to chuck the bow-and-arrow routine and just bang their stupid heads together.

'Drop my sister a thank you card, sure, that'd be great, I'll give you the address,' she said now to Liz. 'But what about lover boy, who's carted this stuff all the way up the A1 for you? You know what men are like. They need to have their efforts appreciated. In triplicate.'

'Oh crumbs, didn't I . . .? But you seemed to be saying all the right things for me.' Liz bit her lip. 'Anyway, it's so silly calling him lover boy. Really. You mustn't.'

'Oh yeah? I'm sure he drives round the North Circular with jet lag and a trailer rattling on the back of his car for anyone at the drop of a hat.' There was a clatter and slam from the front door, and she raised her voice. 'Don't bring the glasses upstairs, Kelvin, we're coming down.'

She turned back to Liz and took her by the shoulders. 'Listen to me, baby. Sometimes, you have to grab your chance, because it may not come around again. Carpe diem. Like all our generation seem to be saying these days.'

'Car-pay what?'

'Roughly translates as bloody well stop messing about and get on with it. You hear me?'

He was in the kitchen, with a misted bottle open in his hand – and winked at her. Annie winked back.

'No, don't pour one for me,' she declared, before he could utter a word. 'I've just seen the time and I have to dash. I promised Dominic, um – anyone seen my cycling helmet? Oh, thanks. Yes, I faithfully promised I'd help my son with – with his physio. This evening. He's having trouble with some of the exercises and I've been neglecting him shockingly, spending so much time down here ... No, no, I wouldn't dream of letting you haul that rattly old trailer a yard further tonight,' she said when Kelvin gallantly offered to run her home. 'Drop it up mine any time suits you. No hurry.' She had arrived on her bike, she continued without pause while zipping up her jacket, and she would depart by the same means. When he began burbling some half-hearted nonsense about not drinking himself, since he had to drive back to his flat, Annie fixed her friend with a meaningful eye.

'I could, um, run you home, Kelvin?' stammered Liz. 'I don't mind sticking to lemonade.'

'Pete's sake, he can get a cab,' Annie cried, flinging open the front door. 'Doss on the sofa, whatever. Go on, man, you've earned yourself a break. Kick off your shoes, drink the night away. I only wish I could join you, but a mother's duty calls. Have fun, children.' At which she pulled the door smartly shut behind her and blew out her breath in one long whistle.

'I can do no more,' she said to herself.

The question was, could they?

It surely says a great deal for Annie Stoneycroft's self-control and, indeed, her selfless concern for the happiness of others, that she did not learn the answer to her question until the following afternoon.

The temptation to telephone 2 Station Terrace later that evening, to enquire whether she had left behind her diary, or her gloves – perfect excuse, yes, her pink gloves? – was powerful. But she resisted. Even though, as she reflected while squirming in her armchair through some grimly stagnant French movie Dominic insisted on watching, she would need no more than a couple of words from Liz to deduce how events were progressing. But *no*. If Kelvin were still there, as Annie fervently hoped he was, she couldn't take the risk of embarrassing the fledgling lovers.

The same applied the following morning, dammit. She visualised them sharing coffee and croissants in a sun-flooded bed. Well, perhaps not croissants, if they'd any sense, because there was nothing less erotic, in her experience, than a sheet full of greasy crumbs. By noon, the urge to take out her mobile was almost overwhelming. But did she do so? She did not. Surely – surely – Liz would be desperate to phone, call round, tell all? That's if there were anything to tell. Or could it just be she was curled in one corner of her splendid new divan alone, weeping into a handkerchief? Oh, please not . . .

At two o'clock Annie had an idea. And hurried out to her bike. Why had she not thought of this earlier? She would cycle along Station Terrace. If Kelvin's car and trailer were still present she would loop directly back home. If it had gone, however?

It had gone. The double parking space was now occupied by a plumber's van and a motorbike. Annie even went to the lengths of pedalling round the block to check he had not moved his vehicle for any reason. No sign. Her own little motor, though, was tucked in neatly two doors down from number 2. So Liz was almost certainly at home.

Her heart was thumping quite ridiculously as she knocked at the door. There was a long wait. Then Liz opened it. Liz, ashen-faced, wide-eyed, with not a scrap of make-up and her hair sticking out every which way. Annie had once seen an elderly woman walk slap bang into the plate-glass door of a shop. Liz's dazed expression reminded her of that quite unnervingly.

'Oh my God, Annie,' she gasped, which itself was shocking, because Liz was prissy about the Lord's name being taken in vain. Whereupon, to Annie's horror, she exploded into sobs.

'Oh love,' she cried, stretching out her arms, and stifling an urge to burst into tears herself. 'Hasn't he . . .?' Nightmarish possibilities were crowding in. 'Or has he and . . . Oh Lord, I'll never forgive myself if . . .'

She was moving forward to enfold Liz, but all at once halted, lowering her arms. She stared harder at her friend. It occurred to her that Liz, between those shuddering sobs, was in fact . . . smiling? Bloody hell, yes. Her friend was beaming like the Cheshire Cat who's cornered the cream futures market.

'Liz?' she said.

'Oh Annie,' gasped Liz, 'why has it taken me all these years to find out sex is so – so *fucking* heavenly?'

II

The Red House might have been designed for the properly Dickensian celebration of Christmas. It was big, it was solid, and it was warm. There was a log fire ready to spit and crackle in the sitting room; the lofty entrance hall was lined with wood panelling which positively demanded to be garlanded in holly and ivy, and the broad staircase leading out of it was perfectly angled to frame a big, fat, festive tree.

This year, in honour of the return of the London Daleys – as well as the horde of relatives and old friends she had invited on Christmas Eve to please her family-minded sister – Annie had secured a Norwegian spruce, fully ten feet tall. This had been manoeuvred into the house with the help of a sweating delivery driver, a limping Dominic and even a hapless stranger who had happened to be walking his dog along Deerbourne Lane, while Annie bellowed directions and whisked vulnerable furnishings out of the way. Such was the height and green abundance of this monster that she had been most delightfully compelled to double her stock of baubles, beads and seasonal spangles.

'Because there is nothing more depressing than a meanly dressed tree,' she instructed Liz who called round on the morning of Christmas Eve to admire the result on her way to Bridlington where she was to perform her own family duty by visiting an ancient cousin. 'I loathe and detest *tasteful* Christmas trees. Pasty silver and white or, yuckety-yuck, purple or blue or something equally out of key with the season. No, no, no. Only the traditional red, green and gold will do and the gaudier the better. Don't you agree?'

Liz agreed. And made a mental note to hide the pretty blue and silver miniature tree she happened to have picked up in the market only yesterday. She was sorry to be missing the gathering here tonight, she told Annie. Sorry to be going to Bridlington at all, actually. Much though she hated to admit it, she was feeling rather tired – exhausted, in fact.

'Too much sex,' whispered Annie merrily.

No, no, Liz protested – but couldn't quite hide her smile. She hadn't seen Kelvin in the couple of days since, well, since *then*. 'I just hope I'm not coming down with a cold. But it does slightly feel as if I might be.'

'Oh you poor soul,' cried Annie, hopping backwards with a haste forgivable in a hostess who cannot afford to court winter bugs at this critical social juncture. She maintained a prudent distance as she ushered her friend out, with much stout advice as to the taking of paracetamol and the desirability of an early bedtime to ensure fitness for the following evening's festive dinner at the Hopkirk Arms. 'I know Kelvin's excited,' she called bracingly after Liz's retreating figure. 'He never stops texting me about it.'

As if she didn't have enough to do without assuring Kelvin Parsons that a tie was not necessary, nor gifts. His latest message was a fatuous enquiry as to whether she had found the trailer outside her garage yesterday. Since her trailer was seven foot high and now blocking access to the dustbins, she was tempted to respond that it had been bloody hard to miss. Of course she actually tapped hasty thanks and apologies for being out when he'd called and had just pressed the send button when she saw Jen and Phil's big BMW nosing up the drive.

'Darling, we're here!' cried Jennifer, not even waiting for her husband to brake before throwing the car door open.

'You should've cut that hedge back years ago,' said Philip.

'Lovely to see you, too,' said Annie.

Her sister and husband were hurrying back to London early in the morning of Boxing Day because their house was due to fill up with their children (they had five) and grandchildren (four and rising) who were scattering for Christmas Day itself to their assorted in-laws or unmarried equivalents. When Annie first learned their plans, she had sighed that they would barely have walked through her door before they had to pack up again. She was, however, reluctantly conscious that the briefer the mergers between her sister's household and her own were, the more successful they tended to be.

This had nothing to do with Jennifer. The sisters' relationship, once they had grown beyond the scraps and scrapes of childhood, was unconditionally affectionate and confiding. Rarely a week passed without a lengthy phone conversation reinforced by emails and texts. Jennifer was younger, taller, rounder and altogether softer than Annie, who loved her dearly. She could not say *quite* the same about Jen's husband. Not that she was not fond of her brother-in-law. Sincerely fond. Philip Daley was clever (brain the size of an oil tanker), successful (shedloads of money) and unquestionably a devoted husband and father. He was even quite good-looking. No, he was *very* good-looking. Tall, square-jawed, straight-off-a-knitting-pattern good-looking. However, although Annie had to concede that Phil was decently modest about his appearance – in fact totally unconcerned, to judge by his lamentable fondness for golfing slacks – the same could not be said for his formidable intelligence. Philip Daley was only too prone to assuming he was smarter than everyone in the room. Even when that room contained, for example, his sister-in-law who was exactly the same age as him and who, if he would only remember this, actually came top of the class ahead of him two years on the trot. His lofty disregard for her abilities naturally had no bearing on Annie's longstanding preference for the company of Philip's younger brother.

Not that she had enjoyed Rob's company recently. They had not spoken at all since their sour quarrel at the foot of Lowgrave Hill. A friendly email from her about tonight's family party at the Red House, along with her carefully plotted timetable of events for the morrow, had received a terse 'Fine' in response. That was it. 'Fine.' No 'Love Rob.' Not even a lousy 'X'. How childish was that? He would doubtless claim to be busy with his precious work. She would like him to acknowledge that she, too, had been busy, flitting hither and thither like a demented Christmas fairy, shopping, tree-trimming, stocking-stuffing, bed-making, flower-arranging – she had even been out rodding the sodding kitchen drain which chose this convivial season to block itself. As drains will. But had she wilted?

'*And*,' she announced proudly, as she hugged her sister and brother-in-law, caught Jennifer's scarf as it tumbled groundwards and flipped it round her own neck while attempting to relieve Philip of his ridiculously small overnight bag, 'by dint of expending staggering amounts of money and charm, I have secured a people carrier to transport us all home from the Hoppy tomorrow night. So no one has to drive.'

'What'd you do that for?' said Philip, and looked round the grandly bedecked hall. 'God, Annie, you've really gone the full festive hog, haven't you?'

'Oh love, it all looks wonderful,' said Jennifer, beaming mistily. 'If only Mum could see. What would she say?'

'That you shouldn't bring ivy indoors,' responded Annie promptly. And they both carolled in unison: 'Ten years bad luck!'

As she led the way upstairs, staggering slightly under the weight of a black plastic sack stuffed with Jennifer's lavishly wrapped and ribboned parcels, she explained that she'd had to splash out on the multi-person vehicle because there were to be seven in their party. They had met Kelvin, of course, when he collected the bed, and her friend Liz would also be joining them.

'Lovely,' cried Jennifer. 'You've told me so much about Liz, and she sent me such a sweet card, I'm really looking forward to meeting her. Is she—'

'Ah, I suppose you will need a cab then,' Philip cut across his wife, as he did rather too often, in Annie's opinion. 'Damn nuisance, but I can only fit three in the back of the Beemer, and if no one else has a vehicle . . .'

'You're not planning to drive?' She halted at the bedroom door and turned to face him. 'Surely you'd like a drink, wouldn't you?'

'I'll be fine. Don't worry, Annie, I shan't be following you into the magistrates' court. Some of us know when to stop.'

And wasn't that just typical of Phil? Not ten minutes inside the house, he was as good as calling her a dipso. And then pulling out his phone and striding away into the bedroom – without so much as a glance at the exquisite vase of roses, mistletoe and holly she had arranged on the chest of drawers – jabbering in German or Chinese or double bloody Dutch, leaving his wife to smooth and soothe in his wake. As per always.

'Don't worry,' said Annie to her sister. 'I'm long inured to your husband. If there's a gene for tact it's missing off the

Daley DNA, that's for sure, because I'm currently at loggerheads with his brother, too. Or rather, I've proffered the olive branch, but Rob's still cutting me dead. Pighead. No, don't ask, it's all too boring and this is the season of goodwill and I intend to enjoy every minute. Come down to the kitchen, Jen, have a gin, and help me with the salads.'

They were soon shouting with laughter as they traded gossip. Far more keenly than her sister did Jennifer follow the lives and careers, births, marriages and deaths of their childhood friends, neighbours and far-flung cousins. Thus Annie could confirm that among tonight's guests were Uncle Dick, new hip notwithstanding, as well as Aunty Sheila, and Jen's friend from her Saturday job at the vet's, remember Joyce? All the old crowd, in fact, in honour of her sister being back in Bucksford. It was a crying shame, yes, that Martha couldn't be with them but, as Annie sighed, even if airfares from t'other side of the world weren't such a rip-off at this time of year, her daughter was working so hard she could barely take more than a few days' holiday, so it simply wasn't worth it. This shopping centre seemed to be going up slower than a medieval cathedral – poor Marth hadn't even been able to get away for Bernie's wedding, and she'd been truly gutted to miss that.

'Oh, me too,' exclaimed Jennifer. 'But we had that huge villa booked for our whole family, they'd all fixed their time off from work, and Phil insisted we couldn't let everyone down. I must say, Bernie and Dave looked blissfully happy in the photos.'

'He didn't show up though, did he, the famous dad?' Philip had strolled into the kitchen unnoticed and proceeded to fill a kettle. 'Where d'you keep the teabags these days? Don't worry, I can look after myself. Do you want me to do something with these peppers?'

Annie would infinitely rather he left them alone to enjoy a sisterly summit. However, since one of the many things that irritated her about her brother-in-law (whom she loved dearly) was his undeniable handiness in the kitchen, she responded rather gracelessly that he could slice them if he wanted, the chopping boards were over there. And, yup, Phil was right. Simon Spencer had not, in the end, shown up at his son's wedding.

'Never thought he would,' he said.

'And what would you know about it?' she longed to ask – *longed* – but she did not. Airily ignoring her own often-expressed doubts as to the reliability of Bernie's famous father-in-law, Annie found herself stating as certified fact that Simon Spencer would be visiting Bucksford soon. Very soon. And that he had written a long and charming email of explanation to Bernie.

'It was rather touching, actually,' she went on. 'I can't give you the full story, of course, because he was writing in confidence.'

'So how come you read it?'

'His wife sounds to be quite a difficult person,' interposed Jennifer hastily, smiling at Annie, as she accepted a colander full of dripping lettuce. 'At least that's the impression you get from the stuff you read in the papers. I suspect he's not the happy-go-lucky soul he seems.'

'Shouldn't think he is,' said Philip, slicing perfect rings of de-pithed pepper with infuriating dexterity. 'Got a bowl to put these in? I actually went to the trouble of looking him up after he failed to show for Bernie's big day, and his career's pretty much in the doldrums. He's done nothing worth mentioning recently.'

'His wife's been ill,' said Annie crossly. 'Anyway, why have you got such a downer on him, Phil?'

'Because he knows I think Simon Spencer's edibly bloody gorgeous, that's why,' said Jennifer, grinning. 'I've been besotted with him for years, as I have often told my husband. Now listen, Annie. You've got to promise to let me know if and when he does turn up in Bucksford because I'll be on the train from King's Cross like a rat up a drainpipe.'

'Heartless harpy,' murmured Philip Daley, wrapping his arms round his wife as she placidly sliced a red onion and kissing the back of her neck. 'I don't know why I love you so much.'

That was the thing. He really did love Jennifer, adored her, you couldn't fault him on that. On everything else, however . . .

'You can't want to go to Phuket,' said Dominic earnestly, working his way through a fistful of crisps, 'it's a disaster. Fuck-ed, as they say. Although, stone me, it's no joking matter.'

They were all gathered in the sitting room. Carols were trilling, tinsel twinkling and candles glimmering as they scented the air with spices and pine. The more senior of the friends and rellies filled sofas and armchairs, while youngsters milled around with their beer bottles and phones. Dominic was propped against the back of a chair, injured leg outstretched, as he talked to his Uncle Philip. Conversation between them flowed as convivially as you would expect between a paid-up member of Actors Against Capitalism and an international financier who had been known to declare that, as far as he was concerned, theatre was a dressing-up game for overgrown children.

'Have you been to Phuket, Dominic?' he enquired now.

'Christ no.'

'Have you, in fact, travelled to Thailand at all?'

'Why would I?'

And why, thought Annie, couldn't Dominic see that his uncle, like a circling shark, was cruising in for the kill? 'More fizz, anyone?' she trilled, thrusting herself between son and brother-in-law with bottle aloft.

'Then I wonder how you contrive to be such an expert on the place?'

Her son stared back at his uncle, blue eyes as innocent as the sky. 'Haven't you met my friend Kit Grayson? Aunty Jen knows him. I tell you, he's really made me see what an eco-nightmare tourism is in that part of the world, the damage it does to developing economies—'

'Strangely enough, I know just a little about developing economies,' said Philip, the heavy irony wasted on his nephew. 'Perhaps even almost as much as your friend.'

'Never mind the carbon footprint of flying, Phuket's all paedos and potheads anyway. You seriously need to look at Kit's website.'

'Somehow I believe we can book a holiday without the benefit of Mr Grayson's wisdom,' said Philip, tight-lipped.

'Time to eat!' cried Annie before her son could entertain the elderly aunt reposing in the chair behind him with further talk of pot, paedophilia and unfortunately named holiday resorts. She fixed her brother-in-law with a steely eye. 'Phil, help your Aunty Sheila to the kitchen, will you?'

If she said so herself, the supper table looked sumptuous, from the molasses-crusted ham to the cucumber-scaled salmon, with a carnival riot of other delicacies in between. And if most of these had rolled up the drive in a caterer's van, so what? Annie had plated, prinked and parsleyed every last dish to perfection. And made the salads. Well, mostly.

'You spoil us, Annie love, you do that,' rumbled 'Uncle' George Daley – uncles and aunts having long been shared between Daleys and Royds – as, without waiting to be asked, she produced his preferred English mustard ('Can't be doing with that foreign muck') and pointed him towards the plain boiled potatoes. Meanwhile, the younger members of the party, which is to say those under the age of sixty, helped themselves lavishly to the carpaccio of tuna and quail's eggs with noisy admiration. This was one fantastic spread. As always. Annie was amazing. Even Philip, with a sliver of fish and a teaspoon of tabbouleh on his plate, conceded that she knew how to put a good table together.

'And to think this were t'lass used to come by my house cadging Eccles cakes,' said her mother's younger sister.

'I'd still be doing that if you were baking them, Brenda,' said Annie, smiling not just at her Aunty Bren, but with satisfaction over the whole room. Everyone was chattering, laughing, drinking, eating, enjoying themselves – everyone except Rob. He had arrived late and was now propped against the door-frame, glass in hand. She hadn't spoken to him so far. But this was silly. She put down her serving tongs, squared her shoulders and threaded across to his side.

'So?'

His smile barely flickered. 'Well done, Nan. Good party. Your friend not here?'

'Do you mean Liz? No, she's doing her own family duty with an elderly cousin. But I gather there's a host of great grandchildren being brought along, so that will keep her happy. She's a great baby-cuddler.' She caught his expression and burst out: 'I know, I know, she could have shared armfuls of grandchildren with the bishop.'

'Caradoc. He does have a name.'

'Rob, it's Christmas. Can we have a ceasefire? I know we don't see eye to eye on this, but we've neither of us a personal axe to grind, have we? We're both just trying to do our best for people we like.'

He frowned as he drained his glass. 'I don't claim to be doing anything at all. If you ask me, most folk are better off if you leave 'em to get on with their lives the way they choose.'

'Whereas I like to give a helping hand? Oh, Zoe love, sure. Second door on the right down the passage. Here, let me look after your plate for you while you go.'

'The ever-helpful hand?' But his face had softened.

'Piss off, will you?' She sighed. 'Look, I don't wish any ill on the – on Caradoc Swallow, of course I don't. Have you seen him since, you know, Liz gave him the heave-ho?'

'I have actually. Bumped into him on York station of all places.'

'And?'

'Well, he wasn't going to say much, was he? He mumbled something about having been over-hasty with the wedding invitation – made a joke out of it, really. Cardy's not the type to wear his heart on his sleeve, and we were on the station concourse when all's said and done. But ...' He shrugged. 'Yeah, to be honest, I'd say he's pretty cut up. He looked older. I felt for him.'

'I'm sorry. Really, I am. Still ...' She shot him a sideways glance. 'I'll bet you there are pews full of cake-baking, flower-arranging, brass-polishing widows who are just dying to get their claws into an ex-bishop. I'm amazed he hasn't been trampled already in the stampede.'

He gave a bark of laughter. 'Aye, you might be right at that. Watch this space, eh?' He smiled properly now. 'Friends again, Nan?'

She beamed in return. 'We're always friends, Rob. How could we ever be anything else?'

'How indeed?' he murmured. And if there was something off-key in the way he said this, Annie did not notice because she was restoring plate and cutlery to young Zoe and complimenting her on her glamorous butterfly tattoo.

The guests had gone. The sweet-scented candles were guttering in their nests of holly and the carols long silenced, but still the quartet of brothers and sisters was gathered at one end of the kitchen table, a cluster of half-empty bottles between them. When Dominic had stumped off to bed, Philip too had half risen, declaring it was surely time they all followed his nephew's example, but Annie and Jennifer caught one another's eye, giggled, and refilled their glasses. Phil was welcome to take himself off to bed, they said, to watch telly, to read the paper, to do whatever the hell he liked – and they spoke as they had done as children, with one finishing the other's sentences.

'But we're sticking here—'

'—just a little longer, darling, this is our sisterly catch-up time—'

'—*serious* sisterly catch-up.'

'After all, I haven't seen Annie for ages and ages.'

It made Rob laugh, and he looked up at his brother, who had the grace to shrug, fall back into his chair, and reach for the jug of water. Jennifer patted his hand but kept her eyes on her sister.

'You were saying about poor Trisha. Still soldiering on in Chatsworth Close?'

'Still smoking her head off and boring for Britain you mean?' said her husband. 'No, don't glare at me, Annie. I do know Trisha Hough has a godawful life. If I were her, I'd have put what's he called – Johnny?'

'Joey.'

'*Joey*, into a home, long since.'

'Phil, darling, that's a terrible thing to suggest. Would you say that about one of ours?'

'I don't mean necessarily full time. The boy might even be happier with some of his peers round him. Less claustrophobic than that little bungalow anyhow.'

'Phil might have a point,' said Rob. 'But it's academic. Trisha could get more help from social services – respite care, that kind of thing. I've talked to her about it. But she insists Joey doesn't like other folks messing him about, as she puts it.'

'Except her sister, of course,' chipped in Annie. 'Wonderful Cate, the golden girl.'

Philip let out a crack of laughter. 'You never did like Catherine Blackwell, did you?'

'I don't *dis*-like her,' said Annie, enunciating with the care required after a certain quantity of wine. 'I just – never find 'nawful lot to like.'

'She speaks very highly of you,' said Rob. 'Don't pull faces, Nan. She does. How clever you are and that.'

'She's *frighteningly* clever,' said Jennifer. 'Cate, I mean.'

'Attractive, too,' Rob said. Annie rolled her eyes while her sister let out a whistle. 'Give over, the pair of you,' he said. 'Back me up, Phil. Cate Blackwell's pretty sexy, in a sort of dark, smouldering way, don't you reckon?'

'Answer with care, my darling,' said Jennifer.

'Actually, in my humble opinion—'

'When'd you ever have an opinion that was humble, big brother?'

'In my opinion, then, I'd say she was a bit of a cold fish.'

'Thank you, Phil,' cried Annie. 'Course she's a cold fish. And particularly, 'sfar as blokes are concerned, because I still say she's a closet lesbian. Oh don't start, Robbo, we've had this argument before. No I don't *know*. Just saying, that's all.'

'I think I heard her on an arts programme on the radio not so long ago,' offered Jennifer, laughing as her sister and Rob scowled at one another across the table. 'But she's still over in the States, isn't she, Annie?'

'Yeah, Berkeley. I heard that programme too; fact just about everyone in Bucksford did after Trisha put out a three-line whip. Some dirge about Jane Austen. So boring my brain switched off three words in.'

'Not that you're prejudiced,' said Rob.

'Piss off.'

'Is that the second time tonight you've told me to piss off or the third?'

Annie beamed sleepily at him. 'Yeah well. I'm only rude to the people I love best.'

12

'Ho ho ho, boys and girls, have I got a surprise for you!'

Mr David Eastman's mighty person filled the doorway of the Hopkirk Arms, his beaming face almost as ruddy as his Santa Claus suit. The costume looked to have been shrugged on in haste between kitchen and doorway because chef's whites bulged here and there and his beard, already dangling from only one ear, tumbled into Annie's bosom as he clasped her in tree-trunk arms and waltzed her across the threshold.

'And how's my second most favourite girl in all the world?' He planted a smacking kiss on her cheek. 'Honest to God, if I wasn't such a happy husband, I'd be dragging you straight under the mistletoe now, Annie Stoneycroft.' As he allowed her to totter away with a squashed toe and a snowy armful of beard, he turned to her companions. 'You're never still limping around on that stick, our Dominic?'

As they squeezed into the side bar, her heart sank a little when she saw that Dave had been unable to resist inviting several of his favoured regulars to this supposedly intimate party. Add in his sisters, along with their spouses and offspring from babes in nappies to phone-clutching, sulky-faced teenagers, plus Bernie's darling Liam with his new girlfriend, and it looked as if they could almost fill the dining room. What was more, for all it was past five o'clock, that end of the pub was still roaring and rollicking with the remains of the paying lunch crowd, paper-hatted, streamer-bestrewn and, to judge by the noise emanating from the open doorway, as drunk as lords.

'Can't seem to get shut of the buggers,' Dave declared with pride.

His wife snorted. 'It'd help if you stopped trotting round offering 'em fancy liqueurs to try.'

He gave Bernie's shoulders a squeeze. 'What's the rush? We're having our cocktails and bits and bobs through here, aren't we?' Beaming, he touched a finger to his nose. 'Along with Santa's special surprise – and it's a proper Christmas cracker, I'm telling you. Any road up, there'll be time and plenty to clear the tables. Our venison's only just gone in the oven.'

'Oh, marvellous,' Annie heard Philip mutter, as did his wife.

'Absolutely, how marvellous, *venison*,' Jennifer exclaimed, with a baleful look in his direction. 'Your favourite, isn't it, darling?'

'Never in a million years will you guess what Father Christmas has arranged for you first off, though,' continued Dave, oblivious. 'Once we've all got a drink in our hands. Ho tiddly ho ho ho.'

'Jesus, not the karaoke again,' breathed Dominic, not quietly enough.

'I am breathless with anticipation,' said Philip.

Annie and Jennifer looked at one another. 'Lovely,' they cooed, in determined unison.

Annie had been philosophical about waking up that morning with a heavy head. Too much wine, too late at night. However, any admission that her tolerance of alcohol had declined with age would have hurt more than any headache, so she briskly reminded herself it had been an excellent party, and she had all of Christmas Day to convalesce before serious festivities resumed. Thank God it was a late dinner and she was not cooking it.

More of a blow was a text from Liz, excusing herself from tonight's do on the grounds of flu. Any suspicion that she might be over-dramatising a seasonal sniffle was banished as soon as she answered her phone. She sounded so pathetic that, after only a few moments' reflection, Annie informed her loved ones they could sort out their own breakfast. Loading her bicycle basket with soup, fruit juice, tasty leftovers from the previous evening and assorted medicaments including whisky, she slung a bag of Liz's Christmas presents over her shoulder, refused all offers of motorised transport and sailed down the hill into town. Rather unsteadily, given how heavily she was laden.

There was no denying, however, that she felt pleased with herself. Smug is not too strong a word. Cycling along near-empty roads in sharp winter sunshine is a joyous way to clear the fogs of over-indulgence. And she was aglow not just with exertion, but with virtue, congratulating herself at every turn of the pedals for so selflessly forgoing the warmth and brioches of family breakfast in order to bring succour to her ailing friend. That she had thereby delegated to Jennifer the thankless role of umpire between Dom and Philip was quite incidental.

On arrival at Station Terrace she found her friend looking so wretched – red-eyed, pasty-faced and shivering despite multiple cardigans – she was ready to remain all morning, if Liz wished. The plan had been to join Rob for a brisk walk up Abbey Mill way, but she could always give that a miss. No, of course she would not be bored. She was never bored, only boring people got bored. While Liz snoozed under a quilt on the sofa, she could make herself useful about the house. As a matter of fact, the mere act of brewing a pot of tea had suggested to her how much more efficiently this absurdly small kitchen would function if the contents of the upper cupboards were swapped around and the larger worktop cleared of all that junk. Did not Liz agree? Who, after all, had any use for a plastic bread bin in this day and age? She would have gone on to dazzle her friend with her projected master stroke (doubling the cramped floor space simply by sawing the overhangs off the kitchen table) only the poor soul began to weep. And, bless her unselfish heart, she sweetly insisted that Annie must – truly, truly *must* – return home to the bosom of her family. She would be fine.

Annie might have persisted with her philanthropic mission, however, had Liz not gone on to confess, in a hoarse whisper, that Kelvin was imminently due to arrive.

'Why didn't you say so at once?' She eyed her wan and crumpled friend. 'Lord, you must be desperate to change and get a bit of colour on your face. Don't worry, I'll finish my tea and scoot. The last thing you need is me playing gooseberry. Gosh, I've already managed to downgrade the people carrier to an ordinary cab. I wonder if I dare cancel even that now?'

Liz looked up in bleary puzzlement. 'Sorry?'

'Well, if Kelvin's on his way round, once he realises you're not coming out to the Hoppy tonight, I doubt he will either. I'm sure he'd sooner curl up in front of the fire with you and soothe your fevered ... whatever.' She chuckled. 'For goodness' sake, tell him not to feel obliged. We'll quite understand.'

'Oh, hello Kelvin,' she said, as his sharply perfumed and stylishly shirted form squeezed alongside her in the crowded bar. 'Where's Liz? Is she feeling better?'

'No, no, I had to drive myself,' he said, planting a damp kiss on her cheek before releasing her to shake hands with Rob.

'It's a pain in the butt, because she told me you'd fixed the cab back and I'll need my car tomorrow but, what the heck, huh? I guess someone will run me out to collect it. Hey, Jennifer, Phil, great to see you guys again. Oh man, cocktails? Cool.' So saying, he flipped out his mobile, held it at arm's length and snapped a picture of the sugar-frosted glass into which Dave was pouring a brilliant green liquid. His thumbs spidered to and fro over the screen at adolescent speed. 'Sorry, gotta post this one. What's it called, can I ask?'

'Good Golly Miss Holly,' said Dave promptly, handing the glass to Dominic. 'Down the hatch.'

'Christ,' gasped Dominic, after swallowing a mouthful.

'May I have a fruit juice?' said Philip.

'But, how is she?' persisted Annie, accepting her own cocktail, but not taking her eyes off Kelvin.

'Liz? Oh, streaming with bugs, poor old dear. Wowee, is that mine?' He took a gulp of the green concoction and promptly doubled over, spluttering.

'I should have warned you Dave's drinks are lethal.' She sniffed her own and winced. 'But when you say—'

'Laydees and gennelmun. Yewer hattention puh-lease ...' Ripping off his scarlet jacket and tossing it behind the bar, Dave stomped across to a large screen which Annie belatedly noticed had been suspended on the back wall. 'Now, for anyone who missed Her Majesty's ho-fficial broadcast this afternoon ...'

'Tell me he's joking,' muttered Phil. 'Please.'

'... we have an exclusive royal message all of our own. Mrs Eastman? House lights down *hif* you don't mind!' The sudden gloom was startling. 'Bloody Nora, I can't see a thing. Hang on a tick, sweetheart ...'

'Hey, I'm already getting likes.' The screen of Kelvin's phone glowed bright, while their host fumbled with a laptop. 'Yo, and green cheers to you too, dude!'

'But you did go round there?'

'Where?'

'To see Liz, of course.'

'Sure thing. She'd promised to take up these pants for me. They were just that maddening inch, inch and a half too long, know what I mean? And I really wanted to wear them today, so—'

'Geronimo!' roared Dave as the screen flickered into light. More than that, the pixels resolved into a face – a famously familiar face. A fine-boned, smoothly tanned visage with crisply moulded mouth, dark eyes, and a stylish crop of silver-grey hair, shot with pure white above the ears and in a distinctive flash over the right eyebrow. The only discordant note in this vision of elegant masculinity was a cardboard crown, wobbling atop the debonair coiffure.

'My loyal subjects, in faraway Yorkshire,' trilled Simon Spencer, in a passable semblance of the royal soprano. 'It is my pleasure and privilege today to broadcast seasonal greetings to you from this benighted outpost of one's former bloody colonies . . .' At which, the crown toppled over his nose and he shook it away, laughing.

'How's that, my dear boy, will it do?' Now he leaned towards them, dark eyes smiling directly into the camera. 'Seriously, you good people, my son asked me to record a little Christmas joke for you on the old Skype or whatever they call it. Which I'm delighted to do, because I've been wanting to say "hi" to you all for a long time.'

'Shit, that's – *Simon Spencer*?' Annie was amused to hear Kelvin gasp. 'You telling me he's, like, related to Dave?' He was groping for his phone again.

'No, no, forget *hi*. That's just the native lingo out here in la-la land. This sunny, crummy, funny farm known as California. Personally, I'd rather grunt "how do" as we do in

God's own county, where you lucky chaps are now. And where, believe me, I hope to be joining you one fine day that can't come soon enough for me. But, oh, how I'd love to be in Yorkshire, now that Christmas is here. What I'd give at this moment to see a scattering of snow on a moor top. To sup a pint of beer. Proper bitter, of course, not the frozen cat's piss they serve over here. Gosh, I could rhapsodise for hours about the things I miss, from cobbled streets to fish and chips – wrapped in the *Daily Mirror*, goes without saying – and as for a decent cup of tea . . .'

'Three flat caps, two pigeon lofts and a whippet up a pear tree?' whispered Dominic into his mother's ear. Philip over-heard and, in a rare moment of accord with his nephew, guffawed loudly.

'Quiet,' hissed the sisters in concert.

'O-M-G Sly Spencer himself.' Kelvin Parsons was tapping away furiously at his phone. He glanced round. 'You do know who this guy's married to? I am so not believing this.'

'Although I dare say you're all laughing your heads off, as I witter on about Blighty. This daft old bugger, you're thinking, with his swimming pool and his fancy orange trees, what t'bluddy hell does he think he's on about?'

Annie and Jennifer shot identically triumphant looks at son and husband.

'But I promise you I mean every word. However, you don't want to listen to my twaddle when my talented son is cooking up a storm for you.' He leaned forward to pick up a glass, then tilted it towards them. 'So permit me to do now what I so shamefully failed to do back in July at Mr and Mrs Eastman's wedding, and propose a toast. First of all, I ask you to raise your glasses, please, to David. My son. He knows how immeasurably proud I am to call him that. To beautiful Bernadette and her handsome boy, Liam – I'm counting on you, you know, *Doctor* Saville, to look after me in the years ahead as I fall apart. To my two little granddaughters, Megan and Emily, big kisses and cuddles to them. And – hang on a minute, sorry, the old anno domini catches up with us all in the end . . .' He groped for a piece of paper at which he squinted to read the names of Dave's sisters and their children who, according to age and sex, cheered, giggled or squirmed in turn.

'What is this, a rehearsal for the Oscars?' Philip caught his wife's glare and threw up a hand. 'OK, OK.'

'And finally . . .' He lowered the paper, and smiled directly into the camera again, 'I must say a special hello to Annie. Mrs Annie Stoneycroft, no less, Bernie's dear friend. I have my own reasons for looking forward particularly to meeting *you*, Annie.'

'Noooo!' whooped Jennifer. 'I may have to kill you for this, sis.'

'Even Dave doesn't know what I'm talking about, because it's a connection I made only very recently. But that story will have to wait until I'm in Yorkshire. In the meantime . . .' All at once, his smile faded, and he twisted to look over his shoulder. A distant voice, female, but as husky and thrilling as a tiger's growl, could be heard calling his name, demanding to know what he was doing.

'Holy shit, that's *her*,' squawked Kelvin, so loudly Annie nearly dropped her glass. 'That is actually Viola Hood herself you are hearing. I cannot believe this.'

There was a crash. She spun round to see Dominic stumping past the door he had so violently flung open, ignoring the protests as an icy December gale blasted through.

'So may you all have a happy Christmas and an even merrier new year . . .' Simon Spencer was speeding up, as there came another howl from his wife, still out of camera range but audibly closer. 'Looks like that's all for now, folks. Bye-ee!'

The screen blacked out just as the door slammed behind Dominic.

'Dear me,' chuckled Philip Daley. 'I'm no fan of Simon Spencer, but I didn't think his performance was *that* bad.'

Annie grimaced at her reflection in the loo as she swabbed a muddy ring of mascara from under one eye. Christmas, she thought, was like coffee. Which never tastes as good as it smells, does it? Christmas Day, likewise, never quite lives up to its twinkly promise. This year should have been about as good as it gets, with only Martha missing, so why the vague sense of disappointment?

It had nothing to do with the meal, which even Phil had admitted was superb – before asking Jen if his indigestion tablets were in her bag. He had, of course, refused any more than a sip of Dave's finest wines in favour of water. Tap not fizzy. Still, given that on the twenty-fifth of December even Philip Daley couldn't assuage his boredom by closeting himself with a phone to reconfigure some hapless third-world economy, he had been almost sunny-tempered. Unlike his brother, who had seemed exasperatingly morose all evening, and so surly about Dave's precious message from his dad that Annie was ready to take him to task. Her soft-hearted sister, however, had whispered that this first Christmas without wife and children must be very hard for him, and allowances should be made. Which was fair enough, Annie supposed. Up to a point.

Besides, they'd had to wait so long for their dinner that anyone could be forgiven for growing tetchy, particularly someone with Rob's appetite. By the time the dining room was finally emptied and re-laid most of the younger children were snoring like puppies on nests of coats, and several of the adults too drunk to tell a haunch of venison from a fish finger.

Dominic, unsurprisingly these days, was one of them, and as if his drinking weren't concerning enough for his mother, there had been his crashing exit from the bar earlier. He had been sober then, or so he had sworn after she pursued him outside. Less credibly, he tried to tell her there was nothing amiss, he'd just wanted a fag. Only when pushed did he mumble something bizarre about Viola Hood's voice having triggered memories of that night. Yeah, yeah, yeah, the night he came off his bike, what else?

'Not the accident,' he had snapped, in response to Annie's bewildered enquiry. She noticed that the hand shielding his lighter from the bitter wind was shaking alarmingly. 'Just, you know, the whole fucking nightmare.' He sucked hard on his cigarette and glanced sideways at her. 'You don't really want to hear, do you?'

'Of course I do,' she protested, shivering even before a squall of icy rain smacked around the corner of the building. The weather had turned with a vengeance since this morning. 'Well, maybe not just here and now. My hair's going to be wrecked unless I get back inside. And you should too, if you don't want to catch your death.'

She had returned to find Kelvin and Dave in a corner of the bar not so much conversing as hurling words at one another over the hubbub. Dave was predictably excited to find a new audience for the tale of his parentage. Kelvin was extolling that parent's wife for her courage in so publicly baring her troubled soul. That she featured as heroic poster girl for psychotherapy in one account and Wicked Witch of the West Coast in the other did not blight the fast-blossoming friendship between the two men, since neither could hear much of what the other said and both preferred talking to listening.

'She's given a voice to thousands of silent survivors,' declared Kelvin.

'Yup, mad as a box of snakes,' cordially agreed Dave. 'Can I top you up, mate?'

That Kelvin had gone on to embrace everything else with equally noisy relish – food, drink, company, even the jokes in the bloody crackers – had increasingly irritated Annie. She did not expect him to don sackcloth and ashes just because Liz was absent with a cold, but she did think he could show concern, particularly after the cheeky monkey had hauled the poor woman off her sickbed to put a hem on his trousers. He obviously sensed her disapproval, because he had been swift to explain that their friend had insisted.

'You know how she loves to make herself useful, yeah?'

Annie could not deny this. But she was less impressed by his boisterous contention that Facebooking all these flash-bleached snaps of himself, his dinner plate and his dining companions would allow the invalid to enjoy the party from afar. He was drinking too much, laughing too loud and generally arsing around like a self-obsessed adolescent. Worse, as she forced a smile for yet another photo, it was occurring to her – belatedly perhaps – that while sex with Kelvin Parsons had been a very big deal indeed for an innocent like Liz, their night of passion might not have meant . . . quite as much to him?

This disturbing possibility had been niggling ever since. Even now, as she snapped shut her bag and left the ladies' loo, she was asking herself whether sixty-odd-year-old Kelvin could still be playing by the same easy come, easy go rulebook their generation had followed in their twenties. In fact, why should he not be? Annie herself, in joking to Liz about reviving her own love life, had made clear she wasn't for a moment contemplating remarriage, although . . . But they hadn't really discussed . . . Well, not properly . . . Oh crikey, should she have given Liz a little lecture on the facts of modern sex life?

'Your chum seems to be having a whale of a time,' commented Philip, who stood back to let her pass him in the corridor.

'Sorry, what?' Annie was taking out her phone because she felt impelled to compose a comforting good-night text to Liz. 'I mean, who is?'

'I must tell Jen she owes me a tenner.' Seeing her puzzlement, Philip smiled, not at all pleasantly. 'Hasn't she told you? I said when he called round to pick up the bed that he obviously had a thing going with you.'

'You don't mean Kelvin?' cried Annie, so loudly she clapped a hand over her mouth, glancing over her shoulder towards the dining room. But she could have dropped a grenade and no one in there would have blinked.

'Your sister wouldn't have it. Or to be strictly accurate, she said she'd be surprised, because he didn't seem your type. Well, how wrong can she be?'

Without hesitation, Annie pushed her brother-in-law into the deserted bar and kicked shut the door behind her. 'Bollocks,' she said. 'Complete and utter bollocks. Yes, Jen's right, of course she is, about him not being my type. The very idea. I mean, *please*, do me a favour. But you're both way off the mark if you think he's interested in me. Ha!' Her laugh was splendidly derisive. 'I assure you I'm the last woman alive to attract Kelvin Parsons. I was once extremely rude about his precious occupation, and he's never going to let me forget it. He was still getting the odd sly dig in after weeks of doing up Liz's place.'

'Yes, he was telling me how much fun the two of you had *decorating* together.' Philip imbued the word with ludicrous significance, looking happier than he had all evening.

'What? That man couldn't decorate a cupcake, besides which there were three of us at all times. Because, if you must know, it's Liz and Kelvin who have a *thing* going, as you so inelegantly phrase it.' Annie's conviction wavered only for an instant. After all, even if Kelvin was more laid back about sex than her friend, a relationship could still develop, couldn't it? 'Early days, of course,' she said stoutly, 'so who knows? However, the one thing you can be totally bloody sure of is that I don't enter into the equation.'

Whereupon the bastard actually laughed in her face. 'Care to put a tenner on that, sister?'

13

Since Philip Daley possessed the emotional intelligence of a vacuum cleaner, Annie assured herself she need pay no heed to anything he said about human relationships. Nor to his opinion on any matter at all, in fact, which could not be expressed in algorithms. Whatever an algorithm might be.

Moreover, she did not believe that Jennifer had entertained for a second the idea of Kelvin as a possible partner for herself. She would have confronted her sister with this nonsense at once, if Jen had not been sitting a mere two places away from the pillock himself. Who, she could not help but notice, beamed rather soupily at her as she returned to her chair. The next minute, he had risen and shuffled up the table to plant himself beside her, loudly demanding to know where she'd been all this time. Even Bernie heard and twitched a quizzical eyebrow.

'Loo,' snapped Annie, covering her glass with one hand as Dave shoved yet another bottle in her direction.

'I meant – all my life.'

'I beg your pardon?'

'Where've you bin, lovely Annie? Setera, setera?'

With some relief, she realised the man was just very drunk. No wonder, given the gusto with which he had been syphoning up everything his new chum Dave poured into his glass. Only in tomorrow's nauseous dawn would he realise that Dave Eastman's friendship should come stamped with a health warning. Her relative sobriety made her even less inclined than usual to humour drunken ramblings, so she gathered up bag and glass at the first opportunity and decamped to the far end of the room where there was a conveniently empty chair beside Bernie's son, Liam. Oh, lovely Liam. Personable, sweet-natured, sober, non-smoking, starry-prospected *Doctor* Liam. Not that she would ever draw comparisons with her own beloved son. Although speaking of Dominic . . .

'Last I saw him, he was heading outside with a fag packet,' began Liam, in answer to her question. But he was interrupted by the sudden dimming of lights. Mingled cheers and groans heralded the arrival of the blazing pudding – whose fumes alone, he murmured, were enough to anaesthetise a rhinoceros.

Of course everyone protested they could not manage a mouthful. Of course almost everyone managed a bowlful. But not Philip. He was already jiggling his watch meaningfully at his wife. Annie was pleased to see that her sister was in rebellious mood, however. In response to Phil's grim predictions about tomorrow's motorways being clogged with moronic sales shoppers, she responded sunnily, with only a couple of hiccups, that she was having the time of her life and didn't give a stuff. So they had to get on the road before eight, so what? He was driving, she intended to sleep all the way home. At which she turned back to Bernie, with whom she was engaged in an intense analysis of historic plotlines from *The Archers*.

Annie herself, politely trapped in a conversation with one of Dave's brothers-in-law about the (alleged) joys of caravanning, was so intent on trying to catch Rob's eye as he talked to Liam's teacher girlfriend that she forgot Dominic's prolonged absence. Nor did she notice Philip quitting the room as the coffee cups were produced. No one, though, could miss his return when he strode to the head of the long table, shaking the rain out of his hair and smiling broadly as he announced first, that he had peeled Dominic off the picnic bench outside, where he had been snoring in the downpour for heaven only knew how long, and, second, that Annie's taxi was also outside, doubtless clocking up a fortune in waiting time.

'I would have shovelled your son directly into the cab,' he continued, turning to Annie, 'but the driver said he wasn't – and I quote here – having some soaking wet piss-head dripping all over his nice clean vehicle. So I have, with reluctance I may say, installed Dominic in my own car. Fortunately, I had an old mac I could spread under him to protect the leather.'

'Oh that poor boy!' cried soft-hearted Jennifer. 'Lying out there in the rain all this time while we've been enjoying ourselves without giving him a thought. I hope you've put the car heater on full blast, darling. He could be seriously ill.'

'Serve him right,' said his mother, but she relented enough to observe that he'd been wearing an overcoat when they arrived. She supposed she had better go and retrieve it from the bar so they could throw it over the silly bugger. Since there were half a dozen youngsters dozing on settles and cushions, with a tangle of coats, scarves and shawls over and around their little bodies, her search took time and tiptoeing care, but proved fruitless. She could only assume, she declared, as she marched exasperatedly back into the dining room, that Dominic must have been wearing his bloody coat when he took himself outside – hadn't Phil noticed?

'But where is everyone?' she said. By 'everyone', she was speaking only of her sister and brother-in-law, because the room was still crowded. 'Rob, too? Where's he?'

'Phil's dropping him off,' said Dave, lifting a brandy balloon invitingly. She gestured it away.

'You mean they've all gone – without me?' Even as she spoke, she was aware of sounding absurdly like an abandoned child at the school gates.

'You've got a taxi, haven't you?' offered one of Dave's sisters. 'Jen said they'd see you at home.'

Annie pulled herself together. 'Sure,' she said. 'My cab. Which, as my brother-in-law was so keen to remind me, is clocking up the fare with every second that passes. I must go. No, dearest and best host in the world as you are, Dave, this truly is home time for me.' She looked down the table. Kelvin Parsons beamed back cross-eyed. 'Oh, and for him, too, I suppose. Kelvin? Come on, sunshine, up you get.'

Dave was equally pressing in his attempts to persuade this new chum to remain and sample a particularly fine cognac he was about to produce. Annie would have been happy for Kelvin to succumb. It was his liver. But no. Staggering to his feet, he insisted it was his pleasure and priv-lish to eshcort Mrs Shoney-Stokey-Stone . . . *Annie* safely home.

'Too kind,' she said, prodding him away from the swing door to the kitchen and re-directing his steps towards the exit.

'Will you be all right, love?' whispered Bernie. 'With this eejit?'

'Are you kidding?' she said. 'No one's had more practice than me at managing the drunken male of the species. And compared to Jake, this one's a pushover. Come on, now, Kelvin. One foot in front of the other.'

This was not the conclusion to the evening that Annie had planned. She had expected Philip would want to quit early, and even anticipated that Dom, from drink or boredom, might go with him. That would have left herself, Jen and Rob to share a cosy family nightcap with Bernie, before the three of them coasted home together in the taxi.

She sighed when she saw that there was already the best part of fifty quid on the meter as she shovelled Kelvin's left foot after the rest of his limp and lanky body into the back of the cab. If not for this paralytic buffoon, she too could have travelled home with Phil and saved herself a packet. Still, money was only money. She tossed her handbag into the front passenger well and was about to clamber in after it, when the driver, a dour-mouthed elderly gnome with a flat cap and a bulging boil on the side of his neck, informed her that they were going nowhere unless she got in t'back with her friend. No he blinkin' well were not joking neither. He'd already refused to tek t'young lad on account of he were roaring drunk as well as sopping wet, and this bugger didn't look in much better shape. So she was to stick close by and give fair warning if he looked like throwing up, because he'd another shout come midnight, and he was not mopping his bloody vehicle out tonight, were that clear?

'And a merry Christmas to you, too,' murmured Annie, retrieving her bag and clambering into the back seat instead. 'Shove up a bit, will you?'

Kelvin Parsons did not puke.

Instead, as soon as the car pulled away down the lane, he flopped an arm round Annie's neck and planted a slobbery kiss on her right ear, a kiss that might have landed on her mouth had she not turned aside in time.

'Get off, you fool,' she said, irritated but not much perturbed by this outpouring of drunken affection. 'Watch it, you're nearly strangling me – *oh*! Now that is quite enough. Stop it at once.'

Somehow his hand had slipped from her shoulder and was squirming over her breast. She twisted away indignantly, but his embrace only tightened, arms clamping round her like a bloody octopus.

145

'C'mon, babe, less've some fun,' he said thickly into her neck. 'You're quite a sexy li'l piece, y'know?'

His leg had now locked across both of hers and the next thing she knew, he was pressing her hand on an unmistakable lump in his groin, and smothering her outraged squeal with his blubbery, booze-stinking mouth. The driver must have heard something, however, because he glanced over his shoulder.

'Nay then, act yer bloody age, the pair of you,' he grunted. 'Save it 'til you get home.' So saying, he stretched over to the dashboard and a brass band blasted out of multiple speakers.

The sudden racket did at least surprise the creep into slackening his grip enough for Annie to wrest one arm free. With all her strength, she pushed herself away from his chest, but to little effect. When he shifted to envelop her afresh, however, she managed to yank back her hand and, after only an instant's hesitation – could she really do this? – whacked it across his face as hard as she could. This was not so very hard, thanks to the cramped space and awkward angle. She happened, however, to be wearing both a charm bracelet and a trio of fashionably chunky rings, one or more of which must have found its mark because Kelvin let out a shriek of quite startling anguish. It certainly startled the hell out of the taxi driver, who craned round, as he was later to relate, to see who was after murdering who in his flamin' back seat – and drove slap bang into a traffic bollard.

It could have been worse. Modern road furniture, after all, is designed to absorb impact and capsize gracefully, but the crunch was serious enough for the enraged cabbie to insist on pulling over and climbing out to inspect every inch of damage by the wavering glow of his mobile phone.

'I'm bleeding,' gasped Kelvin Parsons, lifting his hand away from his cheek and staring at it in horror. There was indeed a dark stain on his palm, big enough to be visible even in the dim light from the street lamp.

'Well, there you go, sorry about that,' said Annie briskly, reaching inside her bag. 'Here, have some tissues. But you were being a complete pain, you know. I had to do something. Don't worry. I realise it's only because you'd drunk yourself silly. I won't breathe a word to Liz.'

He took the tissues and clamped them to his cheek. A trickle of blood was zig-zagging down from his eye. 'This – some kinda joke?' he grunted. 'You trying to make out you weren't up f'rit?'

'What on earth are you talking about?'

The shock seemed to have sobered him somewhat. He straightened up against the back of the seat and dabbed the wad of tissues delicately round his eye. 'Quit fooling, huh? You've bin giving me the – the big come-on f'weeks. Fuck knows whatcha think you're playing at now.'

'I beg your pardon?'

'Gagging for it one minute, the next—'

'Are you mad as well as drunk? All we've ever done is argue.'

'Come round for a drink, Kelvin.' He was affecting a fluty falsetto. 'Come help me dec'rate, Kelvin. Doing anything Christmas, Kelvin?' He broke off to burp loudly. 'Jeez, you've pract'ly been stalking me.'

'How *dare* you?' shouted Annie. 'This has nothing to do with me whatsoever. This is Liz you're talking about, her house we were doing up, her—'

'Oh my Gaaad,' he suddenly burst out, and lifted the bloodied tissues away from his face. He even tried to laugh. 'Is that it? We jealous?'

'*What?*'

'She tell you what a good time I gave her in the sack? Yeah, yeah, bet she did.'

'You—'

'Forget that, sugar-babe. Mercy fuck, strickly one-off. I mean, she's not in bad shape but 'slike screwing your mom. She's 'cross sixty, for Chrissake.'

'So are you!' Annie shrieked. 'And—'

'C'mon, y'know what they say. Gotta halve the guy's age, add seven and – ding-dong. Forty's good for me.'

Annie's mouth dropped open. She drew a long, long breath. And when she spoke again it was very quietly. 'Is – that – so?'

There was actually a smile creeping across his face. 'But, y'know, I was ready to make 'ception. You and me. Thought we could have a sweet thing going, yeah?'

'Oh but you're too kind. At my great age.' She was delving into her bag again, riffling through her purse.

He gave a little laugh. 'Yeah, well, 'stough on you older ladies, guess. But thass the way the world rocks. Us guys can still pull when you're—'

At that moment, the taxi driver, chuntering darkly, climbed back into his seat. Annie promptly thrust a wad of tenners over his shoulder, informing him that she would walk the remaining distance. Swinging herself out of the car before he could object, she turned back to smile down into Kelvin Parsons' bleary and bloodied face. 'Well, all I can say to you, lover boy,' she whispered, 'is that there must be some suicidally bloody desperate forty-year-olds in this rocking old world if they're prepared to be *pulled* by the likes of you.' Her voice was rising. 'But tell me, do you bore the poor souls into submission – or just feed treats to their fucking guide dogs?'

14

She shouldn't have said it. Treats for guide dogs indeed. Not just the hoariest of old gags but, as Dominic would doubtless tell her, gratuitously offensive to the visually impaired. Their dogs, too, as likely as not.

Besides, there were many more apt insults she could have flung at Kelvin Parsons. As she twisted and squirmed in her bed, sleepless for much of the night, she came up with plenty. The humourless, conceited, squelchy-mouthed, garbage-spouting lech – how *dared* he? To even suggest she could be – what did he say, *gagging* for it? With that preening, prancing, self-deluding dimwit? She hoped, oh how passionately she hoped, that she had left him with a Technicolor sunset of a black eye.

Phil had evidently hauled his wife to bed by the time Annie bashed open the kitchen door. After her rage-fuelled stomp up the lane – never had she climbed Deerbourne Hill faster – she couldn't even vent her wrath to Jennifer. Although perhaps that was just as well. Because if Phil had gleaned the least hint of what had happened from his wife then that, frankly, would have put cherry and candle on the Christmas cake, never mind the sodding icing. Even if he never said a word, just knowing he suspected would have been intolerable.

Likewise, iron determination to avoid arousing curiosity impelled Annie out of bed at some dank and sepulchral hour the following morning, wan-faced, wild-haired and foul-breathed, only to assume a shiny smile along with her best dressing gown as she gaily offered fresh-ground coffee and toast to her departing guests. The effort required was shattering. And wasted because, before joining her husband in the car, Jen drew her aside in the hallway to ask what on earth was wrong.

'Crap night's sleep,' she answered instantly.

Jennifer frowned. 'I do sometimes worry about you, sis. You're so clever, and funny and good at everything you take on . . .'

'More, gimme more, I love it.'

'I'm serious, Ants.' God, childhood nickname, must be *very* serious. 'It frightens me that you've nothing to – to *anchor* your life, not any more. I don't mean just your business, I mean deep roots like kids, and Mum and Dad – Jake, even. And of course Bernie's not here, either. All of a sudden you've nothing and nobody left to . . . oh, to keep you grounded, darling, put a shape to your life.' Before Annie could respond to this startling outburst, her sister had turned away to raise her voice. 'Yes, Phil, I'm *coming*. Lord, if I don't let him get on the road he might just have the coronary I've been expecting these past twenty years. Bye, love. Think about it. We all need anchors.'

Annie pondered this over a solitary mug of tea after waving them off. An anchor. Was this Jen's way of suggesting she needed a man? A nice, steady, husband-type man – like her own, perhaps? Yeah, well, if the choice were between Phil and a nunnery, bring on the wimple. Much as she loved him.

What was more, she reflected, if it weren't for bloody Philip, she could have confided the events of the previous evening to her sister. Leading this poor sap on – apparently! Being pounced on in the back of a taxi – imagine! How wonderfully absurd was that, in this day and age? She had no doubt that recasting the incident as comedy would have left her feeling considerably less frazzled this morning.

God's sake, she was no ditsy snowflake, screaming sex abuse because a drunken oaf had groped her tits. She had inflicted a sight more damage on him. Far more upsetting was the man's patently genuine conviction that she had actually wanted him to jump on her. Had she really put out such grossly misleading signals – or did the creep just take his knicker-dropping irresistibility for granted? Well that was possible, given he reckoned blokes like him could still play sex god when poor old dears like herself and Liz were long past their shag-by date. Bastard.

Oh shit, she thought. *Liz.*

She was going to have to tell her friend something, wasn't she?

Not about the tussle in the taxi, not even the comic version. None of this was a joking matter for Liz. Mercy fuck indeed. She should have punched him again for that. Instead she was going to have to find some gentle way of demolishing all Liz's shy hopes, hopes she herself had so assiduously fostered. No way was a phone call adequate. She must get on her bike and pedal down to Station Terrace. At once. Well, as soon as she was dressed. OK, maybe when there was a break in the weather ... The rain, however, continued to blast in thick billows of grey across the valley. By lunchtime she decided she could legitimately resort to the telephone and steeled herself.

Ringo Starr answered – or someone remarkably like him – which was a bit of a shock, but at least there could be no mistaking this gruff Liverpudlian drone for Kelvin's voice. It turned out to be Hank Damon, Liz's jazz-hatted boss from the Woolshed. And like Liz, reportedly asleep in her bed, he too was thick with flu. On top of which, as he wheezed and coughed to Annie, his boiler had died last night, leaving him without a drop of hot water in an attic flat as cold as a morgue. Anyway, Liz had taken him in, thank fuck, and let him make up a bed on her settee. They were wallowing in misery together, but at least they were warm – oh, and by the way, he thought what Annie had done to this pad was really fab. Could he pass on a message?

'No,' said Annie. 'I mean, yes. Give her my love, of course, and tell her, um, that I'll be down to see her. Soon.'

'If I were you, love, I'd keep well away,' croaked Hank. 'This bug's a pig. I wouldn't wish it on my worst enemy.'

In the end it was a fortnight before Annie was able to execute her painful duty. Early on, she braved barely better weather to cycle down, only to find Hank Damon still in residence – Bucksford's entire plumbing fraternity, according to him, having taken off for Poland, Florida or, in one case, the graveyard. In such a small house, conversation was of necessity general.

Then, unsurprisingly perhaps to anyone but Annie herself, she also succumbed to the flu. Diagnosing a trivial cold which would be thrown off within forty-eight hours by someone of her robust constitution, she was as indignant as she was astonished to find herself in bed throughout the New Year holiday, and still spluttering days later when Liz had recovered sufficiently to drive up Deerbourne Hill. If nothing else, however, prolonged incarceration had given her time to edit the necessary revelation as tactfully as possible.

'Yes, well. I'd guessed something was – awry,' Liz whispered, after Annie gravely explained that, when drunk, Kelvin Parsons had revealed himself to be one of those ludicrously Neanderthal males whose ego could only be satisfied – long term – with a partner much younger than himself.

'If he can find one,' Annie could not refrain from adding. 'But I'm afraid it does seem your fling with him will be just that. A one-nighter. Something to be, um, chalked up to experience, you know?'

'That's probably the best way for me to look at it, yes.'

Annie stared at her. 'Are you OK? You seem to be taking this very calmly.'

'Well it's not exactly a surprise. He unfriended me on Facebook more than a week ago.'

'He did *what*? God, he's so juvenile.'

Liz's voice was quaveringly brave. 'And as you know I never really believed he could be attracted to someone like me.'

'Rubbish. He should be so lucky, the cocky little toe-rag.'

'But I thought you liked Kelvin. You said—'

'Before his, um, inner caveman emerged,' said Annie hastily. She took a deep breath. 'However, you're quite right, Liz. There's no denying I encouraged you. I should stop trying to run other people's lives for them. As Rob has been known to tell me. Frequently.'

'But you're so good at everything.'

'Not in this case.' Having embarked on the confession of her sins, she was not to be deflected. 'It was me got Kelvin round to decorate, me who posted him off for that bed. Dammit, it was me practically threw the pair of you into it.'

'Oh, I could never blame you for that.'

'No?' she said. 'Well, that's good to hear. I think. But – oh Lord, I don't know what more I can say.'

'There's nothing more to say.' Liz's smile was as sad as it was forgiving. 'I shall be fine.'

'Gosh,' said Annie, awed by such saintly forbearance. 'Do you really mean that?'

It became clear, however, that while Liz might claim with perfect candour to have abandoned any hope of rekindling relations with Kelvin Parsons, she was far from consigning him to history.

Chancing to glance over her shoulder a good two weeks later, Annie was startled to see him leering back from the home screen of Liz's tablet – flanked, admittedly, by herself and Liz.

'I've only got it as my screensaver because it was such a lovely jolly evening,' Liz stammered, scarlet-faced. 'You know, when everyone came to see the decorations? I can't remember ever having felt so happy.'

Annie couldn't remember ever having felt so guilty.

Worse was finding two narrow strips of grey fabric tucked inside a rose-gilded china egg on Liz's cluttered mantelpiece. In an attempt to lighten her friend's spirits, Annie was rationalising her knick-knack collection for her while she was at work, by way of a surprise. She wasn't throwing anything out, of course. Just finding one or two items a more appropriate home. Such as the cupboard under the stairs. She would have binned these scraps of cloth, though, without a second thought – offcuts of trouser legs? – until it dawned on her from whose trousers these strips must have been cut. On Christmas morning.

Most pathetic of all was the crumpled bit of paper she then felt obliged to retrieve from the bin. It turned out to be a list of Thai takeaway dishes in a hand Annie knew must be Kelvin's because she remembered dispatching him to collect that very meal.

As the days went by, she became ever more aware of how often his name figured in Liz's conversation. Kelvin always used to say this. Kelvin liked that restaurant, this television programme, such and such a flavour of bloody potato crisp. She was reminded of herself, as a spottily besotted teenager, impelled to utter aloud at every opportunity the name of whoever happened to be her equally spotty love object at the time. Such behaviour was tiresome in a fourteen-year-old. In a woman of bus-pass generation, she was finding it excruciating.

'Who cares what that narcissistic dickhead thinks?' she was driven to demand, but then had to bite her tongue. It was harder, though, to stick to a resolve not even to confide in Bernie.

Her beloved friend rolled up unexpectedly one bleak February evening with a glum face and a bottle of Irish whiskey to say, hey-ho, in spite of all his fine talk, Dave's dad would not be crossing the Atlantic any time soon, by the sound of things. In fact, it wasn't clear when they might expect him. Maybe not until May, when Dame Viola was supposed to be coming over to do her play.

'Although you can bet it's her fault he can't get away sooner,' she went on. 'Honest to God, when I saw my fella's face crumple up again, just like a kid's, I could have throttled that woman with my bare hands, so I could. *However* . . .' She shook herself, as though to banish the image, and patted Annie's knee. 'Enough of my moans. He'll come when he comes, as I keep telling Dave, and fretting won't help. Tell me about yourself instead, and Liz and Kelvin, of course. Lord, we haven't had a proper chat for ages. How's things going with the lovebirds?'

How Annie yearned to tell her friend the full story. How she would have loved to see Bernie laugh, howl, cringe and swear she'd give that randy, dandified bag of wind more than a feckin' black eye, so she would. But she could also hear Bernie telling her husband that his new chum, Kelvin, was no longer welcome in their pub. There were no half-measures with Bernie. You were either in with her or – heaven help you – you were out. She couldn't bar Kelvin Parsons without explanation and, no, Annie most definitely did not want her tussle in the taxi to be shared with Dave. Dear soul that he was, his indignation was only too likely to spill out among his late-night cronies in the side bar.

'No go, I'm afraid,' she said lightly. 'I, um, get the impression Kelvin has other fish to fry.'

'Well, isn't that a terrible crying shame.' Bernie cocked an eyebrow. 'You wouldn't be one of them, I suppose?'

'Do me a favour,' cried Annie, rather too vehemently, but Bernie only chuckled and agreed she didn't fancy the fella either, looker though he was – or at least not half so much as he seemed to fancy himself.

'You could see Liz had a real touch of the old starry eyes, though,' she continued and shook her head. 'She's bound to feel it, because you know what they say: love's like the bloody measles. The older you are, the harder it hits.'

'Right,' Annie barked the following day.

They were at the kitchen table. Liz had given up pecking at her sandwich and was drawing listless circles in the foam of her untouched cappuccino.

'We need to get out,' she went on. 'Both of us. Out of this house. We must do something.'

Liz looked up warily. 'Like what?'

'Deep-sea diving? Don't panic, I'm joking.'

'We could go swimming. I suppose.'

'The pool in town's a stinking soup of chlorine and athlete's foot. And the smart one out at Rob's place would give a gold-fish claustrophobia. Anyway, we're not members.' Annie paced over to the glass doors and stared out at the grey and winter-withered shrubs. 'Besides, it's our brains that need exercise. We are lacking stimulation, Liz. We need to sharpen ourselves up.'

'I've still got the evening-class brochure,' said Liz dolefully. 'I think.'

'Huh. Accounting software or conversational Spanish, and we're hardly planning a trip to Benidorm.'

There was a silence. Then Liz said: 'I don't suppose you'd fancy the knit-lits?'

'What?'

'The book club? They knit too, you know. While they're talking.'

'You're kidding me.'

'I'm sure you once said you'd nearly joined. Last year some time?'

'Oh, you mean Trisha Hough's outfit?'

'She's the secretary, yes. She was asking about you just the other day, actually – I meant to say. She came into work to stick up a poster about it.'

On the verge of retorting she would sooner build a model of the Taj Mahal in matchsticks, Annie was silenced by Liz adding wistfully that some of the books under discussion looked rather interesting. 'I did think about signing up,' she said. 'But I wouldn't want to go on my own.'

'That's it then,' said Annie instantly. 'Come on, get your coat on.'

'Why?'

'We're going to see Trisha Hough,' she said. 'Put our names down. Just don't expect me to knit.'

15

They could have phoned or emailed. However, as Annie explained to Liz during the short drive into town, she had been guiltily aware for too long of neglecting poor old Trisha. When in her store, a mere stone's throw round the corner from Chatsworth Close, she had used to call by regularly on her way home from work, if only to drop in a bag of wallpaper or fabric offcuts.

'Big crafter, is Trish,' she continued. 'Finds a use for almost anything and sells the results by the shedload. Bizarre, really, because you have to wonder who wants a felt cover for their laptop. A felt anything, come to that. Still, it's all for charity, so who am I to quibble?'

Behind her car seat now was a box of odds and ends left over from the work on Liz's house, along with a bottle of sweet pink fizz some cheapskate had palmed off onto her. And no, she was *not* just offloading likewise. She happened to know Trisha Hough was partial to this tipple. Even so, at the last minute, she'd been moved to stuff beside it a tub of truly ritzy chocolate truffles that her extravagant sister had brought up from London.

'Which isn't generous of me at all,' she said, as she pressed this largesse upon a happily protesting Trisha. 'You're saving me from myself, because I'm still fat as a pig after Christmas.' Realising that this was a shade tactless, given Trisha's monumental bulk, she hurried on to ask if they had been decorating. 'The place feels different somehow?'

And yet she could see no changes. The bungalow, which was always suffocatingly overheated, was configured entirely around the needs of a severely disabled person. Such furniture as Trisha owned was squeezed against the walls to allow passage of Joey's motorised wheelchair. This was parked as usual in the centre of the lounge on a mat of ribbed plastic, flanked by a wheeled table in the depressing wood-effect melamine so beloved of social services. Head lolling against a cushioned neck brace, Joey appeared to be dozing while Los Angeles Police Department vehicles smashed into each other with siren-blaring gusto on the television.

Trisha put a finger to her lips as she tenderly detached a remote-control handset from her son's twisted fingers and adjusted the volume downwards a shade before placing it back on his lap. 'It disturbs him if I turn the sound off,' she whispered. 'Shall we sneak out and put the kettle on? I can wake everyone up when the tea's brewed. Now don't go tripping over that shopping bag, Lizzy – honestly, what am I like, dumping things here, there and flippin' everywhere, just where they're bound to . . .'

As Trisha chattered Liz away into the kitchen, Annie held back and gazed round the stuffy lounge. This is what hell looks like, she was thinking, not for the first time. How does Trisha bear it? Dear God, if this were my home, my life – my poor son in that chair – I'd want to stick my head in the gas oven. Or drink myself senseless.

Or at least paint the walls anything but that bloody pink.

The bungalow had been built by the council in the 1960s with a kitchen scarcely bigger than Annie's downstairs loo. Liz was pressed against a sink piled with pots as Trisha squeezed past to flip a switch under the kettle. She then kicked open the door to a small lean-to porch where she kept her washing machine, under a sad forest of brown pot plants, and retrieved a cigarette packet from behind a geranium corpse.

'Trying not to smoke in the house,' she muttered, indistinctly because she already had a fag clamped between tight-stretched lips and was holding a wavering flame to its tip. 'Got to be careful with invalids now. Bit parky in here this time of year, but still . . .' As she sighed out a stream of smoke, Annie belatedly recognised what had struck her as different on arrival. The familiar fug of stale tobacco was disguised with some lavender-ish aroma, ersatz but not wholly unpleasant.

'Fabulous, isn't it?' exclaimed Trisha when Annie remarked on this. 'It's one of those thingies you plug into the wall. I mean I'd always fancied one, seen them on the telly and that, and you look at them in the supermarket and they don't seem to cost much but, oh-ho, that's where they catch you out, don't they just? The plugs are cheap as chips, but the refills cost a flippin' fortune, just like printer inks, Lordy-lordy, it's wicked what these companies think they can get away with charging, once they've got you hooked, and I did look on eBay of course, but honestly what with the postage and so forth, and besides how d'you know it's the real thing? That's what I say, Annie. Can't sniff it over the internet, can you? Course, eBay's great, I'm not knocking it for a minute, where would we all be without good old eBay? Look at this top of mine, Marks and Sparks, brand new, four ninety-nine postage free, which I thought was marvellous because I'm not a one for wasting money on myself, Liz, as Annie would tell you, never have been, but I don't have a lovely slim figure like yours, and it's very tricky to get things that fit properly, if you know what I mean, I can't be doing with tops that pinch under the armpits, well, they give me sores, actually, bit like eczema, I've had to go to the doctor more than once for cream, and they get a proper bashing – my clothes, I mean, not doctors, ha ha, just my little joke – because everything's in and out of the washing machine all the time, with Joey spilling stuff, well, he can't help it, poor love, not with his hands being like they are, but air freshener, no, that kind of thing eBay does let you down on. And what's more—' She broke off to lean aside and knock her ash into the nearest dead plant, but barely drew breath before resuming. 'I'm very particular about smells, which is funny, because you might think I couldn't smell a thing with the old cancer sticks, but I can, got a nose like a bloodhound, I have. I know, I know, don't tell me, Annie, I really should give them up.' She was waving the glowing stub in the air as she spoke. 'Just like the doc lectures me every time he calls by. Bless his cotton socks, he's so good with Joey, Doctor Ed, patience of a saint, but he doesn't mince his words, our Ed, he gives it you straight, and he tells me they'll kill me, one way or another, and you know sometimes I think I wouldn't mind, honestly I would not because we've all got to go sometime, haven't we? Only if I wasn't so worried what would happen to Joey without me, it doesn't bear thinking about, really doesn't, that's what keeps me awake at night, as I said to the doc, just the thought does my head in, and that's why I smoke so much, ha ha.'

Laughing triggered a paroxysm of gut-wrenching coughs, and Annie seized her chance to point out that the kettle had boiled. A couple of minutes ago, actually. If Trisha would just remind her where she kept the teabags? She had learned long ago that when Trisha was in spate – and when was she not? – an hour could slide by before the promised cup of tea or coffee was brewed. Even then, it could moulder to tepid on the worktop before milk was retrieved from the fridge. Annie had no particular desire for a drink at this moment. Still less did she want one after inspecting the brown rings inside the mugs on the draining board and wondering if she could surreptitiously re-wash her own. Leaving before the statutory social rituals were observed, though, would be to hurt Trisha's feelings. So tea had to be poured and drunk.

'Yes, that's right, lovey, you've remembered Joey has his in the plastic beaker, must be a lid somewhere, oh, you've got it, well done, but you really shouldn't, Annie, honest to goodness, I ought to be doing all that, you've enough on your plate, busy-busy-busy as you are, well, me too, because we've a bloomin' packet to raise for this new studio thingy at the theatre, Lordy only knows how we're going to do it, and I'm sure you must be keeping yourself occupied, I mean, how long is it since we saw you down here? We miss your lovely shop, you know, Joey and me, we always used to go round that way to have a good stare in the windows on our walks, and it's all being turned into these luxury flats now – loft apartments they're calling them, if you don't mind – reckon they'll be open for business by Easter— Can you see my sweeteners, they're usually over by the microwave. No? Well, never mind, I'll just have to have sugar, it's in that pot shaped like a strawberry, three spoonfuls, please, Annie – oh, go on then, I'll have another quick ciggy whilst Joey's still asleep and I've got the chance, because he won't drink his until it's cooled a bit anyway. Oh, and Cath doesn't have milk in hers these days, which you won't know. Actually, she sometimes likes a bit of lemon, if you can see, there should be one kicking around . . .'

'Cath?' About to pour, Annie halted, teapot poised. 'Surely you don't mean . . . Is Cate over here?'

'Didn't you hear? Why, I thought that was what'd brought you running round,' said Trisha, enthusiastically sucking her newly lit cigarette. 'That's why I put it straight on good old Facebook yesterday, because I knew everyone'd be wanting to see our girl.'

At that moment the shouting and gunshots of the television snapped to silence, there was a moan from Joey, a low-pitched, teasing laugh – and here she was in the kitchen doorway. Five foot ten with no shoes. High-cheek-boned, vampire-pale and inky-haired, she was draped, as ever, in one of those bleak, black smocky things which looked to have been cobbled up from a horse blanket but somehow hung with architectural stylishness on her wide-shouldered frame.

'Trisha, love, you'll end up with pneumonia if you insist on smoking out there, you poor soul. It's very sweet of you but . . . *Annie.*' The voice changed. 'I didn't know you were here. Well, hello, how are you?' Doctor Cate Blackwell squeezed out an approximation of a smile. 'Good to see you. It's been quite a while.'

Annie's answering beam was as bright and hard as a fluorescent strip light. 'Cate!' she cried. 'What a lovely surprise.'

No, she didn't mean it.

As Annie would later assure Liz, it was not that she *dis*-liked Cate Blackwell. Not at all. Well – not exactly.

What possible reason could she have for disliking this beautiful and brilliant woman more than a decade her junior? This internationally acclaimed feminist academic; this dutiful sister and aunt; this most distinguished old girl ever (allegedly) of Laurel Park High School? That Annie herself had attended Laurel Park, and indeed had been head girl of the same (which was more than Cath Blackwell ever managed) was neither here nor there. Obviously.

She was amused but not surprised to see that Liz was glancing from Trisha to her sister with poorly concealed incredulity. No one would take Cate Blackwell and Trisha Hough for sisters with one being so tall, dark and spare, t'other short, fair and very square – never mind Cate being a non-smoking, non-driving, barely drinking vegetarian. Or a juice-swigging, soya-munching planet-saver, as Annie had been known to describe her.

They were only half-siblings, of course, with different dads, neither of whom had stuck around to see their daughters grow up, and there was a full sixteen years between them. Their mum, a sadly feckless character, died of a drug overdose when Catherine, as she was in those days, had barely started school, so Trisha had been as much a mother to her as a sister, and a sturdily ambitious mother at that. Propelling the young Cate along her stellar path to Oxford and beyond was big sis back home, staunch, loving and proud. And all credit to Cath (said the sages of Bucksford), she had never forgotten it. Whatever the heights to which she had risen, she had remained equally devoted to her sister and her nephew, even if her visits had necessarily been fewer since she'd moved to the States. A shame, because along with all her other talents, Cate was famously good with Joey.

So when there was a thump from the lounge, followed by an anguished bellow, it was Cate who spun round and was first through the doorway. Joey had flung himself half out of his chair and across the wheeled table, which had careered into the sideboard. His arms were flailing, and he was roaring like a bear in a trap.

'Darling, what's the matter?' said Cate, hastening to his side. 'Oh Lord, was it the remote control you were after? Because your thoughtless aunty turned the television off, didn't she? I'm so sorry, darling. Look . . .' She retrieved the device from the floor and wrapped her arms round Joey's squirming body to help him upright again. Almost at once though, her grip slackened, and it seemed to Annie she staggered.

Before she could offer assistance, Trisha muscled past. 'What's all this noisy carry-on? Here, you big lump,' she said fondly to her son, grasping him expertly under the armpits and heaving him back into his seat. 'Silly girl,' she said in exactly the same tone to her sister. 'What're you thinking of, trying to pick our Joey up, when you can't hardly stand up yourself, you poor old crock? Go and sit down this instant, and I'll fetch you a nice cuppa.' She leaned confidentially towards Annie and Liz. 'Shocking state she's in, our girl. Worn to a thread and look what's happened. Glandular fever you can bet your bottom dollar, whatever the doctors say. I mean, I'd known in my bones something wasn't right, but only from reading between the lines, because Cate being Cate, she never actually said a word, so I'd no idea how bad she was, not a clue, not 'til she turned up on this doorstep, day before yesterday. Well, talk about gobsmacked, half past two in the afternoon it was and I opened the door, thinking it was the postie, because he does sometimes run very late these days, with that many packages and parcels from all the internet shopping, and he's a proper love is Tony, always signs for us if I haven't heard him shout, or I'm busy with Joey, and he knows where to put stuff if—'

'I say,' interposed Liz timidly, 'do you think Cate's all right?'

Annie glanced round to see her slumped on the sofa. Her eyes were closed, she was breathing fast and there was sweat glinting on her brow and upper lip. Given the tropical temperature, this was perhaps unremarkable, but she was moved to pre-empt whatever Trisha was about to say with a suggestion that her sister might benefit from that cup of tea sooner rather than later and not to worry, she would go and get it.

When she returned with the tray, however, it was Liz who now occupied the sofa, alone. Cate had taken herself off to recover on the bed, said Trisha, tutting as she dabbed a smear of drool from her son's chin, and pretending to cuff him when he moaned a protest. So if Annie wouldn't mind taking the cuppa through – Aunty Cate would like that, wouldn't she, Joey? Whilst his mum had a little sit-down and kept a beady eye on him just in case he was thinking of trying another mad dive – who'd he think he was, flippin' Superman?

Annie duly carried the milk-less tea across the narrow hallway into what she knew was Trisha's bedroom, and nearly plummeted over an inflatable mattress, complete with quilt and pillows, immediately inside the door. But where else could Cate sleep? The bungalow had only two bedrooms, with Joey occupying the larger of those. She was lying on her sister's bed now, though, with her eyes shut, as still and pale as a marble effigy.

Annie carefully positioned the mug among the clutter on the bedside table. 'Tea?' she said softly.

Cate did not respond. Could she really be asleep already? Annie shrugged and picked a careful retreat round the blow-up bed. Trisha's bungalow was always piled high, but only now did she notice that in the hallway, alongside the usual barricades of polythene crates, bulging carrier bags, laundry baskets and the like, there were two large suitcases with airline labels looped round the handles, as well as a couple of smaller bags in smartly monogrammed leather. A lot of luggage, in other words, and classy luggage at that.

'Looks like Cate's back for a nice long visit,' she commented as she re-entered the lounge.

Trisha was urging her son to drink his tea. 'And we'll put the telly on again for you in a minute.' She turned towards Annie, eyes wide. 'Oh, better than that,' she said. 'Our girl's come back for good.'

'So she's jacked it all in,' marvelled Annie to Liz, as she pulled the car door shut. 'The States, the high-powered job at Berkeley, the whole shooting match. Well, that proves it, as far as I'm concerned. Whatever Rob and Bernie say.'

'What do Rob and Bernie say?' Liz craned round to execute a neat three-point turn. 'Gosh, I've just realised we completely forgot about the book club.'

'What a pity,' said Annie, with no audible regret. 'The club, I mean, not about her being gay. Hey, careful.' She waited until Liz had steadied the steering wheel. 'Rather, about Cate *not* being gay, according to my friends. While I've been saying for years it's a no-brainer, ever since she took off for California straight after her very close *friend*, quote-unquote, Siobhan was head-hunted by one of the studios over there. She's a big cheese in the television industry, this Siobhan – you'll have seen plenty about her if you ever look at the business pages, smashing glass ceilings and all that. She and Cate were at Oxford together and shared a flat in London for years before they headed west.'

'Is this the friend Trisha was saying had just got married?'

'Exactly.'

'So she can't be—'

'To another woman, didn't you clock that? Siobhan's always been up front about her sexuality. As she should – who gives a stuff? Except Cate, apparently. And don't try telling me she had boyfriends years back—'

'How, when I've never met her before today?'

'—because she wouldn't be the first woman to see the light in her thirties. And the fact she's cut and run the moment Siobhan weds is a mighty big coincidence, wouldn't you say?'

'She's come home because she's ill,' retorted Liz with unusual asperity. 'Glandular fever – all right, suspected glandular fever. But even without knowing her, I can see how poorly she is. She's as pale as a dishcloth.'

'Always was. Dab of make-up might help, but it's probably against her religion. Oh don't cluck like that, it was only a joke. I'm just saying it's mysterious. Great job, great life, tons more dosh than she'd ever earn in a British uni, and what's she coming back to? At her age, too. Sorry?' Annie had to think for a moment before answering Liz's query. 'Mid-forties? I know I was pregnant with Dom when she was at Oxford because she came to interview my famous author husband for her student mag. I remember feeling like a bloody hippopotamus as Jake gazed entranced at this super-brainy nymph in a see-through blouse telling him what a genius he was.'

'Is that why you've got such a down on her?' said Liz tartly. This was when Annie delivered her standard riposte about not *dis*-liking Cate Blackwell.

'Although if I just once heard her swear, or crack a bad-taste joke or something, I might like her a lot more. But she just glides through life like an iceberg, no clue what's going on underneath. I find that kind of person hard to love.'

'Maybe she's just shy?'

Annie snorted. 'You should've heard her knocking ten bells out of some bloke on the radio last year. Hell hath no fury like a feminist defending Jane Austen. *But* ...' she patted Liz's knee with a chuckle, 'before you tell me I'm just a crabby old crone and totally unreasonable – yup. You'd be right. Cate Blackwell is clever, lovely and admirable in every way. It's a sad reflection on me, not her, that her squeaky-clean sheer fucking perfectness makes my teeth ache. OK?'

One unexpected but welcome effect of Cate Blackwell's reappearance, however, was that it seemed to cure Liz overnight, if not of her aching heart, certainly of her lingering flu. Her cough vanished, she emerged from her woolly chrysalis of scarves and the once permanent tennis ball of tissues stuffed up her sleeve shrank to a ripple. It was as though her aches and pains melted away in the face of real illness.

Even Annie could not deny that Cate Blackwell looked ill. She did not need Trish to confide that she could scarcely persuade her sister to eat a crumb, although she suspected that Trisha's notion of a crumb might constitute a square meal for an average family of four.

She was not surprised, then, that when she scrambled out of the car at the surgery to collect a prescription for Dominic, she caught sight of Cate's ashen face bent over a book in a corner of the waiting room. She raised a hand in greeting and, remembering Cate didn't drive, and being pretty sure she hadn't spotted Trisha's distinctive Joey-carrier as Liz turned into the car park, she began to walk over to ask if she needed a lift home after her appointment. A friendly and – so she congratulated herself – very thoughtful gesture.

She could swear the younger woman had seen her, but what did she do? She hunched a shoulder and buried her head deeper in her book. Yup – Cate Blackwell downright cut her dead.

16

'You're making a mystery out of a molehill,' said Rob Daley. 'She'd been given a sabbatical to work on a book, anyway, and she was ready for a change.'

'And how,' retorted Annie.

They were in the cafe-bar downstairs at the Woolshed. This was a fashionably rugged cellar, with bare stone walls, gnarled beams and cobbled floor. The counter was a slab of burnished concrete, and the seating slices of raw tree trunk bolted onto iron legs. Eye-catching, Annie would concede, but a very literal pain in the bum as far as the benches were concerned. What do you expect, though, if you entrust interior detailing to an architect, and a man to boot? Not that she resented the failure of the Woolshed's management to consult herself, obviously. Their loss. Obviously. She and Dominic were here at Rob's invitation to see a touring production of *The Tempest*.

'Shakespeare?' Annie had said, when he rang to suggest it.

'You have any other Tempest in mind?'

'Don't get clever with me, sunshine. It's not a Shakespeare I know, that's all. I don't suppose it's a bundle of laughs.'

'You're such a pleasure to invite out, Nan. Hey, Rob, theatre trip, brill idea. Thanks for thinking of me, Rob. Be nice to see you again, Rob.'

'Still,' she said, ignoring him, 'it might do Dominic good. In fact, it could be just what he needs. You know he's muttering now about packing in acting altogether? I ask you, where's his ambition gone, all that crazy passion? It can't be just because he fell off his bike.'

'I guess work's hard enough to find for young actors, even if they're not limping around on a stick.'

'That's exactly what he says. Then rants on about having to pimp yourself at cattle-market auditions, only to be told you're crap. He never used to get so worked up, he'd just shrug and laugh. I tell you, he's not himself. Look at the way he slammed out of the bar that time.'

'What time?'

'Christmas Day, of course. You know, when we were all watching Dave's dad.'

'Huh, can you blame him?'

'Don't be ridiculous. And when I ask, he says I wouldn't understand. Even if I listened for once instead of always telling him what he should be doing. Can you believe that?' Annie paused. 'Don't answer.'

'Cheer up, love. Once he's fit again—'

'He'd be a damn sight fitter already if he did his exercises, as I keep telling him – OK, OK, very funny, but you wouldn't be laughing if he were one of yours. It's more than six months he's been back at home now, and the latest thing is, he's not just lounging around like a sulky teenager, no, he's writing a play, isn't he? About searing, contemporary issues too deep for trivial old me to comprehend. Although apparently I should be encouraging him.'

'Well – yes?'

'I'd be more hopeful if he'd ever learned to spell. Never mind the only talent he seems to have inherited from his dad is for drinking. Still, yeah, it'd do him good to get out of the house for once, and into a theatre. Who knows? Might give him inspiration.'

'Actually, I only had the two tickets—' Rob had broken off with a sigh. 'I dare say I can swing another. Trustee's perks.'

Two days later, having frogmarched her son out to Rob's car, she was cautiously pleased to see him now, perched on the corner of a table, laughing at Hank Damon's melodramatic rant about screwing dosh out of the local bourgeoisie for some new building project. She was about to thank Rob for his timely invitation when he jumped to his feet.

'Speaking of angels – hello, you two. Coming to the play?'

Peering past him, she saw Cate Blackwell approach, as stylishly black-swathed as ever. Trisha panted along behind, with a cardboard box bulging under one arm.

'Not our cuppa, I'm afraid to say,' she gasped, before her sister could speak. 'Joey and me both nodded off last time we tried old Jerky-Javelin – our little joke, d'you get it? Shaky-spear? But I've just been telling Cate I asked at the box office and they've one or two returns, and look, lovey, you wouldn't be on your own now, not with Rob – and my word, here's Dominic, too, how's your wonky leg, sweetheart? Your old friend Joey's out in the car, so I can't stop to chat.' However, even as she hugged Dominic with her one free arm, she was twisting round to continue her monologue. 'I've only called by to drop these posters in, for our Walk 'n' Wheel day, yes, we're at it again, fundraising for the new studio and—'

'So will you join us, Cate?' said Rob, stepping back and indicating Annie. 'The production's had five-star reviews.'

'Yes, why don't you?' Annie echoed, perhaps more dutifully than enthusiastically, but there was no call for Cate to recoil. She *did*. Annie had not imagined that flash of dismay, whatever Rob might say, and however sweetly the woman now offered some excuse about tiredness. So absorbed was she in storing up this typically bizarre response to discuss with Rob

– 'like I was Caliban, crawled out from under my stone' (she had prudently Wikipedia-ed the plot) – that she didn't realise Trisha was addressing her now, asking if she'd heard about her friend, Kelvin. *Kelvin?*

'What about him?'

'He's not single any more,' Trish declared, with the triumph of one breaking a major news scoop. 'Not according to his Facebook page as of six o'clock this evening.'

'Oh sure, that's right,' chimed in Rob unexpectedly. 'I meant to tell you, Nan. What with you and him being so matey.' There was a satirical glint in his eye. His brother must have been talking to him.

'Don't tell me you and Kelvin are Facebook friends, too?' she enquired acidly.

'You know me, love, strictly a real-life merchant. No, I bumped into the man himself practically on my doorstep. He'd been viewing one of the flats downstairs, he said. For him and his new partner, he said. Looking smug as a slug in the strawberry patch, I'm here to tell you.'

'Oh shit,' she said unguardedly. Of course Rob's eyebrows flew up. She glared at him.

'A whirlwind romance,' said Trisha, oblivious to their locked stares, 'from the minute he saw her photo, he says, because that's how they got together, apparently, one of these internet sites, which everyone seems to be at these days – maybe you should give it a go, lovey,' she added to her sister, 'it's ages since you brought a nice boy home.' Annie's amusement at Cate's face was forgotten, however, as Trish went on to marvel at this funny old turn-up, 'with everyone not so long ago thinking him and Lizzy Jones might be, you know—'

'Your friend, Liz?' cut in Rob sharply. He turned to Annie. 'And Kelvin Parsons?'

'She seemed quite keen,' offered Trisha.

Annie was only defending her lovelorn friend in retorting firmly that it had been Kelvin, actually, who had seemed so keen. Too late did she realise this might have been unwise. 'At least I thought so, at one time. But there was nothing to it.' And now she was just digging herself in deeper. 'Obviously not. I mean, could you imagine Liz with someone like him?'

Rob shook his head. 'Oh Annie,' he sighed. 'It sounds to me like you did.'

Bloody typical. So unlike his robotic brother, this senior wrangler in the mind-reading department had added Kelvin to Liz, multiplied the result by herself and come up with a very fair notion of what had scuppered his friend the bishop's marriage plans.

She was saved by the bell. Literally, because the three-minute bell summoned them into the auditorium. Shakespeare bypassed her as she pondered Liz's likely response to the news of Kelvin's latest squeeze. In the event, it was both better and worse than she feared.

Better, because Liz assured her that this was only what she had been expecting. Worse, because Liz repeated that this was only what she had been expecting – and kept on repeating it, in various forms, with a regularity that was at first touching, then monotonous, and by the end of the second day sanity-endangering. Annie had permitted her only a glimpse of the glamorously backlit, soft-focus portrait of his new lady-love on Kelvin's Facebook page, which – blessedly, as it now seemed – Liz was barred from accessing herself.

'Photoshop job,' she said, snapping shut the laptop. 'Facelift, too, if you ask me, with those cat eyes. A model, he says? Not in this century. As for calling her his Tantric Goddess – puke, puke – what's that supposed to mean? Apart from sex taking a week and a half. Oh, don't cry, Lizzy love. You are so well out of that, my dear, believe me.'

'Yes,' said Liz. And wept on.

After a tear-sodden week, Annie concluded there could be only one answer. Another man.

Not that Annie was going to attempt any more matchmaking. No way, not after the fiasco with Kelvin. Even if she had a potential partner in mind, which she had not. Well, except for a widowed accountant with a droopy moustache and a geriatric poodle who used to do her books and who happened to have telephoned the other day, but – *no*. Neville Mayhew had terrible teeth and an aged mother as well as the poodle, both requiring nursing care.

She did, though, feel obliged to ask herself whether the bishop really had been such a poor prospect. Dispiritingly ancient, of course, but Rob seemed to think there was mileage still in his tank. Dull? As hell, no doubt. But were men like carpets? After all, as she had often advised an over-excited client, the electric blue that's so thrilling as you flip through the sample book may drive you crackers after a couple of years on your sitting-room floor – or even a couple of weeks. Conversely, that boring shade of mouldy porridge you barely glanced at may just live with you happily ever after. Was there, then, something to be said for the beige husband? In fact, given her own experience of marrying the human equivalent of sky blue pink with purple dots, you might find youself wondering whether dullness wasn't actually an asset.

Thus, when Liz chanced to mention that she had received an email from one of Caradoc Swallow's daughters, announcing that several of his grandchildren were to compete in the Bucksford Festival of Music and the Dramatic Arts, Annie, after a moment's rapid thought, urged her to attend.

'Really?' said Liz. 'I mean, isn't it rather awkward? You know, after—'

'Nonsense,' declared Annie. 'What's more, I will come along to support you.'

The lime green leather biker jacket was a mistake.

Annie had pulled this new and extravagant acquisition out of the wardrobe because, after her lacklustre encounter with the bishop amid the dahlias, Liz was going to see her making a proper effort this time round. All prejudice set aside, she intended to give the man and his tribe a fair chance to prove themselves worthy. After much pondering, she paired her jacket with a flirty purple skirt and thick-soled, lace-up boots, a bold combo recommended in a recent magazine feature on age-defying styles for the more mature woman, albeit to be attempted only with tights of industrial density. Her reflection in the hall mirror as Liz tooted the horn without was, she thought, both suitably smart and pleasingly funky.

The first blow was learning that the bishop himself was not coming. Up in Scotland, apparently. So much for that bright idea. Then the echoing, marble-pillared lobby of Bucksford's town hall turned out to be a swampy morass of saggy leggings and sad anoraks. Frazzled young mums staggered under the coats, instrument cases, water bottles and music stands of their nervously twittering broods with barely a flick of mascara between them. Annie looked round and felt like a parrot who has strayed into a chicken coop. An elderly parrot at that.

'Oh my gosh, Aunty Liz, I almost didn't recognise you,' cried one of these mothers, stumbling towards them with a violin case over her shoulder and a cardigan round her knees. 'Whatever have you done to your hair? I mean, it's quite nice, really, just—' Here she broke off and gawped at Annie.

'You've met, of course,' said Liz hastily, 'at the flower show? You remember Rachael, don't you, Annie?'

Rachael's face suggested she didn't expect her aunt's cronies to roll up in miniskirts and platform boots. Perhaps she thought the granny generation should stick to polyester blouses and elasticated slacks while sucking toffees and watching the *Antiques Roadshow*. Embracing her warmly, Annie declared that she most certainly remembered Rachael, and was delighted now to meet her sister Gabrielle. And were *all* these their children? Goodness, hadn't they been busy!

Barely had she launched her charm offensive, though, than it was interrupted by an explosive guitar riff she had uploaded to her phone in an idle moment the other day and had since found impossible to dislodge.

As there were notices taped to every other marble pillar reminding patrons that mobiles were to be silenced, Annie began ransacking her bag. The bishop's daughters feigned polite deafness, while their squad of well-scrubbed offspring elbowed one another and rolled their eyes at the technological incompetence of the old. Muttering apologies, she could only back towards the doors, and was down the steps and out on the pavement before her fingers had closed on the importunate phone. To set the seal on her irritation, an unknown number showed. Well, if this was a solar-panel salesman, he was going to be very, very sorry.

'Who wants to know?' she barked, cutting across the usual smarmy enquiry as to whether this was Mrs Annie Stoneycroft speaking. The reply, however, muffled by the rumble of a passing bus, startled her into clamping a hand over her free ear. 'Sorry, lot of noise. Did you say *Sunday Mirror*?'

She had not misheard, and this was not some market researcher conducting a sales survey. He was called Alan and claimed to be a news reporter.

'You're the one married to a famous writer, uh, Jay Stoneycroft, right?'

'No, divorced. And *Jake* died over a year ago. What do you want?'

Her thumb was a microsecond away from ending the call, when she heard this Alan asking if it was correct she was a close friend of, um, Bernadette Eastman? And that she had been in on the amazing secret of Dave's celebrity dad from the start? 'In fact, can I quote you as saying it was you first got her to contact Simon Spencer?'

'I – what? Who gave you my number?'

'How d'you reckon Dave feels about meeting his dad?'

'Sorry?'

'And what about yourself? Are you hoping to meet old Sly, too?'

'Look . . .' She gulped, tried to gather her wits. 'I can't imagine why – why you're ringing me. I have nothing to say. Except this is a private matter, a family matter. And I'm sure the Eastmans, and, um, Mr Spencer, would wish it to stay that way. That's all. No, absolutely nothing else, thank you, good-bye – goodbye.'

17

Phone flat against her shoulder, she stared across the square at Queen Victoria. A pigeon squatted on the crowned head, ruffling its feathers in the wind. Annie felt pretty ruffled herself. Although perhaps the only surprise was that the hacks hadn't come knocking before, given Dave's fondness for telling the tale in the bar.

Simon Spencer, however, had specifically warned against the press. And if he was so wary of upsetting his wife, might this even deter him from coming to meet his son? Please heaven, no, that would be too cruel. Her phone was at her ear again, but Bernie's must have been switched off because the call went straight to voicemail.

'Bit of a shock, Bernie, I've had a call from a reporter.' Why was she whispering? She cleared her throat. 'God knows how he got on to me. Look, I'll try the landline.' The pub proved to be engaged, however; endlessly engaged. Some Bridezilla booking her wedding banquet, vol-au-vent by sodding vol-au-vent? Or maybe it was just the Eastmans dodging the press themselves by leaving their phone off the hook. Oh Lord.

Annie tapped her mobile against her chin. What could she say that would help, anyway? If the story was out, it was out. Maybe just text for now, and get Liz to run her to the Hoppy, once the bishop's brood had strutted their stuff. Absorbed in composition as she returned to the entrance, she missed a shallow step and bent an ankle over, thanks to her platform sole. Lethal bloody things platforms, always had been, she couldn't think why she'd been dumb enough to fall for them again this time round. The crowd in the lobby had now thinned to stragglers and be-sashed stewards and a piano echoed from the council chamber. She limped across the tiles to the towering mahogany doors where she found Liz waiting. Handbag clutched tight to her ribs, she was checking her watch. Her face relaxed as Annie appeared.

'You should have gone in without me, bless you,' Annie whispered. 'Thing with the Eastmans, tell you later. Listen, they're clapping. Can we sneak in at the back?'

The bishop's daughters, however, had saved two seats in their family encampment on the third row. Under cover of applause, she followed Liz down the centre aisle as fast as she could hobble while trying to mute her phone. Of course, the thing buzzed because she tapped something wrong and even – out of typical bloody perversity – blipped to confirm it was indeed now in silent mode, drawing a beady stare from whatever Rachael's sister was called. Stuffing it into her pocket, Annie squeezed along the row, crashing knees, kicking music bags, whispering apologies and stifling obscenities. By the time she flopped into a seat, a plump infant with heavily wired teeth and cheeks even pinker than her too-tight frilly frock was up on the platform, warbling about . . .

'Daisies?' she said to Liz as they clapped after three interminable verses. 'I couldn't make out a word, but that's hardly surprising through all that orthodontistry. Half the Forth Bridge in her mouth, poor kid. As for whoever—'

Liz's face silenced her before she could voice her views on trussing up tubby little girls like Shirley Temple. The rigid shoulders of the bishop's daughters, however, suggested this warning may have come too late. Sure enough, the chubby cherub came and plonked herself between the two sisters with a steel-toothed beam. Annie shut her eyes – and felt her phone vibrate. She clamped a guilty elbow over the pocket. Within another daisy ditty and a half, however, it had fizzed twice more with incoming texts. Bernie? She would have to check. She did at least wait for applause before surreptitiously sliding it out. Cupping a hand over the screen she squinted down, fighting the temptation to cause more disruption by rummaging for specs.

Dominic. A missed call and a text, asking what the *Sunday Mirror* wanted. So it must've been him gave the reporter her mobile number. Thanks a bunch, son. *Ring me soonest.* Tough. Dom could wait, because the other text was from Bernie. Two of the grandchildren had now clocked the phone in her hand and were smirking. She sank lower into her seat, feeling like the naughtiest girl in the class, as another pint-sized chanteuse shuffled onto the stage.

A chorus line of emojis was even more meaningless than usual without specs, but the words jumped out, not just capitalised, but in bold as well.

ANNIE STOP WHATEV UR DOING AND COME ROUND. PLEASE?????? NEED YOU NOW @ OURS LIFE & DEATH!!!! NO SEROUSLY DONT RING BERNIES' FINE

What? Obviously this came from Dave rather than his less excitable and considerably more literate wife, but why say Bernie was fine? Why should she not be fine? And why did he tell her not to ring?

U KNOW WHAT SHES LIKE [more emojis] **DONT WORRY XXXXXXX**

Worry about *what?*

PS NEED U HERE 11 LATEST

'Shit,' she gasped.

Unfortunately she did so just as the accompanist raised her hands and a resonant hush fell over the hall. Nevertheless, it was hard to believe she'd been overheard four seats away, but the two muppets already keeping her under surveillance erupted into sniggers, provoking death glares from the bishop's daughters, which also encompassed Annie. Whereupon the child on stage – don't say she'd heard too? – chose that moment to have a nervous breakdown. Face a-crumple, voice cracking, she stumbled away to the side of the platform.

Annie took the opportunity to lean towards Liz. 'How long does this go on?' She glanced at her watch. Just after half past ten.

'Half five or so,' responded Liz brightly, 'if it doesn't over-run. With the finalists' concert in the evening, of course.'

'Of course,' she echoed hollowly. As the forlorn performer was consoled in a huddle of parent and pianist, a buzz of chatter arose, and she realised this was her only chance if she were to reach the Hoppy by eleven. She jumped up, forgetting her wrenched ankle and nearly plummeted into the row in front.

'Truly sorry,' she hissed, grasping Liz's shoulder to steady herself, 'but Bernie needs me. Will you apologise for me to' – Goneril and Regan were the names that sprang to mind, but she just inclined her head in the appropriate direction – 'to your friends? Don't worry, I'll grab a cab, but—'

'You will do nothing of the kind.' Liz scrambled up beside her. 'That's your car outside. If they need you at the Hopkirk Arms, I'm driving you there. Come on.'

Since Annie's experience of Bucksford taxis suggested they were least available when most needed – Pete's sake, she'd still have her licence otherwise – she shrugged gratefully and began shuffling back towards the aisle. The next competitor was already squaring up on the stage, so she could offer the sisters only a grimace and a wave of her mobile by way of apology. That they pursed their lips, averted their knees and otherwise ignored her as she brushed past, did not trouble her

– too bad, she'd tried – but she was a little perturbed when they seemed to mete out similarly frosty treatment to their Aunty Liz, and she said as much as she stomped after her friend to the car park.

'They'll understand when I explain,' said Liz. She flicked her key to release the locks before adding, 'At least I hope they will. I did try to whisper . . .'

Annie flashed a smile, but already had her phone out. To hell with Dave's silly diktats, she was calling Bernie. To no effect. Voicemail and engaged tone still. As she lowered herself into the passenger seat, however, the guitar riff jangled.

'Dominic, love. Hi.'

'About time, Ma. What's going on?'

'Look, has Dave rung you? Or Bernie?'

'Fuck's sake, Mum, the guy from the *Mirror*? Did he get hold of you?'

'Why on earth did you give him my number?' Something on the dashboard was bleeping. 'Damn, hold on.' Having re-slammed the door, she now had to grab the handle above, such was the gusto with which Liz booted the car into reverse, growling that she would deliver Annie to the Hopkirk Arms before eleven if it killed her. 'Sorry, what?'

'Did he – did he ask about me?'

If this was a strange question she was too preoccupied to query it. 'In your dreams, baby. I don't think you're famous enough for the tabloids yet. No, it's Simon Spencer, of course. They've got hold of the long-lost son story.'

She heard her son sigh. 'Is that all?'

'*All*? Dave's exploding like a box of fireworks. Liz is running me there now. Laters, huh?'

Abandoning any further attempt to ring the pub, she texted that she would be with them shot;u . . . whorly . . . *shortly*, as Liz swerved in and out of traffic like Lewis Hamilton's granny.

'Dead or alive,' she muttered, closing her eyes.

They screamed into the car park of the Hopkirk Arms at ten fifty-five precisely, and braked in a storm of gravel. As Annie levered herself out, she was too preoccupied with testing the weight on her ankle to question the number of cars here on a weekday morning. A stack of heavy-duty silver crates by the open tailgate of a large estate failed to register on her at all, as did the burly man smoking a roll-up beside them. She did not stop to ponder, as she pushed through the door into the main bar, how it was that the light in here was suddenly super-bright, nor why, at this early hour, the bar should be so noisily overcrowded.

Peering round for Bernie, however, she did recognise several of Dave's most favoured customers, all the familiar old lags. For one indignant moment she wondered if it was just his birthday. But no, that was weeks – months – away. Then she saw, in the midst of the hubbub, a lanky stranger fiddling with what resembled a large camera. A television camera, surely. And the bar, now she came to consider the matter, was illuminated like a shop window at Christmas. Bloody hell, she thought. No wonder Bernie was rattled if telly, too, was on to the story. She stood on tiptoe, craning her head this way and that. Where was Bernie, anyway? With all this going on, never mind so many people jostling and bellowing for service?

'They're a noisy lot, aren't they?' shouted Liz into her ear, as they shouldered through.

'Like a coachload of football hooligans,' Annie responded crossly. 'Excited by the camera, I dare say. Idiots.'

Where Bernie should have been on duty there was only some grey-haired geezer bent over the pumps, tilting a single glass under an amateurishly sluggish flow. Annie rolled her eyes in sympathy towards old Harry Todd as he waited for his pint, and was about to ask why he was winking and nodding at her so peculiarly when Dave materialised in the kitchen doorway. He was wearing blindingly clean whites and such a daft grin that, had it not been for the earliness of the hour she might have supposed he'd been at the cooking brandy.

'About time too,' he roared. 'Come here, gorgeous, get yourself over here.' For once, though, he didn't enfold Annie in his usual bear hug. He grasped her shoulders and spun her round to face the bar. 'What d'you reckon to our new barman, then – will he do?'

The new barman straightened up to place a foaming glass neatly in front of Toddy. But he was looking at Annie. In fact, he was smiling directly into her eyes, as though inviting her to share some delicious joke known only to the two of them. 'So this is Annie Stoneycroft, is it?' he said. 'Well, hello, my old darling. I've been looking forward so much to meeting you. You don't know me, but—'

'Oh my God,' she said. 'You're Simon Spencer.'

The lime green leather biker jacket was a triumph.

Crap choice, sure, for schmoozing daughters of the clergy down the town hall, but spot on – oh, wow, one hundred per cent, heaven-sent *perfecto* – for meeting celebrity actors who just happened to have dropped by from Hollywood. Ditto the purple skirt and ankle-wrenching boots. If nothing else, those bold colours looked terrif on the telly, even if she did say so herself, and even if her moment of glory was just that, a moment. To be accurate, she was visible on screen for thirty-two seconds among the crowd of Hopkirk Arms regulars, all urgently summoned by the landlord, like herself, so that a busy pub could be filmed toasting the health of Dave and his newfound dad in a light-hearted report which closed that evening's *Look North*.

Annie watched the piece half a dozen times, curled in her favourite corner of the sofa with a glass of wine in her hand and – had she but known it – a very foolish smile playing about her face. But why shouldn't she be feeling pleased with herself? It isn't every day you're chatted up by your long-time screen idol – a silver-tongued silver fox who was coming round for lunch tomorrow to continue the conversation. What was more gratifying still, Simon had invited himself – or at least hinted to a very willing Bernie that she should do so on their joint behalf. Because, as he said, there was no way he and Annie could become properly acquainted in the Hopkirk Arms today, overrun as it was with hacks, cameras and microphones.

Even now, Annie could scarcely take in the excitements of the day. According to Bernie, the crew from *Look North* had arranged a couple of days ago to hire the Hopkirk Arms, supposedly as a backdrop for a filmed news piece on pub closures in rural areas. No big deal, and a facilities fee. But no sooner had they set up their camera in the bar, with lights on and phones off, who should walk through the door?

'They were taking a risk, weren't they?' said Annie. 'Sure, *we* know Dave was dying to meet his dad, but—'

'Simon swore to them it would be fine.' Bernie rolled her eyes. 'I tell you, like father, like son. The crack-brained pair of 'em both seem to think there's nothing so great it isn't better wrapped up as a feckin' huge surprise. Look how my Dave insisted on hauling you all round here without a word to the wise. I said to him, I don't mind what you say or don't say to your mates, but there was you, my poor Annie, probably imagining me on my deathbed, eejit that he is.' She gave a mock-weary sigh. 'Well, at least we know now where he gets it from.'

What was almost more astonishing was that Simon Spencer had initiated the coverage himself, or at least his agents had.

Look North was not alone. Press packages had been emailed nationwide and a sharply tailored PR person with mobile welded to her ear was ensconced in the side bar, fielding responses, negotiating dates, times and terms while shepherding Simon between other photographers and journalists. It was a slip-up on her part that had led to the enterprising reporter from the *Mirror* chasing Annie for an exclusive angle.

'Indeed, a media firestorm,' Simon had agreed cheerily with Annie, in a gap between interviews. 'What have we got, the *Dales Gazette*, local radio? Lord, it'll be *Pigeon Fanciers' Monthly* next. Never let it be said my star has faded, eh?'

His self-mockery was endearing but unjustified. The *Mirror* wasn't the only national on the story, and appearances with his son were being agreed for afternoon telly and countless radio programmes. Dave, of course, was revelling in every glamorous, clamorous minute. Bernie, thrilled as she might be to see son and father together at last, was doing her best to become invisible, and quietly asked Simon whether he wasn't worried about the effect all this hoo-ha might have on his wife.

'But haven't you heard me plugging her tour? That's the only reason she's let me off the leash to come over.' He chuckled. 'No, seriously, if there's one thing Viola understands, it's managing publicity. The story was bound to surface eventually, so best break it yourself and try to ride the wave. Preferably without drowning.' His grin was disarming. 'Which I've come close to doing before now, believe me. Sorry, my darlings, here we go again.' He made a camp pantomime of biting his lips and flicking back his hair. 'Better try and look lovely for my public.'

He didn't have to try hard. Sure, Annie's first impression of Simon Spencer had been of a man rather older than she'd imagined. But so alive was his face, so quick his smile, you soon overlooked the wrinkles. More unexpected was how small he seemed. He stood taller than Annie, of course – didn't everyone? – but was comically dwarfed by his son. For while Dave stood six foot plus in his socks and solid as a champion bull, Simon was as spare and fine-boned as a bird. No wonder the camera loved him. There was nevertheless an elusive likeness eagerly traced by them both – a curl to the nostrils, a kink in the hairline; a dimple to their smiles. And it was agreed by one and all that pretty Emily was the image of her new grandpapa.

'My granddaughters,' said Simon, with a choke in his voice and a sudden gleam of tears. 'My very own granddaughters. Isn't this too magical for words?'

Naturally such effusions provoked a good deal of merry joshing round the bar. Actors, eh? Gift of the bloody gab or what? Annie, however, was having none of it, and certainly not from her nearest and dearest. As she sternly informed Rob Daley, whom she rang with instructions to switch on his television, Simon was *not* just your typical bullshitting luvvie. How could Rob even suggest it? He was almost as exasperating as Dom, who had grunted something about preferring to stick pins under his fingernails than join tomorrow's lunch party. She would have the pair of them know that Simon's 'we meet at last' shtick to her was no mere gush. He meant every word, although she was prepared to concede this was not entirely down to her personal magnetism. Such as it was. No, she had learned to her considerable astonishment that Simon Spencer was a serious and knowledgeable fan of her late ex-husband's work. So much so, apparently, that he had once taken out an option on a novel of Jake's, with a view to appearing in a movie of the same. The two of them had spent a memorably drunken night around Soho discussing adaptation and screenplay.

'Brilliant, brilliant book,' sighed Simon. 'And it would have been the part of a lifetime for me if it'd ever seen the light of day. An ageing Casanova with a glittering future behind him.'

'Autobiography by the sound of it,' said Annie caustically, and was gratified by his shout of laughter.

'His or mine, darling? Although I reckon Jake Stoneycroft well outclassed me in the bad husband stakes. You know, several bottles down, he actually told me his ex-wife was a heroine for putting up with him even as long as you did. Swore he could never love another woman in the same way.'

'That's what all Casanovas say – about the one that got away. It's the perfect excuse for unfettered debauchery ever after.'

Simon whistled. 'Such cynicism, madam. Me, I still like to believe in the redeeming power of true lurve.' He swept on before she could respond. 'My God, though, I'd have killed for that role – and I so nearly had the money in place. But you know how it is. Putting together the finance for a movie makes walking on water look easy.'

'Well,' said Annie. 'I had no idea.'

'Jeez, Mum, course I knew about it,' snorted Martha later in the evening, when Annie could not resist telephoning her daughter on the far side of the globe to share the extraordinary events of her day. 'You mean you didn't?'

'Goodness' sake, there were years when I barely spoke to your father.'

'But he was gutted when that movie fell apart. Destroyed. You must remember.'

'I suppose I knew some project had fizzled out, but didn't they always?'

'This was the big one, the one he was sure would get him back on the bestseller lists. And it was only when it collapsed that he really started drinking.'

'Like he hadn't before?' Annie spoke before she could stop herself.

'Seriously. Like he wanted to kill himself,' retorted this daddy's girl hotly. 'So I hope that slimeball Simon Spencer realises he as good as murdered my father.'

Tempted to retort that, far from dying, her father had lived on for years, most of them under her roof, Annie simply declared that it was not Simon who had pulled the plug. 'Couldn't have been, love. He was desperate to make that movie.'

'Yeah? So ask him what went wrong,' said Martha. 'Then you can tell me.'

18

'Oh, it was my wife scuppered the deal,' said Simon, as he held out his glass. 'Of course.'

He was the easiest of guests. Forget all the Californian clap-trap, he had responded when asked what he would or could not eat. Red meat, carbs, chips, bring 'em on – seriously, anything. And since Bernie was kind enough to drive and he'd worked his arse off for the gentlemen of the press yesterday, he was ready to drink himself cross-eyed.

'To be fair, I'd raised the backing on Viola's name,' he continued now. 'A goofy Brit B-lister like me doesn't cut much mustard with the big boys. I say, a real Yorkshire pork pie. Have I died and gone to heaven?' He blew Annie a kiss. 'But there was a great part for her, too, as the avenging ex-wife, fabulously funny. And Vi was forever complaining no one offered her comedy. I still say she would have been terrific.' He sighed, and swirled the wine round his glass.

He was so relaxed, so charming, so utterly and perfectly *himself*. Annie couldn't quite get her head round the idea that this was Simon Spencer, Doctor Cockerdale in person, here at her kitchen table, chatting away like an old friend. She caught Bernie's eye and a complicit smile flashed between them.

'We were all set to swing, until some clot pointed out to Vi that her character had to be well across fifty. As was my lovely wife, of course – but admitting it? Are you kidding? She could not possibly play such an old crone, fatal to her image, all the standard thesp drivel.' He pulled a face. 'Who am I to talk? Over the years, I've fibbed my age down, my height up, and scrubbed out the Yorkshire plumber's son so thoroughly I can almost remember those wizard feasts in the old school dorm. We all construct an image to suit the world, don't we? Or you do if you want to survive in my world, so I shouldn't blame Viola. It was a crushing blow for me at the time, though. And for your husband, too, I'm sure.'

Annie frowned. 'I wish you wouldn't call Jake my husband. We were married for less than three years, and that was centuries ago.'

'But he was living with you when he died, surely?'

'He was living in my house. Which is very much not the same thing, whatever everyone seems to think.' She turned to Bernie. 'You've obviously been filling Simon in.'

'Not a word. Blame my gabby husband.'

'No, no I already knew.' Simon leaned over to cut himself a slice of pie. The merest sliver, Annie noted. And his wine was barely touched. For all the talk of chips and booze, it was clear his elegant physique shape was not maintained without care. He looked up. 'Did I hear it from another Stoneycroft aficionado? Lord, yes, how could I forget?' With a wry smile, he began to dissect his pie into neat cubes. 'Although I was working on an infinitely forgettable movie at the time, a made-for-TV biopic of Jane Austen, if you can believe it. I featured as an uncle, or publisher, or some such. A lousy part, I remember that well enough, and my only half-decent scene went on the floor in the final cut. Probably to accommodate an ad for haemorrhoid cream. *C'est la* bloody *vie* in my profession. Anyway, this steely-eyed academic was advising on set. Quite an authority, we were told, which makes you wonder how she came to be employed on that pile of eighteenth-century ordure, but she was a fellow Brit so I made an effort. And then was tickled to discover, quite by chance, that she shared my admiration for the writing of your late – sorry, your *ex*-husband.' His tipped his glass towards Annie. 'I was even more chuffed when I established she wasn't quite as well read in the Stoneycroft canon as little old *moi* with my three O-levels, because this terrifying female had been ripping to shreds all our feeble comments on the sainted Jane. She could tell me what had happened to Jake, though, because she or maybe someone in her family, I don't actually recall, came from Bucksford. Amazing, isn't it, how these connections happen?'

He broke off, and looked from Bernie to Annie. 'Why are you smiling, what's the joke? I should explain this is years ago, long before I knew I had a son, let alone a son living in Bucksford.'

'This academic,' said Annie. 'She wouldn't be called Cate Blackwell, by any chance?'

Simon's eyes opened wide. 'Could be. Actually, now you say the name . . .'

'Tall?'

'Amazonian.'

'Cool? Very self-contained?'

'Glacial,' he whipped back.

'And terrifying, I think you said?'

'Honest to God, Annie, you do talk cobblers,' said Bernie. 'Don't listen, Simon. Cate Blackwell's a fine creature, once you get to know her. Just a bit on the shy side, that's all.'

He winked at Annie. 'They say the same about sharks. It has to be her. Well, of course it is, because the whole point of my story was that she knew you. At least, she was the one told me Jake was being cared for after a stroke by his, um, ex-wife. Well, well, apologies for the cliché, but it really is a small world, isn't it?'

'Even smaller than you think,' said Bernie. 'You know this sponsored walk Dave's twisting your arm to launch on Saturday, in aid of our local theatre? It's only Cate Blackwell's big sister who put him up to asking you. She's on the committee.' She turned to Annie. 'And I promised Davey we'd call by Chatsworth Close on the way home. I just hope Trisha doesn't have a heart attack when she sees who I've got with me.'

'We'll never hear the end of it.' Annie grinned. 'And Simon, lucky man, can renew his acquaintance with her sister.'

He feigned horror. 'You're not telling me the Berkeley Snow Queen is over here?'

'Got it in one.'

'Well you're coming too, then,' he said. 'I need moral support.'

Simon Spencer's appearance was not a surprise to Trisha Hough, as it turned out.

Perhaps they should have guessed Dave would be unable to resist phoning ahead to break the glad tidings himself. She was waiting for them, resplendent in a billowing yellow kaftan, brand new in honour of their visit. They knew this because she told them so, while apologising in the same breath for an orange stain down one sleeve. Joey, in the excitement of their impending visit, had managed to sit on his juice bottle, which had squirted all over her, would they credit it? Mind, if she'd known how long they were going to take getting down here, she could have rinsed the bloomin' thing out and put it twice through the drier.

It was indeed shamefully late by the time Bernie and Annie ushered Simon Spencer into her lounge. Lunch had meandered into the twilit reaches of the afternoon, although little enough was consumed. Annie was too excited to eat. She didn't even open a second bottle of wine, since Simon relaxed his self-discipline only as far as two glasses. A third, he quipped, would qualify him for the twelve-step programme back in the States. Nevertheless, with only a tepid coffee in front of her, she could have lingered at the table all day, so engaging a companion was he. That smooth charm was underpinned by a quick brain and an acid wit. Who could not be beguiled by tales of Madonna's ex-butler, or Harrison Ford's socks? More surprisingly, perhaps, he listened as readily as he talked, seemingly as entertained by the mundanities of life in Bucksford as the high-calibre gossip of his own world.

Besides, what fifty-nine-year-old female in her right mind could fail to revel in his flirtatious banter? Oh, Simon Spencer flirted only with the flippancy appropriate to a married man of his years. A woman would have to be extraordinarily vain, not to say dim, to imagine he meant anything by it. He probably darling-ed everyone – he was an actor! – but it still gave Annie the most intoxicating buzz.

However, she was equally delighted – well, almost equally – by the rapport he had established with Bernie. The two of them joked like an old-time comedy double act. He mimicked her Irish brogue. She mocked his sepia-tinted Yorkshire rhapsodies. She laughed at her husband's antics. He defended his son with touching pride.

'You see that ugly old mill on the right?' she remarked, as she eventually drove them down to the Houghs. The soot-blackened hulk of the Woolshed loomed over the orange wash of street lights. 'That's the joint our eejit boy has got you fundraising for on Saturday.'

'Sorry, where?' Simon twisted round in the cramped rear seat of Bernie's Mini, which he had gallantly insisted on occupying. 'What is it, exactly?'

'Let's stop and show him,' said Annie impulsively. She had no interest in the planned expansion at the arts centre in spite of – maybe because of – Liz endlessly prattling on about disabled lavs and kiddy drama classes. She just didn't want this day to end at Trisha's front door, not quite yet. There was pleasure, too, in being seen about town with their celebrated companion. Liz might long have quit her desk, but her trilby'd, black-jeaned boss was very satisfactorily astonished and only too keen to show them round.

'Well, it clearly has . . . *potential*,' said Simon, squinting into the chilly gloom of a derelict carpet showroom. Annie poked a pile of rubble with her toe and shivered in the draught from a badly boarded window as Hank Damon rattled through a spiel about this whole end of the mill being transformed not just into a studio space for, like, yer more experimental stuff, but a community facility, great for youngsters, outreach work, dementia-friendly initiatives, blah-blah-blah . . .

'Quite, quite, all that side of things is vital, these days,' nodded Simon, sidestepping a concrete mixer as he edged towards the door. 'I'm seriously impressed.'

Annie might have believed him if, as they followed Hank back to the foyer, he had not whispered that, in his experience, the phrase 'community facility' was to theatre what Dulux bloody gloss was to fine art. She giggled, and had to feign a coughing fit. However, when Hank begged Simon just to take a quick shufty into the auditorium before leaving, she was startled by the change that came over him.

'Now this is something again,' he breathed. To Annie's mind, the dim cavern with seats racked round a starkly lit square resembled nothing so much as an aircraft hangar. But the space had such history, such authenticity, such spellbinding *atmosphere*, Simon Spencer declared. Circling slowly with outstretched arms, he gazed upwards as though communing with an invisible audience.

'*To be or not to be,*' he declaimed thrillingly into the empty air. '*That is the question . . .*' Then his arms flopped down and he shrugged. 'The question I never got to ask – and never will now, for very sure. Ah me, how I'd have loved to work in a place like this.'

'Name yer dates, man,' said the artistic director instantly. 'Whatev. Whenev.'

'Ha.' Simon smiled as he shook his head. 'I'm afraid it's more years than I care to count since I trod the live boards. The idea rather brings me out in a sweat nowadays. Mark you, it's been much longer for my wife, and she's taking the plunge. Or so she swears. Over here, as it happens, lured back by a play that's been written specially for her—'

'Shit, yeah, I've heard,' Hank burst out, to Annie's surprise. 'He's a really interesting writer too, that guy, done some amazing stuff for Flat Out. Word is they're touring the piece round places even smaller than us.' His eyes widened. 'Hey, you don't think there's a chance—?'

Simon was already holding up a hand. 'Sorry, old love, no bananas. Sure, we're keeping under the radar with a soft try-out in the provinces, but there's no way on God's earth Vi would play in the round. She'll only go on with the security of a good old pros arch. That's if she ever actually does go on.' He bit his lip and glanced away. 'Frankly, even at this late stage, I wouldn't put money on it.'

'I'm that disappointed Cate's not here to say hello, she'll be so sorry to miss you, I can't think where she's got to at this hour, but you know what she's like, don't you, Annie? Always been the same, our Cath – once she's got her nose in a book, that's it, World War Three could be starting and she'd never know, although the library's not like it used to be, of course. People natter away in there nowadays just like they was in Asda, drinking coffee and eating crisps, can you credit it? But Cate says there's a side room where they keep the old newspapers that's pretty quiet, quieter than this house any old how, because I'm afraid we don't *do* quiet at 3 Chatsworth Close, do we, Joey? We need a bit of noise to keep us cheerful. Oh, and I mustn't forget to tell you – honest to God, what am I like? – Cate tells me she's actually met you before, Mr – well, Simon, then, if you're sure you don't mind. Simon, yes. Bet you didn't know that, did you, Annie? Actually, I can't believe Cath never mentioned it to me neither, not at the time, not that I recall, and I'm sure I would've remembered, although my poor old head gets more like a sieve every day, the number of times our Joey has to nudge me about his pills, he does, too, he's very good at reminding me, aren't you, lovey? Any road up, Our Cate actually met you over in America, although she says to me, don't you dare mention it, Trish, he won't remember me, he meets hundreds of people, but I says—'

'On the contrary, I remember Doctor Blackwell very well,' cut in Simon. Since he had been hard-pressed to recall even so much as Cate's name earlier, Annie could only admire the brazen assurance with which he informed Trisha that he had been enquiring after her sister over lunch. 'Do tell her how sad I am to have missed her. Perhaps we can catch up another time.'

He winked at Annie. Honestly, he was incorrigible. It served him right when Trisha responded that her sister should be home any minute. She had to swallow hard so as not to laugh at the horrified face he flashed her way. 'We've been expecting her for hours, haven't we, Joey? I texted her to say you were all coming round, but she's a shocker for not looking at her phone. I wouldn't be surprised if she's forgot it again, or let the battery go flat, and it worries me to death, poorly as she's been. Look, can I fetch you a cuppa while you wait?'

Bernie rescued them. They'd be screaming for her at the Hopkirk Arms, she said firmly, and she had brought Simon round only so Trisha could tell him what he was expected to do on Saturday.

'Wave a whistle, blast a flag, dance a paso doble with the Lady Mayoress?' he offered gaily. 'I can manage a rather fine paso I'd have you know. Far be it from me to boast, but you're looking here at a *Dancing with the Stars* quarter-finalist.'

This prompted Trisha, gasping with wheezy laughter, to say how funny it was he should mention dancing, because just last week some folks on the walk committee were asking if she fancied organising a dinner dance next time round, only she'd had to tell them no because—

'Quite right, too.' Annie was nodding Simon towards the door. 'Hopeless idea. Dinner dances went out with velvet bow-ties and Herb Alpert. We must be off. Bye, Joey, bye . . .'

'*Balls*, madam!' cried Simon, exasperatingly blind to her signals. 'I'm talking about charity balls, so I can't imagine why you're giggling, Trisha. How disgraceful of you. No, seriously, dinner dance or ball, it's the same thing with a different name, surely? And I'd have said that's absolutely the way to go if you want to raise proper money. Over our side of the pond they—'

'Bucksford,' said Bernie, taking firm hold of his arm, 'is not Beverly Hills, and I've a pub full of hungry punters who won't get their dinners unless I'm dancing feckin' attendance, so can we get a move on?'

'My God,' he sighed as he curled into the back seat of the Mini. 'That lady can talk.'

'We'd have escaped sooner if you hadn't got her on to balls,' said Annie, tugging her seatbelt down. 'She was still bending my ear on the doorstep, trying to persuade me into getting involved. *Me.*' There was no response from the back seat. 'Simon?'

'Sorry. It's just, Jesus H., that place, the mess – that woman's mindless gabble. It's enough to drive a fucking saint to murder.'

Annie may have said much the same herself before now, but his vehemence took her aback. She even felt a little defensive. Trisha Hough might be a pain in the neck, but she was *their* pain in the neck. Bernie, too, observed that the Houghs had been dealt a mean old hand in life, so they had, and you could only admire the way they soldiered on.

'Yes – yes, of course,' he muttered. 'That was crass of me, I'm sorry. I suppose I was just trying to equate all that with, oh, the fastidious creature I recall, picking her way round our movie set. Like a – like a well-bred cat in Battersea Dogs' Home. And you say she's actually living there? Ye gods.'

Annie flashed a smile over her shoulder. 'I know. Bernie's always telling me off for bitching about the sainted Cate, but I tell you she has my heartfelt sympathy just now. Camping on the floor, too, with not an inch of space to call her own, let alone a door she can shut. You can see why she runs away to the library.'

'And why she still looks like death warmed up,' added Bernie, leaning forward to peer round Annie before pulling onto the main road.

Simon poked his head between the seats and rested his chin lightly on Annie's shoulder. 'Yes, what's all that about? Her sister said something about her being poorly.'

'Glandular fever. Jaysus, the traffic's going to be solid all the way to the roundabout now.'

'Well, that's what they're calling it.' Annie was deliciously distracted by Simon's breath on her neck.

'And what would you be calling it, Doctor Stoneycroft?' said Bernie. 'On second thoughts, don't answer that.'

'Take no notice of my daughter-in-law. Come on, doc, what's your diagnosis?' His voice was close to her ear. She was catching a faint, citrussy perfume. It made her mouth water.

'Oh, Bernie and I have never seen eye to eye on Cate Blackwell,' she said breathlessly. 'I'm just saying that when Cate's long-time friend and house-mate goes off and gets married, bingo, look what happens.'

'And what about you and me, Annie? Hasn't your long-time friend and house-mate just gone and got herself wed?'

'Not to another woman. And it doesn't make me run away and chuck my career down the plughole . . .' Annie faltered as she realised what she had said.

'Exactly. When did you sell up your business?'

'That's totally different.'

'Hang on, hang on, you're losing me.' She could feel Simon's laughter as much as hear it. 'You said another *woman*? Are we to assume the Snow Queen's gay?' She gulped as he brushed against her ear while settling himself back in his seat. He was still chuckling softly. 'Well, of course. Why didn't I think of that?'

'Because you've more sense?' said Bernie. 'I don't give a stuff if Cate's gay, straight or swinging twenty ways from the feckin' chandelier, but I still say Annie's talking piffle.'

'There must have been something, though, come on.' In the face of Bernie's indignation and Simon's mirth, Annie was struggling. 'Some – some emotional volcano to make her rip her life up like that. Why else would a woman like Cate Blackwell come hurtling back to Chatsworth Close, for God's sake?'

'She's got a point, you know, Bernie,' said Simon, evidently enjoying himself.

'Don't encourage her.' Bernie braked outside the Red House and turned to give Annie a hasty hug. 'Will we be seeing you a week today, then?'

'What, next Saturday?' Annie blinked as she climbed out of the car. 'Oh, this sponsored walk.'

Simon clambered out after her. As she turned towards him, though, Bernie leaned across, wailing that they should have been back two bloody hours ago. He shrugged with evident reluctance, kissed his fingers and touched them to her cheek before folding himself into the front seat.

'Are you coming to cheer me on?' He looked up as he reached for the door handle and gave her that famously dazzling smile. 'Let me rephrase that. You *are* coming. Please?'

19

She had not intended to take part in this sponsored walk. But then, she had not been invited to do so, had she? No one had so much as mentioned it to her. Well, apart from Liz.

'Why would they?' said Rob Daley when she rang the following day to complain to this trustee of the Woolshed. 'When did you last go on a walk, sponsored or not? You hate walking.'

About to deny this, Annie remembered her caustic comments on the hiking group she and Liz had tried last year and instead asked whether Rob himself was taking part.

'Yes and no. I'm officiating, as a marshal.'

'You would be.'

'What's that supposed to mean?'

'Bossing people around, of course. As per.'

'Thanks, Madam Pot.'

'Sorry?'

'I'm speaking as the kettle.'

'Very witty. Not. Still, if you aren't walking, you can sponsor me. Once I've got myself a form. I'll need to get a move on, obviously. Who's in charge of the sponsorship forms and stuff, Trisha?'

'I think the Kings, actually, although I don't know much about it, to be honest. I've just said I'll lend a hand. It's certainly Maggie and Hugo running the gig on the day.'

'Christ, that's all we need.'

'What's wrong now, Nan? The Kings are OK.'

'He's half-witted, she's cream crackers, and their kids are glitter-painted savages in wellies and ballet tutus. And that's just the boys.'

Rob gave a crack of laughter. 'No one could accuse you of mellowing with age, love. I shudder to think what a poisonous old hag you'll be at seventy.'

'Remind me to punch you next time I see you,' she said. 'Which is Saturday, so be warned.'

'You're pitching in on the job, then? Excellent. What's come over you, all of a sudden?' His tone changed. 'Oh, hang about. Maggie did mention summat about hoping our local celebrity would graciously consent to shine his face upon us.'

'If you mean Simon Spencer is firing the starting pistol, yes,' said Annie. 'So? I'm always happy to support a good cause.'

'Yeah, right,' said Rob Daley.

This irritating conversation, if nothing else, underlined the need for caution.

Galling as it was to make any concession to age, Annie was clear that affairs of the mature heart are best kept tight-locked in the mature bosom. Dignity is all. Consider Liz's recent lovelorn antics. So, while she might have lost interest in food (no harm in that), had taken to twitching like a racehorse at the faintest pip from a phone (idiot) and was passing her sleepless nights wandering through a Googled forest of Simon Spencer links, she was not about to make a public fool of herself.

Therefore, it was only after days and days of waiting for him to arrive at her door – or at least bloody phone – that she was reduced to ringing the Hopkirk Arms with a cunningly manufactured query about a birthday present for little Emily.

'So what'd you make of him?' demanded Bernie at once.

'He's good company,' she said primly, and had to lift the phone away from her ear as Bernie let out a shriek.

'Good feckin' company? I told Dave I could've lit a fag on the sparks buzzing between the two of you.'

'Oh sure.' She might have sustained this fine air of indifference if Bernie, after thanking her, had not disclosed that Grandpapa had already promised Em Barbie's stable-block when he got back.

'Back from where?' she squawked.

Bernie crowed with laughter. What the hell – Annie reached for her coffee mug and felt herself smiling. Yeah, yeah, yeah, that pathetic juvenile thrill of just being able to talk about The Man.

Apparently, after certain publicity commitments with his son – 'quite the celebrity my Davey's fancying himself now' – and being paraded round friends and family – 'every last second cousin and next-door neighbour but ten' – Simon had to meet his wife's agent in London to tie off details of the tour. 'And let's pray the mad old witch will actually do the feckin' play,' Bernie finished.

Annie yawned. 'Why should we care?'

'Because she'll bring Simon with her, birdbrain.'

'You're talking like he's her pet chihuahua.' With one leg stretched across the table, she was reflecting that she really must paint her toenails. And when a woman of fifty-nine is thinking about painting her toenails, in March, in Yorkshire, that woman is thinking about sex. 'He's a big boy now. Can't he book his own plane tickets?'

'Maybe.' Her voice dropped. 'But I don't think he'd be travelling business class.'

'Sorry?' Annie swung her leg down and grasped the phone more firmly. 'Come on, he must have earned a fair bob or two.'

'And spent more. He says that himself. Hold on a tick.' There was a pause and Annie caught the click of a door being closed. 'From what he's let slip, Dame Viola's lawyers have the purse strings tied up tighter than a nun's knickers. Every last thing's in her name.'

'Is that so?' With a stab of longing, she recognised afresh what she had been missing this past year. Liz was sweet, of course she was, but no one could replace Bernie. She shouldn't be at the end of a phone line. She should be in her favoured chair across this very table, gripping her mug between both hands, currant eyes bright over the rim as they didn't so much talk as dissect and analyse any given subject with relish and forensic attention to detail. 'She may be mad, but she's not daft?'

'She's bloody smart at keeping him running in rings, isn't she? And if you ask me, he goes along with it in the hopes of an amicable divorce. He as good as told us he can't afford a fight in court. Maybe it's his only chance of a decent divvy-up.'

Annie frowned. 'That's – a bit sad.'

'Oh, I don't blame him, not for a minute.' Typical Bernie. Once she'd embraced someone into the clan her loyalty was absolute. 'Who wants to end up skint at his age?'

'I suppose.' Annie, however, could not help feeling there was something undignified in a man jumping to the whims and whip-cracks of a neurotic wife just to secure his pension. 'So he's been away all this time dealing with her agent, has he?'

'Ah, well that's a bit of another story, so it is.' At which Bernie fell most unusually silent.

'Come on then. Give.'

'If you must know, he's taking a couple of days off. At a spa. Getting, um, his Botox topped up. And such.'

'You are not serious.'

'And his eyelashes tinted – oh, swimming in volcanic feckin' mud baths, for all I know. I mean, we took the mick something terrible, but he just laughed, said a man's gotta do.'

'Well, I don't think it's funny. Beauty treatments. Honestly.' Annie may even have added that she was disappointed in Simon Spencer – while neglecting to mention the couple of hours she had spent only the previous morning behind the barbered bay trees and bronze doors of a very smart salon off the high street.

'He's an actor,' offered Bernie feebly. 'He says, you know, Dave's tools are his knives and pans, his are his face and bod. So it's only like putting your car in for service.'

'Huh.' Annie knew she sounded curmudgeonly, but she was not best pleased to learn she figured below the colour of his eyelashes in Simon Spencer's priorities.

'And he's not a bit precious when you're with him, is he? He's forever telling us how he's sick of the glitz and wants to come back to Yorkshire. If only—'

'He wasn't tied to his bloody wife's apron strings. Her purse strings, rather.'

'If he could settle here with the right woman, actually. Honest to God, those were his very words to my Dave. The right woman. So what about *that*?' finished Bernie triumphantly.

Annie swallowed hard. 'What about it?'

'Look, madam, if you've not got half your wardrobe spread on the bed this minute wondering how to doll yourself up come Saturday, I'm the bloody Queen of Sheba.'

She had to laugh. 'I just wish Dave had asked him to open a jumble sale. I look like Minnie Mouse in my new walking boots.'

*   *   *

Had she ever got round to obtaining a sponsorship form – helpfully headed 'Walk 'n' Wheel Appeal' – Annie might not have felt obliged to purchase the boots. Nor would she have been so taken aback, when Liz came to pick her up, by her well-mannered friend's snort of something remarkably like derision at the equally new rucksack and waterproof poncho she had laid out ready in the hall.

Only as they drove into town did Annie learn that the event was designed for those citizens hoping to benefit from the planned development at the Woolshed. Since this included the very young, the seriously old and the variously disabled, the route was a mere four miles long and flat enough to be navigable by buggy or wheelchair. Walk and Wheel indeed.

The crowd they found assembling in Victoria Square, however, turned out to be a riotous carnival of conveyances, with wheelbarrows and supermarket trolleys as well as more conventional modes of transport. A customised council dustbin trundled alongside kids' tricycles, and an old-style hospital bed carried a ruddily healthy patient, bandaged head to toe, with a gin bottle dangling from his drip. The rattling structure was propelled by a squad of grinning muscle-mountains from the rugby club, as were several of the wheelchairs, including Joey Hough's. And while some were garnished merely with balloons and collecting buckets, others had been disguised as anything from a Tardis to a giant flowerpot of crepe-paper daffodils, with the elderly occupant beaming out through one of the blooms.

'Fun, isn't it?' shouted Liz, as party poppers exploded, football rattles twirled, and kazoos blasted tunelessly around them.

'Bit bloody chaotic,' returned Annie, as King Kong on a scooter tangled with a writhing Chinese dragon. Even so, and exasperated as she was at having dressed more for an assault on Everest than this mobile fancy-dress party, she had to smile. The Buck Vale Silver Band, who had played at every event in the town's history since Mafeking – 'with the same membership, by the look of 'em,' Annie shouted in Liz's ear – was gamely if largely inaudibly tootling selections from *The Sound of Music* on the steps of the war memorial while the Honourable Hugo King, beaky and tousled as ever, with trousers even pinker than his cheeks, gesticulated at fluorescent-vested henchmen from a rickety platform, bellowing instructions about health, safety and passing cars into a microphone. Meanwhile, a pair of police constables, looking too young to drive motor vehicles, never mind direct them, waved traffic round the back of the square.

'Total feckin' mayhem,' shouted Bernie, as she dodged a swaying lighthouse to reach their side.

'What'd you expect with that nincompoop in charge?' returned Annie, inclining her head towards the hapless Hugo King.

'Tell me about it. And my crackpot husband has just invited him and his entire committee, husbands, wives, kids and pet feckin' poodles for all I know, back to the pub for a jar and a butty at the finish. As if the kitchen isn't busy enough with him skiving off down here. They're over by the platform. Both of them,' she added, having correctly deduced that Annie was scanning the crowd for her father-in-law rather than her husband. 'See, talking to Trisha? Or listening, anyhow. Speaking of Trish, though, have you heard—'

Liz caught her arm. 'Sorry to butt in, but I think that car's pipping at you, Annie?'

She turned to see a familiar dark grey Range Rover nosing along behind the police barriers. 'It's only Rob,' she cried, and waved in return. 'What's he doing in a car? He's supposed to be marshalling.'

'Aha, I can tell you that,' said Bernie. 'He's been to collect Cate Blackwell. She was all for sticking at home, because Trish says there's no way she could manage even this little stroll, but you know Rob. He said to hell with her missing the fun, she could sit cosy in his car at the marshal post and help him with the crossword. And off he went to fetch her.'

'Good old Robbo.' Annie grinned. 'Sooner him than me.'

Bernie leaned towards her. 'But has it never crossed your mind, Miss Clever Clogs,' she said, 'that they make a rather lovely couple, those two?'

'Shame, though, because if I'd only known what a jamboree this was, I might have asked him to round Dominic up as well, and they could – sorry, what?' Annie halted abruptly. 'You're not talking about Rob? And *Cate*?'

At that interesting juncture, the band reached a discordant cadence, there was thunder from the speakers while Hugo King extracted himself from a tangle of cable, and Simon Spencer could be seen nimbly scrambling onto the platform to relieve him of the microphone, amid a storm of cheers and whistles.

'Friends, Bucksfordians, *Yorkshiremen*,' he bellowed, over the crackles of the ancient tannoy. 'Lend us your money, hey?'

Annie wasn't listening. She was staring at her friend, who grinned back, as beady-eyed as a blackbird who has just seized the fattest worm in the lawn.

'Cate and Rob?' she repeated. 'That's absurd.'

'For why? In fact, I can't think why we never thought of it before, with you fancying yourself so smart at the matchmaking game.'

'... worthwhile cause, and don't you all look marvellous, in your costumes? Go on, give yourselves a big round of applause ...'

'He's frightfully good at this sort of thing, isn't he?' exclaimed Liz, clapping madly. They both ignored her.

'Gorgeous people, the pair of 'em, both with brains coming out of their feckin' ears, and when you think about it, Cate's quite like Frances in a lot of ways – cool, classy . . .'

'. . . how happy I am to be back in the county where I was born . . .'

'I just wish I could hear what he's saying because it's frightfully crackly, isn't it?'

'Sorry?' said Annie blankly, looking from one to the other.

'Plus they go back forever, because Rob's parents only lived a couple of doors away from Trisha's mum, did you know that?'

'*Know* that?' cried Annie, recovering her voice. 'Bloody hell, Bernie, I've known Rob Daley since he was in nappies. Well, almost. Sorry, Liz, what? Yeah, crap amplification, can't hear a word, typical of the Kings. I tell you, if I'd been in charge – still, never mind.' She turned back. 'That's exactly what I'm talking about. Rob's my age.' She paused fractionally. 'Well, my generation. If nothing else, Cate's too young for him.'

'What's between them, ten years? How much older than you was Jakey?'

'That's beside the point. Or maybe that's exactly the point. Because if ever there was a marriage made in hell – no, believe me, Bernie, you're on the wrong track here. Big time.'

Bernie just tapped her nose with an infuriatingly knowing air and before Annie could set her straight once and for all, there was a pop from a starting pistol so feeble it provoked a storm of derisive whistles, the band resumed honking and she saw Simon Spencer hop deftly down from the platform with a wave and begin shouldering a smiling path through the throng. Towards her? Yup – absolutely, definitely, towards her.

'Hello,' she said. 'It looks like we're off.'

20

'Half past three yesterday afternoon, this low-loader rolls up.'
Trisha Hough was struggling to keep abreast. 'Well. You
could've knocked me down with a feather.'

'Some feather,' said Annie under her breath, but her words
would have been lost anyway as they milled along, dodging
ankle-nipping buggies, kamikaze mobility scooters and rugger
buggers racing their wheelchairs, while an open-top van
blasted Abba. Having exchanged no more than a wave with
Simon thus far, she now had Liz in one ear, marvelling at
what a wonderfully genuine sort of person he seemed to be,
while at her other side Bernie was reminding her of two previous occasions when she had (allegedly) failed to detect a
burgeoning romance. Since one of the couples cited had
already passed through the divorce court and the other, in her
view, would end up there sooner rather than later, Annie was
unimpressed and said as much. Trisha meanwhile had puffed
up to join them fifty yards ahead of Simon who, shepherded
by son and granddaughters, was being accosted every few
steps for the inevitable selfies and autographs.

'And he's so good-humoured with everyone,' said Liz, turning on tiptoe to monitor his progress. Annie found herself
wondering whether a little crush on Simon might not be such
a bad thing for Liz? At the very least it might cure her of
panicking when, as had happened a few yards back, some
woman with a bad perm and a mean streak slyly asked if she'd

heard about her friend Kelvin and his new lady taking off for three weeks in Antigua.

'Yes, he's a sweetheart, isn't he?' sighed Trisha, diverting seamlessly from her monologue to agree with Liz. 'So easy to chat to, makes you feel you've known him years. I was telling him about this hut, just like I've been telling you – that's what they're called, by the way, huts, for all it's got wheels, although of course it didn't arrive under its own steam, it was on this truck, as I said – anyway, he was really interested, wanted to know every detail, even when I said I'm sorry, I know I can go on a bit sometimes, he just laughed, and it's not like he's laughing at you . . . Oh my Lord, will you look at my Joey over there, being charged along like he's in bloomin' Formula One.' She halted, to wave and hoot.

'What's she on about now?' hissed Annie.

'Glory, *yes*, that's what I was trying to tell you before.' Bernie leaned closer. 'This is fantastic, so it is. Cate's been given one of these trendy shepherd huts, you know? So she's somewhere quiet to work on her book while she's convalescing at Trisha's.' She turned, raising her voice. 'And didn't you say it's even got a pull-down bed, Trisha? Now, how thoughtful is that?'

'A shepherd hut?' Annie tried to picture what she had seen of these pretty bucolic follies in the scrubby back garden of 3 Chatsworth Close. 'Like the one, whatshisname, David Cameron had?'

'That's right,' panted Trisha, now several steps behind. 'A surprise present from one of her kind friends back in the States, that's what it said, love from your friend in California – I mean, it didn't come all the way from there, only from Milton Keynes, but . . .'

Annie was intrigued enough to halt and let her catch up. That she thereby increased the chances of Simon Spencer doing likewise was quite incidental. 'A friend in *California*?' She tried to catch Bernie's eye but was ignored.

'Flippin' miracle what you can fix up over the internet, isn't it? I mean, I've probably told you before about Pam, one of our crowd at the book club, when she wanted a zip for the jacket she was knitting, lovely thick yarn so it had to be a chunky zip, oh, and double-ended, that was the trouble, now I think about it, anyway, she searched high and low and where did she finally get one? New York, if you can believe—'

'But you were telling us about this hut?' interposed Annie firmly.

'You'll love it,' she said, without drawing breath. 'I said that the minute I clapped eyes on it, Annie will love this, I said, all in your sort of wishy-washy greens, and I'm like, bloomin' heck, all I ever get sent when I'm taken poorly is a bunch of flowers.' Laughing at her own joke, however, triggered a coughing fit which allowed Annie to enquire sharply which friend, exactly, was responsible for this handsome gift.

'Trust you to ask the sixty-four-thousand-dollar question,' whispered a long-awaited voice close behind her ear.

Liz may have melted into blushing giggles but Annie – dignity-is-all – Stoneycroft scarcely blinked. She even managed to sound surprised. 'Simon. Well, hello stranger. If I may say so, you're looking' – she pretended to peer at his face – 'remarkably the same.'

'What? Oh, don't you start, darling. Bernie's as good as told me I'm either mad or gay. But your face is your fortune in my job. Costs a bloody fortune, too.'

'I dare say it did and all. Mind, even though the lumps and bumps have been tidied up very nicely, you can see it's been around a bit, secondhand you know . . .' Trisha looked from Annie to Simon. 'What's so funny?'

'Idiot,' Annie whispered, as he clutched his jowls with a grimace of mock-dismay.

'But you've not heard the best of it yet – I didn't get round to telling you this, did I Simon, the little secret the driver whispered to me?' She leaned towards them. 'Our caravan used to be on the telly. Yes, that makes you stare, Annie, doesn't it? Series on Channel Four, apparently, living with nature or summat, and I wish I'd seen it now, but Joey can't be doing with that kind of thing and it's finished now which is how they're selling off all the bits and pieces. So. What about that?'

'How *fascinating*,' breathed Annie, wide-eyed. 'Sorry, I mean, yes, wonderful for Cate, exactly what she needs just now, I'm sure.' She could not resist glancing Simon's way however. 'It must be, um, a very *close* friend, out in California, to come up with such a perfect present.'

His eyebrows flew up at a speed that suggested his forehead, at least, was a Botox-free zone. Then he began laughing again.

'Indeed, yes. With – dare one suggest? – excellent connections in the television industry?'

'Pardon?' said Trisha.

'Shush,' said Annie, beginning to feel a little uncomfortable at having provoked this tease. 'Take no notice, Trish, we're only talking nonsense.' Simon, though, was not to be silenced.

'What did you say was in the mysterious message?' He was looking at Annie, however, inviting her to share the joke. '"*California is a desert since you deserted us*"?'

'Stop it,' she hissed. Fortunately, Trisha was oblivious.

'You're such a comedian, you are. I told you, just love from her pal and that bit, you know, about a room of one's own.'

'Virginia Woolf,' said Annie promptly, always happy to display a little erudition. 'Well, at least it makes a change from bloody Jane Austen.'

Simon let out a shout of laughter.

'Oh, I love you, Annie,' he said, throwing his arm round her shoulders. 'A woman after my own heart.'

Despite her earlier lack of enthusiasm for any event involving walking or the King family, Annie – unsurprisingly – was now having a high old time. How could she not? If strolling along beside Simon Spencer were not exhilarating enough, there was the exquisite pleasure of feeling herself envied by every other sentient female over the age of forty.

Every forty-plus female with the exception of Cate Blackwell, as it turned out.

By the time they reached the top of Lowgrave Road, where Rob Daley was handing out water and sweets while exchanging cordial insults with a trio of former pupils, she joined in their mockery of Rob's vast orange tunic, without noticing his car parked on the nearby roundabout between two banks of spindly daffodils.

'So are you meant to wear it, or use it as a tent?'

'Give us a break, Nan. One minute you're telling me cycling kit's too tight for a bloke my age—'

'Actually I said you'd quite a decent bum for Lycra, although—'

'Stop there, while I'm winning. Cheers, you guys, good to see you.' Rob was waving the men away when he stepped aside to stare past Annie's shoulder. Turning, she saw Simon leaning over the passenger door of Rob's Range Rover, where a half-open window framed a long, pale face.

'Of course, you went to fetch Cate, didn't you?' said Annie, studying them with interest. Simon seemed to be doing all the talking. Cate was as inscrutable as ever. Mona Lisa, minus the smile.

Rob frowned. 'That's him, isn't it, Simon Spencer? What's he want with Cate?'

'They know one another. From years back.' She spoke abstractedly because Rob's unmistakable displeasure at seeing the actor beside his car brought to mind Bernie's continuing insistence that he and Cate Blackwell would make a fine couple. Only minutes earlier, while Simon was being pulled aside to pose with the beaming ladies of the Rose Vale Choral Society, Annie had whispered to her friend that – if nothing else – Siobhan *surely* had to be the donor of this hut. Whereupon Bernie had retorted that it all sounded to her like a fairy story, and her money was on Rob as the mysterious benefactor. Yes she feckin' well was serious.

'You know how he hates fuss, and he's always been clever with presents,' she went on. 'Generous too. Look how he came up with that bike for you, Annie.'

'Rubbish. Totally different.' Simon, by then, was edging back towards them and Annie had to resort to a fierce under-tone. 'Anyhow, why splash money on a fancy shed when he's got a whacking great flat? If Cate needs somewhere to spread her books, he could just ask her up to his place. No, Bernie, no way.'

Bernie, dammit, had simply tapped her nose again as Simon rejoined them. And one thing she had said tweaked a nerve: she was right, Cate was indeed in something of the same mould as Rob's departed wife. Annie had suffered nigh on thirty years of her friend being married to a woman who gave the impression – however sweet her smiles and whatever drivel Rob offered about shyness – of viewing her as a fluffball with not a thought in her head beyond tassel trims and waterfall taps. So, no, she did not want to see him paired up with just such another lofty-minded blue-stocking.

As she reflected on this now, she saw the window of the Range Rover glide upwards and Simon jerk away, as though startled.

'Looks like the famous Spencer charm has failed there,' remarked Rob, with audible satisfaction. Annie swivelled towards him. Unaware of her scrutiny, he was smiling to himself.

Never let it be said that Annie Stoneycroft dodged the hard questions. She did, however, have to swallow a couple of times. 'Well, well, Robbo. Do I detect a touch of the old green-eyed monster?'

He jumped. Comically, as if she'd stamped on his toe. 'What?'

She shrugged. 'I've heard it suggested you and Cate would make a good match. And I suppose I could see the pair of you together, you know, swigging your orange juices and – and swapping T. S. Eliot quotes.'

He stared at her for a moment, then his mouth curled into a sardonic grin. 'I thought Cate wasn't interested in men? In your expert opinion.'

She lifted her chin. 'I am capable of admitting that I can be wrong. Sometimes.'

'Well, you can be damn certain she isn't interested in me.'

She could feel blood flooding into her cheeks. 'Sure. Of course. I never thought she was.'

He gave a crack of laughter. 'Then why ask?'

Having come this far, however, Annie was determined to rubber-stamp all available evidence for conclusive presentation to Bernie. 'So it wasn't you gave her the hut?'

'What? Oh, the gypsy caravan job. Lord, Nan, if I had, at least I'd have made sure it would fit into the bloody garden.'

She cocked an eyebrow. 'Sorry?'

'Haven't you heard? There was no way of getting it down the side passage without demolishing the porch, so the thing's just been dumped out front. Trisha's putting her usual cheery face on it, but Cate's mortified because it's blocking the garage doors and half the light to Joey's bedroom, so she tells me. And as she also says, the flip-down bed's just great if you're five foot nothing, and don't mind hiking over to the front door in your pyjamas every time you want a pee in the night, never mind dodging the drunks taking a shortcut back from the Sportsman. Honestly, talk about a cock-eyed waste of money . . .'

Annie giggled, as much from relief as amusement. These were not the words of a would-be lover. 'Poor Cate,' she said magnanimously.

'God, yes,' said Rob. 'I just hope she'll see sense yet and come to live with me.'

'But I thought we'd be making loads,' Trisha was wailing, waving an arm around at the crowds. 'It's like the whole town's come along.'

'Warm me up,' said Simon Spencer, casting an arm round Annie and hugging her close. 'Severe case of hypothermia.'

'Sorry?' Annie was too startled by the sensation of his body tight against her own to point out that it was a notably warm day for March. Trisha and Liz were only a step behind, however, in vociferous argument with a top-hatted, green-faced vampire, so he released her, gesturing back at the round-about. She turned, and saw the wan face in the car window immediately swivel away. 'Oh, I get it. Dr Blackwell. Frozen out by your old friend, were you?'

'You can say that again,' he retorted, with such savagery she laughed. 'Who's the guy walking up there now?' he added.

'In the orange? That's only Rob. Rob Daley.'

'So that's him, is it?' he said thoughtfully. 'Big friend of yours. I'm told.'

'Sure. Why the funny look?'

'Yeah, yeah, I *know*, Trisha love.' It was the vampire breaking across their conversation, a fiend improbably mounted on roller skates whom Annie only now recognised, under the fangs and lurid make-up, as Hank Damon. He had a poster pinned round his top hat advertising the Woolshed's current show. 'But half this lot aren't registered for sponsorship, and the buckets won't bring in zilch. Well, nowhere near enough anyhow.'

She turned back to Simon. 'A big friend to one and all, old Robbo,' she said with a touch of asperity. 'It was him insisted on wheeling Cate along today.'

She was, however, prepared to believe that his offer of a bed – *a* bed, please note, not *his* bed – sprang from simple kindness. As he said, he was away so much Cate would have the flat to herself half the time, with no obligation to make polite chit-chat over the cornflakes. Nor even, he had added, to deconstruct *The Waste Land* over the bloody orange juice.

'Ha very ha,' snorted Annie.

'You said it,' he had retorted, and spun on his heel.

'Hey, what's with all the glum faces?' Dave Eastman was striding up to join them with little Emily jubilant on his shoulders and Megan swinging from Bernie's hands. 'Count Dracula here looks like he swallowed the bloody garlic.'

Annie politely joined in the laughter, but as Hank returned to grumbling about money, her gaze drifted back to the roundabout. Cate had turned down Rob's offer of accommodation, apparently. It would be different if she could drive, she had said, but there was no way she could give her sister long-deserved help with Joey if she were miles out at Abbey Mill. Besides, she was afraid of hurting Trisha's feelings. Typically admirable of the woman, of course, particularly as Rob said she had refused with real reluctance – although Annie doubted his claim she'd been close to tears. Cate Blackwell? Excuse her.

'. . . yuh, 'sreally great so many people've come along,' Hank was saying, flashing a blackly mascaraed smile at Simon. 'Big thanks to you, mate. Trouble is, the effing Arts Council'll only match what we raise ourselves, like, and the target's—'

'Forsooth, ten thousand curses summoned be upon the Old Farts Council,' Simon suddenly declaimed, startling everyone including several nearby strangers. 'As Shakespeare didn't quite put it. Sithee, how say you, fair Mistress Stoneycroft?'

Annie blinked. 'Pardon?'

'Pay attention, old love. This is a financial crisis. Summit conference.'

'I blame myself,' Trisha began, only to be drowned in protests and reassurances. She was not to have known how all the daft health and safety regs would increase the expenses, even without Hugo King cocking up the insurance. (There's a surprise, commented Annie.) Anyway, according to Hank, the real problem was that most of this merry procession hadn't actually collected any sponsors.

'On account of Maggie taking off for a last-minute skiing trip when we thought she was dishing the forms out.' He glanced round and lowered his voice. 'She's a laugh a minute, is Maggie, with a good heart and that, but I've been kicking myself for leaving the money side to her. If it's any bugger's fault, it's mine.'

'What'd you expect with the Kings?' Annie declared, omitting to mention that she herself hadn't even tried to obtain a sponsorship form. Well, she'd had so much on her mind – like buying hiking boots – and her wealthy bro-in-law was going to cough up a round five hundred, even if he didn't know it yet. 'That pair couldn't organise the proverbial in a brewery.'

Simon guffawed. 'Don't mince your words, will you?'

'Not everyone's as efficient as you, Annie,' said Trisha reproachfully, and even Bernie shot her a warning look before observing that she'd read the smart advice these days was to kick-start appeals with one or two major donations.

'Tell me about it,' said Hank laconically. 'Ideas on a post-card pur-lease.'

'Find some bloke with an ego as big as his wallet and prom-ise to name the – whatever it is – after him,' said Annie. A perfectly intelligent suggestion, which was warmly endorsed by Simon – until Trisha had to beam inanely and say, gosh, yes, wouldn't it be brill to call it the Simon Spencer studio?

The silence lasted a mere flicker of a second, but it was excruciating.

'Me?' he stammered. 'That is, sweet of you, darling, so flat-tering, but I'm not, as it were . . .'

Bernie was looking aghast, Hank bewildered and even Trisha sensed she might have blundered because she plunged on to compound matters by claiming she hadn't meant Simon should actually, you know, lumme, not at all—

'Put me down for a grand,' bellowed Dave, 'and a plate with my name on it inside the gents' – give 'em summat to aim at, hey?'

Liz meanwhile was prattling about a ceilidh that had worked wonders for their parish hall appeal, 'And you'd be astonished at the success we had with our safari suppers.'

Tempted to retort that she would indeed be astonished, Annie was forestalled by Simon. 'Clever old Liz,' he exclaimed, only a faint flush betraying his embarrassment. 'But I don't think a ceilidh will pull in the big bucks here. Besides, Irish fiddlers give me a migraine.' Deaf to his son's bluster that they were wasting good drinking time and should save their ponti-fications for the pub, he seized Annie's hand.

'What you need is a ball,' he informed a round-eyed Hank Damon, before turning to Annie. 'As you and I were discussing just the other day, weren't we? Yes, my super-efficient friend here and I will organise you a fundraising gala ball.'

21

'Make mine a large one,' said Annie, struggling out of her jacket. The Hopkirk Arms was already hot and noisy. 'My brain's in overdrive.'

'Sure, it'll be fine,' said Bernie with less confidence than Annie could have wished, before squeezing past her. 'Nothing for me, my love,' she called to Simon. 'I need to get myself behind that bar before there's a riot.'

He followed her, smiling and back-slapping his way through the press of bodies. Annie remained by the door, ignoring incomers buffeting past as she totted up what they had decided during the last hour. More accurately, what *she* had decided. Because, even if this ball had been sprung upon her, a deep breath and a vision of collaboration with her co-organiser – collaboration of an interestingly close kind – had fortified her quite sufficiently to embrace the challenge. With, naturally, many a modest protestation as to her abilities and an insistence on this being a team effort. Oh, totally a team effort.

Minutes later she was steamrollering across arguments about black or white tie with a decree that dress was to be strictly formal, although themed costume was a possibility (Hank's dramatic get-up having inspired her, 'But I shall have to give that some thought, obviously'). Over her dead body would the event be housed in the dreary town hall; this once-in-a-decade highlight of the Bucksford social calendar would be staged – 'note, *staged*' – in the auditorium of the Woolshed

223

itself, the atmosphere of which had so impressed Simon, had it not ('So will you email me your schedule ASAP, Hank?'), while it went without saying that a sumptuous dinner – yes, a sit-down dinner, not any common-or-garden buffet ('Stop scowling, Bernie, these things can be pulled together in a twinkling if there's a will') – could be entrusted only to the Hoppy's own acclaimed maître de cuisine. Furthermore, the climax of the evening, as well as the major earner – by the grace of God and her own contacts book – was to be a grand auction, chaired by her distinguished partner in the enterprise.

'Do I hear five thousand for this superb example of an empty Coke can?' Simon had obediently cried, brandishing the item on high. '*Gone*, I thank yew, to the vampire on my right.' He had fronted many a charity auction, apparently. 'Uh-huh. Far be it from me to brag, but the last lot under my hammer – at the Beverly Hills Hilton, if you don't mind – was an all-in week for twelve on an oligarch's yacht.'

'More likely to be a coach trip to Bridlington here,' commented Bernie. 'Bingo included.'

Also on the plus side she had a ready-made committee. On the minus side, the founding member thereof was Trisha Hough, who had instantly declared her determination to support Annie in every possible way. Liz had equally readily volunteered as her secretary and treasurer; Hank of course was in charge of the venue; Dave hastily excused himself from the yakkety-yak side, but assured Annie that the day he dished up a rubber drumstick or leathery quiche, she could book him in as roast of the day down the crem, and Bernie consented to join as his representative. If only to keep an eye on the rest of these mad hooligans.

'Lost in thought, Nan?' Rob had appeared beside her, balancing two brimming glasses. He laughed when she raised an eyebrow at the contents. 'Yeah, yeah, Dr Blackwell and I are once again hitting the orange juice together.'

'Stone me. You've never lured Cate into a pub?'

But there she was on the window seat, her straight spine and even straighter face reminding Annie of the Queen in the royal box at a command performance, even more so when the woman visibly cringed as Dave's voice blasted from speakers: '*Testing-testing-testing-huhwon-huhtwo-huhthree-are-we-all-ready-for-a-good-time?*'

'Not the karaoke,' groaned Rob. 'At this time of day?'

'You love it really. Who can forget your rendition of "Y.M.C.A." on Bernie's birthday?'

'I'm still trying to,' he said, sidestepping a cluster of balloons. 'Come on, let's get out of the scrum.'

She was ready to follow, not least because, out of the corner of her eye, she saw Trisha waving. Even Cate Blackwell's company had to be preferable to more advice from her sister on the management of charity gigs. Besides, Rob was always telling her she should make an effort with Cate. She'd show him. She pulled up a stool with her beamiest beam.

'So, I gather you and Simon are old friends?' OK, not the smartest opening gambit after the frosty reception Cate had accorded him at the roundabout.

Rob scowled. 'I notice you seem to be getting on with the guy like a house on fire.' Before she could ask what he'd got against her new friend, he had turned away. 'What d'you reckon to him then, Cate?'

Annie hoped he would get his nose bitten off. But oh no, not a bit of it.

'People seem to find him likeable,' she pronounced. 'He can be quite entertaining.' Talk about damning with faint praise. 'We met when I was advising on a film.'

'And I hear bonded over your shared enthusiasm for my late ex, of all things,' prompted Annie. This surprised an actual smile out of her. A warm smile.

'We did, yes. And I'm so sorry, Annie. I meant to say something before – about Jake. It must have been terribly hard for you—'

'Thanks,' she cut in. Realising how ungracious this might sound, she hurried on to observe that life couldn't have been easy for Cate herself recently, with such, um, upheavals. 'How's it feel, returning to the old home town?'

The woman looked taken aback, as well she might at the brusque change of subject, but Annie never talked about Jake if she could avoid it, particularly with a long-time fan like Cate. Seeing her thus close-to, however, in the bright light from the window, Annie was surprised by a stab of compassion. Bernie was right. She really did not look healthy. Older, and even if there was still barely a line on that lily-white brow, there were grey shadows under her eyes. It was a moment or two before she answered.

'I suppose I feel in limbo,' she said slowly. 'Disconnected from the past. Incapable of seeing into the future. If that makes any sense.'

Even if it didn't, Annie sensed anguish underlying the words. Well, if the woman she loved had gone off with someone else ... 'It must be a wrench,' she said with genuine sympathy, 'leaving Berkeley – for this.'

Since at that moment Dave's voice belted out the opening bars of 'Delilah', she moaned theatrically and was pleased to find Cate laughing with her.

'Oh, give me Bucksford over Berkeley any day.' Simon had arrived, with a condensation-dripping bottle and a fistful of glasses. He kicked a stool up to their table. 'But you know I never had the impression Dr Blackwell felt the same tug on

226

the heartstrings from the old country.' He cocked an eyebrow. 'So tell all, Cate. Why'd you up sticks?'

Of course her laughter had died. Even Annie winced at his bluff irruption.

Cate shrugged. 'Some things just reach a natural end.'

'Is that so?' He waggled the bottle.

She and Rob both shook their heads, but Annie immediately seized a glass. 'Real champagne, too. My, you're pushing the boat out.'

'My son's finest,' he said, pouring lavishly. 'To celebrate our partnership.'

'What's this?' said Rob.

Before Annie could dazzle him with her ball plans – that'd teach him to harp on about worthwhile sodding occupation – Simon raised his glass. 'A toast to new beginnings. For all of us, in our different ways.' So saying, with a sly wink at Annie, he leaned forward and adopted the furrowed brow and earnest East Coast drawl of an NBC anchorman. 'But, Dr Blackwell, may we clarify for our viewers exactly what is implied by "things coming to an end"? Is this a response to recent events, or a strategy you had been contemplating for some considerable while?'

Annie smiled uneasily, but Cate visibly recoiled and reached for her orange juice. Devil that he was, he didn't let up, although at least he abandoned the drawl. 'No, seriously, darling. You just got out of bed one morning and – Geronimo? Surely there must have been someone or – what was it you said, Annie? – some seismic eruption?'

'I'm sure I said nothing of the sort,' she declared, all the more vehemently for knowing she had said something very much of the sort. Couldn't he see Cate was tensing like a cornered animal? She frowned at him. To no effect.

'Well, far be it from me to trample in where angels what have you,' he began, and she was actually stretching out a leg to kick him in case he might even be mad enough to name Siobhan, when rescue arrived in the beefy form of Dave Eastman.

Thrusting head and shoulders between them, fists on the table, he commanded Annie to her feet, announcing that the mic was warmed up and ready to rock 'n' roll, and she needn't think she could escape without treating them to her celebrated impersonation of Tammy Why-not.

'Isn't that right, folks?' he roared, to a spatter of whoops and whistles from the bar, and he began a rhythmic hand-clap. 'We want Annie, we want Annie . . .'

Annie had been persuaded onto the karaoke stand before now, although only with a lot more drink inside her. Never, though, had she marched up to the mic with less reluctance than this afternoon, sober or not. Hell, she'd have stood on her head reciting limericks if that's what it took to shut Simon up. She was astounded that a man who had struck her as being particularly fine-tuned emotionally seemed to have no sense of when teasing should stop.

Taking a gulp of champagne as the intro began to pound, she cleared her throat, glanced across at Cate's stony face – and reflected that, sometimes, it might indeed be hard to be a woman.

'Fantastico!' roared Simon Spencer, on his feet, arms in the air. 'Bravissimo!'

Actually, Annie was gratified to earn pretty much a stand-ing ovation all round. Hers might not be the greatest singing voice in the world (although it was not as bad as her son claimed) but she liked to think she could sell a song, give it a bit of welly, you know? Even Rob, for all he rolled his eyes, was still clapping as she returned to the table and gave her a swift hug.

'You missed your way in life, kid,' he said. 'You'd have gone down a storm in the old working men's clubs.'

'You sure know how to make a girl feel good, Bobsy-boy. Thank God Dominic's not here. He threatened to disown me last time I did "Stand by Your Man".'

'Your signature tune?' Simon was holding out the bottle. 'Very apt.'

'Come again?' she said. 'No, top me up in a minute. I need a pee.'

'Well, you stood by your man heroically, didn't you?' he said. 'To the bitter end.'

He doubtless meant it as a compliment, but she could understand why the famous feminist on the other side of the table pursed her mouth. Nor was Annie flattered. Maybe she should sing 'D-I-V-O-R-C-E' next time.

'Back in a tick,' she said, picking up her bag.

Given the crowd, there was a queue for the loo. By the time she emerged, the karaoke was booming the opening chords of 'I Will Survive', instantly recognisable to Annie, because it was another of her favoured party pieces. Some other woman had got in first, however, some woman with quite a voice. A blast of a voice, in fact, operatic up top with a lower register like the roar of a Ferrari. Startled – and not a little miffed – she squeezed between the grinning blokes in the doorway, peering on tiptoe. And that's when she saw who was singing, who was claiming she used to be afraid and petrified, as she belted every word with the ferocity of a Valkyrie, and the lungs to match.

Cate bloody Blackwell.

Annie shoved her way back to their table. 'Did you push her into this?' she hissed at Simon. But it was a daft question. No one was making that woman sing. Clutching the microphone two-handed to her chest like a dagger, Cate was giving her all with a gusto to rival Gloria Gaynor herself.

'I just looked round,' he muttered dazedly, 'and there she was. Gone.'

'She – is – *phenomenal*,' breathed Rob, with quite unnecessary fervour. Annie plonked herself down beside Simon to enjoy – or endure – the rest of the performance. To cap it all, she could swear Cate was bloody well singing at her. Seriously. Every note, as she hollered out her determination to survive, was fired Annie's way.

'Fuck me, the lady sings like she means it, doesn't she?' Simon murmured into her ear as the final chord sounded. Rob was already jumping out of his chair, shouting 'incredible' and 'marvellous' and so forth and so on. He wasn't the only one. The whole pub was erupting. Annie had never heard such stamping and cheering. Simon obviously felt obliged to join in, and even began demanding more, an encore.

'Sorry, my loves.' Bernie's voice rang out over the tumult. 'That's your lot. Cabaret over. I need to clear away before the dinner crowd rolls in.'

'Just one more,' shouted Simon.

Rob, however, was already ushering a dazed-looking Cate towards them, an arm round her shoulders. 'She's knackered herself, can't you see?' he said to Simon. He smiled at her. 'Come on, you crazy canary, where's your coat?'

'That's right, lovey, you let Rob run you home.' Trisha, proud mother hen, was following her chick. 'I've got to pick our Joey up yet, from his mates down the rugby club – they're very good with him, bless their big stripy socks, that's what I always say to them, big stripy socks, you know, and it always makes them laugh, and besides' – she beamed expectantly – 'I know Annie here's bursting to talk turkey and, oh, look, here's Liz and Hank as well, turning up just in the nick, like your two bad pennies. And we've got our Simon, of course, well this is great, we can have our first committee meeting, can't we?'

Bernie bustled over, holding out a mobile phone to Simon. 'It was ringing where you left it behind the bar.' She leaned towards him. 'You know who. Sorry, couldn't help seeing with the screen lit up. You off, my lovely?' She embraced Cate. 'Aren't you a dark horse? We'll have to have you back, so we will, and I'll be selling tickets next time.'

'This can wait.' Simon thrust the phone into his pocket. 'Well then, goodbye, um, Rob. Hey, Cate, that was – quite something.'

She looked at him as though he were deranged, turned and followed Rob out.

They weren't the only ones quitting. There was now a general shuffling up of bags and coats and shouts of thanks. After staring at the door for a moment, Simon sighed and pulled out his phone again. 'Oh well. I guess if the party's over . . .'

'Bet that'll take a while,' said Bernie in a low voice to Annie as Simon sidled out of the bar, mobile already at his ear. 'That wasn't the first call he's missed, and she was on at him for an hour or more last night. I shudder to think what their phone bills are like.'

He had not so much as glanced over his shoulder at her, Annie was thinking. He'd just walked out without a word. One tug on the string from the wife and – *pouf!* – off he trots.

'Never mind,' said Trisha brightly, 'we can start without Simon, can't we?'

'What?' she said. 'Oh, not now, for God's sake.' She hadn't intended to speak so sharply and would have apologised if Liz hadn't claimed her attention with something about the promise of a lift.

'He needs to get back to the theatre by six for the am drams, so I said he could come with us?'

'Sorry, what? I mean who?'

'Hank. Only if you're ready to leave now, of course.'

With a spurt of surprise, Annie realised that she might indeed be ready to go. Hell, yes, she was more than ready.

Two could play the sudden exit game.

22

Fortunately, the next morning was bright, with the sun melting a milky sky to blue.

Fortunate because, this being Sunday, Liz's services were retained by the Almighty and Annie was going to have to pedal herself into town. She had packed a satchel with a shiny new box file and her raggedy old client book, along with wads of computer print-outs on everything from swing bands to the latest trends in table centrepieces. There were also sheaves of her own scribbles. So fat was her bag as a result, it refused to lodge in her bicycle basket.

Her time since quitting the Hopkirk Arms the previous evening had been fruitfully employed. She had been at her desk until midnight, combing information and inspiration from the internet. The bullet-pointed action list she had typed for herself was almost as long as those she had compiled for her fellow committee members. However, this plotting of the most successful fundraiser ever to support the arts in Bucksford (watch and learn, Maggie King) had not occupied quite the whole of her evening.

She had also given a certain amount of time and thought to Mr Simon Spencer. Did she regret quitting the Hoppy in something very like a huff? Well, perhaps. When, sitting at her desk with a cup of tea and a tuna sandwich, she found herself idly imagining the dinner *à deux* she might instead have been sharing with him over a candle-lit corner table. (Bernie would always squeeze her into even the most overbooked dining room.) But then again, *no*, she did not. Her departure had served him right. What did he think he was playing at? One minute he was all over her, the next scooting off for bloody beauty treatments. Or jumping at the whim of a wife, in a marriage he had led them to understand was as good as over. What was a woman supposed to think?

It occurred to her this morning, as she grappled with her overloaded basket, that he was just as capricious with other people. Look at him seemingly going out of his way to ooze charm over Trisha Hough yesterday – the woman he'd declared would drive a saint to murder. Still, she was in no position to criticise bad behaviour towards poor old Trish. Why else was she getting on her bike?

Hurrying back into the kitchen, she rummaged in a drawer for a length of string to secure her satchel. She was not about to see all her hard work scattered over Deerbourne Hill.

'I'm popping down to Chatsworth Close,' she shouted up the stairs. Dominic, typically, had yet to roll out of bed. This reversion to adolescence would have to be addressed, but just now she had no time to take her son to task. 'I need to get this ball rolling. Ha ha,' she called to empty air, before adding in an undertone to herself, 'and mend my fences.'

She had reached home last night conscious she'd left Trish looking like a kicked puppy. Not for a moment was she fooled by her cheerful farewells and assurances that she understood how busy Annie was. At the top of her sheaf of notes, therefore, was a list of questions on which to consult her exasperating old comrade, with the firm resolve of listening most attentively to her advice. If not, perhaps, of acting on it.

She grasped her bike, kicked away the prop, flipped a leg rather too high over the saddle and had to stifle an unforgivably aged grunt before hoisting herself aloft and sailing down the drive.

On swinging nonchalantly into Chatsworth Close the first thing she saw – how could she not? – was the much talked-of shepherd hut. Just as Trisha had said, this exquisite toy was painted in muted greens (Farrow & Ball's French Gray and Lichen, unless she was much mistaken), with a curved roof, chintzily curtained window and iron wheels picked out in precisely the right shade of cream. It sat in front of number 3 looking as pretty as a picture on a calendar – and as incongruous as a cherub on a chip pan.

The second thing she saw – well, almost the second, but enough to distract her from the surprise of Bernie's Mini being parked at the kerbside – was Simon Spencer's bum. A bum decently clothed, it must be added. She knew it belonged to him because Trisha told her so, although so flustered and full of self-reproaches was she that it took some time for Annie to ascertain that, no, Bernie wasn't here – apparently she'd lent the car to her father-in-law – and even longer to establish exactly how the upper part of Simon's torso came to be thrust through a window at the front of the Houghs' bungalow. A shattered window, although since it was ajar he was not actually having to squirm over shards of jagged glass.

'Don't you dare laugh,' she heard him gasp, when told of her arrival. 'And if you take a picture, old love, you're dead. Don't worry, Trish, I'm nearly through. If I can just hoist my knee that leetle bit further . . .'

The problem was that the window was blocked from opening to its full extent by the folly-lolly hut parked in front, leaving only the narrowest of apertures for manoeuvre. It gave into Joey's room, apparently.

'I swear I was only in the bath ten minutes, well maybe a bit longer, bit stiff after all that walking yesterday, you know, and Cate, bless her, had toddled off round the corner to pick up her Sunday paper, and there my poor Joey was, roaring blue murder, but of course I had the radio on – well, I like the music Sunday mornings, you know, on the local station, they play all the goldie-oldie stuff at the weekend—'

'Is Joey all right?' interrupted Annie, glancing at the window where Simon continued to wriggle manfully.

'You're all right, aren't you, sweetheart?' bellowed Trish at once, and a muffled groan from within suggested Joey was, at least, still in the land of the living. 'Little tinker, he only went and got himself pickled as a parrot with his mates down the rugby club yesterday, not that I blame the lads, bless 'em, he had a high old time, and he's a grown man now, as I keep having to remind myself, but I told him he'd regret it come this morning, didn't I lovey? Didn't your old mum tell you you'd be sorry?'

As far as Annie could gather, Joey had woken, presumably with the raging thirst of a hangover, knocked his water beaker over, flung himself out of bed in pursuit and not merely landed awkwardly on the floor, but – according to the limited information Trisha had been able to discern – managed somehow to jam his heavy wheelchair hard up against the door.

'One – more – heave,' gasped Simon.

'Don't worry, darling.' Only now did Annie hear Cate's muffled voice from inside the bungalow. 'Not long now.'

'. . . clue what to do, I mean I had to smash the glass just to get at the handle and open the window, but there was no way I could climb in, bloomin' heck, I couldn't hardly squeeze along between the hut and the wall to get the thing open in the first place, and even Cate looked a bit iffy, well I said to her, we don't want you knocking yourself out, love, don't you even think about trying, I'll ring our Rob, which I did straight off, only of course he's on his voicemail, isn't he? So I'm just thinking, right, it'll have to be the fire brigade, nine-nine-nine here I come, when——'

'Yay!' roared Simon, suddenly slithering out of view. There was a disconcerting thump and crash, as of falling furniture, and a stifled yelp from him. 'Don't worry,' he called, sounding rather less perky. 'No bones broken, just a few scratches and . . . Ah well, I guess we can fix the television stand. Come on then, old chap, let's see if we can shift this chair of yours away from the door, hey?'

'So you rang *Simon*?' said Annie, following as Trisha pounded off into the hallway. 'You could've called me.'

She was already issuing breathless thanks, reassurances, congratulations, promises of hot drinks and warnings to Cate, who was braced with her ear to the bedroom door, ready to shove. 'Pardon, what, Annie love? No, Simon just rolled up, didn't he? In the very nick of time and – oh, *there* we are!' The door swung back and she surged past Cate into the bedroom with Annie in pursuit, to find Joey curled on the floor in his pyjamas, his face shiny with snot and tears. 'Come here you daft lummock,' she crooned, stumbling down onto one knee to cradle his head. 'Let's get you back on the bed. That's right, Cath, lovey, swing the hoist over here. Simon, I could kiss you, honest I could.'

'Feel free,' he said, brushing himself down as he stood a little unsteadily by the fallen television. There was a rip across one knee of his jeans and a graze on his forehead, which he touched gingerly after Cate pointed it out. He held up a hand with a trace of blood.

'Hail the wounded hero, huh? Dear Lord, I am definitely too old to perform my own stunts these days.'

'Thank you, Simon,' said Cate, which was not what you'd call effusive, but she spoke as though she sincerely meant it.

'That was – truly good of you. Shall I go and put a kettle on, Trish?'

'I'll do that,' said Annie. 'High time I made myself useful.'

It was more than half an hour before Trisha and Cate between them had Joey cleaned up, dressed, rehydrated with beakers of squash and dosed with paracetamol. He looked under-standably sorry for himself as he slumped in his chair in its usual station in the lounge.

'Serve him right,' said his mother fondly. She flopped into her own chair, delved into her bag for a long overdue cigarette and had it to her lips before remembering herself and lower-ing it again with a glance at Cate.

'For goodness' sake, have one,' said Cate, shaking her head. 'I've told you a hundred times this is your house.'

'Well, I suppose you've your own little smoke-free zone out there now, haven't you?' said Trisha, happily touching her lighter to the tip. 'Your lovely caravan. Have you shown it to Annie and Simon yet, because I know—'

'She sure has,' said Annie, pouring tea into mugs she had scrubbed until the pattern nearly lifted off. She had also swabbed down the sink, the worktops and – while she was at it – the fridge door, by way of penance for having snubbed Trisha the previous night. Simon meanwhile had insisted on gathering up the broken glass from the window. Not alto-gether skilfully, to judge by the curses she heard emanating from Joey's room. Between their respective labours, however, they had indeed been shown the shepherd hut, even if Cate's notion of a guided tour only went as far as throwing open the door, standing aside and inviting them to see for themselves. She was not being unhospitable, Annie realised on clamber-ing up the steps. There was barely room for one body inside, let alone three. But the hut was as pretty within as without and, as Simon remarked, it was at least a civilised bolthole in which she could write – her laptop and a stack of books were evidence of that – as well as sleep.

'I'm not so sure about sleeping,' Annie had said, and leaned out of the doorway, eyebrows raised.

'Not an ideal bedroom,' admitted Cate. 'But I don't want to sound ungrateful,' she added hurriedly, 'because of course I can work in there, and – and it was a very, um, kind and generous thought. Very.'

Annie was already withdrawing into the hut to fix Simon with a scowl. 'Don't even think of asking *whose* kind thought,' she mouthed. 'Not a word.'

'*Moi?*' His smile was more piratical than angelic, thanks to a large blue sticking plaster over his right eyebrow.

Annie had affixed this herself, but their conversation had been fragmented. He had just begun whispering reproaches to her for abandoning him in the pub the previous evening when Trisha had tottered into the kitchen with an armful of sheets for the washer. At least it reminded Annie why she had come down to Chatsworth Close.

'It's Trisha I should apologise to, not you,' she said. 'I abandoned you too, yesterday, didn't I, Trish? It had been a long day, and I'm afraid I was tired and ratty.'

He waited until Trisha trundled away to the lounge again – protesting that Annie could never be ratty, the very idea – before he turned back to whisper that he knew full well he was the one who should be apologising, for exiting the bar so rudely last night. In fact, he said, he'd been headed for Annie's house this morning, to do just that, when, at Bernie's request, he had called here to drop off some stuff Trisha had left at the Hoppy.

'And as I've been saying to Simon,' Trish had declared, unexpectedly reappearing, 'I could swear I told Bernie, well, I meant to tell her any rate, just to chuck it all in the bin. It's only a few banners from the walk, which is all done and dusted now, thank you very much, and full steam ahead for our ball, eh? Is that tea brewed, Annie love? Because I tell you what, I'm gasping.'

Only after Annie had topped up the pot and was embarking on a round of refills did she halt at Cate's mug, which was in any case barely touched.

'Lord, I'm sorry, I forgot. You drink it black, don't you?'

'Doesn't matter,' said Cate, with a fleeting frown. Polite as ever, she immediately took a sip of what must have been very tepid tea. 'This is fine, truly. Milk just seemed to disagree with me. For a while.'

'The ball, then,' said Annie, resuming her seat. 'Now I was thinking—'

'Hello?' shouted a gruff voice from the hall, and here was Rob. Sweaty in his cycling gear, helmet a-dangle, he blinked as he took in the crowded room. 'What's this, Sunday morning prayers?'

Trisha, of course, had to recount the saga, interspersed with grunts from Joey who chuckled as Rob seized his shoulders and pretended to shake him. When he could get a word in, Rob explained – unnecessarily given his apparel – that he'd been out on the bike, and was miles up the moor by the time he picked up Trisha's message. 'But it seems everything's sorted now,' he said, and gave Simon a curt nod. 'Thanks to our athletic friend here.'

'Exactly so,' said Annie. 'Hurray, hurray, all's well that ends well, and we're about to discuss our ball.'

'Your what?' Rob looked round. 'Any more in that pot, Nan? Don't fret, I'll fetch myself a cup.'

Annie followed him to the kitchen, however, teapot in hand. 'A fundraising gala ball,' she announced triumphantly, 'for the new, uh, thingy rooms at the Woolshed, you know? And *I* am organising it.'

'Well, blow me down Nora,' he said. 'What's got into you? It was a bonny day yesterday, but I'd not have thought hot enough for sunstroke.' Some people might be underwhelmed, but not Annie. This was a Yorkshireman offering high praise, and his smile was warm.

'To be fair, it was Simon's idea,' she felt obliged to admit as she led the way back into the lounge. 'But we're in joint charge.'

'Absolutely,' chimed in Simon. 'Partners in crime.'

'How's that work?' Rob perched, with caution, on the edge of Trisha's cluttered table. 'Tricky with you on t'other side of the Atlantic, I'd have thought.' He looked at Simon over the rim of his mug. 'At least, I'm assuming you're headed back for the States?'

'Sadly yes,' he said, 'but, hey, not imminently. And not for long, with people in this town so dear to my heart. If that doesn't sound unutterably slushy.' The bashful smile was pure Doctor Cockerdale, just as Annie remembered it from so many Sunday nights. But there was no shyness as he continued: 'And now that I've found them, I don't intend to lose touch again. Ever.' He pulled a face. 'You'll soon be sick of the sight of me.'

'Get away with you,' cried Trisha. 'Dave and Bernie will be thrilled to see you back here. Well, we all of us will, won't we?'

'Sure,' said Annie. She was puzzled, though, by the earnest way he'd spoken, as if he felt he had to convince them of his sincerity. Perhaps he did, at that, after keeping the Eastmans dangling for so long. 'But I dare say we'll muddle along without you somehow,' she added drily. 'Just so long as you swear to turn up on the night in your best bib and tucker. I stood in for you at your son's wedding. I warn you now, I'm not doing the same at this ball.'

'*Nothing* will keep me away me this time.' Even if he wasn't looking her way, Annie did not doubt the emphasis was intended for her. 'Besides, distance doesn't mean a thing these days, does it? Not with planes and phones and email.'

'Well, while we have you here in person – ' Annie reached for her satchel ' – maybe we could take a look at one or two of the ideas I've jotted down.'

'As a matter of fact,' he said slowly, glancing round, 'I've just had rather a bright notion myself. In fact, a perfectly brilliant notion, if I say so myself. Why don't we move our discussions down to the Woolshed? Do a proper recce of the venue? It's Sunday morning, so the theatre's bound to be dark, and I'm sure that sweet guy – Hank, is he called? – I'm sure he'd come down to let us in. Do you have a number for him?'

'Yes, but . . .' Annie chewed her lip and consulted her watch. Trish would mean Joey and Joey meant the wheelchair and all the attendant kerfuffle. Typical bloke, Simon, not a thought for the practicalities. Although if Cate could nephew-sit? And anywhere had to be preferable to this stuffy lounge. 'Well, it's a thought,' she said. 'How about you, Robbo? Fancy joining my committee, to give us the benefit of your wisdom? God knows, you sit on every other committee in the north of England.'

'Count me out on this one.' He rose and set down his mug, but must have realised how surly he sounded because his voice softened. 'Balls aren't really my thing, Nan. Anyway, you're right, I already waste too much of my life holed up in meetings – including the Woolshed board, come to that. But you can rest assured I'll fight your corner with my fellow trustees, if needs be – and roll up on the night, to cheer you on.'

'Trisha?' said Simon. Only then did it occur to Annie that she might have misjudged the guy, because he was looking concernedly at Joey in his wheelchair. 'Although perhaps you feel . . .?'

'No, lovey, that's right. I think me and Joey best stick at home, after all the hoo-ha this morning. Hadn't we, you silly sausage?'

You crafty sod, she thought triumphantly, scrambling to her feet and stuffing her papers back into her satchel with alacrity.

'Not to worry, though,' continued Trisha, just as Annie was contemplating the unexpectedly beguiling prospect of a morning flirting her way round an empty theatre in the company of Simon Spencer. 'Cate will come along with you, won't you, love? Then you can tell me all about it, and what's been decided. Go on, pet, it'd do you good to get out for an hour or two.'

'Excellent idea,' said Simon with a heartiness so patently hollow Annie had to swallow a giggle. 'Come on, Cate, this committee needs you to report back to your sister. Haven't I earned it, after my heroics this morning? It's the least you can do.'

Ha. Fat chance. However, to Annie's surprise and considerable irritation, Cate – after a moment's grave-faced reflection – said yes, maybe she would accompany them.

23

Was it as early in proceedings as that very morning when Annie began to wonder if she might manage this ball committee more successfully without the assistance of her distinguished co-chair? Perhaps.

For starters, Simon had evidently forgotten that the back seat of Bernie's Mini was folded down and the rear of the vehicle piled roof-high with broken seating destined for the recycling depot. There was, he said glumly, space for only one passenger.

'No prob,' Annie chirruped, not averse to presenting a youthful image of herself as a keen cyclist. Minus the Lycra, naturally. 'I'm on my bike, so you take Cate. I'll see you round at the theatre.'

Then, however, the silly pillock had to take it into his head that Bernie, too, must join their deliberations, she being the key voice on catering. Which was *so* vital, he insisted, airily declaring they'd clear the back seat by dumping all this junk back at the Hoppy. Nor would he listen when Annie assured him there was no chance whatever of digging her friend out of the bar with Sunday lunch imminent.

'But she'll be hurt if we don't at least ask,' he insisted. Touching, if boneheaded. Even Cate murmured a protest about their keeping Annie and Hank Damon waiting around for them, but he was not to be dissuaded. 'I'll drive like the unfettered clappers,' he said, throwing open the passenger door. 'Fasten your seatbelt, honey, gonna be one bumpy ride.'

By good fortune, Hank had already been in the theatre when Annie phoned to propose this impromptu meeting. She found him there, supervising the get-out of Bucksford Amateur Operatic Society's latest production, which had closed the previous night, only too willing to roll down his sleeves and leave them to their packing-up. Yesterday's top hat and fangs had given way to jeans and trilby, although a flip of mascara remained – which was quite becoming, actually. As he led the way into the auditorium, he said he hoped it was OK, but he'd just left a voicemail for Liz asking if she wanted to rock round too, after church. Kinda made sense, if they were serious about brainstorming this gig, yuh?

'The more the merrier,' muttered Annie, who had already relinquished any notion of wandering around in theatrical twilight and intimate conference with Simon Spencer. Not just was their party growing by the minute, she now saw that their ballroom-to-be was as fluorescently bright as a supermarket, and a-bustle with the show dismantlement operations. She had to dodge a scaffolding pole swinging from the shoulder of a lanky youth whom she could swear she recognised from behind the counter of her bank – except his hair seemed to have turned jet black.

'Sure, dyed it to play the Count. *Dracula*: the musical you never heard of,' said Hank laconically. 'Set in a Romanian nunnery so it's God's gift to yer amateur soc with ten mad-keen women for every tongue-tied bloke. Might not be Sondheim, but you tell me another show only needs three guys up to croaking a tune. Played a blinder, too. Ninety-six per cent capacity across the week, and bar takings up a third.'

Annie began to think she might have underestimated this Hank Damon, who approached the ball with equally hard-headed pragmatism. Board of trustees? No prob, he'd square the chair. Bands? Piece of piss, he'd give her a list. Seating banks? They could be rearranged every which way or just concertinaed up against the walls, yeah, dead clever, cost a bomb, thank fuck for the Lottery. Atmospheric lighting? *Puh-lease.* So impressed was Annie with his gung-ho attitude she found herself hoping Simon wouldn't return any too soon. They were accomplishing more than she suspected might be possible if he were here clowning around.

They had reached the critical question of a date, however, for which they certainly did need his input, and were squinting at the calendar on Hank's pad when Simon eventually sauntered into the auditorium and gazed round, as wide-eyed as a kid in a toyshop. 'God, don't I adore this space? And totally glorious for a ball.' Following him was not just Cate Blackwell, but Liz, who had apparently pulled up beside them in the car park and now squeaked a blushing protest as he seized her by the hand.

'*Shall – we – dance?*' he sang, waltzing her across the floor, effortlessly bypassing two women staggering under a stack of gravestones. 'Da-da-da, dumdy-dum-dum-dib-dib-dah! And one, two, three!' He had a fine tenor voice, and was nifty on his feet, gracefully releasing Liz before stretching a hand to Cate with a fluid panache worthy of Astaire. It goes without saying she declined the invitation, but the corners even of the Blackwell mouth twitched up a millimetre.

'*Dates,*' said Annie.

'Oooh, she's a slave driver, this one.' With a tap shuffle and a twirl, he bowed low. You could almost see the top hat and tails. 'Sorry we were so long, my darling. We got stuck behind every tractor in the north of England, and you were right, of course. Our lovely Bernie was immovable. So, dates. Diary, diary diary ...' He produced his phone and made a comedy of donning a pair of horn-rimmed specs. Too right progress was faster without him, thought Annie, although there was no denying he added gaiety. However, even as his phone lit up, the light in his face seemed correspondingly to fade. She thought she heard him curse under his breath and raised an eyebrow, but Hank was already talking.

'Soon as we can. To hit our target we've gotta get the fund over the quarter mill mark by July, and it's nowhere near yet. So wotcha reckon to that Saturday we looked at first off, Annie, early May?'

'May?' squealed Liz. 'Surely not *this* May?'

'Think of it as a flash mob thing,' declared Annie, with no precise notion of what a flash mob might be, but liking the sound of it. 'Except, I thought you had some locals booked in that night, Hank?'

'Yeah, mass ukulele strumalong. Silver Stringers, world famous in Bucksford. Can I pull it, though?' He stroked the stud in his eyebrow. 'The Formby fanatics'll be after my blood. With their little bricks of Blackpool rock ...' His mouth twisted in a grin. 'Nah, I'll buy 'em off with cut price on a Sunday and fuck the overtime bills.' He looked round. 'If Simon's up for banging his star-spangled hammer that night? Not bank holiday, weekend after?'

Simon seemed not to have heard. Only when he realised they had fallen silent, waiting for him, did his head jerk up. Muttering apologies, he began scrolling through his phone. 'Um, the second Saturday in May? That seems to be ... OK. And Viola will be over here by then, just about to start rehearsals so, yup, pretty much perfect. Ink it in, guys.' He snapped shut his phone. 'However, blessed nuisance, but I'll have to leave you to it for a short while. No panics, no *peanuts*,' he added, flashing a glance at Annie, 'just a text the length of *War and Peace* from an author with his knickers in a twist. Sweet boy, huge talent, but not happy with the latest re-writes

demanded by She Who Must et cetera and the poor bloody
director sounds to be having a nervous breakdown between
the two of them. I'll have to step in before the situation goes
nuclear, and my copy of the script's back at the pub. My loves,
I am fearfully sorry about this.'

'Can't be helped,' said Annie heartily. 'No need to apologise.'

Apologise he did, however, and at blathering length with
repeated promises of returning inside the hour, if not before.
His reluctance to leave was flattering, to be sure, but she was
keen to get back to business. Hank, too, urged him on his way,
wryly wishing him luck and recommending a bulletproof vest.
Even Liz chipped in, assuring him that he need not drag Cate
away now, no need at all.

'If you don't get back in time, Annie and I can run her
home, can't we? So long as one of you doesn't mind squash-
ing into the back – oh, are you on your bike, Annie? Well,
that's settled then. Because I hate to cast a damper, but if
you're seriously talking about holding this ball in what – not
quite seven weeks? – I hardly dare think what we have to do.
Oh my giddy aunt, surely this is *insane*?'

The haste with which Annie and Hank claimed the date
proposed was perfectly feasible suggested they were asking
themselves the same question. But if Hank flinched a little as
he totted the days remaining in his calendar before the second
Saturday in May, Annie was relishing this sizzle of danger.
She hadn't felt such a surge of energy since taking charge of
Bernie's half-cocked wedding plans.

'Nothing like a challenge for making you feel twenty years
younger,' she declared.

'Attagirl,' called Simon from below the green-lit exit sign,
where he was patting his pockets for car keys. 'See y'all later.'
He blew a kiss and left.

*   *   *

Committee meetings are rarely riveting, even for the most active participants. Certainly not for Cate Blackwell, whose scant utterances and furrowed brow suggested her mind was engaged elsewhere, doubtless with matters more erudite than ticket pricing and table hire. She looked up, seemingly startled, when Annie at length suggested they conclude for the day.

'Oh, are we finished already?'

'Don't time fly when you're having fun?' responded Annie ironically, given the woman's blatant disengagement from proceedings. She herself, though, truly had been having fun. Striding around, querying, asserting, groaning one minute, guffawing the next, she'd felt in her joyous element. And while Liz, scribbling notes, twittered between excitement and terror, Hank Damon had confirmed himself a pillar of sturdy sense and dry wit.

'Between us,' were Annie's last words to him, as she embraced this new and most worthy comrade-in-arms, 'we are going to make our ball happen. And we are going to make it happen *big*.'

Perhaps it was only to be expected that, having climbed off her bike after the haul up Deerbourne Hill – which, battery or no, required leg muscle a-plenty – she flopped into a chair at her kitchen table, as limp as an old cushion. That she felt emotionally as well as physically flattened was also understandable.

There was more to this than a protracted meeting. With every thrust of the pedals on the way home, she had been mulling over Simon Spencer's failure to return to the Woolshed. In spite of his repeated assurances, in spite of their having remained in the theatre a full three hours, he had not reappeared. She may not have required his presence as her colleague in the enterprise. She may even have welcomed his absence as such. But not only was this another instance of the man's chronic unreliability, it also, quite frankly, didn't say much for his interest in her. Had she just been kidding herself? Flattered and fooled by the easy charm? Was she as gullible, dammit, as Trisha Hough? She slumped in her chair, too weary to decide whether she wanted a bath, a snooze or a large gin.

Barely ten minutes later, however, she was flinging open the door to the sitting room where Dominic was toying with his phone, two empty beer cans at his elbow, while some bow-tied toff on the television enthused about Chinese porcelain, look-ing – as he uninterestedly remarked – like she'd been struck by lightning. And she did. Not struck down, that is, but illumi-nated, ablaze, in fact one hundred per cent bloody electrified.

'Are you thinking of going out this evening?' she asked in a voice half an octave up from concert pitch. 'I only ask because I, um . . . well, the fact is Simon Spencer's coming round.'

He was, definitely. Well, *almost* definitely. The text from a number unrecognised on her phone had read:

Will you be home 7-ish? Need to see you. XXX S

And she had coolly texted back, with her thumb trembling no more than a twig in a hurricane:

Sure thing. See you then. X

Only a breathless hour of wardrobe-ransacking later would it occur to her that this message could, just conceivably, have arrived on the wrong phone. Sent in error with a single misplaced digit by one of the ninety zillion other phone-owners in the world whose names began with an S? But no. It had to be him. Not a perishing doubt. Hell, why was she in such a dither? It wasn't because of Simon's imminent arrival – well not *just* that. Her son had been winding her up. Again.

As a cherubically beautiful child, Dominic had possessed an uncanny ability for springing a temperature or spots – even a suspected dose of meningitis – when she had an especially promising date lined up. Small wonder he went into acting. And Bernie – as much a mother to him as Annie ever was – wouldn't suffice at such times. It had to be the real deal at his bedside, whipping off her earrings, mopping up the puke in her best frock, cancelling all her plans. His tactics might have matured, but it seemed the dog-in-the-manger possessiveness had not.

'Do I really have to go out, or can I hole up in the study?' Dominic had said when she so breathlessly informed him of the impending arrival. He was glowering at the television screen if not at her. 'Don't worry, I'll put headphones on.'

'God's sake, d'you think I'm planning rip-roaring sex on the sitting-room carpet?' She was babbling. Stopped. Tried a more conciliatory tack. 'Look, you haven't even met Simon yet, have you? Maybe you'd like to say hello, have a drink? Before you go out.'

'Jeez, it can't be that serious yet? Meet the family time.'

'I meant because he's an actor,' she retorted, stung. 'He knows people, useful people – over here, as well as in the States. Only this morning he had to go off to sweet-talk some brilliant young author who's written a play for his wife and—'

'Darling Clementine?'

'Sorry?'

'*Darling Clementine*, that's the name of the play. If you're talking about the piece Viola Hood's doing.'

She gaped at him. 'How on earth do you know that?'

He shrugged, as though it were obvious. 'I auditioned. Along with every actor in London between nineteen and thirty, I should think.'

'You never told me.'

'Why would I when I didn't get it?' He hunched a shoulder. 'Like all the other cruddy parts I went up for last year.'

'Well,' said Annie, struggling to assimilate this bizarre revelation, 'I guess that at least explains why you've a thing about Viola Hood.'

'What?'

'Don't think I've forgotten the way you stormed out of the pub at Christmas.'

'Oh, Mother, you haven't a clue,' he snapped. 'Not a fucking clue. So she said I was crap, so what? She was probably right. Anyway, history now.' Grasping his stick, he hauled himself up off the sofa. 'That was my last fucking audition.'

Now was not the time for a row, still less for a mother and son heart-to-heart, but she couldn't let this pass. 'Don't be absurd, Dominic. You can't talk about packing in your entire career just because of one bad audition.'

'Bad? You don't know the half of it. And who said I was jacking the job in? Although I might well,' he added pugnaciously. 'But as it happens, I just meant *Clementine* was the last audition before I came off the bike. Same night. And you wonder why I remember the name of the fucking play? Only the worst night of my entire life.'

'Will you stop shouting at me? You've never told me any of this before.'

'Why would I? You never listen.'

'Oh come on, I'm forever asking—' She broke off wonderingly. 'So you've actually met her, have you, the great Viola Hood?'

'Course I fucking haven't. She's in LA.'

'So – I don't understand?'

Now he looked directly at her. There was something in his face she couldn't read, but he was seriously stirred up, that was for sure. 'You really wanna know? It's quite a story.' Before

252

she could even think how to answer, he spun away. 'Forget it. Your *date's* coming round. I'll text Kit Grayson back. He asked if I wanted to go out.' He was already stumping away. 'Have fun, Ma.'

'Thanks,' she snapped, to a slammed door. 'Thanks a bunch, sweetheart.' Then she saw the clock. 'Shit, I need to move.'

At least she didn't have time to fret about her stretch marks. Or how you're supposed to conduct yourself with a member of the opposite sex when you're three months short of your 60th birthday and haven't been out with a man since . . . Oh God, pink sweater or the cream boat-neck? And was he actually going to turn up?

But there was to be no nerve-shredding wait tonight. At two minutes to seven, with her last spritz of scent still wet, she distinctly heard a car pull up, and . . . yup, a trill from the front doorbell. Straightening her pullover (glam but understated), shrugging on the killer heels she could endure for at least the distance from here to the sitting room, she snatched a last glance in the hall mirror, thanked God the lighting was dim, and threw open the door. Yes, it was him. It really was him.

'Hiya, darling,' he said. 'Bad news, I'm afraid.'

24

Annie kicked shut her bedroom door and toppled across the bed. Yanking off a shoe, she tossed it at the wardrobe. A sharp crack obliged her to heave herself up on one elbow to see if she'd hit the mirror. Seven years' bad luck would round the day off nicely. No – no visible damage. She flopped back again.

Oh, she had *quite* understood that Simon couldn't stop, not with a plane to catch at some silly hour in the morning. So she had said. Through a smile so tight her teeth hurt. She might have been more forgiving if his regrets and promises to keep in constant touch from California hadn't rattled out as though his thoughts were already several time zones away. Meanwhile, an engine was ticking over at the end of the drive. That wasn't Bernie's Mini she had heard pulling up. It was a hired Jag, complete with driver, waiting to whisk him down to Heathrow. Madam had clicked her fingers.

'I wouldn't dream of going now except . . . Darling, she *has* to do this play.'

'Why?' said Annie.

'Isn't it obvious?'

'Not to me,' she said, head on one side like an enquiring bird. Of the razorbilled prehistoric variety.

'I thought you of all people . . .' He tugged at his scarf as though it were throttling him. 'Look, can I come in? Just for five minutes?'

They were still on the doorstep. Without a word, Annie stood back while he threw scarf and coat down, and followed him into the sitting room.

The lights were dim, the candles bright, a log fire crackled in the hearth and a guitar whispered from the speakers. Annie screwed up her eyes in one swift cringe before she kicked off her heels and stalked round flipping lamps on and Rodrigo off. She need not have worried. Simon didn't appear to have noticed the scene-setting – didn't appear to be aware of anything much at all, including Annie. He stumbled round morosely, chewing a thumbnail, as she plucked the bottle of wine from its ice bucket. No, not champagne. There's such a thing as a cliché too far.

'Drink?' she said, never doubting he would refuse and pouring a hefty one for herself. But he almost snatched the glass out of her hand and gulped.

'Not driving,' he said thickly, 'and there'll be plenty more going free on the plane. First class, of course – only way to travel, eh?'

'Your wife booked your ticket then?' Whoops, that just slipped out.

'You saying I'm a kept man?' But he didn't sound offended. 'Sure, my wife's *people* fixed it. Viola has *people* for that kind of thing – for every bloody thing – and a motley crew they are too. Her pet snake in London laid on the limo, the creep, but he needn't think he can get round me that way. God, I needed that. OK if I help myself to another? This has been one total fuck-up of a day.'

'You didn't manage to fix the script then?' She was going to sit down, even if he wanted to pace like a caged beast.

For a moment he stopped dead, staring at her, as though he'd no clue what she was talking about. 'Oh that. Lot of what Vi wanted made sense, actually. She knows her stuff.'

He let out a weary sigh. 'No, the problem's not the script. It's her.'

'You don't say,' responded Annie tartly. 'Still, I suppose it must be serious if you have to scoot back to LA at a moment's notice.'

He shrugged. Didn't even glance her way. 'Someone has to look after her.'

Yeah? Or are you looking after yourself, jumping to her every whim in the hope of a decent pay-off? 'So what's up this time?'

'Stage fright. In a word. She's scared senseless by the sound of it, won't even get out of bed.' He clasped a hand to his chest, all at once very much the actor. 'I mean, I understand. God, do I understand. Theatre terrifies the best of us, walking out there, all those expectant faces, and suddenly you can't remember what play you're in, never mind your lines. And the poor old love's barely set foot on a stage since she came out of RADA. It was always film or telly, and she isn't offered that these days. Too old, too difficult – too bloody unreliable. But she has to work, Annie, she has to do this play. It's a gift.'

'*Darling Clementine?*' How much more about his effing wife? Annie rose and picked up the bottle. 'Matter of fact, I've just learned my son auditioned for a role. Isn't that a weird coincidence? He didn't get it, mind.' Another black mark against Dame Viola Hood, now she came to think about it. How dared the woman say Annie's brilliant boy was crap?

'He's probably well out. Not much of a part.' He didn't even pretend interest. He had come to a halt by the fireplace and was scowling down at the flames. 'It's a one-woman show, really, star vehicle. That's what I'm trying to tell you. This is her last God-given chance to prove she can still do it. What? No, no more for me, thanks.' She was turning away when he grasped her arm. 'Go on then, fill me up. Why should I care?'

He wasn't even seeing her. Whatever was going on in his head had sod all to do with her and, in that moment, she'd had enough of playing along. This man had led them all to believe, implicitly, *explicitly*, that he wanted out of his marriage, that it was all over bar the lawyers. And listen to him now: Viola this, Viola that, poor old love . . . 'But you obviously *do* care, don't you?' she snapped. 'You care a hell of a lot. About your wife, I mean.'

He looked at her now all right, and his jaw sagged. 'God's sake, Annie, I've always thought that you – you, of all people – would understand the mess I'm in.'

'I can't imagine why.'

'Look, if she pulls out of this play now, that's it. End of her career. She'll hit the booze again, or the pills. Both, probably. End up a raddled old harridan, forgotten by everyone, die sooner or later in – in a puddle of her own vomit.'

In spite of herself Annie winced. 'Surely – not as grim as that?'

'Toss-up which gives out first, her heart or her liver. And this is a performer who isn't just talented, she's unique.' He was in passionate earnest now. 'Me, I'm only your jobbing actor, light comedian – a safe pair of hands. Viola is despotic, erratic, wild as a kite and bloody dangerous to work with, but she has something that's entirely her own. A kind of magic, really.'

'Well, maybe. But—'

'Don't you get it?' He grasped her shoulders. 'Don't you recognise yourself? Come on, Annie, weren't you married to someone like this? A total fucking monster on the wrong day, but a genius when the sun shone?' He released her and turned aside with a groan. For a light comedian, he had a rare talent for melodrama. 'Only you quit while Jake Stoneycroft was still strutting around, king of his world. Which, dear God, is what I should have done – years ago when the champagne corks and flashbulbs were still popping. And I could do it now, if only she were back on her feet, fighting and screaming and driving directors insane. I'd shut the door on Viola the monster tomorrow. What I can't bring myself to do, although God knows I want to, is walk out on a whimpering, snivelling wreck.'

Don't you recognise yourself?

Far more to the point, thought Annie indignantly, as she lay on her bed, staring up at the crack in the ceiling she should have had seen to months ago, *far* more to the point was how Simon Spencer had recognised a parallel between his rotten marriage and her own. Not that she was admitting any comparison, certainly not to him. Oh, about being married to a drunk, yes. To a monster, if you like. Jake in his riotous prime had undoubtedly been that, in spades. But the other stuff, the latter years?

Annie had confided in no one – no one, not even Bernie – how desperately she had resented the return of Jake to her household. Her broken, shambling ex-husband. But this silence wasn't to do with bravery. It was just that, as her dad used to say, 'What tha can't get out of, tha can only get on with. And least said t'better.'

Good old Dad. Yorkshire to the core. He was also fond of talking about reaping what you'd sowed. Spot on there, too.

Because when Martha had visited her stricken father in hospital and reported back through hot tears that he was about to die in a cruddy geriatric ward, stinking of piss, with Radio 1 blaring and nurses who just sat round scoffing biscuits and talking holidays, of course Annie had felt obliged to drive down and inspect for herself.

She had walked the length of the ward twice before she even recognised Jake, although it wasn't so very long since they'd met. This skeletal figure, yellow-skinned and white-haired, who tried to smile with a face half set in stone? Obviously she'd brought him home, if only after a blazing row with a pigheaded cretin of a doctor who assured her the upheaval would finish his patient off. He was the father of her bloody children and you wouldn't leave a dog to breathe its last in a dump like that.

Except Jake didn't die. He didn't recover much, either, in spite of the fortune she was soon spending on physio and rehab and the rest. Yes, she understood Simon's desperation to haul his wife back into functioning life, understood it painfully well. As he said, you can abandon a monster. But that sad hulk, tottering round the house on a walking frame, that once-dazzling wordsmith struggling to mumble a request for a cup of tea?

As it had sunk in that her ex-husband might be around on this earth not for days, or weeks, or even months, what had she done? Wept? Felt as sorry for herself as Simon evidently did? No, she'd installed another bathroom, that's what. Goodbye lumber room, hello disabled-friendly en-suite. She had told herself this was no more than sensible preparation for the sad day one of her parents was alone and failing. Only for Jake to outlive the pair of them, while time slithered past and her life was stuck in limbo. Her love life, at any rate. As she had been known to comment – if only to Bernie – it was hard to get your head round dating with the Ghost of Nuptials Past stumbling along the landing, listening for your key in the lock at night, looking as scared as an abandoned orphan if ever you got dressed up.

To cap it all, she'd had to suffer the plaudits of friends and neighbours who comfortably – admiringly – took for granted she and Jake were reconciled, after she'd hauled him back from the very jaws of death. What was she supposed to do? Go round proclaiming that if she had never clapped eyes on Jake Stoneycroft until the day she died, that would have suited her just fine? Maybe Simon was more honest. He did at least tell it like it was. She had always chosen to leave the murk at the bottom of the marital pond unstirred. You reap what you sow – you pay what you owe. Simon doubtless had a fair few years of good marriage on his balance sheet from the early days. Her good times with Jake could be counted in months – but she'd still come out owing, hadn't she?

Naturally she didn't share any of this self-indulgent twaddle with Simon. Not least because, as she'd regularly used to lecture herself, what did she have to complain about, really? The house was plenty big enough to accommodate an ex-husband without tripping over him. She'd had money by then, a thriving business and soon discovered there was nothing like a passionate desire to escape your home for tripling your turnover. And when, one morning, with far less trouble than he'd caused in life, Jake quietly failed to wake up, Annie had found herself weeping on Rob's chest at the funeral, although she couldn't have said why. It was not simple grief, that was for sure.

None of this would she have dreamed of confiding to Simon, even if he hadn't had a car idling at the bottom of the drive. In fact it'd been bloody hard to know what she could say after his despairing outburst, other than that she was sorry for him – which she was – and that she, you know, wished him luck. Some such meaningless pieties.

And that should have been that, and everything would have been fine. Well, hardly a bundle of laughs and very much not what she'd been hoping for this evening, but there you go. Only instead of putting down his empty glass, giving her a hug and exiting stage left, the pillock had dithered. He shuffled from foot to foot on the hearthrug, about to say something, then would stop, tugging at his earlobe, looking anywhere but at her. If it weren't for the Californian perma-bronze she could almost have suspected he was blushing.

'Your car's waiting,' she offered.

'Oh, fuck the cab,' he burst out. 'There's so much I wanted – *need* – to say to you.' Catching hold of her hand, he gazed deeply and – no two ways about this – meaningfully into her eyes.

And suddenly there they were. Suddenly, seemingly, headed straight for the clinch Annie had been imagining since the moment he popped up behind the bar at the Hoppy – since long before then, in fact. Since the day she'd bashed out that first email for Bernie, if she were honest, when the chance of her idle fantasy turning into steamy reality had seemed as likely as a lottery jackpot. So why on earth was she gawping back at him now, as glassy-eyed as a rabbit in the path of a lorry, silently screaming for Dominic to come home, for the phone to ring – *anything*.

'Listen, darling, I might regret this in the cold light of day but I'm sick of playing games and today's been such a miserable cock-up, thanks to Vi, I feel I'll explode if I don't say this now, while I've got the chance. At least you understand my bloody marriage situation—'

'Simon, I, um—'

He ignored her. 'Because I don't know about you, but even before we met, I felt you and I were, well, kindred spirits, so I wouldn't be surprised if you've a fair idea what I want to—'

'No,' she squawked. 'I mean, maybe, but . . . Look, do you really think this is the time? Or rather, there isn't time. Is there? Not if you're getting that flight.'

He frowned. Hesitated. Then, with a shrug, he lifted her hand to his lips, touched a feather-light kiss to her fingers and

– oh, thank God – let her go, muttering no, she was probably right.

'But when I come back,' he said. 'Soonest, hey?'

'Simon's gone,' was the first thing Liz said as she walked into the kitchen the following morning.

'Uh-huh,' said Annie.

God's sake, it wasn't just that he'd chuntered on about his wife and, worse, her own ex-husband – great prelude to seduction, that. Nor even that he had a car waiting and a plane to catch – although what kind of a peabrained goon makes a move under those circumstances? What did he have in mind: quick snog and a grope, thank you and good night? They weren't a couple of kids behind the bike sheds. Grown-up liaisons require delicacy, style, a touch of finesse – *non*?

'He went down to Heathrow to get on a plane first thing, apparently.'

Annie, who had her laptop open in front of her, glanced up. 'You're well informed.'

'Trisha's just told me. I called round for a knitting pattern she promised when I dropped Cate off yesterday, such a pretty christening blanket.'

'How'd she know?' said Annie absently. 'Lord, the way news gets round this town. Stick the kettle on, if you like. I'm putting together a Facebook page for us. The ball, I mean.'

She had not accomplished much, however. Sidetracked by her own neglected Facebook page, she had found herself lackadaisically scrolling through pictures the kids had posted the last time Martha was home. She wasn't taking them in. She was still pondering the events of the previous evening.

The thing was, when it had come to the crunch, when there he was, and there she was, nose to nose, her hot little hand clasped in his, and he was about to say – well, who knows the words he might have uttered, his intentions were clear enough – she had felt nothing. *Nothing.* Apart from a lively urge to make for the door. What she had not felt was the faintest tremor of excitement, let alone the volcanic surge of red-hot lust she should have been feeling—

'Shall I put your mug here?' said Liz. 'Oh, is that your Facebook page?'

—with Simon, gorgeous *Simon Spencer*, at last closing in on her.

'What? I mean, thanks. Just shift that pile of papers.' She realised Liz was peering over her shoulder. 'Yup, that golden siren in a bikini is my engineer daughter, Martha, last time she was home. Doesn't the tan make you sick? Actually, we're due another visitation, according to Dom. She doesn't bother to tell her mother, naturally. I wonder if she'll be back by the second Saturday in May?' She glanced round. 'You haven't a paracetamol on you, by any chance?'

'Gosh, I'm sorry. Bad head?'

'Too much hard thinking,' said Annie darkly. 'And it hurts.'

Use it or lose it. That was the obvious explanation. After all these sexless years, had her sturdy old libido just quietly curled up and perished of boredom? Was it to be knitting and boxed sets of *Downton Abbey* from here to eternity, with only the prospect of grandchildren to quicken her pulse?

'No, no, stay where you are,' she said to Liz, who was asking where she kept her pills. 'Easier to find them myself.'

Liz bit her lip. 'I say, if that's your Facebook page, would you, um, mind awfully if I took a quick peek?'

Annie pushed the screen towards her as she rose. 'Help yourself while I raid the drugs cupboard.'

Was there a female version of Viagra?

Then, passing through the hall on her way to the downstairs cloakroom, she saw the scarf on the table. Had Simon left it? He'd certainly pulled one off when he arrived, and she'd been in no condition to notice anything as she waved him away. She picked it up and touched it to her cheek because she was a sucker for a nice bit of cashmere – or Mongolian goat-coat, as Rob called it. That being his way of expressing sincere gratitude for a similarly *luxe* specimen she'd given him a couple of birthdays back. This one smelled faintly good, too, of some half-familiar cologne or aftershave. She inhaled more deeply. And all at once . . . *bloody hell.* Stuff Proust and his biscuit barrel, one whiff of this scarf and she was on fire, gripped with wild longing to be crushed against a solid masculine chest. The sensation passed in a flash, but it was enough. She could have yowled like an alley cat.

As it was, abandoning any thought of paracetamol, she skipped back into the kitchen humming a tune, giving a hop and a twirl as she returned to the table. Apparently there was life in the old girl yet.

'Shall we make a start on the hit list? I have to say our secret weapon here's going to be my client book because I don't want to boast – well, yes I do – but virtually anybody who's anybody this side of York is—' She broke off. 'Liz?'

Her friend was slumped over the laptop, and there were fat tears slaloming down her cheeks.

'Goodness me, whatever's the matter?'

'It's Kelvin,' she gasped. 'Kelvin and – and you know. *Her.* They've got married.'

25

Annie sympathised. Naturally she did.

She comforted her friend with milky coffee and hot cross buns. She clucked, she sighed, and she gave many a mournful shake of the head – while totting up a mental list of affluent locals whose Rolex-bangled arms might be twisted into buying a whole table.

In the lachrymose days that followed, however, she often had to stifle an urge just to suggest Liz give over whingeing and bloody well get on with it. Only the knowledge that she had been responsible for steering her friend into this wretched impasse in the first place restrained her. On the sole occasion she was driven to offer the gentlest hint that it would be nice if she could, you know, brighten up a bit, she was instantly made to regret her words. Through choking sobs, Liz wailed that she wasn't going to ruin Annie's life along with her own, and here were the car keys.

Annie then had to waste an hour assuring her she was indispensable. She could do that wholeheartedly, at any rate, because there was no way she could mastermind ball preparations without the car. Privately, she thanked Providence that, for the time being, Kelvin and his bride were still toasting their nuptials in the Caribbean. Too much to hope for a helpful hurricane. She had immediately deleted him from her Facebook friends to save Liz from any further self-torture. She could even be grateful the creep had blocked her poor friend from his page, which poor old Trisha wasn't to know when she had asked whether Liz had seen his latest post.

However, it's a universally acknowledged truth (according to Annie Stoneycroft) that the surest remedy for a bruised heart is hard work. How fortunate, then, that the ball threw up so many tasks which could be delegated to her melancholy assistant. Liz's spirits must have been bolstered immeasurably by all those hours of address-checking, typing and envelope-stuffing.

Would that her son's troubles could be as easily addressed. Annie had been unable to tackle him about their row over Simon's visit until midway through the day following. A hard drinking session in the pub favoured by the Woolshed crowd had led to his sleeping what remained of the night on Hank Damon's sofa.

'But you needn't worry, Ma,' he had croaked, from behind dark glasses, 'I'm not his type.'

Annie retorted that she would welcome the excellent Hank as a son-in-law any day, compared with some of the peculiar girlfriends he'd dragged home over the years. This had gone some way to breaking the ice. Dominic mumbled an apology for behaving like a jerk and was even moved to give her a hug – albeit only after learning that Simon had been and gone from the house within minutes. He would not, though, tell her anything more about his supposedly traumatic dealings with the actor's wife, other than to snort that the woman had been present at his audition only via the internet. *Obviously.*

'Just forget it,' he muttered. 'Doesn't matter. Well, it does, but – oh fuck, you know.'

Actually no, Annie didn't know, but he remained blackly unforthcoming so, as she brewed him the organic, hand-plucked, quid-a-bloody-leaf brand of green tea he insisted was so much healthier than your standard bags – and never mind the mess in the sink – she instead told him about the ball. After all, as she reassured herself, the cycling accident was far from being the only night Dom had pronounced the worst of his life. There had been many, starting with the fancy-dress party she'd sent him to, aged eleven, dressed as a pixie. Very sweet he'd looked, too.

'Will *he* be there, at this bash?'

'If I have to get on a plane and fetch him myself,' she said. 'Why else is my working title Hurray for Hollywood? But if what you're really asking is whether Mrs Spencer is coming' – she handed him his tea – 'the answer is no. Deffo. That's the last thing the poor sod would want. So, my angel' – she patted his hand – 'there's no excuse for you not to dig out that dinner jacket you conned me into buying before you decided black tie was unutterably bourgeois. And in which you will look drop-dead fucking irresistible.'

He gave a reluctant smile. 'So long as you don't expect me to dance.'

Ten days later, with daffs giving way to tulips as the great day edged closer, Rob said the same. He had called round with a sheaf of risk assessment nonsense, as insisted upon by the Woolshed board. But Robbo, as she sternly pointed out, did not have the excuse of a smashed tibia or fibula or whichever it was.

'Just two left feet,' he said. 'As you've often complained.'

'I'll bring my steel toe-caps. Get a load of this, then. Hot off the press.' The tickets were printed in silver and black on pearly card as thick as a cream cracker. *Hurray for Hollywood* was blazoned across the top. Patrons were instructed to '*dress for the role or the red carpet*', possibly because Annie had spotted the most divine little evening frock in her favourite shop and decided fancy-dress was no longer to be compulsory. 'Bit blingy, yes,' she went on hurriedly as Rob turned the ticket to catch the opalescent shimmer, 'but you know Yorkshire folk. They expect flash for their cash.'

Flash they were to have. Thanks to the hours of charm she had been lavishing down the phone, local businesses and well-heeled citizens were donating all manner of requisites, from fizzy water to potted palms – and including twenty yards of your actual red carpet – along with an impressive array of auction lots, now being catalogued by Liz. Three days' salmon fishing on the Tweed (thank you, Hugo King) currently vied for top spot with a head-and-shoulders study in pastels – by a genuine RA portrait artist, thank you very much. The dinner menu Annie had, on the whole, felt confident to delegate to Dave, although this led to a brief chilling of relations over the vegan option, Mr Eastman having unreconstructed views on the use of butter.

Her most recent triumph, however, as she told Rob when following him to the door, was the securing of a decent band. The panic over this, with all Hank's suggested ensembles proving to be engaged or extinct, had almost derailed the venture because a DJ simply wasn't good enough for a ball, was it? However, she had now booked a very smart outfit indeed, thanks to the wedding of a premier league footballer being kicked into touch by his fiancée, after the *Sun* published photos of his off-field antics.

'That's a piece of luck,' said Rob, fishing for his car keys.

'I shouldn't think Rolando whatever-he's-called sees it that way,' said Annie cheerfully. 'Well, thanks for the forms. I can hardly wait to read them.'

'Spare me the sarcasm, we have to go through the hoops.' He was looking past her. 'Oh, is that my scarf? Not that I'll be needing it in this weather.'

It was the navy cashmere number, still coiled on the hall table. '*Yours?*' Annie began. 'But surely—'

'Cate did say she'd given it to Liz to bring up here. I'd forgotten all about it. I lent it her, day of the sponsored walk?' He was stuffing it into his pocket. 'It was a present from you and all—' He broke off. 'What's so funny all of a sudden?'

Annie was only sorry she couldn't share the joke with Rob. But she wasn't about to embarrass the hell out of her old play-mate by announcing he'd been responsible for restoring her faith in her sex drive. Honestly, how priceless was that?

Well, they always reckoned these perfumery wizards mixed pheromones into their brews, didn't they? Although, since Rob's idea of grooming generally didn't extend beyond a bar of soap, she had quite likely given him the classy scent as well. She'd thought the smell was familiar. Even days later she was apt to chuckle when she recalled the glee with which she had danced back into the kitchen.

It was just a shame the effect couldn't be bottled for future ref. On collapsing into bed at night, try as she might to conjure up a lusty fantasy of the next time Simon Spencer gave her the old deep and meaningful routine, she always seemed to pass out before the action got interesting. Even while conscious, her thoughts had an exasperating habit of mean-dering away to table allocation or crockery hire. She wasn't lacking in desire, she told herself, just sleep and brain capacity.

Besides, while absence is supposed to make the heart grow fonder, Simon scarcely seemed absent. It was true he had regretfully confessed he was not, after all, able to return to the UK immediately (no surprise to Annie, even if it was to her colleagues), in fact not until he shepherded Viola into her rehearsals in London. In the meantime, however, barely a day passed without an email or two pinging into her inbox. They were not all addressed exclusively to her. Most were conscientiously copied round the whole committee – although she couldn't imagine why he felt anyone else needed this constant reassurance of his yearning to be back in Bucksford. Nor why he had to write at such length. She could only assume the poor guy was bored, cooped up in his sunny golden cage, if he could find nothing better to do than bash out daily screeds to anyone with the time to read them. This, increasingly, did not include herself, flattering as his attentions were. Even the links and attachments he forwarded, pertaining to the management of charity functions, tended to be of dubious relevance.

'Yeah, can't say I've been fretting over where to park all the stretch Caddies,' remarked Hank, as he and Annie were concluding one of their regular meetings. 'Fact the only thing gives me the heebies now is him dropping out.'

'Come on. He never stops telling us he's counting the days.'

Annie's ideal committee would in general have a membership of one. In Hank Damon, however, she had discovered an associate of rare merit. And since her respect for his abilities was most gratifyingly reciprocated, they had fallen into the habit of conferring, as this morning, without troubling their valued colleagues.

With papers spread across two tables, they had shifted a hefty roster of business in fifty minutes flat, possibly spurred on by the buttock-numbing nature of the log benches in the cellar of the Woolshed.

Although not as busy as it became in the evening, the cafe and bar did a popular trade in coffee and snacks during the day, and a row of skylights along one wall meant it was not without a pleasant glow of natural light. Several of the tables below these windows were occupied by the senior tea 'n' toastie squad, as Hank fondly described them – 'ten pence tippers but regular as clockwork so who's complaining?' – and the far end of the chamber was noisy with young mothers and dribbling toddlers in buggies being read a story by a plump female in headscarf and kaftan. 'Yer Jesuits knew a thing or two,' he had whispered. 'Grab 'em young, and you've ticket-buyers for life.' Artistic director he might be, but there was nothing airy-fairy about this young man's nose for business. The place was fairly buzzing. A talk or rehearsal was also underway in the theatre itself, to judge by the murmur of an amplified voice Annie had heard as she hurried through the foyer earlier, and the pink leotard-tight gear on a leggy blonde over by the bar suggested a dance class was due. Although, given her thigh-high python-skin boots, maybe not imminently.

'We done then?' said Hank.

'Yup,' said Annie, stretching luxuriously. She was about to observe that plans were shaping up well (always a mistake), when he cocked his head to one side.

'Hello, sounds like he's done upstairs, too. House's coming out.' Indeed, the lift was bleeping, there were voices echoing down the stairwell and people began to clatter through, mostly middle-aged women fishing for purses and staking claims to tables with coats and carrier bags. 'Corks away for the Prosecco stampede,' he whispered, with audible satisfaction. 'That guy might be a dickhead, but he's fucking great for trade. Rainy Tuesday morning and not a seat left in the main block.'

Only when a tall, spare-framed figure descended the last few steps, inclining his silver head graciously towards the tubby matron chattering along beside him, did Annie realise to whom Hank referred. That must have been one of Kelvin Parsons' sessions she'd overheard upstairs, because here was the great guru himself – every inch a linen-trousered, billowy-shirted, sun-gilded housewives' delight. The cocky clown. Unfortunately, he had also spotted her. Out of the corner of her eye, she saw him study his fingernails, patently wondering if he could pretend not to have done so. Feel free, Annie silently urged him, I'm about to go, just as soon as I've packed up my notes. Hank, however, had already risen, fixing a cheesy grin and waving him over.

She watched him step stiffly towards them.

'Hi there, Hank, good crowd today.' Pause. 'Annie. Yo, long time no see.'

Not long enough in her opinion. His too, by the look on his face. However, manners are manners, even if your average etiquette manual lacks guidance on the correct form of greeting for a gent whom, when last encountered, you whacked round the chops. 'Kelvin,' she said. 'You're looking well. Sunnier climes, obviously, and I gather congratulations are in order?'

Before he could reply, a shiny pink arm snaked through his and a frothy curtain of ashy-blonde curls swished past his nose. 'You're a very, very naughty tiger.' A turquoise-taloned finger wagged under his nose. 'Yes you are. Your lonely pusscat's been waiting all this time for you by the bar and you didn't even *look* at me.' It was she of the python boots. And she growled – yes, *growled* – into his ear before turning her gaze towards them. Gaze? Annie had only ever seen such a bluer-than-blue laser beam on screen. In the eyes of the recently awakened dead. 'Are you going to introduce me to your friends, lover? You know how I'm dying to meet *everyone* in this funny little town.'

'Did you know Kelvin Parsons was doing his thing in the theatre today?' demanded Annie of Liz, when she got home to find her assistant already at the kitchen table, studying a spreadsheet.

Liz nodded mournfully.

'And you didn't tell me?'

'I'm trying not to mention him,' she said, with forgivable indignation. 'I thought that was what you wanted.'

'Well, you might have warned me.' Annie dropped her own files onto the table.

She sighed. 'I was just grateful I don't go in on Tuesdays. Besides, why should you mind?'

Fair question. Which Annie would have been hard put to answer even if she did not have weightier issues in hand. She pulled up a chair, sat down opposite Liz and eyed her earnestly.

'Love, you've got to be brave.'

Liz bit her lip. 'Is it . . .?'

'I've met her, yes. Leona, she's called. Came to join Kelvin after his gig.'

'She's very attractive, isn't she? No, no,' Liz hurried on, in response to Annie's look of surprise, 'I haven't seen her myself. Not yet. But it's what everyone's saying. Amazing eyes.'

'Radioactive contacts, more like. Along with rubber tits, a face stretched tighter than a snare drum and a dress sense straight out of *Star Trek*,' said Annie, who had been polishing this portrait all the way home. 'And if she's south of fifty-five, I'm a banana. Backs of the hands,' she added darkly. 'However, I dare say she's – quite attractive. If you like Barbie dolls.'

Annie would concede that the new Mrs Parsons had a remarkable physique. Even if her breasts did look like a couple of bowling balls fighting to escape. And not everyone can aspire to the intellectual heights, can they? Although it surely requires an uncommon deficit of the grey cells to claim, straight-faced, that you must have encountered your husband in a previous existence, because, 'from the very second Kelvin and me met, it was like we'd always been *meant*, you know what I'm saying?'

From the very second Kelvin clocked her diamond-encrusted fingers, more like, was Annie's report to Liz.

Because this rock-flashing, twice-divorced widow must have stashed a packet on her marital travels if, as she had detailed at eye-glazing length, she was ordering all their furnishings from Tempo Italiano. 'That oh-so-exclusive retailer of oligarch chic. Bling? The shop makes Beckingham Palace look like a council house and you should see their catalogue, Liz, you really should. Lush, plush and chandeliers everywhere. If you fancy a working replica of Elvis's giant, gold-embossed lavatory for a cool couple of grand, that's your supplier. All for their new flat – oh, pardon me, for their split-level, New York-style loft. Which I'm here to tell you I was cordially invited to view. That was after Hank told Leona I used to be in the interiors business myself – in what she thereafter referred to as my *little shop*. We *girls* could swap ideas, she said. As in, she could educate a sad little provincial like me in the marvels of high-end contemporary design.'

'She didn't say that . . .'

'It's what she meant. Asking how long since I *retired*. What'd she think I used to sell – crocheted antimacassars? And to cap it all, this pad's actually on the top floor of my own dear old warehouse. At least I could cut her short there, tell her thank you very much but I was already familiar with the view from their Romeo and Juliet balconette. Whatever a balconette might be. I thought it was a bra, myself. But that's not the point.'

'What do you mean?' said Liz warily.

Here we go. 'Thing is, she's mad keen to get involved in – oh, everything that's on offer round here. From Zumba to flower-arranging to Trisha's wretched book club. The entire social whirl of downtown Bucksford. So—'

Liz shuddered and threw up a hand. 'I knew it. It was bound to happen. It's all right, Annie, I'll be fine. Just – give me a minute. She's coming, she and . . . They're both coming. To our ball.'

'Well, yes, I'm afraid so,' said Annie. 'But . . .'

If only that were all. Before Annie had realised what he was about, Hank was gallantly ushering the woman over to the bar to inspect the flyers advertising the Woolshed's myriad clubs and classes. Which had left just her. And Kelvin. She began stuffing papers into her satchel. But he glanced round shiftily, then leaned towards her. 'Wanna say something to me, babe?'

Piss off? Annie raised her eyebrows politely. 'Such as?'

'C'mon. Last time we met, Christmas.'

'Best forgotten, don't you think? Don't worry. I'll take your apologies as read.'

His mouth fell open. '*My*—'

'Too much to drink. All round. In fact,' she continued firmly, 'I'm ashamed to say that I, for one, can scarcely remember a thing from – from after the time the pudding came out.' And how gracious of her was that? How skilful a slalom around this sticky social corner? But the idiot was already starting to protest, so she added with even more emphasis, 'You too. I'm sure.'

No one could call Kelvin Parsons quick on the uptake. His mouth worked for a moment. 'I – uh – if you say so. I guess.' He was still eyeing her resentfully when the other two returned, full of smiles.

'Sorted your, um, Zumba sessions?' Annie said brightly. Kelvin might be a social moron. She knew how to behave.

'Not only that,' said Leona, wafting two pearlescent cards, but glancing sharply from her husband's face to Annie's. 'We're coming to a ball, Tiger. Hank has given me tickets, isn't that just fabbo-tastic of him?'

'Very,' said Annie, glaring at Hank. 'Truly *fab-o-tas-tic.*'

'Yeah, well, least I could do,' he said, avoiding her eye, 'for our star attraction. Kelvin's such an asset to this theatre.'

Leona gave her bluest beam. 'And now you've another asset in me, haven't you? Guess what, Tiger?'

'She's done *masses* of PR. So we were told. Probably draped over the bonnet of a car at the Motor Show in her swimsuit. Oh, and she once organised a charity fashion gig. For the crème de la crème of Croydon, so I think we can safely assume Anna Wintour wasn't in the front row.'

Liz's eyes had never left her face. 'Still, that's neither here nor there.' God, this was like strangling kittens. 'As I said, she's mad keen to get stuck into local life. And your boss is even keener, blast him, on stopping Kelvin taking his psycho-plonkery courses off to other venues. Although you'd think free ball tickets would be enough. But what could I say? The damage is done. So.' The moment had come. 'I'm afraid we have a new member on our ball committee. The only consolation,' she added, 'is that Kelvin looked even more pissed off than me.'

26

Leona Parsons' arrival did not immediately impair Annie's pleasure in her busy days. There is, after all, no small entertainment to be derived from such a worthy object of dislike. Many a merry half-hour passed in sharing her absurdities and offences with Bernie and Hank, even if Liz was inclined to temper the fun with Christian charity.

'I just hope she's making him happy,' she sighed.

Fortunately there was only one scheduled meeting of the full committee to be negotiated, and that was not until the Monday before the great event itself. In the meantime, Annie and Hank industriously contrived, conferred and otherwise carried on as before, and if they somehow forgot to add Leona to their email circulation list, that omission was rectified by the ever-helpful Trisha. This may have accounted for their new committee member sashaying up to their preferred conference corner of the cafe, several days later, in a cloud of purple sheepskin and jasmine scent, with a bulging gold bag over her shoulder.

'So *this* is where you two are hiding,' she said. 'I'm afraid I can't stay, just dashing by with a little idea for our ball, before my photocall.' Trill of giggles. 'I've set up a press launch, you know? At the Century Hotel, for Kelvin's new website. Which is going to be simply a-maaaaz-ing, because we're not just expanding the facilities at his healing centre, as I'm sure you'll have seen on our Twitter feed, but the big news today is that' – dramatic pause

– 'we are going *global*. Yes, Kelvin is taking his mission online at last. I mean, it was always crystal clear to me he's wasted round here.' Flashing smile at Hank. 'In this town, not your sweet little theatre, my love. But, as I've been telling him – because we're dead straight with each other, my Tiger and me, never a cross word, but many a frank one, that's the secret of a good marriage, take my word for it – he's been burying his talents under this bushel too long. With your gift for communication, I said to him, your very unique genius for connecting with ordinary people, you must reach out to suffering souls everywhere. Online counselling, I said, that's the way forward, trust your Leona.' Her laugh, thought Annie, was like silver paper on your fillings. 'But an old hand at the publicity game like me knows these journalists always want the *personal* angle, don't they? With lots of piccies. Which I'm afraid means' – she pointed both index fingers at her own forehead – 'ta-dah! Step forward yours truly.'

Annie, who had been pondering whether Botox alone could account for the spooky smoothness of that brow, was startled when Leona abruptly leaned forward and lowered her voice. 'You're all on edge, lovey, I can tell, but don't you worry. I've told my naughty old Tiger to wait in the car. I'm here all on my little own-e-o.'

'Come again?'

Diamonds glittered as she held a finger to her lips. 'No need to say a word. We girls must stick by one another. Of course it's hard for you, seeing the two of us together. Believe me, my love, I understand.'

Hank glanced alertly from one to the other. 'Am I, like, in the way here?'

'What? No, of course not,' snapped Annie. So outraged was she to realise Kelvin must have spun some tale about his deal-ings with her to his wife – as spurned seductress? as *lovesick old trout*? – she couldn't immediately utter a word, let alone a riposte of sufficiently dignified and crushing nature. 'Clearly there's been a misunderstanding—'

'Yes I *know*,' interrupted Leona, with a pitying smirk, 'and I promise it will stay our little secret.' Whereupon she dumped her multiply buckled and medallion-jangling bag in the middle of Annie's carefully annotated table plan and extracted a wad of glossy leaflets. 'Now, these are what I really called in about, our fabulous new bro-*shaws*, because I thought we could spread them round the tables?'

Annie's flat refusal was out before Hank could even blink. It was some small revenge to be able to state, unequivocally, that advertising material was restricted to major sponsors. And, no, she was afraid she did not think it would be nice for Kelvin perhaps to say a few words instead, during the after-dinner speeches – here she gave a honeyed smile to match Leona's own – gifted communicator as he so famously was. But they had long since settled that there were to be no formal speeches, just the grand auction, which was to be chaired, as doubtless Leona had gathered, by Simon Spencer. Who possibly had the edge for fame and communication skills even over Kelvin? And was there anything else she could help Leona with? Because she and Hank were in the midst of a complicated table plot.

'Hell hath no fury . . .' he murmured as Leona shouldered her bag and stalked away, with a final measuring stare at Annie.

'If you're talking about scorned women, I damn well hope you mean her.'

'Go on,' he said, leaning forward. 'Tell.'

'If you really want to know, the creep jumped on me. So I belted him one.'

'Oh, Annie,' said Hank, taking her hand and dropping a kiss on it, 'I think I love you. Although it'll cost us ten grand a year if he buggers off to Harrogate.'

Annie laughed. 'Quit worrying. That bastard knows which side his bread is buttered.'

As Leona's presence around the town became ever more visible, however, the irritations began to outweigh the entertainment.

That she would take her custom to Annie's hairdresser was probably inevitable, given it was the smartest salon for miles around. That she should already have booked a four-hour appointment ('Extensions take forever,' said Rosie apologetically) for the day of the ball at exactly the time Annie herself should have been sitting in her favoured stylist's chair was another matter. And while Leona persuading Dave Eastman to prepare for her an organic, free-range, salt-free, egg-white omelette might be little short of a miracle, it was a bloody nuisance when Annie urgently needed him to come to the phone and explain a mix-up over cutlery requirements.

'One flash of those tits and he'd have laid the feckin' eggs himself,' Bernie had said. 'Can I help?'

But the crowning insult came with the *Bucksford Advertiser*, the weekly free rag in which Annie generally wrapped her compostable rubbish without reading a word. She was about to do exactly that when her eye was caught by a large photograph of Leona, draped across a sofa in a gown even Shirley Bassey in her heyday might have baulked at. Kelvin was pictured separately above, aiming a gravely empathetic stare at the camera, but Annie ignored him, along with the usual misspelled, apostrophe-free, advertorial tripe about his new website. What she instantly fastened upon was a quote in bold from Leona to the effect that she was glad to be adding a touch of her own unique style to the Woolshed Appeal Ball.

'What's she mean, *her* style?' she snarled, startling Dominic into lowering his phone and coming to peer over her shoulder.

'Besides, that woman wouldn't know *style* if it bit her in the bum.'

'Where's it say that?' He picked up the paper to scan it more closely. 'Healing drumming circles – in dozy old Bucksford, jeez, who'd have thought it? And a load of support groups. What's this one about, "You Too"?'

'Sexual harassment, whaddya think? God, talk about hijacking every trendy bandwagon going, although how Kelvin Parsons has the brass neck . . . I mean, what a joke.'

'Maybe he isn't stuck in the last century,' said Dominic, throwing down the paper. 'Unlike some people.'

'Swimming with dolphins,' said Leona earnestly. 'You really must try it, for your poor boy.' Joey emitted a loud groan, and she edged her chair a few inches further away.

'I'm afraid he hates the water, does our silly man,' said Trisha. 'Don't you, pet? Can't be doing with it getting up his nose, but it's kind of you, Leona. I do know that loads of people seem to swear by it, but . . .'

Had Annie realised Leona was going to be ensconced in the lounge at Chatsworth Close she might not so cheerfully have agreed to meet Rob here. They were to cycle out to the Hopkirk Arms for what he called a proper sit-down lunch. He had handsomely said she deserved a treat in the midst of all her hard work – no, he damn well was not being sarcastic – but there were a couple of questions he needed to run past Cate, so could they save time by rendezvousing in town?

'Save you the climb up the hill to my place, more like,' she had retorted. 'Fine athlete you are. I'm up and down Deerbourne Lane like a yo-yo these days.'

'Yeah well, just remember I've only got legs, not a battery.'

Legs which had so far failed to deliver him to the Houghs. Annie, however, had arrived early, since she had business of her own with Trisha. Having contrived tactfully to deflect all her old friend's ingenious suggestions for hand-crafted table adornments (felt flowers figured large) she had settled, with relief, on custom-made napkins. These were to be cut from a decently weighty linen Trish had ferreted from some obscure corner of eBay, featuring an (almost) tasteful black-on-white reproduction of the famous Warhol image of Marilyn Monroe. Well, since this was the Hurray for Hollywood ball, Annie supposed it was acceptable. Only to discover now that Trisha's finishing touch was a loop of machine-embroidered tape bearing the legend: 'Stolen from the Woolshed Ball'. A tad kitsch, maybe? Mega-kitsch, if Leona Parsons' enthusiasm was anything to go by. Having greeted Annie's arrival with frost-glittered politeness, she had thereafter turned her back, and was now brandishing one of the finished articles, exclaiming they'd had the same kind of idea at her friend's totally *amazing* wedding last year, only with gold embroidery and, like, crystal tags? Her rhapsodies about a Prosecco fountain – manned by semi-naked butlers, apparently, in some hired junket-palace up a Tuscan mountain – were cut short by Trisha excitedly instructing her sister to pay attention: an Italian castle, did Cate hear that? Having urged a very willing Leona to tell them all about it, she promptly embarked on her own paeon of praise to all things Italian, not that she'd ever been there herself, obviously, but . . .

Ignored, Annie selected a napkin from the pile. Better than woolly orchids, at any rate, and Trisha seemed to think they could flog them at the end for a couple of quid a throw. Trust her, she'd said. They'd sell like hot cakes. Annie was inspecting the stitch work – fair play, couldn't fault it – when Rob rolled in. Looking full of the joys of spring, she observed, as he kissed her and Trisha, clasped Joey's shoulder – and then blinked as he took in Leona.

She likewise was giving him the keen-eyed head-to-toe. Actually – jeans, stripy shirt, properly shaved – he did look quite presentable for once. Not for the first time, it flickered across Annie's mind that this was one of the many irritating things about men. They could, some of them, actually improve with age – and how many women could you say that about? But Rob, no question, cut a more fetching figure these days than he had years back, in his desert boots and bloody safari jacket, chalk-dusted, with pens poking out of every pocket. Leona evidently thought so and flashed him the twenty-tooth beam she did not waste on females. 'We haven't met properly,' she cooed, 'but are you this Rob Daley I've heard so much about?'

'Bloody hope not,' he said genially, dropped onto the sofa beside Cate and immediately plunged into a discussion of Jane Austen. What else?

'Look, will *you* have a word with my sister, Annie? You know how highly she's always thought of you, and she won't listen to a bloomin' word when I tell her it'd do her a power of good, few weeks in Italy, bit of sunshine, get some colour back in her cheeks—'

'What?' said Annie. 'Sorry, I wasn't paying attention.'

'You know, I'm wondering if the *queen bee*' – glassy titter – 'of our ball committee has even seen my article in the newspaper, Trisha, because I'm surprised to say I haven't heard a word from her since. Does she realise what a huge plug I gave the ball? Maybe the *committee* would think that, with all my experience, I should organise some more publicity?'

'Well, they'd have been pleased as punch, I'm sure, but we're already as good as sold out, aren't we, Annie? No, but what I was saying to you is Cate's friend – you know, Siobhan? – she's invited her out to this castle in Tuscany they're renting come June. Well, that's what they're calling it, although it's not

283

our idea of a castle, is it, Joey? Not a moat or a drawbridge, very poor do compared to Caernarvon, but it looks really—'

'I'm not going, love,' interrupted Cate, glancing up from the booklet Rob had handed her. Her cheeks were faintly flushed as she continued, 'I'm staying right where I am, in Bucksford. I'm here to see you, aren't I?'

'But there's a swimming pool and everything laid on, you wouldn't have to lift a finger and you and Siobhan have always been such good pals, lovey.'

About which Annie was not intending to say a word. There was no call for Rob to beetle his brows at her. She scowled back.

He turned to Cate again. 'Any road, if you just tell me whether you want a lectern or the big screen or owt else I'll be off, and get Annie and me out of your hair.'

'Gosh, no, I shan't need any fancy equipment. This talk's going to be very much off the cuff.' She twinkled at him. She did, Cate Blackwell positively *twinkled*. 'If not off the wall.'

For a moment Annie wondered if she'd been just a little too complacent about Rob and Dr Blackwell. 'Is this Trisha's book club?'

'Oh yes, your sweet little book club,' interposed Leona determinedly. 'As I said, Trish, I'm *sooo* looking forward to coming along, when I can find the time, in fact I'm sure I gave that a mention, too, when I was talking to the reporter, but—'

'Tiptree Park,' said Rob. 'Come on, Nan, I've told you about it often enough. Adult ed centre up Darlington way? Third age learning courses, great place.'

Annie rolled her eyes. 'You have to say that – you're on the board there too, aren't you? God, *third age learning*. Don't those words just sink your heart? Intellectual tiddlywinks for geriatrics – to take their minds off the grim reaper.'

Rob snorted, but Cate Blackwell actually grinned at her. 'I know what you mean,' she said. But then she was twinkling round at Rob again. 'The things I do for old friends.'

'Hey, you're the star of the show, love. The woman in charge of the courses nearly fell off her chair when I said you'd turn up to her Jane Austen day for fifty quid and a cup of tea. Sorry, what's this?'

Trisha, urged on by Leona, was holding out a crumpled copy of the *Bucksford Advertiser*. Rob obediently took it and began reading, glanced up at Leona and then back at the newspaper – before erupting into a guffaw that he tried, unconvincingly, to pass off as a cough. 'Sorry – sorry,' he gasped, as Leona glared at him. 'Just a daft misprint, um, caught my eye.' He clambered to his feet. 'Bloody newspapers these days. Sub-editors went out with typewriter ribbons. Come on, Nan, we need to be off. On yer bike.'

'Shame on me, I know, but that chest of hers really is one of the wonders of the world,' he said as Bernie levered the cork out of a bottle. 'And when I read that caption . . .'

A typo and an unfortunate line-break meant that the words immediately under her photograph ran:

'Leona Parsons in the *bra* of the Century,' wailed Annie delightedly to her friend. 'I mean it went on, of course – should've been *bar* of the Century Hotel where they were launching Kelvin's precious website, et cetera, but, oh God, I thought I'd die laughing when Rob pointed it out to me. How did I miss it first time round? Probably too busy spitting tacks. For that alone, Robbo, I forgive you everything.'

'And what's he to be forgiven for now?' said Bernie, who had unexpectedly proposed joining them for lunch. If she wasn't in the way?

'How could you ever be in our way?' Annie had cried, embracing her.

'Quite,' said Rob, with an oddly lopsided smile.

So clement was the sunshine as April blossomed into May that they were sitting outside, on the front lawn of the Hopkirk Arms. Their wooden picnic table had been personally clothed over by the genial host himself, only sorry he could not escape his kitchen, but Bernie had declared she'd shifted a ton of work that morning, and deserved an hour off.

'Oh, Cate's apparently turned down an invite from her mate Siobhan to join her and her wife in some luxury Tuscan castellano.'

'Castello, I think is the word,' said Rob.

'Whatev. Robbo here seemed to think I might say something inappropriate. I cannot imagine why.'

'Pack in squabbling,' said Bernie. 'You know my views on lovely Cate.'

'And mine,' said Rob. 'Seriously, Nan, I wish you'd get over this daft prejudice. I swear, you'd like her as much as I do, if only you'd give her half a chance.'

Annie saw Bernie smile significantly at her and she glowered in return.

'Shall we talk about something else?' she said and turned back to Rob. 'Starting with your bloody brother?'

Phil had rung last night, she said. To ask – no, let her get this right – to *tell* her he was arriving, on Monday, with a carload of elderly rellies.

'Just the two,' said Rob. 'Margie and Joan.'

'You're already in on this plot, then? I might have known.' Annie swivelled round to Bernie. 'One of whom's away with the dementia fairies, the other's stone deaf on a walking frame, and they're both at least a hundred and ten.'

'It's for their baby brother's funeral,' contributed Rob, grinning. 'Poor bloke was a mere sprig of eighty-three.'

'If it were only that. Family funeral, fair enough. But oh no, my lovely brother-in-law thinks that, since he's driving all the way up north, and nobly collecting them – for which he has to make a whole ten-mile diversion – he may as well dump them on me for an extra couple of days while he does a bit of business in Newcastle. And,' she continued, before Rob could argue, 'having informed me that Jake's old room will suit Joan nicely, with the disabled loo, he then announces that he himself will be kipping down with our Rob at Abbey Mill. So as not to give me extra work, he says. *What?* So as not to have to bellow in Joan's ear and listen to Margie telling us how she used to dance the Gay Gordons with the Duke of Edinburgh.'

'But you're so good with people, Nan,' said Rob, grinning even more, 'that's why everyone loves you.'

'And you can quit laughing,' she said, 'because you needn't think you're escaping. I mean, OK, I wouldn't mind normally, but I've got this ball—'

'No, have you really?'

'Shut up. At the end of that very week, and it's our last committee session, with everyone round at my place just as your family rolls up the drive. I can't rearrange, Monday's the only day Bernie and Dave can manage, so I'll have to expand a plate of sarnies and a bag of crisps into lunch for everyone. And you, my friend,' she said to Rob, 'will be there, believe me, along with your brother, to look after your ancient aunts, while I cope with the committee. What's more,' she concluded unguardedly, 'I won't even have Liz to lend a hand.'

'Oh,' said Rob. 'Why's that then?'

Annie eyed him defiantly. 'She has – other commitments.'

27

'Unless you really can't manage without me,' Liz had said, with the quavering bravery of a staked-up martyr eyeing the flaming torches. 'I know I shall have to face her on the night at the ball. But here, in this house, with so few people . . .'

So few?

Annie had been counting on ten to feed even before Trisha said Cate was keen to attend (a likely story) although she wasn't strictly speaking a member of the committee, but then what could they do about Joey? Of course Annie was happy to welcome Joey, too, and not just because he, at least, was unlikely to disrupt her tightly plotted agenda. She duly ushered the Hough contingent to join Bernie and Hank at the big oak table where Trisha, proudly deputising for Liz as secretary of proceedings, shuffled papers into important piles and flipped open her laptop. Only for Leona to sashay in with Kelvin at her four-inch spiked heel.

'I told Tiger I was sure you wouldn't mind one more,' she said to Annie, with a smile so steely it could have carved the ham. 'You know what us newlyweds are like, we can't bear to be apart.' Tinkly laugh. 'If you can remember so far back?'

Which made thirteen. How appropriate. Not that extra mouths mattered, since Bernie's car had come stacked with chiller boxes, courtesy of her ever-bountiful husband, who would himself be following after he'd fed his own lunch customers. Anyway, Annie didn't give a damn who attended this meeting, committee member or not, because the agenda was less a template for discussion than a list of what she and Hank had decided. All that remained was to delegate tasks appropriately.

She had not allowed for Trisha's conscientious insistence on minuting every last raffle prize, hand-towel and parking cone. Although, OK, she had a point about change. 'Fivers,' she had said, 'never enough.'

'Interesting you went for *this* marble in your kitchen,' murmured Leona. 'I've always felt the white's a bit fishmonger-ish, you know?'

A heated dispute over the relative values of auction lots meant that the list had been reordered several times even before Dominic limped in to enquire about lunch, capsized into a chair beside Hank, and – thank you, son – promptly argued that a balloon flight had to be worth more than a box at a City match, any day.

'Hank and I will finalise the order later,' she began, only for Cate – *Cate* – to chip in that Simon was pressing for details of the auction lots, to prepare his patter. Didn't Trish say he'd asked, in one of his emails?

'Because the best ad-libs are the ones you scripted earlier,' quoted Annie wearily. 'Yes, now you mention it, he did.'

'I hope nothing's gone wrong,' muttered Bernie. 'By the sound of it, madam's been getting herself in a rare old lather . . .'

'Dame Viola? Yes, we were just saying – weren't we, lover? – what a crying shame it is you couldn't persuade Simon to bring his wife. Of course, if I'd been involved from the start, I would have told you she's what you needed to *really* put this ball on the map. After all, who's Simon Spencer compared to a star like Viola Hood? In fact, Kelvin's wondering—'

''Scuse me a second, Leona. Auction list, yes, Annie love, I'll make a note of that. Final version ASAP for Simon. Now what's our prize for the best fancy dress costume?'

'When's he back?' demanded Dominic, looking round as though he expected Simon to walk through the door.

No, said Annie, there was no costume prize . . .

'Flies into London this afternoon . . .' Bernie was holding up crossed fingers.

'. . . because if we could include some personal message about her rich experiences of therapy on his new website . . .'

Well, OK, a bottle of champagne then, if absolutely necessary . . .

'He's promised to let us know when they land, so he has, but you know what he's like . . .'

Annie's head was swivelling in all directions. They weren't organising a kids' fancy-dress party, for Pete's sake, this was a gala ball; dead right, Hank – who wanted to make a pillock of themselves in a Bugs Bunny suit all night? Oh, Leona was entering into the proper spirit of the evening, was she? Marvellous. But could they *please* agree who was to be in charge of flogging the red-carpet arrival photos?

The front doorbell rang.

'Steady on,' said Philip Daley, when Annie flung her arms round him, 'anyone'd think you were pleased to see me.'

'Believe me,' she said, as she broke away to greet the two stout little ladies he was helping up the step. 'You've arrived just in time to stop me committing murder.'

At least, once lunch was served, people dispersed round house and garden with their plates and glasses. Between explaining what an avocado was to Aunty Joan, and sympathising with Margie over the demise of her favourite horse (which she apparently rode alongside Her Maj when they were trooping the colour) Annie was able to vent her frustrations to Rob.

'Democracy,' he said. 'It's a bugger, isn't it?'

His brother had drawn up a chair beside Cate on the terrace. As Annie passed their way with a basket of bread, he was explaining that Jen wasn't with him today because their fourth grandchild was about to pop. But he abruptly broke off to ask – with unusual percipience for a robot – whether Cate was all right; she was looking uncomfortable?

'Touch of backache, that's all,' she said, waving away the bread.

'I'm not surprised,' said Annie, 'sleeping on a lilo.'

'Good God, *fatal*,' cried Phil, with the heartfelt sympathy of a fellow sufferer. Thanks to bloody computers, he said, he'd wasted hours and a small fortune on osteopaths, chiropractors, fancy ergonomic chairs – you name it, he'd tried it.

'Water beds,' stated Leona, whom Annie had already observed circling her brother-in-law with interest. Well, Phil, as she had never denied, was a handsome specimen. 'Believe me, there is nothing like the simple purity of water for supporting and balancing the spine.'

'Been there, done that, mended the punctures and it's a load of tosh,' he said shortly – rarely had Annie felt so much in charity with her brother-in-law.

'I don't think we'd manage one of those contraptions in Trish's room,' said Cate with a wry smile. 'As it is, we're forever tripping over the airbed.'

'You're sleeping on the floor?' squawked Leona. 'Sweetie, you have to get professional help. *Kelvin*!'

'Two minutes, babe. Just asking Hank—'

'Your pusscat needs you here and now, Tiger. I want you to tell me the name of that masseur who does the native American—'

Annie moved on.

'. . . give me an old-fashioned letter any day.' Rob was sitting beside Bernie on the bench by the rose bed. 'The written word, on a decent sheet of paper, preferably composed with a fountain pen.'

'Hark the dinosaur,' snorted Annie, albeit affectionately.

'Emails are written, so they are. And you can always print 'em off if you're so keen on a bit of paper.'

He was shaking his head. 'Sorry, Bernie, but it's not the same at all. There's summat about a keyboard seems to disengage people's brains. Instead of folk thinking what they're writing, you just get this half-baked stream of tripe spewing straight out through the fingers. Reams of it, too.'

'No one could accuse you of that,' said Annie. 'I once had an email from you which was just the letter K. Obviously too much effort to type an O first.'

He had to grin, but pointed out that, in its way, this was a faultless piece of prose. Comprehensible, succinct—

'Get away with your nonsense,' said Bernie. 'Simon writes the most fantastic emails. It's like you can hear him talking, wouldn't you agree, Annie?'

Conscious of several lengthy screeds barely scanned in her inbox, Annie nevertheless was reluctant to hurt her friend's feelings. 'He's . . . certainly an enthusiastic correspondent.'

Rob eyed her. 'Uh-huh?'

'I wish he'd be emailing me now,' said Bernie. 'Their flight's supposed to have got in to Heathrow an hour back, and you can't help fretting.'

'He won't let us down,' said Annie. 'Not again.' She wished she could feel as confident as she sounded. 'Oh look, here's Dave. Lord, whatever's the matter with him?'

Emerging from the kitchen, floral shirt clapping over his capacious abdomen, Dave thundered across the terrace towards them, arms stretched wide.

'He's come!' he bellowed.

'The Messiah?' said Rob.

Almost in the same instant, Annie felt a soft buzz in her back pocket, and saw that Bernie, then Trisha, now Hank – even Cate – were likewise glancing up or behind them, groping in jackets, reaching for their bags, as an email pinged around the committee.

Hurray, back in Blighty at last. Yorkshire next. Can't wait. See you Saturday, amigos, if not before . . . XXX

'Oh thank *God*,' breathed Annie, closing her eyes, phone slack in her hand.

For all she had refused to admit as much, even to herself, let alone her colleagues, she'd feared that something – *someone* – would stop Simon returning. Never mind his promises, she knew – didn't she just know? – how a chronically dependent spouse could swing a wrecking ball through the sturdiest of intentions. But Simon was now, at last, on this side of the Atlantic again, barely more than a couple of hours away. Whatever his wife might try, short of imminent death, he could surely escape to Bucksford for the vital night at least. 'Now I truly can look forward to our ball,' she sighed, heartfelt, and looked up. 'Oh, are you going somewhere?'

Rob had jumped to his feet. 'I need a drink.'

'Dead right,' she said. 'This deserves celebrating.'

In that moment, the ball became *real*. Annie couldn't quite explain what she meant by this, but it was how she felt. Until now it had been so much talk and paper, a stimulating maze of problems, compromises, minor triumphs, major frustrations. Now it had solidified into an *event*. As the day hurtled ever closer, with everything bar a few frills in place, she perversely found this less pleasurable. She did, however, sleep better.

The aunts were despatched with Philip, Margie complimenting her graciously on the first-class service in this hotel, Phil typically unconcerned by having missed the arrival of his new granddaughter.

'They don't get interesting until they can talk,' he explained.

'Or do quadratic equations,' said Annie.

She was amused and rather touched, though, that on the afternoon he arrived to collect his relatives, he struck up something of a bond with Liz. Preoccupied as she was with rounding up the pill packets, cardigans, reading specs and a dozen other items the elderly ladies had scattered round the house, she caught only snatches of their conversation, but gathered they were talking grand opera. She already knew Liz was a fan – yeah well, droopy heroines, doomed passions, it figured – but was surprised to learn that the android himself had become a regular at Covent Garden these days; Glyndebourne, too.

'Which only the likes of you can afford,' she commented.

'The tickets are horribly expensive,' sighed Liz, 'although I truly believe they're worth every penny. But of course, once one adds in the cost of getting down to London, and accommodation and so forth, I mean, *gosh.*'

'Come and stay with us,' he said genially. 'Any time. Jen's never happier than when she's got a houseful.'

Annie embraced him even more fondly on departure than she had when he arrived.

There was just one small jolt to her final preparations. It could have discomposed her more than it actually did, but perhaps by now she had learned, with Simon Spencer, to expect the unexpected.

Late on the Thursday afternoon, with a mere forty-eight hours to go, she was with Hank in the foyer of the Woolshed, hammer in hand, mouth a-bristle with tacks, studying two giant boards covered with hessian for the display of the official photographs. Patrons were to be greeted on arrival by the star attraction himself, under an arc of glamorous spotlights yet to be rigged round the doors to the auditorium, for their handshakes and cheesy grins to be snapped and the results pinned up for (she trusted) immediate sale.

'Won't do, not this colour. It needs painting grey, a really soft grey, to make the photos pop,' she was murmuring, tight-lipped. 'Bit darker than—'

'Hello, darling,' whispered a familiar voice in her ear.

She spun round, nearly swallowing a tack. Simon began neatly gathering up the three she had spluttered out. 'What the hell are you doing here?'

He grinned up at her as he retrieved the last pin. 'Nice to see you too.'

He was looking smart, sun-gilded and – untroubled? As it sank in that he sounded neither apologetic nor wary her panic ebbed, the breath seeped back into her chest and blood thundered to her head. She felt quite dizzy, in fact, and this had nothing to do with Simon kissing her overheated cheeks. He, meanwhile, was genially asking Hank if he'd run across a BBC producer in Manchester – nice chap, fellow Liverpudlian? – to whom he'd been talking about some chat show Viola was booked to do in a couple of weeks' time . . .

'So you haven't come to tell us there's a problem,' she cut in, just to be absolutely sure, 'with your wife?'

He pulled a face. 'No more than usual. No, no, cool down, old love, all's well. I left Vi safe in the care of her devoted aconites.'

Annie relaxed enough to laugh. '*Acolytes*, I think. Aconites are plants. Poisonous, what's more.'

'Right first time, then, because her agent is one very poisonous little weed. But hey, Mac's keeping her on the straight and narrow, so I'm not complaining.'

'And you've come up early? Brilliant.'

'If only,' he said. 'Just zipping here and back in a day, I'm sorry to say. *Officially* to Salford, as I was telling Hank, but the chat show's a piece of cake, only radio, and Viola's always happy to talk about herself. Until the cows come home – dear oh dear, did I just say that? Hush my wicked tongue.' He was weirdly exuberant, as though he were drunk. 'So I tied all that up in a ten-minute phone call, and hopped on the train to York instead, to deliver my son's birthday present in person. And before you say a word, Annie, I know the actual day's a fortnight away, and that I shall be seeing him again in a mere forty-eight hours. *That*, my dears, is the point. I am on a mercy dash to stop dear Dave spraying himself green.'

Hank grinned. 'Yeah, meant to tell you, Annie. Old Dave suddenly had this great idea, right, about coming as Shrek? Bernie's going mental.'

'Aha, not any more. After hasty covert ops with a tape measure by her and a trip to a well-known theatrical costumier by *moi*, my boy will now be appearing in a civilised and, if I say so myself, rather magnificent smoking jacket. Silk brocade with all the trimmings.'

'Wow,' said Annie. 'Sounds fantastic. And you've trekked all this way to deliver it? What a star you are.'

'Any excuse to come to Bucksford, darling, and worth it just to see his face. Besides, I urgently needed to decode Trisha's byzantine running order for the auction.'

She and Hank exchanged glances. 'But I thought we'd emailed you our final list?'

He was holding up a hand. 'Don't worry, all clear now. As mud – no, joking, joking. Bernie ran me round to Chateau Hough, and I have sorted out everything. *Everything*. Actually, she'll be here any second now to wing me back to York and the

London train – so, my brave comrades, tell me quickly, how goes it in the front line?'

Sure enough, after a couple more minutes of merry nonsense, his phone trilled, and he had vanished again. In a puff of Bulgari, according to Hank, sniffing the air appreciatively. *Thé vert?*

'Doesn't do anything for me,' said Annie abstractedly, returning to her hessian.

Only later did it occur to her that, flattered as she was, she hadn't exactly been *fluttered* by Simon's sudden appearance. Good to see him – yes. Reassuring – big time. And truly heartwarming he should go to such lengths for his son. She could just imagine Dave walking ten feet tall in brocaded splendour, courtesy of his dad, the day after tomorrow. But why wasn't she imagining herself floating around the dance floor, à la Ginger Rogers, in Simon Spencer's manly arms?

Perhaps it didn't help that her ballroom skills had yet to advance beyond the hokey-cokey.

28

It is often said you can't enjoy your own party. Annie Stoneycroft had never uttered anything of the kind, and she certainly wasn't about to do so tonight. She was having a ball well before the ball actually began.

She inspected the steaming kitchen alongside Dave, checked the trays of flutes stacked ready for the welcome champagne, and patrolled the expectantly empty ballroom while the band twanged and joshed as they tweaked their sound levels. Ah, that ballroom. Dear Hank had worked theatrical magic. Coloured spotlights played over a glitterball as big as a planet, exquisitely laid round tables flickered with *almost* convincing battery candles (bloody health and safety) and a gleaming dance floor positively impelled her to pirouette across while gazing up at the movie greats flickering from giant screens high on the walls. Liz Taylor smouldered, Spencer Tracy winked, Clark Gable didn't give a damn – and Viola Hood glared down and pointed a pistol.

'Up yours and all,' Annie retorted and twirled into Simon and Bernie.

'My sentiments exactly,' he said, planting a kiss a considerate inch away from her pearly powdered cheek. 'Will I do?'

Tanned, tuxedo-ed and twinkling, he certainly would do, she said as she hugged an equally elegant Bernie. 'Told you your wedding dress would come in again. No, we cannot try

298

out the dance floor,' she added to Simon. 'The punters will be rolling up any minute. Action stations.'

As the first arrivals trod wonderingly up the red carpet in their finery, blinking with very satisfactory amazement at the dazzle of popping flashbulbs (members of the Woolshed Youth Theatre equipped with stage-prop cameras, paparazzi macs and trilbies), only to be posed and photographed properly alongside the star guest, she was dodging hither and thither, charged with purpose. Hank had to be consulted about light levels in the doorway, a stern frown was required for gossipy waitresses (more teenage wannabe thesps) and, God help her, there was a stray dog threatening to cock a leg over the far end of her precious carpet. Annie's most testing challenge, however, turned out to be retaining her celebrity in his allotted station. No sooner was there a lull than the itchy-footed twerp kept dodging out to the pavement, craning round to see who was coming in next.

'Looks like another triumph for you, Nan,' said Rob, who arrived obediently on time, in austerely plain dinner jacket, bringing with him Trisha (as a rotund but jolly Mary Poppins) and Cate (as, no surprise, Cate). Joey, for once, had been left at home in the care of a couple of the steadier members of the rugby club.

'Where's Simon *now*?' she cried. Peering round Rob's outstretched arms, she saw that he had gravitated to the outer door yet again. OK, yes, he might be greeting Trish and her sister, but they were neither here nor there. He should be fixed in the photo-opportunity hotspot. About to plunge off and corral him back to his duties, she halted.

'You look really good, Robbo,' she said. 'I mean, seriously. Terrific.'

'Do you have to sound so bloody amazed?'

She laughed as she moved on again. 'Evening dress. Always does wonders for a man.'

'You don't look too bad yourself,' he called, then turned with a shrug and strolled off into the ballroom.

During the hour timetabled for pre-dinner drinks, she was glad to see him chatting to Liz, who had been a quaking wreck in Annie's bedroom just a few hours earlier, but was now – thanks to a large gin and a little bullying – looking very slinky indeed in a black number Annie had recklessly bought at the start of a crash diet last year and never quite managed to zip up. Meanwhile, Kelvin Parsons, caped and wrinkly-tighted, sheepishly padded in as – oh bliss – Batman, behind Catwoman, all silvery whiskers, spike-heel boots and spectacular cleavage.

'She who pays the piper hires the costumes?' murmured Hank, as they watched the purring Leona drape her tail round a wide-eyed Simon for the photographer.

'Talk about cat and mouse,' Annie said a few minutes later, hauling Simon away from their table where he had been about to pull up a chair between Liz and Cate. 'You looked bloody petrified by Mrs Parsons. Come on, no slacking. I need you to charm the Loadsadosh Lumleys.'

Simon sighed. 'Haven't I earned a break yet?'

'Not until we sit down to eat.'

Even after the starters were served when, with heavy irony, he thanked her for so magnanimously allowing him this brief respite to zip up his grin, give his over-shaken right hand a rest and say 'fuck' if he fucking well felt like it, Annie herself did not let up. There were raffles to be monitored, drinks to be supplied to the jazz pianist soulfully thrumming away, tardy wine waiters – no end of distractions for an OCD, power-crazed hag, as she cheerily described herself to Rob who was seated beside her, when she returned once more to her place during the pudding course.

'I wouldn't say hag,' he responded. 'Harridan, maybe.'

'Sod off. Is your mandarin tart OK?'

'Spot on. Want me to help you out with yours?'

She pushed her plate towards him, as she had the earlier and equally sumptuous dishes, too taut-strung to eat. Fortunately, her table was composed entirely of committee colleagues and loved ones – well, if you included Cate in that number – but no one whom she could not cheerfully abandon half the time. Or say fuck to, as Simon put it. Thank the Lord, too, that they'd opted to hire tables for ten, and she had thus been able to banish their newest committee member to the far side of the dance floor, where Leona was now flashing her considerable assets at a puce-cheeked Hugo King.

Not that she had ignored the Kings herself (salmon fishing, dear friends, *so* generous), nor, she trusted, any other of their esteemed patrons and donors. Throughout the meal, she had made regular excursions round the tables, beaming, laughing, hugging, thanking.

'Being *nice*,' she said darkly to Rob now.

'Highly unnatural,' he agreed with a grin. He nodded towards her untouched glass. 'When can you let rip?'

'I may permit myself a modest libation,' she declared, 'when we've done the fucking auction.'

'. . . your final chance, ladies and gentlemen. Yes, my hammer is about to fall for the very last time. So if you're getting sick to the back of your expensive teeth at the sound of my voice . . . Look, if our respected dental surgeon over there on table eight – oh indeed, I know who you are, Mr Taylor, and if you can splash out on that hot-air balloon trip you're obviously making far too much money out of these fine people's gnashers. No, seriously now, if you're all dying to shift me off your bloody stage so you can crack on with the dancing, come on, then.

This is your chance to be rid of me. Shout out a thousand smackers and I'll be gone in a flash, I promise. No seriously, do I hear five-fifty? Five then? Sir, you are a hero. Six – yes six hundred pounds. *Respect*. Seven? Six-sixty?'

'Isn't he marvellous?' said Liz, as Annie tottered back to their table from her post beside the auctioneer, to whom she had been whispering the identity of the bidders while scribbling, issuing payment chits to the young runners and stabbing her calculator. The crowd was still hooting and cheering as Simon took a last bow, tossed his gavel into the air, caught it one-handed, and skipped off the platform.

'Give or take the odd hundred, I think we might have doubled our target for the auction,' she said dazedly. 'Oh no – not a chance.' This was addressed to the triumphant auctioneer who, as bouncy as a squirrel on amphetamines, had pranced up to her, hand imperiously out-thrust for a dance, even though he could surely see her own arms were piled high with clipboard, calculator and a crumpled wad of cash. 'Find yourself another partner, sunshine,' she said, setting down her load and clamping a hand over the fluttering banknotes. 'I need some recovery time.'

Poor Simon, because Cate, to whom he politely turned next, refused – what a surprise – citing back troubles. She might actually have been telling the truth because even Simon, hyper as he was, couldn't miss the spasm that twisted her face as he tried to seize her hand. Giving up, with an exaggerated sigh, he appealed to Liz instead. Much better idea. Annie hadn't seen her friend's face light up like that since the days before *you know who* entered their lives. Thus far, thankfully, the tighted superhero had remained largely invisible in the crowd across the room.

'Everyone looks very happy, don't they?' observed Cate. Annie had heard ashes-to-ashes and dust-to-dust delivered with more party spirit.

But Liz and Simon were indeed looking happy. They made a handsome couple and Liz, surprisingly, was no slouch when it came to matching his fancy footwork. Years of training in the hard school of parish tea dances, no doubt. Dave, meanwhile, mightily magnificent in crimson brocade, was whisking Bernie across the floor in a complicated fandango yet to be recognised by the *Strictly* fraternity, while Hank performed nifty disco manoeuvres around a sozzled Maggie King. Even Trisha and Dominic were out there, tumbling against one another, and laughing their heads off.

'You going to give us a whirl then, Nan? When you're recovered.'

'Never tell me you're offering to dance, Bobsy-Boy?'

'You know me. Half a glass of wine and I'm anybody's.'

'I'll hold you to that, once I've checked my sums. Yeah, and got my breath back.'

In the event, however, it was to be a full hour before Annie could seize Rob by the hand and tug him, mock-protesting, onto the floor. She didn't even manage a dance with Simon, besieged as he was with invitations from coyly smiling fans. As she said to him, when he briefly returned to the table and pretended to cower behind the stiff-spined Cate, it was a shame they hadn't thought of hiring his services out. Tenner a dance would've been a nice little earner.

'Fifty, if you don't mind. My body may be for sale, honey, but no one's gonna call me cheap.'

Even Cate had smiled.

It was not other partners, however, that so postponed her dance with Rob, nor the charm and smarm circuit, as Simon described her labours round the room. It began with an enigmatic summons from Hank, who linked an insistent arm through hers and tugged her out into the empty foyer. He was black-clad, head to toe, an inky mandarin-collared shirt under his DJ and pipe-cleaner scrawny trousers, with the trilby pushed back on his head.

'Yo there, preacher man,' declared Annie merrily, who had by then gulped down a restorative glass or two. On an empty stomach. A cold draught from the door left ajar by smokers was making her head swim. 'I'd been wondering what you reminded me of – in a Western, you know? Quite a sinister vibe, actually.'

'Yer what?'

'Cool, though. *Love* the earring.'

He rolled his eyes. 'Be serious, will you?' He lowered his voice. 'Thing is, uh, you're the one really knows Sly and, like, the situation with his wife? Better than me, any rate, and I'm wondering is this just a wind-up? That's why I need a word before I go opening my big gob.'

Annie was squinting back into the ballroom. 'Wow, will you look at Catwoman doing the twist? I hope we've a doctor in the house because some of the blokes round her look like they might be on the verge of a coronary—'

'Listen, man, this is *big*,' Hank moved closer. 'I've just got an email, right, from a guy called Randolph Mackley? I mean, I know the agency, everyone's heard of Sparmont, and Viola Hood's only one of the names they handle. But this dude reckons she's offering us an interview – on stage, y'know with film clips on a screen if we want, follow-up Q and A from the floor? A whole fucking evening of Dame Vi, totes free and gratis, in aid of the appeal. Here in this theatre.' He whistled. 'Can you get your head round that? *Us*, hosting a live audience with Viola Hood?'

He had her attention now. 'Come again?' Annie stared at him, blinking away the swirl of wine. 'She wants to . . .? Nah, rubbish, Simon would've told us.'

'That's what I *mean*, Annie. Am I gonna put my foot in one big pile of shit here? Simon doesn't know fuck all about it.'

It transpired, however, that Simon did know something, at least, of his wife's proposal.

She and Hank scooped him out of the arms of a disconsolate Lady Mayoress and, whispering, led him into a huddle at the rear of their table.

'Excuse us, darling,' he said, leaning round Hank to grimace at Cate, who was the only other occupant at the time. 'These two are hell-bent on talking shop. I'd go find yourself more entertaining company if I were you.'

With a thin smile, she turned aside, but remained in her chair.

Sure, he resumed, swivelling back to them, Vi had floated this crackbrained notion past him. After he'd returned from, ahem, arranging her chat-show in Manchester, clean out of the blue she'd proposed doing a similar gig here. Since she was travelling north anyway, she said – and never mind him pointing out that Manchester was a hundred miles t'other side of the Pennines. She felt she should support his charity work, she said – so strangely keen as he seemed to be on this joint in the back end of nowhere . . .

'Keen as *she* is to see what you've been getting up to here, more like,' interposed Annie. 'Oh c'mon, Simon, don't play shocked. You've moaned enough about her keeping tabs on you. Maybe she thinks it's time she met your son?' She took a reckless swig of wine. 'Come to that, maybe it *is* time.'

'Since Viola's yet to mention my son by name, I doubt it,' he retorted sharply. 'No, she . . . Well, God knows what she's about. Anyway, I told her it was a non-starter. Hank here can't re-jig his programming just to accommodate her whims.'

The artistic director stared at him. 'You kidding? When all I've got to switch is a choir rehearsal? Which this Randolph Mackley already knew from checking the website.'

'Look, I don't want to be rude about Viola.' Simon glanced round, lowering his voice further, but the people nearby were dancing, drinking, laughing, paying no heed to them – save, perhaps, for Cate Blackwell who, Annie noticed, was making a poor pretence of not earwigging. Couldn't blame her. More interesting than Trisha and Dave attempting to pogo. 'She is a remarkable artist—'

'No need to tell me that, mate.'

'—and even more temperamental than most, so if she pulled out on you, at the last minute? Which I'm afraid she's only too famous for doing. Christ, I even felt obliged to drop a warning in the ear of the guy at the Beeb, but it's a pre-record so he was willing to take his chances. Frankly, with the noises coming out of the rehearsal room, I wouldn't be surprised if she got on a plane back to LA tomorrow, and to hell with *Darling Clementine.*'

'So . . .' Hank shoved back his hat. 'So – we make it pay on the door, why not? Top prices across the house, mind. And what with that, and tonight, we won't just get our new community studio, I could be looking at an upgrade for the frigging lighting grid, too. Guys, this is *awesome.*'

Annie looked from one to the other. Excitement might be blinding Hank to Simon's reluctance, but not her. Before she could ask why he was so opposed to his wife coming to Bucksford, though, he threw back his head. 'To hell with it,' he said. 'Once Vi stamps her foot there's no stopping her. Besides, if she does this gig, *if* . . .' He spoke more loudly now and deliberately, as though convincing himself. 'Why should it matter? No big deal.'

'Fuck of a big deal for us.' Hank was already on his feet. 'You saying I can announce it tonight?'

Simon scowled. 'Why not? Line up your rich punters. Just make sure you warn them it might never happen. Offer 'em a coach trip to Loch Ness while you're at it,' he added, raising his voice as Hank hurried away, mobile already in hand, saying he must ring this Mac pronto, double-double check the offer was for real. 'They might have more chance of seeing that monster.'

'What's this about – a Mac?' asked Dominic as he lowered himself into the chair beside them, frowning at Hank's retreating figure.

'Believe me, you don't wanna know,' said Simon. 'Someone like to give me a drink? And make it a large one.'

Even Annie could not have plotted a more spectacular climax to the evening. They had determined Hank would make the announcement at eleven, when the band took a break. Tiring of Simon's grumpy insistence that he would have nothing to do with this crazy scheme – *nothing* – she seconded Cate Blackwell's tart observation that she, for one, would be intrigued to see the famous Viola Hood.

'Because it's quite something, isn't it, her offering to come here?' Annie said to Rob, as she finally led him onto the dance floor. 'A real coup for us, whatever Simon says. In fact, I reckon this has been a pretty good night all round.'

'Understatement of the century,' said Rob and, to her surprise, yanked her into his arms.

'Blimey, I thought this was supposed to be a jive—' She was interrupted by a burst of protesting laughter behind her and twisted round. 'Uh-oh, just when you think nothing can go wrong . . .'

Dave, dear Dave, had clambered onto the platform and wrested the microphone from a bewildered band leader.

Rob released her. 'He's not going to sing, is he?'

Dave was not going to sing. No, full of bonhomie and burgundy, he thought it was time to shake the party up a bit. Didn't they all agree?

The cheers of assent were wary.

He just beamed as he boomed on. 'So gents, listen up. You've to let your ladies go – that's it, hands off, step clean away. Girls, stay right where you are. Now then, men, close your eyes. No sneaky peeking – yes, I'm talking about you, Brian Humble.'

'Did he train at Butlin's?' said Rob in an undervoice.

'Shush!'

'Three steps forward, gents, and keep them peepers tight. Turn to your right. Ladies, you're allowed to give 'em a prod if they tread on your fancy frocks. Now another two steps. Turn again. And . . . open your eyes!'

'Bet you didn't cover this in your risk assessment,' said Annie when Rob, unlike his fellow males who were blundering around in gales of laughter, somehow arrived neatly back at her side as they were instructed to bow to the nearest lady and ask her nicely to dance. 'You *cheated.*'

'I certainly did,' he said, taking firm hold of her. 'I'm an old hand at this game. You forget we Daleys actually went to holiday camps, unlike you posh types up—' He broke off. 'What's going on there?'

Batman, wings outspread, had swooped to a halt and opened his eyes in front of – oh God – plumb in front of Liz, who had originally taken to the floor with some elderly codger from St Stephen's.

'This some kinda sick joke?' he snorted, and spun on his heel, sneering something about leaving dumb kiddy games to the geriatrics. To make matters worse, Liz was frozen to the spot, eyes wide with shock, chin a-quiver. Annie hurried towards her, but Rob got there first.

'Mrs Jones,' he said, with a deep bow, 'will you do me the honour?' He winked. 'Seeing as how the Caped Crusader's obviously been caught short. Prostate trouble at his age, I shouldn't wonder, so let's hope the poor sod can get out of his tights in time.'

There was laughter from the surrounding couples, but Rob permitted himself only a flicker of a smile as he curved an arm round Liz. Leaning forward, he whispered something into her ear, which – bless him – even surprised a watery giggle out of her as they started to dance.

Annie could have hugged him.

29

The revels were dwindling to an end before she encountered Rob again.

People were draining their glasses, ambling around in search of discarded fancy-dress hats, scrawling cheques for auction lots and mumbling into phones for transport. There remained a happy buzz about the place though, thought Annie, the warm afterglow of a good time had by all. Hank said that the massed gasp of awe which followed his announcement of Dame Viola's forthcoming appearance gave him the biggest kick he'd had out of an audience his whole life. And if, to his regret, he couldn't accept advance bookings, tonight's money was still flowing freely. The photos had sold well but – no denying it – not half so fast as Trisha's napkins. The determination of certain dinner-party hostesses to acquire a round half-dozen or more had triggered a black market and (reportedly) a near punch-up at one table. Annie had just accepted another roll of tenners with due gratitude and a weary kiss, and was heading towards the band to thank them as they packed away their gear, when she felt a hand on her shoulder and spun round rather too fast.

'Robbo!' she cried, stuffing the money into her cleavage so she could grab his arm. Not that she required support, as she was anxious to assure him. Her legs were wobbly from exhaustion, not booze. Well, chiefly. 'Been wanting to talk t'you for *hours*. That was so brilliant of you. Juss brilliant, brilliant, brilliant. Poor Liz. She's so grateful.'

'I've been down in the bar with her, actually, having a chat in the quiet.' He shook his head. 'I got your friend all wrong, you know. I thought – well, forget what I thought. The old working-class chip, like as not. I should've listened to you, Nan. She's all right is Liz, and she damned well does deserve to spread her wings. A nice woman, a good woman. And a sight brighter than she lets on.'

One confession deserves another, particularly when tired, a little drunk and feeling benevolent towards one and all. 'It was all my fault, the thing tonight,' declared Annie. 'Him, fucking Batman, I mean. I did try, you know, to pair those two together. But—'

'I was wrong about Kelvin Parsons and all,' interrupted Rob. 'I used to think he was just a harmless idiot. Now I real-ise the guy's a total prick.'

'Oh Rob,' she said. 'I do love you.'

'You always do when you're pissed – oh, Trish, yeah, with you in a tick. Got your coats, have you? Look, Annie, love . . .'

But her shoulder had now been grabbed by Simon. 'So my old darling, has this boy done good? Have I earned a great big smacker?'

'You bloody well have,' she said, and tottered into his wait-ing arms.

Didn't mean a thing, of course.

Simon Spencer was kissing everybody, and he was a lot drunker than Annie. He must have been applying himself to the bottle with gusto in the latter part of the evening. Actually, she wasn't really pissed at all – thank you, Rob Daley – just *tired*, one hundred per cent cream-crackered. She slept as soundly as a dormouse, which proves sobriety, does it not?

And, moreover, woke as bright and early as a robin. All set to go bob-bob-bobbing straight back to the Woolshed on her bike, to assist with the clearing-up.

Actually what impelled her down the hill long before the Sunday bells started clanking was her urgent desire to establish exactly how much money they'd made, when every last crumpled fiver was included. Just you wait, Hugo and Maggie King. This was going to be the Big One.

'Can't tell you 'til Liz gets here,' said Hank. 'She's the spreadsheet queen.' He threw up a hand. 'Man, we played a blinder last night, didn't we?'

'We sure did,' she said, high-fiving him with gusto.

'And, uh, is Dom OK?'

Annie realised she'd scarcely given a thought to her son since adjusting his scrambled bow-tie prior to the ball, and observing (lovingly, of course) that he could have done with standing closer to his razor, because if he was so much as dreaming of growing a beard she would disinherit him. 'Well, he hadn't surfaced when I left. Naturally. Although as a matter of fact I don't think he drank a huge amount. For once. He was quite subdued in the cab home.' She chuckled. 'I was the one singing. Why d'you ask?'

Hank shrugged. 'He was a bit . . . Well, late on, it was like he wanted to say something to me, kept starting and stopping, then . . . Oh, I dunno, probably imagining things. You see his mate Kit Grayson snogging the Chief Constable's daughter, by the way? With a fucking spliff sticking out of his back pocket?'

'Never!' cried Annie. 'What was Kelvin bending your ear about as I left? Too much to hope he was apologising, I suppose.'

'What for?'

'Doesn't matter. Made a pig of himself on the dance floor. Where'd you want this stand to go?'

'Foyer. Here, I'll give you a hand. Nah, he was on about the Viola gig like everyone else. Big fan, obviously. And did you clock that weird frock on . . .'

They continued to discuss the previous night – outfits, overheard conversations, speculations, scandal – as they stacked chairs, folded tables and gathered up debris, a post-mortem so entertaining Annie had almost forgotten what had brought her down here at such an early hour until Liz appeared in the entrance to the auditorium.

'About time, you slacker,' she called, straightening up with a stifled groan. 'Come on over, love, we're dying to hear the glad tidings . . .'

Then she stopped. Liz was chalk-faced and visibly shaking. And now here was Simon a step behind, with a steadying hand under her elbow.

She and Hank exchanged glances. 'Oh Lord,' Annie murmured to herself, 'has the Caped Crusader struck again?'

Fortunately not. If fortunate was the word – because it seemed Liz had been mugged. Well, had nearly been mugged. Or, as it disjointedly emerged, had thought she *might* be mugged. She was barely able to string two syllables together, other than to thank Simon, over and over again, for coming to her rescue.

'It was nothing. Truly,' he said, keeping a bracing arm round her as Hank administered tea, and Annie tried to establish what had occurred.

Her friend, it seemed, had been walking home from matins – *church*, of course. No need to keep apologising, she told Liz, they now understood why she had arrived late. So?

Apparently, she'd diverted to draw some cash from the hole in the wall – outside that little convenience store round the corner from Trisha, did they know the one she meant, with the steel shutters?

'Sure, sure, cheap booze and lottery cards,' said Annie, restraining her impatience with difficulty. '*And?*'

'There was a gang of them came up to me, all shaved heads and, you know, tattoos.'

'Four,' said Simon quietly. 'Just lads really, mooching around.'

'With cigarettes hanging out of their mouths, and cans of beer. And on a Sunday morning, too,' said Liz.

Simon suppressed a grin. 'I know, shocking. So far as I can gather, they were asking Liz if she could spare a tenner.'

'They were *threatening* me.'

'I happened to be driving past, saw her looking a bit upset.'

'I was petrified.'

'So I stopped, got out and, as it were, suggested they move along.'

'You were so brave.'

'Oh, massively. The one with the guns and roses on his neck said, hey, you the bloke off the telly? Doncher read the news or summat? I said, got me in one, mate, and if you don't want to find yourself featuring on it for harassing this lady, best move along, eh? Rather a stupid thing to say, now I come to think about it, because there's nothing most people want more than to get their ugly mugs on the box, but it seemed to do the trick. A knight in shining armour, I think not. However, dear Liz, before I clamber back on my white charger and return to London, are you going to produce your sums and tell us the grand total? We're all on tenterhooks.'

'I'm still gobsmacked,' declared Annie a few hours later, as she clamped the lock on her bike and strode past Liz into the sitting room at 2 Station Terrace. She was referring to the success of their fundraising, not to her friend's recent trauma. She had, however, insisted on following Liz home to make sure she was fully recovered. Nobly suppressing a query as to how that pair of china dogs had found their way back onto the mantelpiece, she now repeated her offer of supper and a bed at the Red House, if her friend felt the least qualm about being in her house alone.

'I shall be fine,' said Liz, pale but resolute. 'And I have something for you, Annie.' So saying, she produced a creased bundle of white cloth from a drawer in the sideboard. Catching a fold between her teeth, she pulled a small hole, dug her fingers in – and ripped. 'I'm sure you could use some dusters. It's pure cotton.'

Annie stared at her. 'Well, I dare say. But—'

'This is a pillowcase,' she said, still tearing. On reaching the tougher area of the border, she bent over, wedged one corner under her foot, and gave an even mightier tug. 'The pillow-case – *he*, you know, slept on.'

'You mean—'

'Kelvin' – *rip!* – 'Parsons.'

'Bloody hell.'

'Which I have been foolish' – *rip!* – 'sentimental' – *rip!* – 'in fact totally insane enough to keep all this time. Unwashed. So I'd put it through a boil cycle if I were you.' She gathered up the pieces, and held them out to Annie. 'I wanted you to have it.'

'I will – clean the floor with these cloths,' Annie said solemnly. 'Better still, the lav. Love, what can I say? Other than *well done*.' However, she could not help chuckling. 'My oh my, your face. You didn't so much tear that thing up as bloody well eviscerate it.'

Even Liz smiled. 'I did rather, didn't I? And I feel an awful lot better for it.'

As she stuffed the discarded relics into a carrier bag and made for the door, Annie couldn't resist pausing to glance back at her friend. 'There wouldn't, I suppose, be someone else now, someone who has, you know, earned your gratitude?'

Liz did not reply immediately but Annie saw the faint blush, the way her gaze dropped to her ring finger.

'No need to say a word,' she continued hastily. 'I didn't mean to embarrass you.'

'No, no, you've every right to ask.' Liz's tone was serious. 'After all the stupid fuss I've inflicted on you. But I've learned a great deal, these past few months, thanks to you, Annie. No, really, it's true. And I'm deeply grateful. So I don't need you to tell me this is just another silly pipe dream – well, even sillier. Out of the realms of all possibility, I dare say. You've taught me how much wiser it is to keep this sort of thing to oneself. Believe me, I am never, ever going to make such a nincompoop of myself again.' She managed a tremulous giggle. 'And nor am I going to make your life hell by moping around and – and crying into my cappuccino. Not this time.'

'Liz,' said Annie, embracing her warmly, 'you are a star. I salute you.'

It came as no surprise, of course, that Liz should now be nurturing a shy pash for Simon. Annie had foreseen just such a possibility, had she not? And, fingers crossed, it did indeed seem to be having a beneficial effect. Just so long as Liz remained realistic about her non-existent chances.

Only when she was in her pyjamas and preparing to drop into bed that night did it occur to Annie to ask herself how she would feel if ever – in some crazy alternative universe – Simon were to decide that Liz was the agreeable, elegant and blessedly sane woman with whom he could one day settle in his beloved Yorkshire.

Wouldn't that be a turn-up for the books? Swabbing off her mascara, she grinned a little shamefacedly at her reflection in the dressing-table mirror as she acknowledged that such a reversal of what had always seemed the natural order might take some getting used to, accustomed as she was to playing beneficent queen bee around Liz. Grandly glorious Mrs Simon Spencer would be a different proposition to humbly grateful Mrs Elizabeth Jones. Still, that was neither here nor there. Serve Annie right, even. Rob was always hinting, if not actually saying, she would benefit from a few set-downs. Smug bugger, what did he know?

No, never mind how she'd feel about Liz. The shaker was that this led her to examine exactly what she felt about Simon. Or rather . . . did *not* feel? Because when she looked deep into her own soul – and she *did* look deep; she peered, she poked, she prodded the murkiest old corners – she found she . . . wouldn't give a stuff. Not if he waltzed off with Liz, nor indeed with anyone else.

At this moment, she could look herself in the face – very literally, and was that a spot erupting on her nose, dammit? – yes, she could look at herself and state, with wondering reluctance but absolute truth, that she no more wanted to welcome Simon into her bed at this moment than she wanted to cut off her undeniably spotty nose.

Was she *mad*? This was Simon Spencer. Not just drop-dead delicious and smart-as-a-whip Simon, but famously sexy and (let's be honest) sexily famous Simon. Even without that seductive aura of celebrity, though, the man himself was surely everything a woman could desire, from the mischievous spark in his eye to the shine on his faultlessly well-chosen shoes. Admittedly, he could on occasion be a bit of a pain, with the mistimed jokes and endless twaddly emails, but so what? No one's perfect, and he was still gorgeous. And yet, somehow, it seemed she no longer ached for him. In fact, had she ever wanted him, *seriously*? God, had she grown too wedded to the luxuries of single life, the old loo-seat-down, top-on-the-toothpaste syndrome? Please God let it not just be her ageing hormones. She was bone weary. Maybe she'd feel differently tomorrow?

She shook her head in sad bewilderment, let out a body-wrenching yawn and flopped into bed.

'Don't even try to talk him out of it,' said Bernie, casting up her eyes. 'Isn't it just our luck, that the very day her ladyship deigns to descend on Bucksford has to be my boy's birthday? So of course he's got to roll 'em together with another feckin' party. No, poppet, thanks for the offer but much as I'd love a coffee and a good old gossip, I've the girls in the car. Anyway I need to get home before I find he's booked a bloody marquee, for all I keep telling him the council might have a thing or two to say about *that*.'

A week had passed. A rather flat week, inevitably, in the aftermath of the ball, although there was plenty to occupy Annie who, perforce, had been neglecting too much of the mundane business of day-to-day life recently, from overdue gas bills to an audible skitter of what she trusted was only mice in the attic. Crawling behind a sagging chaise longue she had been intending to reupholster these past several years to lay traps, however, she did at least stumble upon a dusty bin liner containing more handsome oddments from her former business. She dutifully carried it downstairs for sifting and onward transit to Trisha, when she had the time and patience. Patience that was wearing thin with her morose son.

'How's your play coming along?' she had enquired with something of a satirical edge. And was not surprised when he blinked at her in palpable bewilderment.

'Oh, that.' He hunched a shoulder. 'It's, you know, really hard. Gut-wrenching, if you're trying to write honestly.'

'So your father regularly claimed,' she had retorted. 'Before taking himself off to the boozer. Maybe it'd help the creative flow if you tidied the rubbish tip formerly known as your bedroom?'

At least Liz was a transformed creature, as chirpy as a cricket, actually singing as she instructed Annie in the correct method of training a climbing rose. Yeah, life was as ditchwater dreary as that. Gardening, for pity's sake – yet another stop on the highway to the hereafter. It'd be carpet bowls next. Even so, she found it difficult now, with Bernie, to evince much enthusiasm for this proposed birthday bash of Dave's.

'I can't quite get my head round this,' she complained. 'You say he's planning a picnic – in the *park*?'

'If you can call that scrubby bit of grass next to the town hall a park. Where my husband's grand notion is we all stand around in our finery and drink too much before we stagger along to the Woolshed to watch Dame Viola's star turn in the interview chair.'

'But coming right on top of the ball . . .' She handed her friend two of the empty chiller boxes she had called to collect after leaving them here on what now seemed the very distant day of their committee lunch, and picked up the third herself, to follow her out to the Mini.

'I know.' Bernie threw open the boot. 'Only a week away – well, a week tomorrow. And it's another bank holiday weekend, what's more. God, don't the bloody days fly. It'll be June before you can blink.'

'But it's not as if Dave's ever had a good word for the woman. Understandably, I dare say, under the circs, but even so . . .'

'Tell me about it. Mad old bag is the polite version. The rest I couldn't feckin' repeat with—' She stopped, and smiled radiantly at the two little faces strapped into the back seat. 'With you in a minute, my lovelies.' She turned back to Annie and lowered her voice. 'But Viola Hood coming to this town is a historic event. He says. All Bucksford is going to be at the Woolshed to see her. He says. And as he also says – purple in the face, because the words will stick in his throat, you know? – she is his stepmother.'

Annie nearly dropped her box. 'He's never inviting her to join us for his picnic?'

Bernie guffawed. 'He was talking last night about sending her in a nice little peanut butter sandwich, just in case she gets peckish in the interval. Such a wicked boy as he is. No, he won't be asking her along. But you know my Dave. Any excuse for a knees-up. And to peacock around in his lovely jacket again, from which, by the way, I have miraculously managed to remove the cream he sloshed over it . . .'

Annie shrugged. 'Well, I suppose we might as well meet somewhere, since we're all going to see Viola anyway . . .'

'Exactly. Quick drink and a butty *al fresco*, before we troop into the theatre, that's all it's going to be. Or that's what I keep telling him. Sunday, five o'clock, bring your own rug – and an umbrella, if you've any sense. The long-range forecast's terrible – course it is, it's a bank holiday weekend – but will he listen?'

30

'Wow, Mum, your social life these days.'

'I know, I know,' groaned Annie, but she smiled as she lolled back in her chair, phone at her ear. 'Shame you couldn't get back for the ball, though.'

'I had to say I'd extend my contract a couple more weeks. Honestly, these tosspots couldn't build a sandcastle in the Sahara. Someone has to take charge.'

'That's my daughter. So there's no chance you'll be home for this birthday thrash of Dave's on Sunday, obviously. Bernie can say what she likes about a few sandwiches, but we all know Dave. Foie gras and caviar is probably the least of it.'

'I'd be well up for a party, but you surely don't think I'd want to watch that vile woman boring on about herself and her glittering career?' snorted Martha. 'Apart from the fact she's about ninety-two and I can't remember a thing she was in, you're the one told me it was her stopped them filming Dad's book. I'd only go to chuck a brick. But don't worry. I'll be home in time for *your* birthday, deffo.' She laughed with the cheery insouciance of youth. 'I've actually booked my flight. After all, it's the big six-O, isn't it?'

'Thank you so much for reminding me,' said her mother.

'Darling, can't you persuade my adorable but pigheaded son to forget this party?'

Another day, another phone call. This one from an ultra-luxe serviced apartment in Knightsbridge, as rented by Dame Viola during rehearsals. *Darling Clementine* was apparently due to premiere ten days after her imminent appearance in Bucksford. Ticket sales for the tour were selling just fine, said her husband sourly, but unless some foolhardy impresario wanted to bring the play into town, receipts from venues specifically chosen for being small and low key were unlikely to cover Vi's manicure bills, let alone five-star hotel suites up and down the country. Why should he worry, though? She could afford to take the hit and it cost less than rehab . . .

'. . . to keep her off the hooch. So far, anyhow. But if she sees Dave – my bastard child, as she so charmingly refers to him – hosting a jolly great junket on the theatre doorstep Sunday night . . .'

Moan moan moan. When he was in this self-pitying mood, Annie found it hard to remember why she'd ever fancied her chances with Simon in the first place. Once, she would have been thrilled to serve as his confidante. Now she was glancing at the clock so see if she was missing *The Archers*. However, tempting as it was to suggest he man up – and shut up – she merely pointed out that the proposed picnic was actually a couple of hundred yards round the corner from the Woolshed, so his wife need never know anything about it. 'Although I can't see what difference it makes. Dave's going to be in the audience for her interview. We all are.'

'Yes and I wish you weren't. Sorry, I don't mean you – in fact, not you at all, darling, it's just . . .' His voice rose to an Oscar-worthy wail of anguish. 'Why oh why did I have to go on to Viola about this being such a little gem of a theatre? I mean the Woolshed's great, sure, but pitching in with the appeal was just an excuse for coming back to Bucksford. I never imagined she'd want to clamber aboard the bandwagon herself.'

'You should've told her this gem of a theatre's actually a sooty old mill.' Annie grinned into the phone. 'Given her the dark, satanic, grim-up-north routine. Eeh bah gum.'

'It isn't funny, Annie.'

'Lighten up, will you? The last thing we want is her pulling out now. For goodness' sake, there's only three days to go and Hank's already planned how to spend all the extra dosh she'll bring in. What's your problem?'

'If you knew Viola, you wouldn't ask. I've tried everything to put her off, warned her the theatre's in a very rough part of town—'

'Excuse me?'

'I even told her about Liz getting mugged on her way round there.' He had the grace to sound ashamed. 'Vi's touchy about personal security.'

'You told her that with a straight face, you bastard? Pete's sake, you'll be claiming next Kit Grayson runs the town as a drugs cartel.'

'That the kid got his cannabis farm raided?'

'*Mugged*, my foot. As if—' Annie stopped laughing. 'Come again – Kit? Are you saying he's had the police round?'

He wasn't listening. 'I should never have allowed it to get this far. I must've been off my head letting Hank talk me into it. I'm serious, darling, don't you understand? My whole life could be at stake here.'

'Your life,' she said, before she could stop herself, 'or your pension for life?'

There was a silence. 'Well, thanks a bunch,' he said, even as she began to apologise. 'So I don't want Viola stripping me of every penny in the courts, is that such a crime? Although for your information, I'd already come round to thinking I'd give the lot up.' His voice rose. 'I would, truly and honestly, darling. I'm willing to sacrifice everything if I can just to be with the woman I love, the only woman I could ever love, and God knows, I've been wanting to say this to you for so long but . . .'

What? Annie's phone actually slipped from her hand and bounced from table to flagged floor. He surely couldn't mean . . . Ridiculous. Sure, she knew he liked her. She *liked* him. Well, when he wasn't being a pain in the arse. But to talk of love? When they'd never so much as . . . She hastily scrambled down to retrieve her mobile – uncracked, phew – and re-clamped it to her ear only to find he was still gabbling away like a man possessed.

'. . . going crazy stuck here in London, with half my emails ignored and even when I'm in Bucksford, it's bloody impossible to snatch ten words together without other people muscling in, and the Vi situation's such a tinder-box, do you wonder I sometimes behave like a total see-you-next-Tuesday? Don't argue, Annie, I *know* I have, and I've tried and tried to explain but . . . Anyway, I've made my mind up now. I'm going to write. A letter, I mean, a proper old-fashioned paper job, not a rubbishy email that never gets read. Won't that prove I mean it, that I'm not just fooling around?' Just as well he didn't wait for an answer, because she was incapable of speech. 'Jesus, darling, I'm sorry, I never meant to get into all this with you now before I've written the thing, but you'll understand, I know you will, because I've always felt you guessed how I felt even if I never found the right moment to—' He broke off. 'Oh, *shit.*'

Quite. At the same moment, however, she heard Dominic's voice calling up the stairs.

'She's back.' Simon was now whispering. 'I thought she was going on to dinner with Mac but . . . I'm so sorry, Annie, I've made a pig's ear of this. We need to talk properly.'

'Don't worry,' she said uncertainly. 'My son's shouting for me, too. Anyway – anyway, I'll be seeing you in a matter of three days.'

'Not if I can help it,' he retorted. 'Sorry to spoil everyone's fun, but if I can stop Viola coming to Bucksford, believe me, I damn well will, even now.'

'Was that *him*?' Dominic, with typical male inability to open more than one cupboard door, had merely wanted to know where she'd hidden his green tea.

'What makes you say that?'

'Stupid look on your face?'

'Much you know,' she retorted, handing him the box. 'Either I'm crazy – or he definitely is. I say,' she continued swiftly, before her son could comment, 'what's this about your friend Kit? Something Simon said, about a police raid?'

'Fuck's sake, Ma, don't broadcast it.'

Annie rolled her eyes. 'We're alone in the house, kiddo, and I doubt the feds are on the case. It's true then?'

'No. Well, yes, but he's not being charged. I mean, he doesn't just grow the weed for himself—'

'This gets worse.'

'Listen, will you? There's a couple of people with MS – they know about it down the surgery, OK? It's cool. But no one wants it shouted all over town.'

'By the way, Bernie, just whilst I remember, my son seems to think we shouldn't gossip about Kit Grayson's little attic pharmacy.'

'Fat chance of that since I wouldn't be having a clue what you're on about.'

'Oh really? Forget it. Simon must've got the story from someone else.' Glancing up from the phone, she mouthed thanks to Liz who had just placed a mug of coffee beside her. 'So which room exactly are these curtains for?'

'Been talking to lover boy, have we? Bet you're on tenterhooks 'til Sunday, even if he will be with herself.'

Annie winced. The only thing keeping her on tenterhooks was the prospect of a letter landing on her doormat. A fat, hand-addressed envelope that very morning had brought her out in a cold sweat, but proved to contain only a petition for speed bumps on the bottom road. Much as she ached to share with Bernie her feelings for Simon Spencer – or apparent lack thereof – she was nervous about doing so. Her friend would be incredulous, probably exasperated and certainly disappointed. Besides, now was not the time. Bernie was ringing from the haberdashery stall in the market hall for advice on rufflette. So she deflected the enquiry by observing that he'd got himself into a quite ridiculous stew over his wife coming to Bucksford.

'Hasn't he bent my ear about it until I'm half deaf? Do you think she's twigged about you and him?'

'But what happens to Dave's party,' said Annie hastily, 'if he does manage to put her off? Please heaven not, at this late hour, but he's still threatening.'

'Come on, you surely know my boy'd sooner party on all night than traipse into a feckin' theatre. Remember dragging him to *The Phantom of the Opera* and the only time he stopped snoring was when the light fittings fell down?' Bernie chuckled. 'He won't care tuppence if Viola cancels. I'd be sorry, though. Holy Mary, we've heard enough about her. I'll feel properly cheated, so I will, if I don't get to clap eyes on the woman.'

'Me too,' said Annie, but abstractedly, because what actually concerned her was missing the chance of seeing Simon. The more she'd thought about that alarming telephone conversation, the more she'd realised she needed to talk to him, face to face. Never mind flowery letters, the time had surely come for plain speaking. Yes, yes, one almighty feather in her cap if he had fixed on her as the woman for him but . . . Had she *really* fallen so totally out of love with him? God, how cringe-making that sounded, even when she was talking to herself, never mind to Bernie. Had she ever been in love with him anyway? Trying to recapture the glow of their first meeting was downright embarrassing. Fruitless, too, because much as she'd like to claim he was the answer to her matronly prayers, she couldn't bring herself to believe it. But there was no denying she had given him every encouragement, and if he truly were about to ditch wife and alimony for her sake? Hell's teeth, she *had* to see him, in person, and sort this tangle out before it was too late.

An idea occurred to her. Even as she compared the merits of pencil and box pleating down the phone, she had flipped open her laptop and begun tapping.

'Definitely, and triple fullness if it's only a lightweight cotton and you want them to look really lush. But listen, Bernie.' She now had the BBC website open in front of her. '*In a special edition of the Movie Show,*' she read, '*legendary Hollywood actress Dame Viola Hood talks about her life and career in conversation with author and film critic* – et cetera. With an audience, just as I thought. So. How d'you fancy a sneaky trip over to Manchester to make sure we do get to see the great dame?'

'Well, maybe . . .'

'Just you and me, I mean.' How brilliant was this? Not only did it guarantee an opportunity to tackle Simon, she would have the luxury of a drive over the Pennines alone with Bernie to unburden herself. 'Six thirty. Day after tomorrow.'

'Saturday? But she'll be here in Bucksford the next day.'

'But *will* she?' said Annie impatiently. 'That's the point. Simon made no bones about doing his damnedest to throw a spanner in the works.'

'Anyway, I can't do Saturday. We're off to Tiptree Park. You know, for Cate's talk?'

'What?' she cried. 'Well, can't you get out of it?'

'I've been looking forward to it for ages,' protested Bernie. 'And what's more my Dave's coming, too. I've told him if I can juggle the bar staff for his party on Sunday, he can bloody well sort his kitchen Saturday and get on that book club bus with me. It's high time he took me for a day out.'

Annie scowled at the phone. 'Since when were you in the book club?'

'Did I not tell you about joining the Knit-lits? It's great, so it is. Just my kind of books and even though it's years since I picked up a pair of needles, I've already started a pullover for Megan. Mind, I've told her not to hold her breath because she'll likely be at uni before I'm done. I've finished my home-work, though,' she said proudly. 'Re-read *Emma* from cover to cover.'

'Congratulations,' said Annie crossly. 'I did that sodding dreary novel for O-level and I'd as soon swot up on the phonebook.'

'Get away with you, it's a hoot. She reminds me a bit of you, you know?'

'I say, Liz,' Annie ventured a few minutes later, as they were about to set off for the supermarket, 'you wouldn't fancy a jaunt over to Manchester?' Nowhere near as ideal a compan-ion as Bernie, obviously, but at least she'd be a chauffeur, if not a confidante.

'Is this Viola Hood? I heard you talking to Bernie about it.'

'Bit of a hassle for me without a car, and I thought you'd jump at the chance of seeing Si—' Annie caught herself just in time. 'Simon's wife?'

Liz looked mildly surprised. 'I suppose so. But it's the same day as Tiptree Park, isn't it?'

*   *   *

'You're joking,' said Hank. 'I mean, sure, I'd be up for it like a shot – but she's arriving here in forty-eight hours and counting and I'm tearing my bloody hair out. They don't like this, she won't have that, will the guy I've lined up to do the interview stick to the brief – and as for the list of stuff this Mac's sent of what she has to have in her dressing room . . . Organic grapes, jasmine candles, hypo-allergy-whatsit soap, it's as long as your arm, and I've never even heard of the mineral water. Should've been personally passed by Gwyneth Paltrow, at that price. Still, anything for Viola, that's what I keep telling everyone. By the way, you haven't got a chaise longue you can lend us, have you?'

'Actually, it's funny you should say that . . .'

She hadn't the heart to tell him that, if Simon had his way, it wouldn't be required.

'You'd be amazed what I've got buried up in my attic,' she said.

But this was to a delighted Trisha Hough the following morning, as she handed her a fat carrier bag of the remnants recently found under the battered chaise longue, now duly despatched to Dame Viola's dressing room.

'The skeletons of ex-lovers?' enquired Rob.

With no great surprise, perhaps, but a frisson of disapproval – Robbo really was a bit too chummy for comfort with Dr Blackwell – Annie had arrived to find him seated on the sofa beside her in the lounge of 3 Chatsworth Close.

'Personally I prefer burying their heads in a pot of basil,' said Cate, with a most uncharacteristic giggle.

'*For cruel 'tis, said she, to steal my Basil-pot away from me . . .*' returned Rob instantly. The poser. Only for Cate to whip back that she'd rather have braggadocio Boccaccio any day than soppy old Keats. That set him off in Italian, if you please, and what with this literary tennis match in one ear and Trisha twittering away in the other, Annie began to regret her impulsive decision to cycle down the hill, effusively grateful though Trish was for her bag of offcuts, saying this was just what she'd been crying out for, the way orders for her craft work were piling in. Annie's visit, however, was not purely philanthropic. When, eventually, she could get a word in, she casually enquired what time tomorrow's lit-fest at this Tiptree place might be expected to finish.

'Oooh, are you wanting to come along?' Trisha exclaimed, but thankfully saved Annie from manufacturing excuses by sweeping on to say she *thought* she had a couple of spare seats on the minibus, now the Parsons were driving themselves, with poor Leona afraid she'd get carsick in a bus, but, honestly, she didn't know if she was coming or going, what with another couple dropping out – had Annie heard about poor old Mary Cornford breaking her hip? Plus she was stitching and glueing 'til all hours to keep her customers happy, 'I mean, don't get me wrong, Annie, I'm not complaining, not for a minute, I'm pleased as punch at people wanting to buy my funny little bits and pieces, all in a good cause, isn't it? Not that I'd charge Simon, I told him I wouldn't dream of it, and it's just lucky I'd some of the fabric left over—'

'Simon?' said Annie sharply, and Cate and Rob looked up from their erudite argument.

'He never got his souvenir serviette from the ball; can you believe it? Not a bloomin' one left, so of course I said I'd run up another, specially for him. Well it's the least I could do, isn't it? And I've promised I'll have it ready to give him on Sunday, because, like I said, I've a yard or two of—'

'Is the Viola Hood thing still on, though?' interrupted Rob. 'Touch and go from what Bernie was telling me.'

Annie turned. 'Do you have to sound so pleased about it?'

'Oh no, I'm sure it is,' said Trisha, looking from one scowling face to the other. 'He only rang us this morning.'

'Well, he might have let me know,' said Annie grumpily. 'Saved me a load of hassle. No, no, Trisha, don't you stir, I'll put the kettle on.' However, when she checked her phone while waiting for the water to boil, there was indeed a text from Simon. In spite of her irritation, she had to smile.

The Met Office has issued a storm warning to residents of Bucksford. Sadly, it has now been confirmed that Hurricane Viola is set to sweep across the Pennines on Sunday. Residents are advised to remain at home and batten down the hatches. X

By the time she handed round the tea, Trisha had the contents of her carrier bag spread over a table, scissors snapping, and Cate was murmuring something to Rob about people at the health centre being a bit embarrassed by Kit Grayson's recent, um, problems.

'What's that about Kit?' called Trisha.

'Trouble with his pot plants,' offered Annie merrily, quite forgetting her son's injunction. 'And we don't mean greenfly on his geraniums.'

Trisha spun round, her face creased with distress. 'You're never talking about *cannabis*, not young Christopher?'

Yes, well, maybe Annie should also have remembered the sensitivities around drugs in this house, given their junkie mother, but there was no call for Rob to glower at *her*. It was his chum, the sainted Cate, who'd started it.

'I heard you asking about Tiptree Park, Annie,' he said, changing the subject with all the subtlety of a bulldozer. 'You coming to see Cate's star turn, then?'

'What else could I say, with her sitting there?' she complained, as he pulled shut the front door behind them and she kicked up the stand on her bike. 'Still, I suppose there are worse ways to spend a day. Everybody else seems to be bloody going.'

He grinned. 'Don't over-enthuse. And it's not my fault –
you did ask Trisha about it.'

'I only wanted to know what time you'd all be finished, on the
off chance someone could run me over to—' She broke off.
'Anyway, it doesn't matter, not now he's definitely coming here.'

Rob's grin vanished. 'Simon?'

'Sure. There's no keeping track of the guy.'

He didn't respond. He was staring into space. Frowning.
'Rob?'

'Look, Nan, I don't want to talk out of turn . . .'

'That sounds ominous.'

'Seriously. You notice Cate at all, when his name came up?'

'Should I have done?'

'Maybe I'm putting two and two together and making a
baker's dozen, but have you ever thought there might be
something going on? Between those two, I mean?'

In the very act of swinging her leg over her bike, Annie halted
and a pedal bit hard into her shin. 'Simon?' she squawked. 'And
Cate?' Then realised they were still outside the bungalow and
hastily lowered her voice. 'What are you on about?'

'Probably rubbish,' he said. 'At any rate, I hope it is. For her
sake, if nothing else. But I've thought once or twice, you know,
can't quite put my finger on it, but summat about the way
they act round each other?'

'Not in a million years, Bobsy-boy,' said Annie. She began
to laugh. 'Wow, I've had a few doubts about Simon Spencer's
sanity myself recently, but that really takes the biscuit.'

He didn't laugh with her. 'You reckon you know the guy
pretty well?'

'I dunno about that,' she said, climbing onto her bike with
more care this time. 'But well enough, for sure, to tell you
you're talking cobblers.'

31

'Now I wonder if you're expecting a feminist perspective from someone like me on this much-loved novel? Perhaps even, dare I say it, a radical critique?'

Whatever, thought Annie, slumping lower in her uncomfortable chair. Before the coffee break (instant, lukewarm and served in Pyrex beakers) she had suffered an hour and a quarter of the blessed Jane in Bath. With slideshow. OK, this being the modern world – not that you'd think it to look at this audience – slides had been superceded by a laptop-powered flip through endless shots of Georgian buildings (acceptable, if not what you'd call gripping), and even more photos of people who had forgotten to discard their bifocal specs and digital watches before tripping off to assorted stately homes in bonnets, tall hats and – worse still, for few of them were in the first blush of youth – bosomy bodices and tight pantaloons. So they could re-enact Ms Austen's greatest hits. They actually had a society devoted to such dressing-up capers.

'Certainly it would be easy for me to argue that this story, if you think about it, presents one or two challenges to our modern sensibilities.'

'Only one or two?' breathed Annie.

'Emma Woodhouse. Famously handsome, clever and rich. She might seem at first glance to be a fine heroine for the twenty-first century. She's very much her own woman, isn't she? She values her sturdy female friendships. She's content to contemplate life without a husband. But hold on a moment. What about that cherished friend who will ultimately become her husband, Mr George Knightley? Are we women supposed to admire this man? He's much older than Emma, remember. We're told he's been her mentor since childhood, a quasi-parent in effect, guiding and chiding her as she grows up. Is that relationship sweet and touching? Or, these days, might we rather call it – *grooming*?'

Annie, hearing the politely suppressed tuttings and mutterings from the card-carrying Janeites around her, began to anticipate with pleasure some heckling from the floor. No such luck.

'However, that isn't what I'm going to talk about today,' said Cate, with a glint in her eye that suggested she had judged exactly the effect of her words. Yes, well, Cath Blackwell always had been a clever little bugger. 'I thought instead we might explore the potential in this novel for a well-hidden murder plot. Let's call it "Who killed Mrs Churchill?"'

'All right, I admit it, I was wrong,' said Annie, before Rob could open his mouth. 'She was great. Terrifo. The hour whipped along totally painlessly.'

Well, perhaps this last statement was an exaggeration, given the plastic chairs, but there was no denying Cate Blackwell knew how to hold a crowd. And she was disarmingly modest about the inspiration for her literary take on Cluedo. The distinguished crime novelist, P. D. James, she said, had long ago suggested that *Emma* was very like a detective story in construction, with clues cunningly implanted at every turn as to what was really happening, unsuspected by the smart and self-possessed heroine.

'Just think about it,' she had said. 'The entire plot hinges, and ultimately resolves, on the death of one woman. Yes, I'm talking about the dreaded Mrs Churchill. Whom we never actually get to meet. That in itself is a little stroke of genius. Jane Austen creates this character whom we readers feel we know and are only too delighted to dislike. Snobbish, selfish and imperiously temperamental, blighting the lives of so many people, she exerts a malign influence on the whole course of events – yet she remains invisible throughout. And then, conveniently, she drops dead. Oh, so *very* conveniently does she drop dead. Now, has it never crossed your mind to consider how understandable it might be – how strangely satisfying, even – if someone had given her a little helping hand into eternity?'

'Which I can't say ever had crossed my mind,' continued Annie, as she surveyed a vinyl-clothed table of cold sausage rolls, shrivelled quiche, and bowls of unidentified rubble drowning in pools of too-yellow mayo. 'All I could remember from school was a cosy bunch of neighbours with too much money and nothing better to do than give endless dozy parties for each other. I'd have enjoyed English Lit O-level a sight more if I'd had Cate lining up the suspects like Hercule Poirot, asking how and why they might have done the old bag in. It almost made me want to go back and read the bloody book again.'

'Come and tell her. She'll be chuffed to hear you enjoyed it.'

Annie pulled a face. 'You reckon?' After selecting a few spoonfuls of this and that, however, she followed him – more readily than she might, had she realised Cate was already at a table with Kelvin and Leona Parsons, as well as her sister and nephew.

'If opportunity doesn't knock, you must build a door,' Leona was declaring. Looking past Annie as through empty air, she patted the chair beside her. 'That's what they say, isn't it, Robbie?'

'Depends which cracker you pull,' he said, taking a seat at the far end of the table.

A trill of laughter. 'Seriously now, I'm telling Cate she should forget dusty old classrooms and get herself onto the television. Wouldn't you agree?'

'As someone who's spent his career in classrooms . . .' he began, but Leona wasn't listening.

'With all her talent, I can't believe she hasn't looked for a helping hand from this great friend of hers, Siobhan, isn't it? Who, so a little bird tells me' – a flash of teeth in Trisha's direction – 'is one very important lady in the media. Now now, Cate, don't shake your head like that, you naughty girl. We women are always too modest – I'm just the same, forever putting myself down. The main thing is, you've got the bone structure and that's all that matters. The camera loves bones, take it from me. And you mustn't worry about your image being a bit, well, you know – because I could get you styled up in a trice. Your friend Siobhan wouldn't recognise you after one of my makeovers. And when you *do* talk to her, I'm sure you'd like to drop a word in her ear about my Kelvin, because if ever there was anyone just made for the screen – pardon? Oh, not for me, Trisha, thank you. I never touch tap water. Chemical poison.'

'Your talk was brilliant, Cate,' cut in Annie hastily, conscious of having herself reflected that today, for once, Cate really could do with upping her style a bit – that black tabardy-thing was more elephantine than elegant. 'Loved it.'

She cocked an eyebrow. 'So who d'you think dunnit?'

'Oh, has to be Jane whatsername. Miss Goody Two-Shoes. I could even get to like the saintly sugar-babe if I thought she was plotting homicide as she tinkled her precious piano.'

Cate laughed. Yes, Annie actually got a laugh out of Dr Goody Two-Shoes Blackwell. 'Gosh, I'm with you there – Jane

Fairfax is so sweet she makes your teeth ache. But, you know, what intrigues me is Austen calling her by her own name, Jane. Which makes one wonder whether we're supposed to realise she isn't nearly such a saccharine little sap as—' She was interrupted by the muffled trill of a phone. Drawing it from her bag, she glanced at the screen, frowned, hesitated for a moment, then rose from her chair. 'I'm sorry, I should probably, um, deal with this. Besides, I'm not terribly hungry. But please may we come back to ghastly Miss Fairfax?' And the smile she gave Annie, as she lifted the phone to her ear, suggested almost sisterly complicity.

For her part, Annie would have been happy to abandon her own dispiriting plate and follow Cate outside, but Dave had now arrived to plant himself in her vacated chair. Producing a bottle of wine from his capacious pocket with a wink, he said they needed summat decent to wash down their lunch.

'So you can snore even louder through the afternoon,' said his wife, following with Liz beside her.

'Oh, you can't expect men to be as passionate about books as we girlies, Bernie,' said Leona gaily. 'Tiger can't believe what a bookworm he's married. The first thing I said to him, in our new apartment, was that I absolutely had to have a shelf for all my books. Isn't that right, lover? But we were hoping we'd see you in particular today, Dave, because I'm sure you'll have heard about my husband's new website . . .'

Rob had risen and, under the pretence of surrendering his chair to Bernie, adroitly steered Liz away to a place beside him at the adjoining table, with their backs to the Parsons. While Annie warmly approved of this tactful manoeuvre, it left her feeling somewhat adrift. Trisha had commandeered Bernie with knitting pictures on her phone and, while she didn't mind being ignored by Leona and her husband, she did very much wish Rob were beside her to hear Kelvin solemnly inform Dave that expansion online would enable him to shine his healing light 'through the darkened windows of so many more souls . . .'

Why he was treating the palpably baffled Dave to a sales spiel only became clear when Leona intervened. Curling a lacquer-taloned hand over Dave's, she confided that they were hoping for an endorsement they could quote on the website from Viola Hood.

'Such a champion of the healing professions as she's always been, and knowing she's your stepmother, we were wondering if you might introduce us?'

Seeing Dave's face, Annie promptly turned her chair round to the next table to share her mirth with Rob, but was side-tracked by hearing him say he'd set aside his prejudice against audiobooks and invested in the new biography of Roy Jenkins to relieve the tedium of the A1.

'Don't tell me you're going away *again*, Robbo?'

'You mean you'd notice?'

'As a matter of fact, I'd been thinking, I dunno, that we could go out on the bikes, or something? I've been feeling rather loose end-ish since the ball.'

'Well, sorry I can't accommodate you,' he said drily, 'but I'm afraid I'm off to the House of Lords, to try and swing a grant for a sports field. Normally I'd zip down on the train in a day but it turns out Jez and Cassandra are both in London at the end of the week, and Molly's there anyway, of course. My kids,' he added for Liz's benefit. 'So, yeah, I'm having a full ten days of family time. Staying with Phil and Jen, obviously. Which reminds me, Liz, my brother particularly asked to be remembered to you.'

'That's kind of him,' said Liz, blushing sweetly.

'. . . sure you can't mean that, Dave, what a thing to say! She is married to your father. Still, perhaps it might be better if Tiger and I just . . .'

'When are you off?' Annie said disconsolately. 'Not before Dave's party tomorrow?'

Rob grimaced. 'No, I'll be there. Although to be honest, I could do without another social bash.'

'I knew I should've brought another bottle,' they heard Dave exclaim, and his wife point out that he had single-handedly put away three quarters of this one.

'I'm about partied out. What was it you were saying just now, Nan, about a bunch of neighbours and endless parties?'

'Sorry?' Annie was tuning in to the conversation behind her.

'Ha, proves I was right, when kids in Austen lessons moaned I was forever banging on about her world not being so different from—'

'Shhh. I thought I heard Trisha say—'

'. . . our appeal, in the national news.' Trisha was excitedly holding out her mobile. 'And don't they make a lovely couple?'

Annie promptly reversed her chair again to see a photograph of Simon and Viola Hood beamingly entwined.

'May I?' she said, taking the phone.

It was the *Daily Mail* website, with a showbizzy piece about that night's radio recording of the audience with Dame Viola. Skipping over a puff for *Darling Clementine*, she found the reference to the great star generously pitching in to raise funds for this little Yorkshire arts centre. What caught her attention, however, was a quote about the couple's imminent silver wedding. She read, with cynical amusement, that Vi 'n' Sly's marriage, one of Hollywood's most enduring partnerships – yeah? – had emerged from well-publicised troubles 'stronger than ever'.

'Sez she,' murmured Annie. Too late, however, she realised that Liz had risen and was leaning over her shoulder, asking if she could take a closer look. What else could she do but hand up the phone? And wait. Braced.

'That's nice,' Liz said quietly, after a moment. 'Will you excuse me? I might just pop out and powder my nose before the next session.'

And in neither her voice nor the hand with which she returned the mobile to Trisha was the tiniest tremor detectable.

Dammit, Annie was proud of her.

With a scholarly lecture on Jane's unfinished writings promised for the afternoon – probably unfinished for good reason, Annie suspected – she could not blame Leona for her unconvincingly sudden recollection that it was Sunday tomorrow, not to mention a bank holiday weekend, so, with *vital* shopping to accomplish, she was afraid they might have to miss the final session.

Had it not been the Parsons, she would have considered cadging a lift. As it was, with a quarter-hour of freedom to spare, she wandered out into the sunshine to see if she couldn't find Cate and cultivate the unexpected bond that seemed to have sprung up between them.

The grounds, she was prepared to agree with an elderly couple likewise taking the air, were indeed pretty. If in need of a haircut, she added, dodging a low-flying branch. The overgrown jungle was gaudy with rhododendrons and azaleas at this time of year, so she wandered onwards, kicking the odd clump of weed out of the gravel as she searched in vain for Cate. Then, just as she was checking her watch while rounding a shaggy giant of a yew hedge, she almost collided with her.

'There you are!' she exclaimed. 'But I'm afraid it's nearly two. I was hoping you could reassure me this next talk isn't going to be as death-defyingly tedious as I—' She stopped short. 'Hey, are you all right?' Daft question, because Cate was clearly not all right. Blotchy-cheeked, sweaty and breathing far too fast.

'Yes. No.' She wrapped her arms round herself. 'Oh, it's nothing. Stupid, really. I think – I think the talk this morning rather, you know, took it out of me.'

Even as Annie asked what she could do – assist her indoors? summon Trisha? – she realised Cate was staring past her, one hand shielding her eyes against the sun.

'Sorry – sorry, you're very sweet, but I've just seen Leona and Kelvin heading towards their car. It looks – yes, as if they're going. I wonder if they'd give me a lift?' She was already striding away, gathering up a swathe of skirt and breaking into a clumsy run, pausing only to call back over her shoulder: 'Explain to Trish, would you? Tell her not to worry. I'm just – very tired.'

And emotional, thought Annie, watching her exchange a few words with Kelvin before lowering herself into the rear seat of their motor.

'She's so kind, is that Leona,' said Trisha when Annie found her outside the front porch, fag in hand, chatting to Bernie. 'I keep telling our Cate she's not to mind me, she should go and stay in their lovely flat for a bit, like they keep asking her. She'd be a lot more comfortable with that dicky back of hers, because she'll not be persuaded to swap with me in the bed, silly girl, and they're only just round the corner, aren't they?'

'That's – very generous of them,' said Annie, virtuously refraining from adding that, if she were Cate, she'd rather kip in a cardboard box, never mind on a lilo. Only to laugh when Bernie whispered generous her foot, it was ever since she'd heard about Cate's high-powered contacts in telly that Leona had been all over her like a rash.

'She needs a good old rest to be fit for tomorrow,' said Trisha. 'She won't want to miss Dame Vi, I know. I showed you that bit about our Woolshed in the news, didn't I? Oooh, it's one exciting thing after another these days, isn't it?'

'Mmmm,' said Annie, as a bell sounded. 'Whatever next?'

Perhaps it was inevitable, after the sun had obediently smiled over so many of the functions in Bucksford's busy social calendar, that it would sidle behind a fug of darkening clouds for Dave's picnic the following day. By mid-afternoon, much as Bernie had predicted, there was a damping mizzle in the air – and on the spirits of the assembled company.

Definitely a collective dullness, thought Annie, drawing her pashmina more closely round her shoulders. Maybe Rob (killjoy) Daley had a point. Maybe they were all beginning to feel partied out. Besides, even with the famously eccentric British enthusiasm for eating in fresh air and discomfort, she was conscious that they must look pretty idiotic. They were gathered on a square of litter-strewn grass to the side of the town hall, enclosed only by a knee-high fence of wrought iron, missing many a wonky loop, mere yards from a pavement that was embarrassingly well populated for this hour on a Sunday. With coats and cardigans draped over their finery, they clutched their glasses and pretended to be unaware of the puzzled stares and occasional ribald comments from passers-by.

Cate Blackwell perched poker-spined on the arm of Joey's wheelchair beside Rob and Liz, while Trisha twittered away to them. Some distance off, the Parsons were posing under a giant pink umbrella, in shimmering glamour and palpable discomfort. This was not surprising since Leona had arrived both under-clothed and overdressed in a column of silver lamé, the absurdity of which had supplied Annie with her only entertainment thus far in the leaden afternoon. Kelvin was clad almost as inappropriately in a dazzlingly white Nehru suit and was shifting from foot to foot on the mangy sward, squinting anxiously down at his pristine trouser hems. Thus far the couple had only been exchanging whispers in one another's ears, but Annie saw their faces suddenly break into fulsome smiles as they lowered the umbrella and surged forward.

'The man we've been waiting for!' cried Leona, bangled arms outstretched.

It was Simon, of course, pacing up from the direction of the Woolshed. Jumping the fence, he dodged the Parsons with a kiss blown Leona's way and a nod to Kelvin as he hurried over to hug his son and Bernie. If now was not the time to embark on their difficult but essential conversation, it was a chance to suggest a less public word later. Steeling herself, Annie called his name before he could become embroiled with Rob, Liz and the Hough contingent. He turned enquiringly. Even if her heart failed to skip at his approach, she was cheered by the chagrin in Leona's face. His embrace was perfunctory, however, and he broke away to scowl up at the clouds.

'What do these literary types call it, when the weather fits the mood – some fallacy or other? No doubt Doctor Blackwell over there could tell us, if she deigned to notice my existence, because I tell you, that sky now looks just like I'm feeling.' A flash of a smile, strangely lacking its usual charm. 'Still, enough about my woes. How are you keeping, old darling?'

'I . . .' She was disconcerted. This was hardly the greeting of an aspiring lover – and Dave was already thrusting himself between them, bottle in hand.

'So what's the news on Her Highness? Raring to go in there?'

'You're joking, of course. Well, at least Hank can't say I didn't warn him. The latest crisis, before I managed to slip out, was that the fan she'd made him unearth is intolerably noisy. Apparently. Christ, it's a chat show she's doing, not *Hedda* fucking *Gabler*.' Annie had never heard him sound so bitter. 'But we must remember these great artists require Zen-like silence.'

Dave guffawed. 'She could come out here if she wants a bit of hush.' He raised his voice. 'What's up with you lot, cat got your tongues?'

It was true that conversation seemed to have juddered to a halt. There was a spatter of self-conscious laughter now, and Bernie resumed passing damp canapés around, one hand over the tray, while Dave popped the cork on another bottle with a flourish. Rob lifted his orange juice ironically in Annie's direction but Cate, to everyone's surprise, defiantly put hers down and said she'd like a glass of champagne, please. For once.

Her sister, meanwhile, had trundled up and, to Annie's irritation, cornered Simon with some prattle about that lovely picture of him and Lady Viola . . . 'I don't mean Lady Vi, I mean Dame Hood – oh, what am I like? You know what I mean, anyhow, the two of you, with such bonny smiles, and it was the *Daily Mail*, too.'

'Yup, that's the one thing you can always trust the *Mail* for,' he said loudly. 'To get everything one hundred per cent wrong. Fucking British press,' he added in an undervoice to Annie.

'Lighten up, hey?' she said, startled afresh by his bitterness. 'No plans for silver wedding parties, then?'

'I'd top myself first,' he hissed. 'Or her. In fact, definitely her.'

Annie tittered. He didn't. Oh well, she'd best get on with it. 'Look, Simon. I think you and I, um, need to have a conversation?'

'Where's your son?' he cut in unexpectedly, glancing round.

'Dominic? At home.' Annie shrugged. 'He's not exactly a fan of Viola Hood, I'm afraid.'

'You're apologising for that? But surely, I saw him just now, outside the stage door. I meant to have a word with him, actually, tell him he should be thanking his lucky stars he didn't get the job with Vi because from what I'm now hearing—' He fell abruptly silent as Bernie approached with her tray. 'No thanks, darling, honestly. Couldn't eat a thing.'

'Isn't this all fun?' exclaimed Liz to no one in particular, seemingly immune to climate and mood alike. She at least was having a high old time, chattering away to Rob and Cate – and looking a credit to Annie in that slinky black dress again. Bless. Everyone else smiled round at her too – well, everyone except the Parsons. Leona was clutching Kelvin's arm as she struggled to withdraw a muddied stiletto heel from the grass and let out a squawk as he caught the brolly in her hair.

'Watch out, will you? And you've dripped all down my dress now, you clumsy thing.'

Kelvin cleared his throat. 'I, uh, think maybe Leona and I'll go inside to wait for the show?' With umbrella carefully aloft, he supported his wife as she limped away, skirt hoisted round her knees.

'There's another happy couple,' beamed Trisha, watching them go.

'You think?' said Simon and gave a sour laugh. 'Anyone wanna bet how long it'll be before they hit the divorce courts?'

Well, that certainly shut everybody up.

'You're being rather harsh, surely?' ventured Liz. *Liz*, of all people.

'Get real, darling,' he retorted, unabashed. 'These late-life relationships don't stand much chance, do they? Oh, come on, you guys, I don't know why you're all staring me, I'm only stating the bleedin' obvious – pardon my language, Liz. Old Ma Nature designed us to pair up young. We crumblies might kid ourselves the rosy glow's just the same for us but, trust me, it's an Indian summer. One blast of cold wind and – *pfft!* – Good night Irene.'

Annie was bewildered – could this cynical outburst be aimed at her? Had he realised she didn't return his feelings? Bernie, however, was up in arms.

'And what about me and your son, if you don't mind? We're no chickens, and we seem to be doing very nicely, thank you.'

Simon had the grace to look embarrassed but had barely begun to protest that he didn't mean *everyone* when Rob cut in, stating gravely that, although he couldn't speak for the Parsons, he believed mature relationships might actually stand a greater chance of success.

'When you're older, you know yourself. Or you should, and what you truly value in another person. You're not dazzled by lust, let alone all the daft razzle-dazzle glamour of getting wed.' He turned slightly – and his steady gaze met Annie's. 'But I'd argue the main benefit is that you're *not* driven by Mother Nature any longer, if you want to call it that. I'd sooner say plain old biology. Because that's what sends so many youngsters hurtling off in crazy directions, if you ask me, and I'm not talking about sex. It's the urge to reproduce that's bloody well hardwired into us. God knows how many folk end up with ridiculously unsuitable partners just so they can start a family.'

Well. Lust, glamour, babies? As a summary of her own disastrous marriage, this piece of cheap armchair philosophy could scarcely be faulted. Annie felt an angry flush rise up her neck.

'No, no, I can't agree with you there, Rob,' Trisha was protesting. 'Although, I'm a fine one to talk about marriage, aren't I? What with me and Joey's dad busting up so bloomin' quick, although of course I was past thirty when I walked down the aisle, so does that make me old or young? Any road, plenty of people even nowadays still get together when they're young, and as for our mums and dads, well, our mam, Cate's and mine, was only eighteen when she had me, although I suppose that marriage didn't fare too well, neither, come to think of it, but I'll not give in, Rob, no I won't, because I can think of plenty of couples who wed in their twenties and who've stuck together through thick and thin, happy as Larry for forty years and more, in fact I could name you now a whole list of—'

'I'm sure you could, but for God's sake, spare us,' Annie burst out, far more loudly than she realised. Or perhaps there was a lull in the hubbub of traffic and town. Anyway, it was Rob she was cross with, not silly old Trisha. But of course they were all looking at her – and looking shocked. Even Bernie's face was reproachful. As for bloody Rob's . . .

'Am I at my rabbiting again?' Trisha, vivid pink, was trying her best to smile. 'Eh, Joey, I should be sticking closer to you, so you can give your silly old mum a nudge.'

Shit, Annie was thinking. Shit, shit, *shit*. Before she could even begin to backtrack, however, a phone shrilled into the charged air with a tinny rendition of Wagner's Valkyries, so ludicrous, so utterly, crazily inappropriate, she couldn't help herself. She guffawed.

And Simon, the dickhead, winked at her as he delved in his pocket. 'Just my dear wife's personal ringtone,' he said smoothly, lifting the mobile to his ear. 'Excuse me for a moment, would you?'

32

Annie walked away to the edge of the grass, hot-faced and fist-clenched, searching for some way of excusing her eruption. There was a cry of impatience behind her. She glanced round to see Simon clamping a hand over his free ear.

'What? ... God's sake, Vi, I can hardly hear a word. Say again ...' A sigh. A grimace. 'OK, OK, don't panic. I'm sure ... Yes, of course, I'm coming ... Yes, *now.*'

He dropped the phone back into his pocket, realised everyone was watching him and cast up his eyes. 'At ease, you chaps. Nothing to worry about, just me trying to kill the wife again. Or possibly someone else is, the details weren't clear. And God alone knows where spiders come in, because I'd swear she was screaming about arachnids, and that's spiders, isn't it? Still, if there's a tarantula in the washbasin I'm evidently expected to grapple with the beast.' He was already backing away. 'See y'all later, huh?'

With a distracted smile and a wave he was gone.

'Off her rocker,' said Dave. 'Didn't I always say so? Now, who needs a top-up?'

Trisha, fussing over Joey, had turned her back on Annie. Deliberately? She'd every right. God, how could she have been so horribly rude to her poor old friend? And, what was more, laughed? That ringtone was a shocker, but to have burst out laughing *then*, after what she'd just said ... She must be mad – well, she was mad, as in hopping mad, downright

348

bloody furious, with Rob. How dared he? Had she ever – *ever* – inflicted a single word of complaint about her *ridiculously unsuitable* marriage on him? She had not. Never. Not ever. And yet he apparently felt quite free to deliver that priggish homily, right here, in front of everyone . . .

And now, of course, he too was cutting her dead. Leaning forward to catch something Liz said to Cate. Even Dave and Bernie had their heads locked, arguing over a plate of sandwiches, by the sound of it. While she just stood here like a pillock. Worse, a pariah. She must make things right with Trish although she couldn't think how. Claim she was drunk? Just joking?

As she waited for Trisha to look up from tucking a mac over her son, she heard a rumble. Soft but, yes, a distinct rumble of thunder. At least that brought Bernie bustling towards her, declaring she'd always predicted a downpour, had she not? And did her husband ever listen to a feckin' word she said? Him in his beautiful jacket, too, which wouldn't take at all well to a soaking, so it would not. She went on chattering, about this, that and the inconsequential other, all of which floated past Annie's burning ears. As Bernie was obviously aware because, at one point, she leaned forward and told her in a whisper that she was not to fret, they all came out with the wrong thing now and again, she herself more often than anyone. Holy Mary, half the time she couldn't open her mouth without putting her big Irish foot in it.

Annie smiled gratefully but wasn't comforted. 'You're never unkind,' she said. 'And I was. I didn't mean to be, didn't intend—'

'Course you didn't, and Trisha knows it. Come on now, and give me a hand packing up, will you? I've told Dave everyone's eaten all they want, and we may as well rescue what's left while we can. I'll take it home and give the old lags in the bar a treat with their last drinks. Because the real rain is coming along any minute now, sure as eggs.'

By the time they carried the boxes round to Dave's van, parked in the alley beside the stage door of the Woolshed, Bernie was proved right. The spray had swelled into fat flurries of wetness and a flicker of brilliance ripped across the sky, followed almost at once by a cannon blast of thunder.

'In the very nick,' said Bernie, stuffing in the last box and slamming the doors. 'We'd best go and round up the troops.'

'Hang on a moment,' said Annie. She retreated a few steps to the mouth of the alley to gain a better view of the main entrance to the theatre. 'What's going on? Because I don't think those people are queueing to get in. Looks to me like most of them are actually coming out.'

'Can't get seats, very likely,' said her friend briskly. 'Good thing we've friends in high places keeping ours. Come on, shift yourself, pet, before we get drenched to our feckin' knickers.'

But just as the town hall clock loomed back into view, below which their friends could be seen huddling into their coats, with Rob manoeuvring Joey's chair round to the pavement, Annie felt a hand grab her shoulder and spun round. 'Oh, it's you, Hank. Hi, what's up?'

'It's off,' he gasped. 'She's – well, fuck knows, but she can't go on.' He paused to catch his breath. 'Si – Simon asked me to tell you. Sounds pretty bad.' He was already retreating. 'Sorry, but I gotta get back in there. Fucking madhouse.'

Annie stared at Bernie as he pounded away again. 'Pretty bad . . .?'

Bernie cast up her eyes. 'Oh, what a surprise. Actually, I don't know why I bothered booking a babysitter. I might've guessed we'd be home by dinnertime.'

But there was a siren whining, growing louder by the second. Annie saw the blue light, zig-zagging round the traffic, watched it jolt to a stop by the stage door.

'It's got to be for her,' she said. Two boiler-suited figures sprang out of the ambulance and were urgently ushered inside. 'What d'you suppose is up with her?'

'Terminal feckin' hypochondria, of course. Ha, and you say I'm never unkind? Look, here's your lovely Liz coming now, and you're parked in the pay and display, aren't you? Yes, well, you run along with her quick, before you drown. I'll kiss everyone goodbye for you.'

The full force of the storm was cracking overhead as Liz dropped Annie in her drive, and she scurried indoors, shawl over her head. 'Dom?' she shouted. No answer.

She knew almost from the moment she opened the door that he wasn't there, although she still paced round, calling his name. The house was dark, all doors shut, his keys missing from the bowl on the hall table. Hell. Why'd he have to go out this evening? She didn't give a stuff about him getting wet, or drunk, or most likely both. She just didn't want to find herself alone.

That had nothing to do with the tempest outside; Annie had always relished a good storm. When the kids were little, she found herself recalling with an unexpectedly wistful pang as she tossed away her pash and shook the rain out of her hair, they had always turned off the lights at the first murmur of thunder. Then all of them, Bernie and Liam too, would watch the sky, noses pressed to the window, counting the seconds between flash and blast, cheering a particularly fiery display.

No, the weather wasn't responsible for her sour mood. She was appalled at herself for snapping at Trish. She was also furious with Rob, headachey from Dave's champagne and generally, totally, all-bloody-round pissed off. And she wanted to *talk*. To someone – anyone. Well, not to Liz, who had prattled ceaselessly all the way up the hill. Her newfound high spirits were becoming even more wearing than her misery. Bernie would be busy clearing up the party debris. As for Rob . . . Huh. She'd plenty to say to Rob Daley, but not now.

She kicked off her shoes, wandered through to the sitting room – cold, but she wasn't going to light a fire, this was damn nearly June for heaven's sake – so just flung herself disconsolately across the sofa and switched on the telly. Some old-fashioned whodunnit, all gorgeous clothes and still more gorgeous houses. She had dozed off even before the second corpse.

A crash woke her. Not the storm. That seemed to have cleared. It was the front door. A moment or two later, Dominic lurched into the room, bleary-eyed, dishevelled and drenched.

'Oh Dom, honestly,' she murmured, yawning. 'Pissed again?'

'Yurrrs,' he said, managing to make at least four syllables out of it, and hiccupped loudly.

'Well, you can stop dripping over my carpet for a start.' Wearily, she hauled herself to her feet. 'Come into the kitchen. I suppose I'd better make you some tea.'

'Don't want tea. Need 'nother drink.'

'Not likely,' said his mother, taking hold of his shoulders and steering him across the hall. She had just pulled out a chair at the kitchen table into which he capsized like a stringless puppet and was walking away to pick up the kettle, when a sound halted her. A groan? She turned, and saw her son suddenly fling himself face forward across the table, with a great shuddering sob.

'Oh my God. How much have you had?' But she stopped, because this was different. Dominic was wailing, making a weird keening noise – like a wounded animal. She returned to the table, dragging a chair over to his, and tried to put her arm round his sodden shoulders. He shrugged her off. He stank. Booze, fag-ash, sweat – vomit? Terrific. She glanced at her hand. Seemed to be sick-free. 'Come on, you soft ha'porth. Pull yourself together and tell your old mum. What's up?'

'You'll – you'll hate me. Hate myself.'

She sighed. He really was getting too like his father. Jake had been a great one for the sackcloth and ashes routine after a skinful. But she folded her arm round him again, and this time he didn't pull away. He just sobbed all the harder.

'I'm such a – such a fucking coward.'

'Uh-huh?' Any minute now he would surely announce – again – that he was abandoning his acting career. Or maybe the play he clearly was not writing. *But* . . . This was her son, her baby, and besides, the very clumsiness of a man crying always touched her. So she rested her cheek lightly against his shoulder. 'You're no coward, sweetheart. I was the one nearly fainted when they were pulling your leg round in that hospital, remember? We barely got a squeak out of you. Downright heroic, you were.'

He glanced round, and it was his sad attempt at a laugh that really wrenched her heart. 'Only cos I was drugged senseless. Thass all. But – this.' He jerked away from her arm again, screwed his fists into his eyes and tried to sit up. 'Gotta talk to Hank,' he said thickly. 'Need to tell him.'

'What about? Actually, that reminds me. Was it actually you then, that Simon saw, down by the theatre?'

He nodded convulsively. 'But – but I funked it. It'll be my fault.' Fresh tears were dripping down his cheeks.

'What will? Oh love,' she said helplessly. 'Talk to me, please. Is this something to do with her, Viola Hood?'

'It's not her,' he burst out. 'She just told him to get on with it, didn't she?'

'Who?'

'Her fucking agent. Randolph f-fucking Mackley. When he was – when he was trying to rape me.'

Jesus. This is the kind of thing you read about. Hear reported practically every day on the news. Not what you ever, not in a million years, expect to find yourself hearing from your own child. Your weeping, hysterical, grown-up son.

Annie had to swallow, physically choke back the bile, as she hugged and soothed and coaxed the sordid story out. Worse than anything she ever dreamed could happen to Dom, but not as bad – dear God – not nearly as horrific as it could have been.

It seemed that after the auditions had been relayed to the great actress, this scumbag Mac whatever he was called, asked Dominic back to his flat. To talk about him getting the part. Of course. And, wouldn't you just know, slipped something into his drink. Must have done, because the next thing Dom was aware of – not that he could remember much – he was woken by hearing his name screeched by Viola Hood. Yes, by Dame Viola herself, over the phone speaker, saying the boy was crap.

'So have your fun and fucking well get rid of him,' had apparently been her immortal words. Or something of the sort. 'Ten minutes, max. I want to talk.'

'Half my clothes were hanging off, shirt, a shoe.' Dominic shuddered. 'Flies – undone. So when I tried to get up, I just fell over, jeans round my knees. And he chased after me, grabbed me. I kicked him, think I did, in the guts.'

'Bloody hard I hope.'

'Dunno how I got out – down some steps, great long staircase, curling round. And – and all thick carpet, I r'member that, slippery. Nearly made me fall on my arse again. And he was yelling down, y'know, if I said anything, I was finished. Finished anyway, he said. He'd – put the word out.'

'Bastard,' cried Annie. 'But, oh my God, you got on your bike? In that state, that night . . .' She was remembering being woken, so groggy with sleep she could find neither phone nor lamp. Struggling to take in the words of this soft-voiced stranger who claimed to be a doctor. Then, high-wired with terror, racing down the A1, screaming at the sat-nav in the maze of London streets, wandering even more bewildered down deserted hospital corridors, finally finding the right ward – and Dominic, still slathered in dirt and blood . . . 'Christ, if you'd been an inch or two closer to that fucking lorry, you'd be dead now. *Dead*. And it would be his fault. That Mac would have killed you, sure as if he'd stuck a knife in you. And she – she'd be as much to blame. Have your fun, indeed.' Annie was on her feet. 'I'm calling Simon. No, I'm not, this is a matter for the police.'

Dominic clutched her arm, however, and wouldn't let go. No way was he talking to the police, not to anyone. God, he'd had to tell them in the hospital there might be some drug inside him, he'd *had* to tell them, with all the stuff they were injecting, and the doc had looked at him, asked if there was anything he wanted to report . . .

'The way he asked – I felt so fucking stupid. So – humiliated.'

'There's nothing for you to feel—'

'Mum, he's *here*. At the Shed. And I – not just shit scared of seeing him – I couldn't face even telling Hank. I wanted to, meant to, but . . . But if that bastard tries it on with him . . .'

'He won't be spiking anyone's drinks after tonight's fiasco,' Annie declared. 'She was carted off in an ambulance, did you hear? The callous bitch may well be dead, for all I know and I couldn't care less. Serve her right. As for that agent of hers – my God, death's too good for the likes of him.'

*   *   *

355

Viola Hood was not dead. The following morning she was, apparently, creating her customary havoc in the Royal Infirmary where she was being detained ...

... *under what they call "observation"*, Annie read, in a text from Bernie which pinged in while she was scrubbing her teeth. *For which read, fit as a f****** flea. Unlike my poor Megan who's throwing up everywhere with a tummy bug, plus Em's tripped and bust a tooth and their dad's groaning from a birthday-sized hangover. Can I move back in with you? Talk soon. X*

Nothing like someone else's troubles to lighten your own. Besides, with morning had come that edgy clarity which can follow too little sleep and too much strong coffee and high emotion. Inevitably, she and Dominic had talked long and late. A marathon sob-fest but, she hoped, cathartic for both of them. Each had kept protesting the other was not to blame. No way was her boy to call himself dumb for accompanying Mac back to his flat. How was he to have known? Nor was Annie to curse herself as a terrible mother. She was a great mother, Dom said. Well, the best he'd got. That he could manage even a feeble joke was heartening. But, oh, how remorsefully was Annie now recognising her son's attempts to confide in her before. After that drunken woman fondled him under the table at the wedding. When he'd crashed out of the pub at Christmas on hearing Viola's tiger snarl. Whatever Dom said, she'd flinched from stab after vicious stab of maternal guilt.

This morning, however, raking a comb through her hair and blinking into the mirror as she wielded the mascara wand – when in turmoil, slap on the warpaint – she was resolutely assessing the positives. Her son had escaped physical molestation, if not emotional. He was alive, for God's sake. With two legs. And was now sleeping soundly. She had actually found herself tiptoeing along the landing in the middle of the night to check on him. It'd felt weirdly as if life had slipstreamed back a quarter of a century and more to the pale scrap of baby he had once been, with an unnerving talent for lying as still and silent as a wax doll. At least now, with all that booze oozing through his system, he was snoring as reassuringly vigorously as a bull elephant.

And he had mumbled last night – unprompted – that this was the end of it. No more drinking himself brain-dead.

'I'm not Dad,' he'd said. 'Don't even like it much. It was just – you know.'

Yes, Annie did know. Now. And when he earnestly promised a spartan regime of water, exercise – even sodding driving lessons if she wanted – she had laughed as well as wept. The least she could promise in return was that she would contact Hank this morning. And without mentioning Dominic – truly, not a word – she would find a way of warning him about this Randolph Mackley, if the monster was still lurking around Bucksford. Somehow.

She had to brew herself tea of tooth-stripping strength before reaching for the phone. However, simply asking if Viola's agent had followed her to the hospital proved enough. After spluttering that Randy Mandy had, and good riddance, Hank informed her, unprompted, that he'd caught him whispering in the ear of an innocent-as-milk, stage-struck kid on the crew. Just as well he'd been tipped off about the sleazy old git by a mate in London. As he moaned about the chaos following Viola's melodramatic exit, Annie found herself recalling Simon's snide comments about his wife's *people*. Did he know about Mac? Or suspect something, at any rate? Must have done. Why else had he suddenly said yesterday that Dom should be glad he hadn't got the part in Viola's play?

'Never mind the fuzz muscling round. I mean, as if we didn't know—'

This startled her into paying attention. 'The *police*?'

Hank was still talking: '—with it, like, plastered in fucking great capitals, top of the list of what we had to lay on. NO PEANUTS. And I tell you, I'd been through this theatre like a sniffer dog in a crack den. Not just the nuts on the bar, but the salads, everything, I even made 'em take the pistachio caramel tubs out of the ice-cream trays. I swear to you, like I did to Plod, there was not a fucking nut within twenty yards of Dame Viola.'

'So it was her allergy again?'

He gave a sardonic crack of laughter. 'Excuse me. This was a deliberate attempt to murder her. That's what the poor cow was yelling. Honest, Annie, she was out of her tree, with Sly trying to calm her down and shut her up and let the paramedics get her onto a stretcher. But of course some fuckwit has to overhear and get their phone out. So now the press are poking round, as well as the Bucksford boys in blue having their biggest thrill since the bus shelter got burned down. Tying stripy tape over the door of her dressing room, calling it a potential crime scene. Chrissake, the woman's alive and kicking everyone in sight, and I keep telling 'em we need that dressing room. I've Broadsides in for the week, with a cast of fucking hundreds, due any minute. Not that you can get inside there, hardly, for all the bouquets and cards and fucking balloons from her fan club. Stop sniggering, will you? From where I'm standing this isn't funny. I've told Liz here I want a nice quiet job. Like bomb disposal.'

'*Bouquets!*' exclaimed Annie suddenly. 'A bunch of flowers, of course. Cheers, Hank – I mean, I'm sorry and all that, hellish time for you obviously, but . . . Oh God, it's a bank holiday, isn't it? Bloody typical.' She stared in frustration at the phone before grabbing it back to her ear. 'Look – did you just say Liz was there? Phew, yes, any chance of a quick word?'

33

Liz duly arrived at the Red House in the early afternoon, with a photo on her phone of the very large, very beautiful and very costly floral arrangement she had purchased on Annie's behalf from the florist next to the cemetery which, thankfully, was indeed open on bank holiday Monday, if not offering deliveries. Yes, she had personally taken it to 3 Chatsworth Close. Yes, with Annie's message on a card, exactly as dictated.

'And you told Trisha how sorry I am I couldn't get down there myself, because of Dom being, you know, under the weather?'

'Well . . .' Liz eyed her uncertainly.

The side door crashed open and Rob strode into the kitchen, scowling. 'Look here, Annie, I hope you know, all that stuff I said yesterday . . .' He stopped short. 'Oh, Liz. Um, hi love.'

Why did he have to arrive *now*? For sure, Annie wanted to see Rob, and not to argue about his stupid remarks at the party yesterday. That had become the merest irrelevance. He was the person – the only person – who could be told what had happened to Dominic, who could be depended on to advise her, comfort her, bolster her with solid good sense. But not with Liz present. So she found herself staring at him like a complete idiot, lost for words. And he just glowered back, equally dumb. Meanwhile, Liz was wittering on about Trisha being too busy to talk.

'She asked me to thank you, of course, although . . . Well, to be honest, she didn't really have much to say, which is not like her, as you know, but I could see she was worried about Cate. I'm not surprised, as a matter of fact. I thought yesterday, at the picnic, that she looked peaky – didn't you, Rob?'

'I – uh – can't say I noticed anything,' he muttered, not taking his eyes off Annie.

'Still,' she continued brightly, 'the flowers will be nice for her too, won't they? Cate, I mean.'

At any rate this lightened Rob's frown. 'Flowers – from you, Nan?'

'Least I could do,' said Annie uncomfortably. To her relief, though, he was smiling at her now – well, nearly smiling.

'Oh, and the good news,' continued her indefatigably cheerful friend, 'is that they're expecting Dame Viola to be allowed out of hospital later today. So Hank heard.'

'Huh,' snapped Annie. 'They probably can't wait to get shut of her.'

Rob stopped smiling. 'You've seriously got it in for that woman, haven't you?'

'My God, if you only knew,' she burst out, but had to bite her lip and mumble something about the trouble Viola's hysterics had caused at the Woolshed.

'Gosh, you're telling me!' cried Liz with a giggle. 'Hank has been reading us the riot act, because you know some thoughtless person rang the papers? He's made us all swear not to breathe another word to *anybody*. There are journalists poking around everywhere. Shall I put the kettle on?'

Annie could have screamed. And, even as she was preparing to ask Liz please to forgive her rudeness, but she really did need to talk privately to Rob, Dominic chose this moment to limp into the room. He was grey-faced and red-eyed, but determinedly holding himself erect and flexing his injured leg as he walked. He glanced round, flinched perceptibly as he took in the presence of Rob and Liz, but managed a smile, the bravery of which wrung his mother's heart afresh. 'Sorry, um, am I interrupting something?'

'Not so far as I'm concerned,' said Rob, before Annie could open her mouth. 'I'm off and away.'

'What, already?' she gasped.

'Jen's expecting me for dinner and if I don't move I'll be snarled up in the rush hour on the North Circular. I only dropped round to say . . .' His mouth worked soundlessly for a moment or two. 'Well, to say goodbye, I guess.'

To Annie's considerable surprise, instead of his usual brotherly clap on the shoulder, he clamped both arms round her and hugged her tight to his chest. 'Well done, Nan. The flowers, I mean, and . . . Oh, there's things we need to talk about, you and me, but I guess it can wait. You, um, you take good care of yourself, eh?'

She was startled by a ridiculous impulse to burst into tears. Just a sleepless night and mega-stress, obviously. Besides, in the same instant, she was even more startled to feel herself smiling, because she was breathing that elusive scent which had so stirred her innards after finding his scarf. Lord, she sensed a reminiscent twinge even now. She'd have to ask him what the stuff was called. Buy herself a large bottle. 'What's all this?' she managed to say, as he released her. 'Anyone'd think you were going away for good.'

He just grinned, a bit oddly, she thought, and with some comment to Liz about letting her know – soon as poss, yeah? – he strode out.

It was a couple of hours later that the phone trilled.

Liz had taken herself off soon after Rob, declaring with a distinct air of mystery that she had an awful lot to do. *Just in case* . . . She was clearly hoping to be questioned, but Annie was too preoccupied to accord her more than a grateful smile and a wave. As soon as they were alone, she reported her conversation with Hank to her son, but hadn't the heart to press him over his continued refusal to speak to the police. Instead, she tenderly prepared for him – without a joke, let alone complaint – the liquidised concoction of carrot, apple and assorted green gunk he assured her would speed the purification of his too-long abused system.

She herself was now eating double-chocolate ice cream straight out of the tub (there are times when comfort food is a medical necessity) while, as beady-eyed as a mother hen, she watched him sweat and stifle curses on the bench outside, straightening his leg under the weights which had languished neglected on his bedroom floor these many weeks. He might be looking almost as green as his so-called health drink, but he seemed, she thought – hoped – to be at peace with himself in a way he hadn't since his accident.

'Bernie, hi,' she exclaimed, guiltily slamming the lid back on the ice-cream tub. 'Good, I'm glad you've rung. You spoken to Simon? I didn't want to trouble him when he's obviously got his hands full with the wife, but . . .' But, without betraying her son's confidence, she was very determined to talk to him about his wife's agent. She had no chance to say anything more, however.

'He's just rung,' said Bernie. 'She's dead.'

'Let's not bother with any mealy-mouthed crap,' she went on. 'Pity's sake, I couldn't be wishing her or anyone else dead, but I won't pretend I'm weeping. I'm sorry for Simon, though. He sounds half demented, so he does, with the police and I dare say a post-mortem to come and all that hoo-ha.'

'Gosh, yes, I gathered the cops were at the theatre this morning,' said Annie, glancing out of the window again to see Dominic strenuously pushing himself outwards from the garage wall. 'Bloody ridiculous.'

'Well, with her screaming at one and all she'd been poisoned, what'd you expect? But before you ask – sorry, shouldn't laugh – it wasn't my Davey sent her the hand cream in a pretty box.'

'You what?' Annie blinked. 'Hand cream?'

'Haven't you heard? Or body lotion, or something of the sort. Only what d'you suppose the stuff was made of? Peanut oil,' said Bernie, without waiting for an answer. 'Which Dame Viola realises only after she's been slathering the stuff on, when she gets round to reading the label. Hats off to her, mark you, for spotting it, because they don't write anything as common or garden as peanut on their fancy organic labels, do they? Arachis or something, it was.'

'Spiders!' exclaimed Annie.

'*Exactly*, my love. Spiders, just like poor Simon said, when he couldn't make head nor tail of what she was on about. But I'm here to tell you it's a word like arachnid turns out to be Latin for peanut, so that's a handy one to remember for the next pub quiz, isn't it? God forgive me for joking, the woman's dead, so she is. Look, I can't talk. We've the Fishing Association dinner tonight and the place is even madder than usual. But I thought you'd want to know.'

'Yes,' said Annie. 'I mean – thanks, yes.'

'Good,' said Dominic, but immediately shuddered. 'Sorry. No. Of course I didn't mean that.'

'Why not?' said his mother. 'The way I felt last night, I could cheerfully have done her in myself. But no, let's agree with Bernie. We wouldn't wish anyone dead, but we'll skip the crocodile tears. What do you fancy for supper?'

More surprising was that an email arrived almost immediately from Simon. A paragraph, cut and pasted from a news site, just reporting the death, with an even shorter message below.

You know what this means – could mean, please God??? I'm crazy with hope and despair. Even now, not a word!!! Longing to talk to you, but I'm besieged by idiots wanting to cry over me or quote me or even take bloody witness statements. Soonest. XXX

Uh-oh, she breathed. Does he mean what I *think* he means?

'So she's dropped dead?' said Martha. 'How convenient.'

'How in God's name do you know?'

'Jeez, Mother, it's all over Twitter, the web, everywhere. Why'd you think I'm ringing? I suppose this is good news for you.'

Annie winced. 'Not, I assure you, for the reasons you could be forgiven for imagining. Simon Spencer and I are – friends. And that's it.'

'Seriously?'

'Very seriously.' Annie just hoped he could be persuaded to see it that way.

'Shame. I was quite coming round to the idea. You getting yourself shacked up. With someone, anyhow.'

'Why? So you don't end up with a lonely old crone on your hands, expecting you to cook her fish fingers twice a week and run her to the day centre?'

Martha gurgled. 'That's about the size of it. Still, if you and he really aren't an item, at least I don't have to worry that it was you who poisoned her, I guess.'

'You're such a comfort to me, love. In every way.'

'I'm sorry I'm missing all the fun, actually. I mean, it's so fabulously bizarre, straight off the telly.' Her voice dropped to a doom-laden whisper: 'Death in a golden box.'

'What?'

'Come on, Ma, get online. It's all there.'

*   *   *

She was right. The story was all over the internet, although the respectable news organisations couldn't tell Annie much she didn't already know.

Viola Hood had died suddenly, aged sixty-seven – sixty-nine or even seventy, according to other accounts – in hospital, after being taken ill before a staged interview, et cetera, et cetera. *Blazing Star of the Big Screen; Brave Struggles with Cancer* – or with depression, drink, drugs, take your pick, depending on the site; *One of Hollywood's Most Enduring Marriages* – that old chestnut. Amongst the luvvies rushing to gush tributes, the 'rising star' author of *Darling Clementine* described her as an inspirational artist and utter perfectionist *striving ceaselessly to*—

'Drive you round the twist?' murmured Annie.

—portray the fascinating complexities of this woman, remembered now only as the wife of the great wartime leader, but—

'Yeah, yeah.' Yawning, she added 'Bucksford' to the search, which at least brought up a quote from dear Hank. But that was just publicity blurb, pre-dating recent sad events. She yawned again. Small wonder, considering she'd managed barely a couple of hours' sleep last night. Dominic had already returned to bed, with a mug of hot chocolate and a loving embrace from his mum. She was about to shut the laptop and follow him when her eye was caught by the story Martha must have been talking about.

Death in a golden box?

The self-same words, in bold, jumped out at her. Resettling in her chair, she tapped on the site. And saw the picture.

This was not BBC News. Nor even the *Daily Mail*. This was Buckfeed, the town's very own underground news site, although everyone knew it was run by Mo Harrup's nerdy son who sold advertising on the local rag but fancied himself destined for the *Sunday Times*. In his dreams. The site's hour of glory had come last year when it bravely exposed the council's top-secret plot to ban dogs from the Memorial Park. Evidently some bright spark in the Woolshed had whipped out a mobile phone before access was barred to the dame's abandoned dressing room. A wide-angle shot showed the place was, just as Hank had said, thick with cards, bouquets and balloons. But it was the second, close-up photo that riveted Annie. The rich colours and sharp shadows cast by the bulbs round the mirror gave the cluster of objects the charm of a still-life oil painting.

She was not interested in the chunky bottle of lotion, cork stopper carelessly cast aside. Nor in what appeared to be a tablet of soap, ribbon-tied and gleaming in gold wrapper. No, behind them, she was staring at a gift box. A slightly crumpled gift box, half capsized, probably because it was not made of cardboard, as such, but had been constructed from cunningly folded stiff paper. Rather beautiful – *very* beautiful – paper, featuring a tastefully washed-out map of the world as envis-aged by Renaissance cartographers, overlaid with gilded scroll work and sepia italic scrawls, seemingly inscribed with quill pen. Annie could tell you this paper cost well north of four hundred quid a roll, even four or five years ago. And that was with a professional decorator's discount. Yup, she knew that paper well. Course she did. She herself had bought it, had imported it direct from the Italian craftsmen. And to whom had she given the leftover, recently unearthed few yards?

'Morning, Trisha. I just thought I'd—'

'Annie! Lumme, it wasn't you I was expecting. I was sure it must be – well, never mind.' Trisha was holding open her front door, but not moving. Nor was she even looking at Annie. She was glancing uneasily back over her shoulder.

'Is this a bad time, Trish? You're looking a bit harassed.'

'Yes. I mean, I'm always glad to see you' – she didn't sound it – 'but was there anything particular? It's just . . . Oh Lordy, I dunno if I'm coming or going.'

Had Annie not been forgiven? To her dismay, down the hall behind Trisha, she glimpsed a flower arrangement. Still cellophane wrapped and lavishly bowed – lying on the floor.

'And now here's Tony as well, with the bloomin' post,' she wailed. 'As if I'd not enough on my plate.'

A balding, uniformed man leaned past Annie with a grin. 'Only a council tax leaflet, pet. But you found your big parcel, Saturday?'

'Saturday?' Trisha was glancing over her shoulder again. 'What about Saturday?'

'You was all out. And it's that new microwave you've been on about so long by the look of it. I knew you'd not want to wait until today with the bank holiday and that, so I popped it in t'caravan.' He was already stepping back to peer through the window of the shepherd hut. 'Blow me down, it's still sitting there, with the other post and all. Come on, love, I'll fetch it inside for you.'

'No!' squawked Trisha, much to his astonishment – and indeed Annie's. 'I mean, no, don't worry, just – just give it here. I can manage.'

This was no time to be enquiring about fancy gift wrap, although that little gold box had been much in Annie's thoughts since last night. Well, you did have to wonder how Trisha's handiwork came to be in Viola Hood's dressing room – containing the allegedly fatal bottle. How bizarre was that?

Breathlessly refusing all assistance, Trisha tottered indoors with the bulky carton clutched to her chest. Annie gathered up the wad of post that had slipped from under her friend's chin and hurried after her. 'Actually, I've come to say sorry, Trish, properly—'

'Not now,' she gasped, dumping the box and tossing the letters Annie handed her on top of the wretched flower bouquet. 'Any road – any road up, I can't think what you've to be sorry for.' Annie would have felt better if she'd said this with even a trace of conviction. 'So if that's all you called round about?'

'And I was hoping to see Cate,' said Annie – which she was, she truly *was*. They seemed to have embarked on the tentative beginnings of a friendship at Tiptree Park – irritating as it was to concede Rob might have been right all along. 'I gather she's not feeling too great?'

'Sorry, no.' Trisha was ushering her – hell, almost shoving her – over the threshold again. 'My girl's not up to seeing anyone. Not today.'

Annie caught her breath. 'I'm – so sorry to hear that. Is she seriously unwell? I know Liz was concerned about her on Sunday.'

'She's fine. I mean, she will be. Dr Ed's coming round any minute, so if you don't mind, Annie, love . . .'

'No, no, sure.' She was already backing away to pick up her bike, when she heard – unmistakably – Leona Parsons' voice echoing down the hallway.

'The kelp is in the fridge, and I've left the essence of moon-flower on the worktop. Just three drops, morning and night – in pure spring water, mind. But you must give her a big old hug from me, Trisha, and tell her that her nice comfy bed's ready and waiting, soon as she's well enough to pack a bag.' The woman had now appeared behind Trisha in the doorway.

'Oh, it's you, is it, Annie?' she said, with an infuriatingly smug smile. 'No visitors for our invalid today, I'm afraid, even little me – although I don't count as a visitor any more, do I, Trisha? But don't worry, I haven't even put my head round the door, not if our poorly girl's managing to get a bit of sleep at last. I'll pop round later to see what the doctor has to say. Bye for now.'

Trisha stared helplessly at Annie as Leona stalked away down the close. 'She's – very kind.'

'I'm sure,' said Annie, and gave a mechanical smile. 'My love to Cate, too. I hope she's feeling better soon.'

Where was bloody Rob, when she needed him? So Leona was welcome to swan around 3 Chatsworth Close, was she, but not Annie? She wanted his robust reassurance that she hadn't mortally wounded Trisha. Never had her old friend been so unwelcoming, so twitchy – dammit, so unnaturally *quiet*. Where was everybody else, come to that? Liz was off at a prayer meeting. OK, a conference of Anglican women, or some such jamboree. Bernie wasn't answering her phone. No doubt trotting between sickbeds at the Hopkirk Arms. Even Dominic had taken himself off for a physio session followed by more healthful exercise in the town swimming pool. Excellent, of course, but . . .

She passed the afternoon reordering her wardrobe. Even that reliable stand-by failed to soothe her ruffled soul, however. She could not have been more pleased when, towards suppertime, the doorbell sounded, for all she fully expected it to be the window-cleaner or just the Amazon delivery Dom had warned her to expect. A vegan cookbook – how delightful. She'd begun to feel like the last survivor on the planet. To her surprise and satisfaction, however, she found Bernie on the doorstep. And not just Bernie, Dave too.

'Coming to the front door?' she cried, throwing it wide. 'What's all this about – you in training for Jehovah's Witnesses?'

They didn't so much as smile. Just glanced at one another with palpable unease.

'Annie, love . . .' mumbled Dave. Then ran out of words, his face full of anguish.

Terror gripped her heart. 'Oh God, *Dom?*' she gasped. 'What's happened?'

'No – no, nowt to do with Dom, just—'

'Rob, then? Don't say he's had an accident?'

'They're fine. Everyone's fine.' Bernie elbowed her husband aside, and gripped Annie's arm. 'Come on into the kitchen and stop fretting. There's nothing so very terrible.'

'So why are you looking like undertakers preparing to measure me up?' Annie shook off Bernie's hand but followed her down the hall. 'Well? Or do you need a stiff drink before you spill the beans?'

Dave looked hopeful but was scowled down by his wife.

'It's – Cate,' she said.

Annie actually sank into a chair, such was her relief because, in spite of Bernie's reassurances, she had feared the worst about those she loved best. '*Cate?* Lord, I know she's not well, but don't tell me, please, she's—'

'No, no, no. They've sent her over to Leeds, because of the facilities, but Trish says there's nothing to worry about, not really. Although she's in an almighty tizz, of course.' Bernie visibly braced herself. 'She's having a baby. That's all.'

For a moment Annie just stared at her, slack-jawed. 'Trisha?' Then realised how absurd this was and gave a gasp of incredulous laughter. '*Cate?* You're never telling me little goody-goody Cath Blackwell's having a baby?'

'Bit of a bombshell, huh?' grunted Dave but Bernie, weirdly, said nothing. Just clutched his hand.

'You are not kidding it's a bombshell,' said Annie, and let out a long whistle. 'You mean to say she's not ill? All this time she's just been – pregnant? With her white face and her bad back – and milk turning her sick. Hell, it did me too, with

Dom anyhow. Ha! No wonder she wears those flapping great sacks. Even so, you can hardly credit—' She broke off. 'But what's with the glum faces? I mean, it's the most astonishing thing I've heard since – since Trump got elected, but bloody good for her, I say. Good old Cate.' She chuckled. 'Always was a dark horse, that girl. Didn't I say, Bernie Eastman, did I not say to you, time and again, there had to be something fishy behind her charging back from the States like that? And, just this morning, dear oh dear, there was poor Trisha, tying herself into knots with me on her doorstep . . .' Eventually her flow of words and laughter trickled to a halt, however, because neither Bernie nor Dave had uttered a syllable. And they still looked miserable as sin.

'You haven't asked who the father is,' said Bernie quietly.

'Donor? Turkey-baster job? Come on then, anyone we . . .' But she did not finish the question. She was recalling Rob's words, outside the Houghs' bungalow, as the bike pedal jammed so painfully into her shin. 'No,' she said uncertainly. 'Never. You're surely not going to tell me . . .'

Dave heaved a gusty sigh. 'It were my dad rang us. From the hospital.'

'Oh – my – God!' shrieked Annie, clasping her hands to her face.

'Oh love, don't cry,' wailed Bernie, springing to life. She flung herself into the chair beside Annie and hugged her fiercely. 'I feel terrible, so I do, after all I've said, the way I egged you on. I could throttle that sneaky monkey.'

'Cry?' Annie lowered her hands. 'Don't be so daft. I'm laughing my head off. Glory be, what a crazy fucking world this is.'

34

She brewed a celebratory pot of tea. To toast the health of the as yet unborn child. Well, unborn so far as they knew, and Annie was assured that the Eastmans' phones were charged and held close. Dave knocked back his mug in almost a single gulp, mopping his still-heated brow. He had, he swore, been sweating cobs all the way here.

'And you mean it?' he demanded, for at least the third time. 'You're really not holding a torch for my randy old man?'

'I'm fine, truly. Cross my heart.'

She spoke a little abstractedly, though, as she reached for her own tea because, for all her honest response to the wacky combination of Simon and Cate Blackwell had been helpless laughter, she was feeling just a mite less amused as the implications sank in. No, she did not want Simon Spencer for herself, no way. But she'd certainly thought she did, at one time, and ... frankly, she was now feeling a bit of a fool. Correct that. She felt a king-sized bloody idiot; so blinkered, so dim-witted, so puffed up with conceit she'd been quite ready to believe that this star of stage and screen was madly in love with her.

And she'd been well up for it at one time, hadn't she? Recalling the night he'd called round on his way to Heathrow, she slopped tea over the table, so violently did she shudder at the image of herself tarted up to kill, with lights low, hopes high, every nerve a-tingle. Maybe she'd gone on to have

second thoughts, had shut the door behind him with relief –
but what must he have thought of her behaviour? Bloody hell,
what did he think *he* was playing at, coming on to her like that,
when—

But *had* Simon come on to her – really? What had he actually
done or said? He hadn't even kissed her – not as in *kissed* – not
that night, not ever. He'd flirted, for sure. He'd poured out all
that embarrassing guff about being with the woman he loved
– but then, that woman wasn't her, was it? Never had been.

It was sinking in on Annie that, far from being the femme
fatale of Simon Spencer's fevered dreams, she seemed to have
figured chiefly as his favourite bloody agony aunt. To whom
he could confide his frustrated passion for a woman practically young enough to be his daughter. Or hers. Dear God,
not only did Annie feel a fool, she felt *old*. Old as the sodding
hills.

This wouldn't do. Briskly mopping up the spilled tea, she
smiled at her friends and declared, with a warmth that
surprised even herself, that she hoped all was well at the hospital. 'How early is the babe, did you say?'

'Cate's almost thirty-six weeks, which isn't bad at all,'
responded Bernie stoutly. 'My Liam popped out at thirty-five
and look at the steaming great hulk he is now.'

'Eight months plus, and she's managed to keep it secret.'
Annie shook her head in wonderment. 'You're sure even Trish
didn't twig?'

'First she knew was when the contractions came on this
morning. Well, I dare say they were tweaking before, but Cate
didn't let on, not until she couldn't do anything else. I know, I
know, incredible, but I say again, look at me. My mam and
dad didn't suspect a blessed thing until I was practically
exploding, and I'm a shrimp compared to her, tall and broad-
shouldered as she is, swishing around in her long dresses.'

'But – Simon?' With some effort, Annie managed to say the bastard's name quite naturally. 'Did he know? Must've done, surely.' The triple-*triple* bastard.

Bernie hooted. 'Talk about feckin' flabbergasted. Weeping, laughing, he sounded half cracked, so he did, saying at least he knew now why Cate wouldn't let him within a feckin' mile. She'd been cutting him dead all ways, from what I could gather – which wasn't a lot, with him panting to get off the phone and back to the action.'

'No wonder he told me—' But she was not about to mention that proper, old-fashioned letter she had never doubted was destined for herself. Idiot. 'Well, Cate must've relented. If he's there now.'

'Not a bit of it!' retorted Bernie. 'That was all Trisha's doing, and he's so slobberingly grateful to her for calling him in, you'd think it was her he was in love with. Mind, it's a fat lot of use he'll be to poor Cate in that state. If the midwife's got any sense she'll be giving *him* the gas and air.'

'I told him to get himself a bottle of malt and keep well clear of the business end,' chipped in Dave. 'Until it's out and screaming. And he'll need an even stiffer drink then, because I've yet to clap eyes on a newborn that didn't look like a squashed strawberry.'

'Away with you.' Bernie was looking at Annie, however, as she continued. 'It's lovely, of course it is, a baby for Cate, if that's what she's wanting.'

'But is she?' said Annie. 'She never struck me as the maternal type.'

Her friend shrugged. 'All I can tell you is that the papa-to-be's like a dog with two dicks and ten tails. But that doesn't mean he isn't a scallywag. No, hush, Davey, your dad's a bad boy. And so I shall be telling him, leading my Annie up the daisy path the way he did.' She took Annie's hand. 'Oh, darlin',

I can't tell you how glad I am you didn't fall for all his lovey-dovey palaver.'

'Oh, come on, you know I did.' This was no time for pretending. Annie's grin was rueful. 'I lapped it up. He made me feel seventeen again. But, I dunno, the magic – wore off. Pretty quickly, actually. Just as well, since he obviously had me down as no more than a mate, with a handy shoulder for weeping on. Great boost for a girl's ego, huh? Still, he flirts with everyone, I guess.'

'Jaysus, doesn't he ever? I believe he'd chat up a cupboard door if he thought there were sweets inside.'

Annie chuckled. 'Poor Cate, though. Having to watch him cosying up to me. I thought she was just being stand-offish with me. I realise now she was behaving like a bloody saint. Because let's face it.' She braced herself. 'The flirting wasn't all on Simon's side. I should be ashamed of my own behaviour.'

'You should be no such thing.' Bernie was up in arms at once. 'He deserves to be shot, so he does. It's just feckin' lucky for him you're such a – such a—'

'Tough old trout?'

'Sensible woman. I mean, just imagine if you'd been a fluttery little innocent, like your friend Liz?'

'Gosh yes,' said Annie, her grin fading. 'Imagine.'

Still, this was not going to be as bad as breaking the news to her about Kelvin, thought Annie, as she waved the Eastmans away. Nowhere near. Liz barely knew Simon; the hours passed in his company could probably be counted on the fingers of one hand, and she'd been realistic about her chances from the start. Nor need Annie berate herself for steering her down *this* road to heartbreak. She had offered barely a word of encouragement. Nevertheless . . .

Walking back into the kitchen, she wondered whether to ring her lovelorn friend now, and get the worst over. Liz should be back from her conference. She did actually reach for the phone, only to put it down again. Today, tomorrow morning, what did it matter? Tomorrow afternoon, even, because Liz worked at the Woolshed on Wednesday mornings. Maybe someone in that busy hub of town gossip would have heard the news and would do the job for her.

All she wanted now was to contemplate this astounding turn of events, to pick the story apart, thread by fascinating thread. She wished Bernie hadn't had to hurry back to the pub so soon – although Dave's presence would have been a bit of an obstacle. Nothing against dear Dave, naturally, but being a man, he wasn't equipped to join his wife and Annie in the delicate art of analysing their fellow creatures, hearts and minds, rights and wrongs, facts and – better still – fictions.

Exasperatingly, the same went for her son. Dominic was unstirred to learn Cate was currently closeted in a maternity suite, other than to observe, with a shrug, that she was a bit antique to be having kids, wasn't she? There was no point sharing with him her speculations as to why Cate had kept her condition so utterly secret.

Could be, at first, she'd never intended to go through with it? Even if she did, with all the risk factors at her age, they'd have offered her every test under the sun. No way could she have shared that ordeal with Trisha, devoted mother of a disabled child. Poor Cate. But what about later, what about *Simon*, for heaven's sake? Why not tell the father-to-be? After all, he'd been shouting to the world how he'd always longed for children, how ecstatic he was to learn about Dave. Oh, it was enthralling. To her, if not to her son.

What did provoke a flicker of interest in him was the photograph of the gift box.

'It was made by Trisha,' Annie stated. 'Trust me. Odds are a million to one anyone else in the north of England has that paper.'

'What're you saying, Ma?' He grinned. 'That old Trish knocked the woman off?'

'Oh, sure. Prime suspect.'

But for all she wouldn't dream of voicing such a patently barmy notion, she did find herself, well, *pondering*. Trisha, that loyal sister, that fiercely protective quasi-mother? Even if she knew nothing about the baby, might she have suspected – as Rob had certainly done, blast him – there was something going on between her beloved sister and Simon? The shepherd hut, for starters. Well, no prizes now for guessing the identity of the donor, that mysterious so-called friend in California – with 'excellent connections in the television industry'. His very words, the brazen monkey. She could see him now, suggesting this to her and Trisha, face alight with mischief. The nerve of the guy – it took your breath away. Ten to one he was just back from running round these excellent old telly friends, organising his surprise present while ostensibly getting his eyelashes dyed. Which Annie, for one, had always thought was a dodgy story – and at a knockdown price, she wouldn't wonder, given his money problems. Even he might baulk at charging gifts for his girlfriend to the wife's credit card. *Might* . . .

But the memory of that conversation made her cringe, because his teasing had only been prompted by her own bird-brained speculations about Cate and Siobhan. Which he had damn well encouraged. He'd let her make a complete fool of herself, hadn't he? Honestly, Bernie was right, he deserved to be shot.

Had Trisha really been so totally ignorant of her sister's love life, though? If so, how come – according to Bernie – she'd been the one to summon Simon to the labour ward? What was more – again, courtesy of Bernie – it transpired Cate and Simon's affair was nothing new. Seemed they'd been at it, on and off, for years, ever since the Austen biopic. With Simon unable – or unwilling – to leave his wife.

'And to be sure I can understand him not wanting to end up skint,' had declared Bernie, 'but much as I love him – which I do, in spite of everything – I have to say that was a rotten old reason for keeping Cate dangling all these years. I'm amazed she didn't give him the heave-ho long ago.'

'I'm amazed she ever jumped into bed with him in the first place,' Annie had snorted, before feeling obliged to qualify this. Obviously, he was an attractive man, et cetera, et cetera – but for Cate, the famous feminist?

'I mean, can you imagine how mortified she must've felt, ending up as his *mistress*?' she said now to Dominic. 'He'd got her every which way, because she was never going to wreck his marriage with a kiss 'n' tell, was she? So the years go by, with him locked in Viola's golden handcuffs . . .'

'But it can't be Cate wot dunnit,' said Dominic, with a wry chuckle. 'Obviously.'

Oh, what sweet comfort it gave his mother to see the cloud lifted from that beautiful alabaster brow, the shadows banished from his eyes. He was sipping his herbal brew, conscientiously raising and flexing his injured limb. With a copy of *Equity News* spread open in front of him.

'Why?' she demanded.

'*Duh*. Because she really is the prime suspect – and that one's never the murderer.' But then he frowned. 'Shit, Mum, I don't know how you've got me talking like this. I mean, it's not funny, is it? These are real people.'

'You youngsters,' said Annie. 'Where's your sense of humour?'

*　　*　　*

He had a point, though. Of course, she was laughing precisely *because* these were real people, people she'd known all her life, and it was ludicrous to imagine the likes of Cate or Trisha brewing poisoned potions. But when all was said and done, Viola Hood was dead. And someone had apparently sent her a concoction of peanut oil. In a box created by Trisha Hood. From paper supplied by . . .

In spite of herself and alone now, Dominic having yawned off to bed, Annie had to chuckle. Yup, if this were a Sunday night whodunnit on the telly, her contribution in providing the gift wrap might earn her a fleeting moment under the spotlight of suspicion. Particularly when you added in her public flirtation with the dead woman's husband. And her house was quite up to standard for a starring role in the glitzi-est of corpse-operas, if she said so herself.

But then she stopped smiling as she reflected that she could be accused of having quite another motive for wishing Viola Hood ill, a much more plausible motive, once Viola's squalid role in her son's near-death emerged. Heavens, Dominic himself. He would have to figure high on the suspect list, wouldn't he? Quite likely, he would emerge as the penultimate candidate, the one towards whom all clues and accusing fingers pointed just before the real murderer was unmasked. He'd certainly rank above Dave or Bernie. They were just the comedy turn. You always got one or two of those in the line-up, light relief between the surly grudge-bearers and mysterious secret-keepers. Peanut butter sandwiches, indeed. As for *Simon*, who had actually talked about killing his wife – he *had*, on the grass by the town hall, quite likely at the very moment his wife was collapsing indoors – well, it was never going to be him, was it? The angry and adulterous husband. Of a very rich wife. That was way too predictable a solution for fiction, even if, as she found herself reflecting, the spouse almost always did turn out to be the perp – in real life . . . Oh for goodness' sake, all this speculation was just fun and nonsense.

'It could be any one of us,' said Annie to herself with grandiose solemnity, as she ambled round the house, flicking off lights. 'Even though it obviously isn't. Just a freak accident. After all, who would ever guess hand cream was made from flipping peanuts?'

Her last thought, before falling into a particularly soothing and dreamless sleep, was that she had forgotten to add Liz to the list. Wow, yes, lovelorn Liz had to be considered. In fact, given her sweet and blameless demeanour, her being the widow of a vicar and all that, a regular church-goer, kind to everyone – in other words, the most wildly improbable murderer it was possible to imagine – meant that yup, no two ways about it: if this were telly, Mrs Elizabeth Jones would *definitely* have dunnit.

'Liz,' she exclaimed, still foggy-eyed and dressing-gowned when the sweet and blameless murderess almost danced into the kitchen just before nine the following morning, 'I wasn't expecting you. It is Wednesday, isn't it, shouldn't you be at the Woolshed? Or am I going crackers?'

'I'm on holiday. For a whole ten days. And, oh Annie, I do hope you can spare me too. I'm so excited.'

Hell and damnation. Annie really didn't want to do this. Here was Liz, as bright and sparkly as a kid about to take off on the Sunday school picnic, but she had no choice. 'Have you heard the news?' she said carefully. 'About Cate?'

'Crikey pips, yes. Has she had it?'

Annie blinked. 'Well, I haven't checked my phone for texts yet. But I dare say Bernie would've rung if there were anything to report.'

'Bound to, yes. I must say you could have knocked me over with a feather when I heard, but how simply marvellous for Cate. I mean, obviously everyone will be happy for her, but to someone like me, who used so much to long for a baby – I really feel it in my heart for her, you know?'

Annie braced herself afresh. 'So you've probably not gathered about the, um, the father of her child?'

Liz had already swept on, unhearing. 'I'm frightfully sorry, though, just charging in without a word of warning. As a matter of fact, I did send you a text last night, although it was shockingly late, and it doesn't matter anyway, only do please say you don't mind me going away for a few days? And I thought I should leave the car here, because it'll be safer than parked on my street whilst I'm not there to keep an eye on it.'

'Mind? No, of course I don't mind,' said Annie, bewildered by this excitable creature, flitting around the table, chattering nineteen to the dozen. It was as though a dozy pet budgie had not just started to talk but launched straight into a lecture on nuclear physics. 'I mean, how lovely, a holiday. Where are you off to?'

'*London*,' declared Liz, and the awe with which she breathed the word conjured a vision of seething metropolitan glamour. 'Rob rang last night. Phil apparently has spare tickets for Glyndebourne – *Glyndebourne*, can you imagine? And I'm invited. Isn't that too wonderful for words? And to stay as long as I like with your sister and brother-in-law.'

'Terrific,' said Annie. 'Fantastic. But—'

'My friend Carol's very kindly picking me up here' – Liz glanced at her watch – 'golly, any second now. She works in York, so she's giving me a lift. Train down to King's Cross. And off I jolly well go.'

'I won't offer you coffee then. But listen, Liz.' Should she in fact tell her now? Wouldn't it be kinder to wait until she returned?

'It's so sweet of Hank to let me take off like this, because you can imagine what he's going through at the theatre, with all these reporters and policemen in and out.'

'Really?' said Annie, temporarily distracted from the unpleasant duty awaiting her. 'Press I can understand, sure, but do the police really think she was . . .' Somehow, in the cold light of morning, she couldn't bring herself to say *murdered*. 'There wasn't anything suspicious about her death, was there?'

'That's what everyone's asking themselves, of course,' said Liz, with startlingly inappropriate cheerfulness. 'And no one seems to know, but the police have been interviewing the backstage crew, and so forth.' She seemed belatedly to recollect the proprieties. 'Of course, it's terribly sad, just when everyone thought Dame Viola was going to be fine, but I suppose . . . Oh, I don't really know what's going on, and we've all been sworn to total secrecy about *everything*, particularly dear Cate and Simon. I mean, what a shock. Whoever could have imagined that?'

Annie stared at her. 'So – you do know?'

'You'd heard, hadn't you? Of course, you must have done. Although only Hank and I know it's his baby, the press don't seem to have got wind of that, thank goodness, and we must do our utmost to keep it that way. The newspapers are so awful, aren't they? And I hope you don't think I'm . . . well, of course one can't exactly approve of adultery, but by all accounts, it wasn't the happiest marriage, and I gather she could be quite a difficult woman. Not that that should excuse—'

'Liz,' said Annie, forced to cut across the flow. 'Look, I'm probably being rather dim-witted here, but . . .' How best to phrase this? 'You and I had a conversation, not so very long ago, remember, after you tore up that pillowcase?'

'Gosh, yes.' She giggled. 'Maybe Kelvin should recommend pillowcase-shredding as therapy. It worked a treat for me.' Which, for Liz, was really quite a good joke, but Annie was disinclined to smile.

'The thing is, you more or less hinted that, you know, there might be someone else? Not that you were cherishing any great hopes . . .'

'I did say that, didn't I?' She was blushing now. 'Well, you know what I'm like. You're the one who always says I never expect anyone to take a fancy to boring old me.' She pulled a face. 'But it looks as if you were right – as usual. And I was wrong. I mean, it still seems quite mad, and I don't know if I'm on my head or my heels, because I simply refused to let myself believe it, told myself again and again I was imagining things, but then when he rang me, so late last night . . .'

All at once, Annie felt as though the flagstones were crumbling under her feet. Her stomach was lurching upwards, blood was pounding in her ears, and she had to grab the back of a chair for support. Liz, thank God, had turned away, head cocked to one side.

'Did you hear that toot? I told Carol not to come in, so that I can shift my bags straight over from our car to hers. Are you happy if I just pop the keys through the letter box, in case you need someone to move it while I'm gone?'

'What? Yes. Yes, of course,' Annie heard herself saying. And even though she wanted nothing more than for Liz to go, to get out of her kitchen, out of her house – out of her bloody *life* – she had to ask. Had to make sure she wasn't blundering into the biggest misunderstanding of her entire conceited, complacent, pigheaded, peabrained existence. 'It's Rob, then?' she managed to croak. 'You're talking about Rob Daley?'

'Of course,' carolled Liz. 'Who else? And I can see you're trying not to laugh, because I know you two are forever at loggerheads, but I have to say I think he's amazing. The kindest, cleverest, most thoughtful, wonderful man I have ever known. Whoops, I really must dash, or I'll miss my train.'

Dominic found her, still in the kitchen, a couple of hours later. Seemed he hadn't been in bed all this time. He had been out on a walk – a long walk.

'Well, more of a hobble. But I did make it the whole way into town, even though I began to think getting myself back up the hill would finish me off, but listen.' He poured cold water into the sink, splashed handfuls over his face and shoulders. 'I, um, looked in at the Woolshed, you know? And Hank told me, it isn't Viola Hood the fuzz have been asking round about.' He was groping for a towel, grasped a tea towel and clamped it to his nose. 'I mean, thank fuck I was already red and sweating so he couldn't have seen anything in my face . . .' He lowered the towel and glanced round at her. 'You OK, Mum? You seem a bit – I dunno.'

'Hay fever,' said Annie. 'That time of year, isn't it, even for people like me who don't usually suffer? And look at me, for goodness' sake, still in my dressing gown and it's nearly lunchtime. Shocking. I, um, think I might go and get in the bath. Can you sort yourself out a sandwich or something, love?' She paused at the door. 'By the way, Bernie rang. A girl. Seven and a half pounder, too. So, well done Cate, hey?'

35

She was not going to weep into the soapsuds. She was done with tears. She had screamed like a banshee the instant the door shut behind Liz, but at least she'd managed to contain the explosion until then. There was that much to be grateful for. How she had then wailed, though – great wracking, wrecking, raging sobs. Her throat still burned now, her ribs ached, and a spasm gripped her chest as she reached for a nail brush. Why a nail brush? To scrub a smear of bike-chain oil off her ankle, that's why, because bikes meant Rob. Silly cow. She swallowed hard and scrubbed harder.

How could she have been so blind? Oh, not to what was whirling around in Liz's fluffball apology for a brain. Annie shut her eyes, wincing. God help her, she was at it again. Demonising the woman. She was shocked, truly appalled, that her fondness for Liz could seemingly vanish, just like that, popped and gone like a soap bubble. Even so, merely thinking about her *friend* – her kind, sweet-natured friend – had her hands curling into balls of fury. Once more, she had to remind herself that this was not Liz's fault. It wasn't, was it? Who had turned her into this – this manhunter? Who had packaged her in slinky frocks and shiny lipstick, instructing her time and again not to undervalue herself? Anyway, that was beside the point.

She might have been blithely unaware of what was going on in Liz's immaculately coiffed head, but that wasn't Annie's big mistake. No way. Her real failure – her utter, abject, soul-shredding failure – was that she'd remained equally oblivious to what was going on in her own. And in her heart. Because the truth was clear to her now all right, standing out as big and bold as the town hall clock. And just like the town hall clock, it had been there for years and years and years, in fact for bloody ever, which was probably why she'd never given it a moment's thought. You don't, do you? You just know something's there, and take for granted it always will be. And that newly recognised truth – that towering, forever unchanging and unchangeable fact of her whole life – was that Rob Daley was *hers*. Not just her old playmate, flatmate, brother-in-law, friend, advisor, admirer, joke-sharer, sparring partner – but hers. Body and soul, crap haircut and cute bum, nerdy puns and timely wisdom, orange juice, clunky cycle shoes, the whole damn shooting match, he *belonged* to Annie.

Except, it seemed, he didn't. Oh, she had tried to believe Liz was kidding herself. Yeah, right, this is Liz, who had to be persuaded that even a creep like Kelvin Parsons would look twice at her? Plus there was the evidence of her own eyes and ears. Again, Annie had been reviewing the recent past afresh, but – God – with none of yesterday's relish. No, she was hearing Rob confess how wrong he'd been about Liz. That she was – what were his words . . . a good woman? Sensible? Lot brighter than you'd think? Hardly the effusions of a man in love, you might think, but this was Rob Daley talking. A Yorkshireman for whom 'not bad' was a five-star eulogy. Look how he'd rushed to rescue her on the dance floor. Of course he'd become her hero from that moment on. Stupid, stupid Annie for ever supposing Liz had been won over by Simon dealing with a few tattooed louts in the street.

And there was more. Much more. How often since then had she noticed old Robbo singling Liz out, making a point of talking to her? And she'd just thought (how dumb can you get?) that he was being kind, typically thoughtful. The sharpest pang of all came with the recollection of him holding forth so solemnly to one and all at Dave's birthday picnic about the superior prospects for partnerships embarked upon later in life. So he'd been thinking along those lines. Obviously.

But even if she managed to discount all that – and she had done her utmost – she could not forget the odd way he'd behaved when he'd called round to say goodbye just two days ago. Before heading down to London. Hugging her tightly, telling her to take care of herself, saying they had things they needed to talk about – well, they clearly bloody did. Because off he trots and rings Liz with an invitation to join him. At her own sister's house, to heap insult on agony. She couldn't imagine what had passed between them in their conversation last night. Couldn't bear to. But there was no escaping what it all spelled. Rob and Liz. *Liz* and Rob.

'What tha can't get out of, tha can only get on with.'

Never had her father's words rung more hollowly in her head. But Dad was right. Again. And, true to form, she had only herself to blame.

It was a struggle to heave herself out of the bath. As though her muscles had melted in the hot water. As though she'd put on a couple of stone overnight. Or maybe just a couple of decades. Well, after all, she was about to quit even her much-denied fifties in – what? – a matter of weeks, if not days. Oh joy unbounded. *Happy birthday to me, happy birthday to* . . .

She sniffed ferociously, grabbed a yard of loo roll and blasted away. The other thing her dad was dead right about. The least said t'bluddy better.

'You're looking very glam for a Monday morning,' exclaimed Bernie.

You betcha she was. This level of misery demanded the full cosmetic armoury, every flick, shade and smudge applied with fierce determination to look bright – and on the bright side. She'd barely eaten a crumb for five days. The very idea of food turned her sick. Her waistband was loose, even if her chest was iron-banded. Tight with bottled-up tears. Tears she was not going to let out. It had taken stern lectures to self – and fibs to everyone else about a summer cold – but this morning she had ordered a taxi to convey her to the Hopkirk Arms, where Cate Blackwell had taken up temporary residence with baby Grace. A woman's gotta do. Et cetera.

'Simon's popped out to get fresh supplies of nappies,' said Bernie, leading her upstairs to the number one bedroom. That was a minor relief. Bad enough to face Cate, but the two of them together? '*Supposedly*. Ten to one, it'll be another teddy and a shedload more flowers. I told him I've already run out of vases.' She threw open the door. 'Here she is, my lovely, I've brought you a visitor.'

'Annie,' cried Cate Blackwell. And the unexpected warmth, the unmistakable welcome in her voice and face suddenly – inexplicably – made Annie want to weep. Again. What kind of a mush-headed muppet was she turning into? She had to force a cough, blow her nose and thank heaven for waterproof mascara.

'You look – great,' she said, when she could speak. Cate damn well did. Here was a glowing madonna, with a snuffling, crumpled parcel of infant cradled in one arm. 'And, um, so does she. What I can see of her.'

Cate pulled a face as she turned the baby towards her. 'I'm afraid she's still a bit of a squashed strawberry, as Dave says. But, yes – she is pretty amazing. Miraculous, in fact. Would you like to hold her?'

'Well . . .' This was not the reception she'd been anticipating. 'If – if I may?'

She had to will her hands to stop trembling as she grasped the bundle of blanket and baby, clasped it to her fast-beating heart. But then, suddenly – oh, the sensation of that warm, milky-perfumed little body pressed against hers. How sweet it was, how unutterably comforting. A million memories were flooding through her. That exquisitely tiny mouth, opening and shutting like a fledgling's beak . . . Annie didn't care if her eyes were swimming when she looked round at Cate. 'I think it must be time I had a grandchild.'

'Phooey, you're too young and cool to be a granny. But you can have a goddaughter, if you like. Sorry, I put that very badly.' Cate's smile was shy. 'Simon and I were hoping, you know, that you might consider . . .?'

She gulped. Whatever next? 'I don't know what to say. I mean – of course, yes, I'd be thrilled. Honoured. But—'

'I'm so glad you've come, Annie. And that Simon's not here. I've been longing to talk properly to you, not least to apologise.'

This was crazy. 'You? Apologise to *me*?'

'I've been so cold, so downright rude to you on occasion. I can only say I felt I had to avoid you. I was so sure you knew or would very soon guess. Super-sharp about people as you've always been.'

'Are you ever wrong about that,' Annie said before she could stop herself, and hurried on, 'It's rubbish, anyway. I feel – a complete fool, to be honest. And I couldn't blame you if you never spoke to me again. After – after the way I behaved.' She had to say it, get it out in the open. 'With – your man.'

Whereat Cate . . . laughed? She did. She was laughing. Oh God, the mortification. 'Come on. Anyone could see you didn't really give a toss about Simon – even him. Although reluctantly, if I know my lover. He likes to think he's irresistible, of course, but I'd long since set him straight about you.' Fortunately, she swept on because Annie was now bereft of speech. 'I admit, I did get irritated from time to time.' She grinned. 'No, let's be honest, spitting furious.'

'I'm – not surprised,' said Annie faintly.

'But with *him*, not you. I knew who to blame. And you get all that, don't you, better than most? After being married to a randy bastard like Jake?'

Annie's mouth fell open. For the first time, but by no means the last.

She had embarked on this visit only because she had to.

Bernie had been pressing her to call ever since Cate had had the baby. She had promised to pick her up, drop her off, had offered coffee, lunch, four-course dinners – even hot whisky and lemon. Annie couldn't make excuses about cold bugs forever. Besides, it wasn't just Cate. She had to get back into circulation again, to steady herself for the return from London of Rob. Rob and *her*. She must be ready to welcome them back in quite her usual fashion, with suitable astonishment and delight, kisses and congratulations, a little gentle teasing.

So this outing was by way of a testing ground, a dress rehearsal, for playing herself. For pretending to be the same old handsome, clever and rich Annie Stoneycroft. Who was still, as she kept reminding herself, endowed with some of the best blessings of existence. If not the one and only blessing she wanted. Oh, how desolately she wanted that blessing. Another of Dad's little maxims kept coming into her head, but she'd kicked this one right out of court. *Wanting*, she was here to tell you, was not better than *having*. Sorry, Dad, but it bloody well was not.

What she could never have predicted was that, within minutes, she would find herself plunging into an exchange of the most intimate womanly confidences with Cate Blackwell. About her own marriage. More startling still was that straight-faced, strait-laced, butter-wouldn't-melt Dr Blackwell seemed already to understand so much about that misbegotten alliance and expressed amazement only that Annie had stuck it out as long as she had. When she, wincing, said that Cate must surely wonder why she'd ever shacked up with the likes of Jake in the first place – a man who couldn't have been more obviously mad and bad if he'd had a government health warning tattooed across his forehead – she burst into another peal of delighted laughter.

'Tell me about it,' she said. 'Georgette Heyer has a lot to answer for.'

Annie blinked. 'Sorry?'

'You read her, didn't you, the crack cocaine of girly fiction? Well, I know you did because your mum gave me a stack of tattered paperbacks when she was clearing out your old room, and I devoured every last one. Oh God, don't we all fall hook, line and suspenders for that myth of sexy, sardonic rakes just waiting to be tamed by clever women like you and me?'

Annie managed a cautious smile. 'Whereas in real life . . .'

'Wolves don't change their spots.' Cate leaned forward, eyes alight with mischief. 'There's definitely something to be said for preferring women.'

'Shit.' Annie felt her face burning afresh. 'Did Simon . . .?'

'Pass on your speculation about me and my beloved Siobhan? Naturally he did. Thinking it was a huge joke, the poor sap.'

What? Annie only thought this. She was beyond speech.

'Such a dinosaur as he is, bless him, so unreconstructedly *binary*. Unlike razor-sharp you, but that was aeons ago, you know, just a rather lovely phase in our enduring friendship. I danced with joy at her and Amanda's wedding, in spite of the most ghastly morning sickness. Also, I have to admit, their less than enthusiastic opinion of my own relationship. But Simon's not so bad, you know.'

'No . . .' Annie clutched baby Grace tightly because she'd begun to feel she was free-falling through space. 'I mean, no, of course he isn't, but—'

'A pathological flirt, goes without saying, and a shocker for wanting his bread buttered both sides – but even sticking with the vile dame wasn't all self-interest on his part.' She rolled her eyes comically. 'Nine tenths, maybe, but I can graciously concede now that she was frail. Well, of course she was – look at what's happened. Although I do wonder, if it hadn't eventually turned out he'd written to me *before* she succumbed, swearing at long last that he was quitting come hell or penury—' She broke off, with a shake of the head. 'I certainly didn't know that when I was in the throes. Three cheers for my sister, eh? Did Bernie tell you how Trisha learned the dreadful truth? Apparently I screamed his name during a particularly vicious contraction – accompanied by several unrepeatable epithets. All richly merited, I assure you.'

Annie laughed.

'He's a scamp – but, for better or worse, *my* scamp.' She hesitated only for a moment. 'Whereas your Jake really was an out-and-out prick, wasn't he? But my word he was sexy with it. That guy could seduce a busload of nuns. He tried it on with me, you know. The time I came up from college to interview him.'

Annie bit her lip. 'Does – that make us quits?'

Cate's smile was both warm and strangely wistful. 'I'd like to think it makes us friends,' she said. 'God knows, we've one fuck of a lot in common.'

This woman was amazing. How had Annie never realised it before? Not only laser-bright but funny, rude, self-deprecating – such a jewel was surely wasted on Simon Spencer. As they settled little Grace in her cot, she was not surprised to learn that Cate had told him several times they were finished. It seemed he just refused to listen, even when, as Cate gaily reminded her, she'd resorted to blasting the message over a microphone in a crowded pub.

'Your star turn on the bloody karaoke,' cried Annie. 'Gloria Gaynor with added venom. And I thought it was me you were gunning for.'

'Chump. It was him I wanted out. How's it go?' Cate opened her mouth as if to sing, but glanced at the cot and lowered her voice. 'Out of the door – out of my life for good and all. At any rate, that's what I'd been telling myself for years I should want. Particularly now I'd finally managed to get myself pregnant.'

'You *what*?' Annie squawked so loudly the baby stirred and whimpered, and she had to wait a moment before continuing, in a lowered voice, 'You're telling me it – this little piece of perfection – wasn't just an accident?'

'Do me a favour. I worked longer and harder at getting myself *oop t'duff*, as they say round here, than I have at anything since my finals. No hardship, I admit, because Simon's quite something in the sack.' That wicked grin again. 'Hung like a prize ram, my dear, as I'm glad to say you never had the chance to find out. Besides, I did love him.' Cate's face softened. 'Rather, I *do* love him, beastly old charmer that he is. But I'd about given up hope, at my age, and most definitely given up on him and all his dithering when – hallelujah. I'd cracked it. Of course, I didn't tell him. No way was I letting him back in, just so he could share our child. If he wasn't prepared to leave Viola for my sake alone, then he could fucking well forget it. I handed in my notice and booked my plane ticket. So, in answer to your question – no. Believe me, I did not get pregnant by accident.' She paused, then looked intently at Annie. 'How about you? Chance – or design?'

Annie stared back. She felt a pounding in her chest, a choking lump rising in her throat. Yes, well, she was light-headed from starvation and tiredness and misery and she thought for one panicked instant she might actually be sick, but that wasn't what was surging so inexorably upwards. It was the truth.

'Design?' she heard herself gasp. 'Fuck me, Cate, I'll say it was designed. I plotted pregnancy like a military campaign – both times.' What was she saying? Never, never had she admitted this to anyone before. She had barely acknowledged it to herself. But the words were pouring out. 'I mean, Martha was a piece of cake. I just decided it was time for a baby, that I was going to *have* a baby, and to hell with Jake. Because Jake did not want kids. He absolutely, explicitly did *not*. So what did I do? I coolly waited until I was four months gone, then told him he could either have both of us – or sod off.' She faltered. 'Isn't that appalling?'

Cate just laughed. 'Why? You were thirty, the clock was ticking, here was this glorious alpha brute slavering over you, as brilliant as he was beautiful – and about as likely to commit as an adolescent chimp. Besides, he loved them once they were there, didn't he?'

'He loved them a whole heap more, once they weren't,' she retorted tartly, which only made Cate laugh louder. 'Or so he kept yelling, after I *kidnapped* them, off to Yorkshire. Oh, he could get misty-eyed cuddling Martha. When she was a sleepy bundle of talc and teddy. But he seemed to think babies were like goldfish. That you should be able to stick them in their cot, tap a bit of food over, and forget them for a week.'

'While he carried on boozing, partying . . .'

'He invited a bloody rock band to rehearse in our spare room when she was barely three weeks old!'

'And I'll bet he spun you the hoary old yarn about the pram in the hall rendering him incapable of writing a word?'

'Ha. Anyone would think you were there. But you haven't heard the worst.' Now she'd begun, she couldn't stop. 'According to my masterplan, of course, one sprinkle of baby powder would have magically transformed him into the perfect lawn-mowing, pipe-chewing, doting dad straight out of the Ladybird books. I'd grown up, so why couldn't he? When it sank into even my stubborn brain that pigs would take off from Heathrow first, I had to reconsider my options. I knew I wanted *out*. I was quite clear about that.'

'You don't say.'

'But I desperately didn't want my Martha to be an only one. I can't imagine life without my sister.'

'You and me both.'

'I was so *calculating* about it, though. Half off my trolley with grizzly-baby exhaustion, probably, but as I sat there, with Martha at my breast, I assure you I was coolly weighing up the pros and cons of scooting straight back to Yorkshire and finding myself another source of sperm. I think the only thing stopped me was that the idea of sex at that point with anyone, let alone a stranger, made we want to scream. Stop sniggering, will you? Wait and see how seductive you feel with cracked nipples and piles. Anyhow, I concluded better the devil you know and proceeded to get myself blind drunk – and Jake drunker. Several times, God help me, but it worked in the end. Just as well one of his many talents was that, even when he couldn't string two words together, alcohol never seemed to impair his working parts.'

'Priceless, Annie, *priceless*.'

'Ruthless, more like,' she declared grimly. 'Only it didn't quite run to plan because I'd intended to quit the moment I was safely preggers. Just my luck I found myself sick as a dog, second time round. I'd sailed through with Martha, but now I could barely pick up a teaspoon, I was so wretched. Once

Dom was out, though, that really was it. I packed my bags. Mission accomplished.'

She said this with defiant gaiety, but realised Cate was no longer laughing. To Annie's bewilderment, she reached across and took her hand. 'You'd packed a ton-load of guilt into those bags, though, hadn't you? So much so that, twenty years on, you felt you had to take him in, after the stupid bastard did his best to drink himself to death.'

'I'd – abandoned him. Stolen his kids.' Annie drew a quavering breath. 'Ruined – his life.'

'*Bollocks!*' cried Cate. 'Oh, I can believe that's what he claimed. Typical bloody male, shovelling the blame our way. Yes, it was tragic, the way the drink rotted his brain – and his talent. But that had eff-all to do with you, Annie. He drank like a fish before he even met you; Jake Stoneycroft's benders were legendary when you were head girl and I was still playing with plasticine. No, listen. I used to run into him years after you'd left, on the literary circuit, and that guy was having a ball. He'd fallen straight back into the good old sex, drugs and rock 'n' roll routine, happy as a pig in a midden. Ruined his life indeed. You know, I always wanted to talk to you about all this. But, somehow, I never could. You seemed to freeze over just at the mention of his name.'

'According to my daughter, I've airbrushed him out of history,' muttered Annie, flinching. 'Declared him a non-person.'

'And of course I've always been so much in awe of you . . .'

This at least startled Annie out of her introspection. 'In awe – of *me*?'

'Come on. Smart, sexy, mega-successful businesswoman, two great kids, fabulous house, loved and admired by everyone for miles around—'

'In my dreams.'

'And on top of all that, you had to turn yourself into a

bloody saint, by taking him back. I thought you were insane, frankly. But . . . maybe I understand why.'

'Yes,' said Annie uncertainly. 'I mean – oh God, I don't know what to say.'

Because amidst all the bleakness of recent days, here was a spark of consolation. Cate surely did understand. And almost made Annie believe she hadn't botched quite everything in her life. She returned the clasp of her hand with speechless gratitude, and might even have shed a few thoroughly thera-peutic tears on her shoulder, and everything would have been fine, just fine – if Cate had not gone on to whisper, with a little smile:

'So. When are you finally going to make an honest man of poor Rob?'

Dammit, the woman always had been too bloody clever.

Fortunately, even as Annie began to croak something as inane as it was untrue about old friends, there came a thundering up the stairs, a triumphant shout followed by a wail of mock-despair from Bernie, and Simon burst into the room clutching a stuffed giraffe, as tall as himself, which he planted beside the cot.

'Darling!' he cried. 'Darlings, plural!' He kissed Cate and then the baby, who promptly broke into howls, before turning to her. 'My other favourite girl in all the world.'

'You are *so* like your son,' she observed, the noisy panto-mime of his entrance having given her time to recover her composure. 'I must go. Cate' – she was aware of a tightness in her throat and swallowed hard – 'it's been wonderful. Truly. Let's get together again, soon. Simon . . .'

He was not to be dismissed, however, and followed her down the stairs. He would have insisted on running her home if Bernie hadn't said one of the sous-chefs was about to drive into town on an emergency watercress dash and would give Annie a lift, if she could wait just five minutes?

'Five lousy minutes?' cried Simon. 'But Annie and I have so much to say to one another.'

'Not really.' She looked at him. 'Except, well done. You lucky bastard.'

'I am, I know I am, the luckiest chap on earth. Amazing Grace, hey? Isn't she the most exquisite thing you've ever seen, almost as beautiful as her mother. Oh, Annie, I can hardly believe—' He would doubtless have continued in this euphoric vein, had not Bernie glared meaningfully at him before hurrying back to the kitchen.

He broke off. 'Sorry. Yes. Should I be begging your pardon?'

'Probably,' said Annie, 'but I'll let you off. Oh, except for failing to show up at your son's wedding and upsetting all my perfect plans. You bloody well do owe me an apology for that. In fact, to all of us, considering you didn't actually show your face until Cate arrived in Bucksford. By some amazing coincidence.'

He made no attempt to excuse himself. 'I know, I know, I'm a bum.' He let out a hoot of entirely unrepentant laughter. 'Glory, and I laid on that whole media circus, didn't I, just to make sure she knew I was in town? Little realising, round here, she'd have heard on the grapevine within ten minutes. But Dave's wedding – be fair, Annie, I had no choice. Vi was at death's door, even if she had brought it on herself with that bloody ice cream. How spiteful can you—' He broke off. 'Still, mustn't speak ill and what have you, and I guess she's paid for it now. In spades, God rest her.'

It was occurring to Annie that in her long conversation with Cate, they'd barely spoken of Viola, ill or otherwise. 'Was it that again, then?'

He looked blank.

'Her peanut allergy?'

'Oh, the hand cream nonsense? Lord, no. That's what frightened the wits out of her, absolutely, but nut oil's everywhere, it seems, only so purified and refined and generally buggered around with, it's safe as houses. Arachis hypogaea, if you're interested. I'm practically a world expert on the stuff now. Besides, the paramedics kept telling her this wasn't an allergic reaction, nothing like, just her dodgy ticker playing up again.' He grimaced. 'I shouldn't say *just* . . .'

'So why were the police round the Woolshed for so long afterwards?' She heard her name being called. 'Hi, Dale. Yup, with you in a minute.'

'Ah. That's rather a different matter.' Simon waited until the youth had passed through the bar, keys in hand, and lowered his voice. 'The night Viola was taken ill, the, um, the young actor she'd been working with in London . . . oh, to cut a long story short, the poor kid took an overdose. Not enough to kill him, thankfully, but—'

'This got anything to do with Randolph Mackley?'

His eyes widened. 'You know about Mac?'

'That monster— ' She stopped just in time. 'Hank tells me he's notorious.'

'Christ, I wish someone had told me,' he burst out. 'And what's absolutely unforgivable is that it's crystal clear – to me, anyhow – Vi *knew*. Must have done. She knew what her filthy little chum was about and she did fuck all. I've told the boy I'll support him all the way, obviously, but you know what hell making these charges stick can be, even now. Still . . .' Just like that, worries dismissed, he was beaming again. 'Let's be honest. That responsibility isn't all I've inherited from my wife.'

Before Annie could say a word, he leaned forward, not just to kiss her, but to murmur in her ear pretty much exactly what she was thinking. 'Yup. Not just a lucky bastard, but a filthy rich one, too.'

36

Annie Stoneycroft invites you to . . .

Celebrate? As if.

Hey, guys, how d'you fancy coming to a wake, to mark the passing . . .

Of all hope? Of any reason for living? Oh, stop piddling around, Stoneycroft. Forget gags about wakes for the passing of your fifties, the official unveiling of your bus pass, all those jokes are as tired as last night's salad.

Besides, Annie didn't want any sort of sodding party. This past year seemed to have been one long medley of festivities and fizz and fancy frocks and she'd had enough. More than enough. It was time for some quiet. After all, she was going to have to get used to *quiet*. Dom was talking about returning to London. Bernie was lucky to find five empty minutes in a day. Rob was . . . but let's not think about Rob. And even more let's not think about Liz. Although she'd be gone, too, obviously. Which left . . .?

Maybe she should take up gardening. Grow – marrows? She loathed marrow. Green water in a leathery jacket. Or perhaps she could do something useful, something socially valuable. Organise outings for the disabled and elderly. Was she too old to get a licence to drive a minibus? Probably. With a drink-driving conviction to boot. Next thing you know she'd be a passenger on that bus. Stuff it, she was not going to fret about her age. Age was all in the head. What was the difference anyhow? Fifty-nine today, sixty tomorrow. Well, sixty a fortnight on Friday. And, frankly, all she wanted to do was ignore this birthday. Pretend it wasn't happening.

So why was she sitting here at her desk, drafting a bloody invitation? Which was destined to circulate by email only, none of your pearly stiffies for this event. Far too late to get anything printed. Besides, SHE DID NOT WANT A PARTY.

Just her misfortune, then, that her beloved Martha – her interfering, micro-managing, deaf-to-all-protests daughter – had not merely booked a flight home in plenty of time for the said event but had already invited at least two dozen of her own old cronies.

'Don't be silly, of course you're having a thrash,' she had informed her mother. Where did she get it from, this unshakeable conviction she knew best? 'How would you feel if you woke up on your birthday morning with only a mug of tea and baked beans in front of the telly to look forward to? Don't worry, I'm organising the eats, if that's what's bothering you. I was thinking a hog roast'd be good.'

'A whole pig? That feeds hundreds.'

'Half a hog then. Actually lamb probably would be better. Pulled pork's such a cliché these days. Leave it to me, Ma. And I've told Dom he's in charge of sound and music. He's well up for a party.'

Dominic might be. But Annie could explain to neither son nor daughter why she herself was so resolutely not. Nothing to do with the big round O on the end of her age, dispiriting though that might be. It was the big round hole in her foolish, bleeding heart.

She had received a postcard, if you please, the day after her visit to Cate. Who in the world sent picture postcards in this digital age? A pretty watercolour of the Glyndebourne gardens on the front might be a clue.

Dearest Annie, don't be cross with me, please. Rob will have broken the news by now (as I had to make him promise!) and I'm afraid, whatever kind things you say, you'll be rather upset, but I'm so blissfully happy, I don't care. Is that awful of me? I'd so like to think you could be happy for us one day. Anyway, all this can wait until I – we! – come home, and this is just a scribble to say sorry, because I'm staying down here a few extra days. Do hope you can c . . .

The last word was doubtless 'cope' but she had run out of space. 'L *xxx*' was crammed in spider-scrawl up the side of the card.

Well, thanks a bunch, *L xxx*, but you can rest assured Annie could *cope*. Annie Stoneycroft was fighting fit to cope with losing a bloody sight more than you so kindly driving her round the shops. Not to say round the effing twist. No, no, enough of that. Because – deep breath in, slow breath out – Liz and Rob getting together was no big deal. It wasn't. Really. Life would toddle on much as it always had these past umpteen years. She'd be here in lovely Red House, as ever. Her finest and dearest old friend Rob would be just a few miles up the road, as ever. Assuming Liz could settle in the steel and granite penthouse which, now she came to think about it, seemed a bit of a stretch for a frills and florals merchant like her. The vision of china pomanders and silver tea-strainers in Rob's space-lab of a kitchen almost made her smile. Almost. Anyway, she and Rob would continue to enjoy their sturdy companion-ship just as they always had . . . wouldn't they? Oh, come on, he'd been married to someone else ever since the dim and distant mists of her own marriage. And Liz was an *improvement* on Fran, wasn't she? She unreservedly loved Annie, which was more than you could ever have said for his first wife.

. . . short notice, I kno, but this ittt just a few fiends . . .

Fiends? Not so much a typo as precisely what she felt, if Liz were going to sail triumphantly home in time for the event. Delete-delete-de-bloody-lete. Get it right, Stoneycroft. This email has to be sent out, because there's no way you're capable of issuing invites over the phone.

'Hello? You up there, Nan?'

Her heart stopped. It did. And for a moment she couldn't speak at all. Certainly couldn't move a muscle. You can't. When you're dead.

'Because the garden door's wide open, and I could be a burglar walking in.'

She cranked her frozen lips as wide as they would go – not very – into something that could not possibly be resembling a smile. And she was just heaving herself cautiously upwards from her chair – would her jellied legs take the weight? – when he crashed open the door to her study. 'There you are. I've been shouting my head off.'

'Rob,' she said. 'You're back. Early.' And she couldn't, absolutely could not, would not, ask if Liz was following. But her gaze remained riveted on the empty doorway, ears a-twitch for that lighter tread on the stairs.

'Sure. Well, only by a day. But I had to come home, you know, with – with the news.' He couldn't meet her eyes. 'I'm so sorry, love. This must be hell on earth for you. What can I say?'

Oh God. So he knew. Rob actually *knew* what she was feeling. But hadn't he always read her like a book, damn him? And somehow this was the most unbearable pain of all. She'd tried so hard, rehearsed so intently, practised the astonishment, the cheery jokes, everything. Total waste of effort. She crumpled back into her chair and – she just couldn't help it – why pretend when he already knew? She didn't so much weep as bellow her head off.

He was beside her in an instant on his knees, clumsily bundling his arms round her.

'Don't,' she gasped, making a feeble attempt to struggle free. But this was the most exquisite agony, the closeness of him, that familiar old shoulder, the very *smell* of him, that same sodding, sexy scent.

'The bastard,' he was muttering. 'That slimy, two-faced, two-timing piece of . . . I could kill him. Oh, my poor old love.'

It took a moment for these words to register. 'You – what?'

'I always knew he was a wrong'un. I told you, didn't I? I tried to warn you, but – honest to God, I'd have made myself dance at your bloody wedding, I would, I'd told myself. If that's what you wanted.'

Now Annie lifted her head – with reluctance, because there was nowhere she more wanted to be than squashed against Rob's chest – but she did manage to detach herself just a few inches. 'Oh, f'God's sake, don't be so—'

'I still can't believe I only found out this morning, when Liz let it slip – and to Jen, too, not even to me. You OK, love?' Annie had shuddered so violently at Liz's name, she could only give a mute shake of the head and he wrapped her close again. 'Why couldn't the soft ha'porth have told me the minute I picked her up from the station? I mean, keeping it out of the press is one thing, but not telling a soul, never mind I'm on the board of that bloody theatre. Still . . . I dare say I'd given her one or two other things to think about.'

And Annie could swear she was hearing – no, physically *feeling* – a chuckle deep in his chest. Can you credit it? She did shove herself away from him now. He *was*, he was smiling to himself. The thoughtless, heartless brute was downright *smirking*.

'Thank God it tumbled out in the end, though,' he was continuing. 'Cate – and him. Honestly, love, I got straight in my car.'

'I can't think why.' She wanted to hit him. 'I should think you'd be – you'd be congratulating yourself all the way home, spotting it ages ago like you did. But if you're dumb enough to imagine I give a flying—'

'Beats me, Cate taking on that shifty little stoat, after the way he's treated her. But that's nothing compared to what he's done to you. My poor girl.'

If Annie hadn't been choked with snotty tears, she would have managed the most magnificently contemptuous laugh. As it was, she could hardly get the words out. 'Wrong end of the stick this time, Robbo,' she said thickly. 'Very kind of you, 'n all that, but I assure you I do not care twopence about Simon Spencer.'

And what did Rob do? He grabbed her and hugged her even more tightly. 'That's my Nan. You always were the bravest little scout I ever knew.'

Idiot. 'Leggo, will you, I need a tissue.' She was reassured to find she could sound almost like herself. Because the real challenge was yet to come. He'd see just what a brave little scout she was then. As in *not*. Big time not. 'There's nothing between him and me, never was. Where's the sodding Kleenex? Even Cate thinks it's one big joke.' At last her hand landed on the tissue box. She grabbed a fistful and blasted ferociously. 'You were right about her, though,' she said thickly. 'Amazing. I love her.'

It was his turn to pull back now and look flummoxed. He blinked several times. As though he couldn't quite take in her words. 'You – you're not just saying that? About – Simon Spencer, I mean, not Cate?'

'Do me a favour. And I'll tell you something else: she's got his measure. Simon's bad boy days are well and truly over.' She was in command of herself again. Just. 'So, Robbo. Out with the great news.'

'What news? That's it. Cate, the babe.' He said this distract-edly, as though his mind were elsewhere. Yes, well, probably having to brace himself.

'About you, you pillock.' She still couldn't quite bring herself to name Liz, but there you go. One step at a time.

'What about me? Look Nan, I walk in, you have screaming hysterics all over me—'

'Well, I . . .' Bit late to claim it was the wrong time of the month. Like, ten years too late. Parents – long dead. Sad kitten pics on the internet? 'Oh, I dunno. I was just feeling a bit emotional.'

'A *bit*? You haven't blubbed over me like that since Jake pegged it.' He winced. 'Sorry, tactless.'

'Why? It's high time I stopped being so clammed up about Jake. And y'know who's made me see it? *Cate*. That woman's so smart, so wise, she really helped me to . . .' Enough. This was just babble, putting off the dread moment. Annie blew her nose again, for good measure. 'Anyway, she made me feel better, that's all. She said I was mad for taking him in, but at least she completely got why.'

Rob shook his head. 'Yeah, well, we all thought you were off your rocker taking him back but—'

'I did not take Jake *back*,' she snapped. 'Fuck's sake, not you too?'

He frowned. 'Look, I know Bernie reckons—'

'Everyone else in this town might've been dumb enough to think we were all hearts and flowers and happy ever after . . .' Indignation spluttered into a coughing fit. 'But *you*? You were – *here*. You've always been here. You were the one picked up the pieces in the first place, after I ran home.'

'Do me a favour. When were you ever in pieces? All you did was say that the bugger – sorry, that *Jake* wasn't suited to family life.'

'I never came out with anything so prissy.'

'You did and all, or summat very like. And the next minute you were charging round like a merry bat out of hell.'

'I *was* coming out of hell, if you don't mind. Complete and utter hell, as at least Cate had the wit to—'

'So bloody hyperactive I used to think I'd have to peel you off the ceiling if—'

'I had a bloody family to bring up, support, a house, a business, never mind the years of pent-up aggro and—'

'Will you stop yelling at me?' yelled Rob.

'Who's yelling round here?' she screamed back.

'Are you . . .' With visible difficulty he moderated his tone. 'Are you saying you really were done with the bloke? For good and all, when you left him?'

She hunched a shoulder. 'I cannot believe that you – you, of all people – are asking me such a stupid question. And what's it matter now, anyway?'

'Give me strength . . .'

'Yes,' she hissed. 'Yes, yes, yes, of *course*. That marriage was over the day I walked out. Before then, in fact, long before. Extinct, expired, dead as the proverbial fucking parrot. Satisfied?' She charged on before he could utter a word. 'And don't you try telling me you don't know this, Rob Daley, because I may have chosen not to burden my nearest and dearest with all the bloody stupid ins and outs of my bloody stupid marriage, but I was always quite clear I'd no regrets about quitting. Not for one tiny minute. How often have you heard me say that? Come on, how often?'

'But . . .' He was staring at her in the most peculiar way. Rather as she imagined an enraged bull might look after charging nose first into a stone wall. 'Well, maybe, but I thought you were just putting on a brave – oh, you know.'

'No, I don't know. And I don't care. Go on then. Out with it.'

He looked even more stunned. 'Whaddya mean?'

'With – whatever it is you're bursting to tell me. I'm ready.' She wasn't. But she was gearing herself up.

'I – I dunno if . . . Any road, how'd you know what I was thinking?'

'Pete's sake, just spit it out.' She was getting crosser by the minute. Good. Helped a lot. She could do this.

'If you want the honest truth, I guess I'd found myself remembering . . .' He looked at the ceiling, the floor, anywhere but at her. 'Well, if you must know, I was thinking about the last thing Fran said to us.'

'*Frances?*' This threw her completely off her stride. 'Where's she come in?'

His face was contorting every which way. 'Look, d'you want me to say this or not? Make a damn great fool of myself? Because if not . . .'

Make . . . a fool of himself? Annie opened her mouth, then shut it again and for a moment or two they just stared at one another.

'Fran?' she ventured. Very cautiously.

'When we bust up. You know, after your – after Jake died. She said to us . . .' He actually let out a groan. 'She says to me, so there you are, Robert. You can marry her at last.'

Then he fell silent. So silent she could hear the whine of her laptop.

'M-marry . . .?'

Try as she might, she couldn't get the crucial word out. Against all rational hope and expectation, it was dawning on her that everything might just be . . . all right? No, no, a thousand times better than *all right*. But while a brass band might be assembling to blast a fanfare in her head and the entire Huddersfield Choral Society readying themselves to bellow hallelujahs, with a sky chock-full of fireworks thrown in … this was Annie Stoneycroft. She wanted it confirmed, spelled out and signed in triplicate, preferably witnessed by lawyers.

Oh dear God, she'd expelled two babies into the world with less effort. She took a very deep breath.

'Marry – *who* exactly?'

37

'Whom,' he said later that day. Much later. 'Marry *whom*.'

'And you can promise to love, honour, cherish – and stop correcting my fucking grammar.'

Annie is not having a birthday party. She has not issued a single invitation, emailed, written or spoken.

'Well you needn't think you're getting away with any of that cherishing crap. Prayerbook says obey. Only for the women, naturally.'

'Since when did a heathen like you know anything about the prayerbook? And can I just remind you I got an A in my A-level English?'

'Did they have A-levels back in your day? I thought it was School Cert.'

'Watch it, sunshine.'

'When d'you qualify for your state pension, by the way?'

'At least I'll live to draw it. Which is more than you will, the way things are going.'

So why is her house and garden overflowing once again?

The sun is bright and everyone you'd expect is here. All the usual suspects. This, incidentally, is a peculiarly apt turn of phrase, given Annie's misplaced speculations about the demise of Viola Hood. Even so, for all it is widely known that the great actress expired from the natural cause of her long-diagnosed heart disease, you may be intrigued to learn that it has never been established from whom came that supposedly fatal hand cream. Or body lotion. Or whatever it was – most people have already forgotten. Although Annie heard the stuff was called something like Everlasting Youth, so this reluctant birthday girl, for one, can *quite* understand why Viola gave it a go. And Trisha has been heard saying only minutes earlier to someone or other that she can't understand it, not for a minute, because – yes – she'd made half a dozen or so boxes straight off from that lovely paper Annie give her, but she could swear she'd not sold a blinkin' one, not before, *you know* . . . So how did it end up in that dressing room? Oooh, it brings her over all shivery just thinking about it. Still, she concluded hastily, they shouldn't be talking about sad things like this at a party, should they?

But it is *not* a birthday party. This was a bit of a blow for Dave Eastman after he'd spent several pleasurable if increasingly befuddled hours creating a cocktail in honour of the event, having chanced upon a stash of blackcurrants at the bottom of a freezer. Unable now to christen his indigo-dark and indecently strong concoction Birthday Blues, he is instead mixing, shaking and pouring the retitled Black Magic for anyone fool enough to accept a glass. The bunting strung above the French windows gives the game away. Hand-stitched – by Trisha, naturally – it spells out ANNIE & ROB in candyfloss pink on a green so lurid Annie has to avert her eyes. Still, it's better than having to look at the figure 60, a milestone that she did her best to ignore, the day before yesterday. Rob gave her a copy of the *Oldie* magazine and a senior railcard. She has not invited anyone to their *little* engagement celebration today because her affianced – in cahoots with Martha, Dominic, Bernie, Dave and even her sister and brother-in-law – took the affair clean out of her hands. Her garden – never mind the kitchen, sitting room, *everywhere* – is thus crammed tighter than St Peter's Square with the Pope due.

It takes her ten minutes of dodging, nudging and apologising just to get from fish pond to kitchen doors to greet the latest arrival. Not merely have Martha and Dominic's friends turned up, in whooping, high-fiving, hunting packs, so have all Jennifer's, albeit less rumbustiously. It's also thanks to her sister that the extended Royd and Daley clans are gathered, although Jen cannot be blamed for inviting what seems like every neighbour from within a half-mile radius. That was the ever-efficient Martha's insurance against complaints about noise and parking. So somewhere lost in the throng are eye-watering golfing slacks and a spaniel last seen digging up the rose bed.

Here's dear Hank, though, chatting to Maggie and Hugo King amid a glittery clutter of their androgynous, colt-legged offspring. You might even have spotted Leona Parsons – well, you could hardly miss her in that outfit – alongside a suavely linen-suited Kelvin. Surprisingly perhaps, even had she known Mr and Mrs Parsons were invited, Annie would not have protested. She is exhibiting (as Rob has remarked) a most uncharacteristic benevolence towards one and all. He claims to find this unnerving.

Just arrived, however, is a tall and notably distinguished-looking female whom you may not recognise. She has dark hair barely threaded with grey, cropped stylishly short so as to tuck under a wig, and she is kissing one of her three grown-up children, all of whom are also here. Naturally they are, because this is Frances Daley QC. And while one cannot say she returns Annie's embrace quite as warmly as it is offered, she is – pretty remarkably under the circumstances – present. Smiling as graciously as ever.

'But I still can't get my head round this,' Annie had said, one elbow propped on the pillow. 'You're telling me Fran knew?'

Unusually modestly for Annie, she was blushing. 'That you, well, had a bit of a thing about me, all these years?'

'Come on, it wasn't like that. Sure, I thought you were, oh, beyond amazing. Always had, but . . .'

'I never knew you had such good taste.'

'Only because you'd been brainwashing me from infancy. But be honest, Nan. Back in the day, when we had that flat, and I was teaching out at Willesden . . .'

'Ha, in that disgusting safari jacket you always used to wear. Worse, your blessed suede boots.'

'Bloody cheek. I loved those boots. You can't get 'em now.'

'Thank God.'

'While you were prancing off round town, three parties a night, new bloke practically every other week . . .'

'Those were the days.'

'Cow. But you never once, not ever, saw *me* as boyfriend material. Did you?'

She raised her chin. 'More fool me.'

He grinned. 'Nah. If we'd got together back then, we'd have ripped each other apart.'

'You reckon?'

'Whereas now that you've mellowed with age – hey, stop hitting me. Whereas now—'

'Don't tell me, you pompous fart, I've already suffered this sermon. Now that we're old enough to know ourselves, and what we truly value . . .'

'What's so wrong with that?'

'And are no longer dazzled by lust, of course . . .'

'Speak for yourself.'

'Get off, you sex-crazed beast.' But she kissed him enthusiastically enough. 'Anyhow, you're seriously telling me, Fran *knew*?'

'What was there to know? Oh, she'd get narked, time to time, at you and me joking around. But the fact is . . .' He sighed. 'I guess the bottom line is Fran and I never did really have that, you know – that extra bit of how's-your-father.'

'Hark the romantic Yorkshireman. That bit of how's-your-father.'

'Piss off, will you? It wasn't a bad marriage. I hope.' He was in earnest now. 'We were both of us ready to settle when we met. Well, you'd taken off with your glamour boy, hadn't you? And Fran was as keen as me to start a family, so we did, and it worked fine.' Rob's hand closed round hers. 'I wouldn't have left her, you know, Nan. Ever. And she knows that too. But with the pair of us working all over the place, it'd long since become marriage by notes on the fridge. Jake dying – well, maybe that blew the final whistle, but it'd probably have happened sooner or later, once the kids had flown. High time to call it a day, she said. While we were both still young enough to make good lives apart, that's what she said. And, OK, the business about you. I don't think she meant it bitterly.'

'If I ever uttered a bad word about Frances,' declared Annie fervently. 'I take it back now.'

'Where's that Simon?' Bernie is asking, with a frilly-frocked, sun-bonneted infant clasped to her shoulder. 'Where's your naughty daddy, hey? Are you smiling, my poppet, or just filling your nappy?'

'Some things never change,' says Annie, gracefully declining the proffered goddaughter whom, to be sure, she adores and upon whom she has already lavished any number of gifts, as impractical as they were extravagant. But who can resist a miniature cashmere cardigan? Those teensy-weensy sheepskin bootees? However, smelly nappies she can do without against her equally new and expensive frock. 'So here we all are, once more waiting for Simon to appear. Surprise, sur-bloody-prise.'

'Huh!' snorted Bernie. 'I've had enough feckin' surprises recently to last a lifetime. What with Cate about to turn into my stepmother-in-law, and you, my precious' – she kisses the crown of the bonnet – 'being Dave's little sister, never mind Em and Megan's aunty? I mean, try getting your head round that. The whole world's gone topsy-turvy, so it has, even before you and himself . . . Oh, talk of the devil.'

For once she is not referring to her husband, who at this moment is vigorously arguing the finer points of spit-roasting lamb with Annie's daughter, while his own daughters splash and shriek in the paddling pool that same Martha has so thoughtfully installed for the entertainment of the younger guests. No, Bernie is talking about Rob, who has rolled up to throw an arm around her and baby Grace. But his smile – that unmistakable glow of how's-your-father – is for Annie. It's hers and hers alone.

'Give over your mooning, will you?' says Bernie. 'And don't try getting round me, Rob Daley, because I'm still not after forgiving you. If you'd only pulled your socks together and sorted things out with my Annie earlier, you'd have saved me a bucketload of worry.'

'How could I, when she was running around with your father-in-law? Where is Simon by the way?'

'Much you care,' says Annie.

'I misjudged the man,' he declares, with a benevolence to match her own. 'Anyone who can sire this little cherub,' he says, lifting Grace from Bernie's arms, 'can't be all bad. Pooh, you stink, kiddo.' But he doesn't recoil, he just cuddles her closer. Yeah, well, Rob always was a big softy with babies. He shoots a sideways glance at Annie. 'So which of our kids do we put the squeeze on to give us a babe of our own to spoil rotten? By the by, d'you fancy getting hitched in the abbey? We should be able to fit most of your closest friends in there. What's it seat – six, seven hundred?'

'*Fantastic!*' But it's Bernie whooping this.

'Not bloody likely,' says Annie.

'Now don't be squabbling again, the two of you. And I suppose you've got his eminence lined up to do the honours, have you, Rob?'

It was not until late at night that he had even remembered.

'Hell's teeth, *Liz*. I promised her faithfully I'd ring you straight off, and that was a week or more back.'

Annie was wide awake, bolt upright, in an instant. 'Liz?' In all the dizzying, dazzling glories of these past few hours, she now realised she had not given a thought to her friend. 'Lord, what?'

'I kept putting it off, because – oh, I knew you'd jump down my throat.' She flipped on the bedside lamp to find him staring up at her, shamefaced. 'When I think of the times I've had a go at you for just this kind of thing, trying to fix other folks' lives for them.'

That silly, happy postcard. Annie's cheeks began to burn, so acutely did she feel Liz's mortification if the poor soul had confessed her joyous hopes to Rob. No matter how kindly, how gently he would have tried to let her down, it must have been agony. For both of them. Small wonder he was squirming. 'Just tell me. Quickly.'

'It hit me clean out of the blue. All of a sudden, I found myself thinking this was a chance too good to pass up, what with him meeting me in town for the grant application. And Phil had the two tickets, didn't he? Not that he gave his up easy, I'm here to tell you – I practically had to wrestle it out of his fist. He was going to take Liz along himself, because opera's no more Jen's idea of fun than mine. She says she only goes for the picnic and the gardens. But you should've seen old Cardy's face when I mentioned Glyndebourne.'

'Cardy?' said Annie. 'You're never talking about the bish?'

'Course, Caradoc. Luckily the meeting was at the House of Lords, so he was in his clerical clobber, and you can get away with that anywhere. Phil's DJ wouldn't have gone near him, even if he'd been prepared to lend it, which I very much doubt, knowing my bro.' Rob chuckled. 'He'd already nearly burst a blood vessel when I said I was playing Cupid, and what's more I'd lend 'em my car, so the least he could do was hand over his ticket. Bloody generous of me that was too, because I didn't see my motor again until this morning. Well, yesterday morning now. Fair play, they did ring and ask before they tootled off. Not so much an early honeymoon, more a victory parade round half the parsonages in the south of England, by the sound of it.'

'Are you seriously telling me that Liz has got together with – Caradoc Swallow?'

'Listen, I know you say he's too old, but you don't—'

'I never. Well, OK, maybe I did. So I'm an idiot. God, am I an idiot.'

'Can I have that in writing?'

The very Reverend Caradoc Swallow is indeed here, beaming benignly (through his beard) at one and all. He has been putting away – Annie observes in passing – a surprisingly unbishoply quantity of red wine. Her estimation of him rises with every glass. Liz, of course, is a fluttery, chattery bundle of bliss. She is wearing a brand-new pair of scarlet stilettos. These also strike Annie as interestingly unbishoply. She sneaks a sideways glance at his grace. Yes, from that nifty cross of the feet as he kicks a beach ball straight back to one of the King sprogs, it looks as if this Swallow will make a good few summers yet.

There has been no need for Annie to assure Liz her secret is safe, because her confession of passion for Rob never happened. That's what they are united in pretending, with barely a word exchanged. Liz may have said something about Rob being a wonderful man. Annie – well, Annie just agrees with her, doesn't she?

So she can enjoy Liz's moment of triumph, when they happen to overhear Leona sighing that it's such a crying pity dear Rob (no mention of his bride) won't be able to tie the knot in any sort of style. That is if, as she understands, they're determined to marry here in Bucksford. The register office is such a dump, isn't it? And she's sorry to say this, but she happens to know that the C of E is still very sticky about divorcees. Evidently, she hasn't twigged that the beardy geezer refilling his glass ten paces away is a prelate of the same.

Liz smiles seraphically as she announces that, since Rob and Frances were themselves married in a register office, and therefore not in the sight of the Almighty, he can re-wed wher- ever the hell he likes. 'Caradoc and I are trying to persuade them the abbey's the place.'

Over Annie's dead body, frankly – the tears and tulle routine, at her age? But she winks at Liz. Rob raises an enquiring eyebrow as he rolls up and hugs her tightly. Again. But this reminds her – reminds her of something she's been meaning to ask him for ages.

'That aftershave,' she says. 'I got a whiff of it again then. Did I give it to you?'

He looks at her, pulls a face. 'What aftershave?'

'Cologne, scent, whatever you've got on.'

'Nowt on me, love. Shower gel, Lidl's best. What's so funny?'

★   ★   ★

'You know I seriously used to worry that after all this time, it might not *work*. That I'd been without sex for so bloody long I'd just lost the urge.'

'Yeah well, any day soon. Best make the most of it while we can, eh?'

'Pillock.'

'You seem to be managing, anyhow.' He was smirking. Oh, the smugness of the post-coital male. 'I got the impression you've quite enjoyed yourself, actually.'

'I know – staggering, isn't it?'

His head jerked up from the pillow. 'Sorry?'

'*You*, I mean. Turning out to be so amazingly good at it. Last thing I'd ever have expected. Oh, c'mon, don't look at me like that, you know what I—'

'Here he is. Here's the man at last.' Dave is waving his barbecuing fork, a chubby, red-faced devil in a stripy apron.

'Sorry, sorry, sorry,' cries Simon.

'How many times have we heard that before?' murmurs Cate to Annie, who has just settled on the bench beside her. They exchange glances of womanly complicity.

'Don't you two gang up on me,' he protests, looking from one to the other with a shade of unease. He drops a kiss on Annie's forehead. 'Congrats, old darling, but about bloody time, eh? Cate's always said you two were made for one another. And you can spare me the evil eye, Dr Blackwell, you've no idea what I'm having to sort out – funerals, memorials, lawyers, never mind estate agents. My stress levels are through the roof.' He lowers his voice. 'And I won't even start on Randolph Mackley.' He looks round. 'God's sake someone gimme a large drink. Or a shot of tranquilliser.'

This is Kelvin's cue. He has followed Simon across the lawn.

'Drugs are not the answer to life's troubles, man.'

'Sorry? I mean, just joking, hey?'

Leona now sidles up and takes hold of Simon's arm. He may twist like a puppy in the coils of a python, but Annie and Cate are as one in ignoring his desperate signals because they have business in hand. Although Annie has already been persuaded, without difficulty, to step out of retirement to supervise the décor of the Spencers' marital home, there can be no talk of flooring or window treatments when that house has yet to be purchased. What concerns Cate is her intended's notion of appropriate properties. She is holding out a very large and very glossy estate agent's brochure.

'I mean look at this – just *look* at it.'

'Blimey,' says Annie.

'Kelvin and I were hoping we'd find you here, Simon, for a quiet word, because I dare say you didn't realise, among all the many cards and gifts she must have received—'

'You've got to back me up, Annie. Do I laugh or scream?'

'My son, you're a lifesaver.'

Out of the corner of her eye, Annie sees Simon gulp half the inky contents of the lethally large glass handed to him by Dave and she winces before turning back to Cate. '*Eleven* bedrooms?'

'You see, we took the liberty of asking your dear wife – I mean, your *late* wife,' Leona flashes a wary smile towards his wife-to-be, 'for a few words.'

Cate glances round from the double-page spread she is showing Annie, of a medieval banqueting hall as reimagined by a Victorian wool tycoon. 'Poor Leona. She does *try*.'

'Shame you never got to experience her ultra-luxe facilities. You could've picked up a host of ideas there, balconettes, gold bath taps and all.'

'You can joke. I'd have sold my soul by then for a decent night's kip and an en-suite loo.'

Simon hiccups. 'What is this stuff? Tastes like Ribena. With added rocket fuel.'

'However, I don't suppose that before she . . .' Leona bites her lip. 'You know, while she was still with us, that dear Viola had a chance to . . .?'

His face is a blank. As will be his brain, reflects Annie, if he drinks the rest of that cocktail.

'No, well, such a pity. I mean, tragic, obviously. But the thing is, my husband has a new website, and since Viola is so sadly departed, we were hoping you might allow us to quote you instead as saying—'

'Simon!' cries Trisha, waddling up, and he hugs her like a drowning man grabbing a life-buoy.

'Trisha, dear, if you don't mind, Simon and I were in the middle of a rather important conversation.' Leona is wasting her breath. Nothing short of a bomb blast can deflect Trisha Hough on a mission.

'Look, you've got to set my mind at rest. I've not slept hardly a wink, ever since I saw that box. It was mine, I know it were, and some folk are still saying that the stuff inside, I mean, it really wasn't that, was it?' She can hardly get the words out. 'Just tell me. Not the flippin' hand cream killed her?'

Annie notices something curious. Not merely has this silenced Leona mid-sentence, the face she turns towards her husband is quite ashen under the orange spray tan. 'Hand cream?' she echoes faintly.

Cate, too, observes, and she casts aside the estate agent's details with a soft chuckle. 'Lord, yes. The dreaded oil of arachis hypogaea.'

'Peanuts?' Rob leans towards them as he strolls past, baby Grace again in his arms. 'If I remember my Latin.'

'Show-off,' says his beloved.

'It won't be the stuff we gave her,' Kelvin can be heard muttering to his wife. 'That was pure artisan-made, totes organic. Can't be that.'

'Oh but I'm afraid it can,' murmurs Cate in Annie's ear, as Rob wanders on to deliver Grace into Trisha's waiting embrace. 'We picked it up in an artsy-crafty barn place Leona spotted, all wind chimes and ghastly wicker hearts. On our way back from Tiptree, you know?'

Leona glares at her husband before turning back to Simon. 'She died of heart trouble, didn't she? That's what I heard.'

'Indeed yes.' However, Simon Spencer's natural devilry and his son's Black Magic are a dangerous combination. 'But what brought the first tremors on, that's the question? Because you can imagine the shock, once Vi realised she'd been rubbing her hands in peanut oil, and I'm very much afraid to say—'

'No!' shrieks Trisha, nearly dropping the baby. 'And it came in my lovely box?'

'Take no notice, love, he's talking his usual nonsense,' declares Cate loudly, quelling his mischief with a single minatory glance. She resettles herself beside Annie. 'Poor Trish. I've never dared tell her it was me flogged Leona that box.' She quite misreads Annie's expression. 'Only for charity, you know. I charged her a fiver, too.'

Hank who has ambled into the group round Simon, observes that the person he really feels for is the playwright. 'Well, apart from Dame Vi, obvs . . .' He shoots an uncomfortable smile at the widower. 'But that poor bastard sweated two years writing the piece for her. I mean, will anyone want to pick it up now?'

Annie grimaces at Cate. 'Good thing you didn't know what Leona was putting in the box.'

'The peanut hand cream? For heaven's sake, she let me choose it for her. Leona's blind as a bat close-to in her contacts, and she wouldn't be seen dead in reading specs.'

'You can't mean . . .'

Cate raises her eyebrows. 'Mmm, 'fraid so.'

'. . . real buzz building round the show, wasn't there, Simon? People saying it was the best thing he'd written. Ace story, of course, because yer Mrs Churchill was quite some woman, but the—'

Annie's mouth falls open. '*Mrs Churchill!*' she gasps, and she can't help but laugh. 'Your talk, remember? Bloody hell, Cate, you're telling me it was you. You killed Mrs Churchill?'

At which the other woman explodes into a roar of delighted mirth. 'My God, of course, *Darling Clementine.* She was playing Clemmie Churchill, wasn't she? Poetic, Annie, just too deliciously, murderously poetic. Why oh why did I never think of that?'

Annie's own laughter falters a little. 'But that wasn't what did for her. Not really.'

Cate shrugs. 'Who knows what triggers a heart attack? And as my tactless lover has just pointed out, once she realised what was in that bottle, so carefully selected by me . . .'

Annie gulps. 'Maybe, but – accidentally. Obviously. Goes without saying.'

Cate doesn't reply at once. She looks very hard at Annie, and then down at her feet, before expelling a prolonged shuddering sigh. 'Well, I can trust you, I know. The awful truth is I read the label on that bottle, every last ingredient. I had to – for Leona. You know what she's like, all her temple-of-the-body nonsense.' She lays a confiding hand on Annie's arm. 'And I was so furiously angry with Viola that afternoon, don't you recall?' Another sigh. 'But I suppose you just thought I was ill when you found me in the garden. Whereas, really, that story on the *Mail* website, going on about their fucking silver

423

wedding, had me in such a' – her voice begins to quaver – 'such a savagely homicidal rage . . . Wouldn't you feel . . . Oh God, your *face!*' She can't continue, she's laughing so much, and has to mop her eyes with a clump of the tissues of which, as a new mother, she has a copious supply in her pocket.

'You monster!' shrieks Annie. 'For a moment, I really believed you.'

'What's with the hysterics?' enquires Rob, who has returned, unnoticed by either of them.

'We're having a literary conversation,' splutters his affianced. 'Way over your head.'

'I blame our lousy school,' wails Cate. 'If they'd only taught us Latin at Laurel Park, like they did the boys, I might have – might've realised at the time, not days later, when Simon told me—'

She's silenced by an all-too-familiar shout. 'Come on now, girls, grab yourselves a fresh glass.' Dave thrusts out a laden tray. 'Toast time coming up.'

'But if you *had* realised arachy-whatever was peanut oil? Oh, thanks, Dave.'

Cate's grin is wicked. 'Trust me, I'd have devised a far more reliable method of despatching *Mrs Churchill.*'

'Mrs Churchill?' Rob looks from one to the other in baffled amusement. 'Cate still trying to convert you to Austen and the joys of *Emma*, Nan?'

'In a manner of speaking,' she says grandly. She takes two fizzing flutes from Dave's tray and passes one to her new and delightful friend, who eyes her thoughtfully.

'So, Annie. Shall we drink to ourselves and our husbands-to-be? Or, how about – to dear Jane?'

Annie considers this. Then lifts her glass. 'Why not, indeed?' she says. 'Here's to Jane *bloody* Austen. And all who sail in her wake.'